Firefly Whispers

Bonny Gainley

ISBN- 10: 1466466413
ISBN-13: 978-1466466418

The characters, events and details about the setting portrayed in this book are fictitious. Any similarity to real persons, living or dead, is coincidental and not intended by the author.

To my family.

CONTENTS

ACKNOWLEDGMENTS

Thank you to my amazing husband Glenn, for being willing to offer critical feedback, suggest major changes, and having the patience to support me through the process.

Thank you to my mother Dory, for reading each revision and offering constant encouragement.

Thank you to my daughter Sydney, for the suggestions, laughs, questions and inspiration.

Thank you to Henry and Susan, for sparking the idea.

1 CALIFORNIA ARRIVES

I swung my trusty old Civic into its usual spot next to the light pole that stands in the center of the school parking lot without spilling my latte, even though my tires slid a little on the ice. Megan Burke – race car driver in training. The deli I work at gives me free lattes and I'm hooked. The latest studies say coffee is actually good for us, so as habits go, this one's not so bad. The latest studies also say kid's brains don't function at seven in the morning, but nobody seems to care about that. School starts at 7:45 a.m., whether we're ready to learn or not.

I was running late, as usual. Today's excuse was that I had to put extra effort into scraping the half inch of ice off my windshield. Spring always meant extra moisture in the air, in western Massachusetts anyway, which meant extra ice on everything. My dad often scrapes my windows for me before he leaves for work, but today I was not so lucky. In any case, by March the routines related to boots and ice scraping have become second nature, so my excuse wasn't much of an excuse. It was just another regular school day.

First period Econ was a classic illustration of why I needed my morning coffee. As we tired zombies slouched in our chairs, Mr. Stanley performed his duty as home room teacher, reading the announcements in his standard monotone.

"Prom is coming in May and tickets go on sale tomorrow. Those interested in track should meet in the commons after school today. The Key Club is meeting tomorrow at noon. The cafeteria is now serving a soup of the day. Today's soup is broccoli cheese."

Mr. Stanley's class was one of those lecture/read the book/answer the questions types of classes. He'd been teaching Economics for twenty one years, and as far as anyone knew, his class format had been exactly the same all that time. It was a required class for juniors, so here we were.

"Broccoli," "cheese" and "soup" were the last interesting words he uttered. After that he lost us completely, droning on about credit policies and the fed. At least we weren't expected to participate in any way. Having to pay attention was the only thing that could have made it worse. Cody Parsons laid his head on his open book and dozed. The rest of us were too polite to be so obviously not paying attention, but Mr. Stanley probably wouldn't have noticed anyway.

Melissa and Jess had their hands under their desks and their faces turned down in the general direction of their open text books as if they were following the lecture. Anyone paying attention, which would not include Mr. Stanley of course, could see they were sending text messages back and forth. I watched them for a while, amusing myself by imagining what they could be chatting about.

Jess glanced around the room as Melissa was intently focused on her hands. Then Melissa's shoulders relaxed and she leaned back in her chair a fraction of an inch. Jess looked quickly to her lap, froze for an instant, and then her body started to shake with silent laughter as she stuffed her fist against her mouth. Melissa glanced at Jess, pleased at the reaction, and angled her body away from where Jess sat in an attempt to keep from losing it herself. Jess composed herself and focused on her lap. I could see she was typing on her keypad. Then her hands stopped moving, so I shifted my attention to Melissa. Melissa's gaze flew to her lap. She was absolutely still for a moment, and then turned to face Jess with wide eyes, mouthed "no way" and returned her attention to her lap. Watching them was far more interesting than lending theory.

The Melissa and Jess drama became boring after a while, so I daydreamed about the far away weekend and the dance on Friday. In a town as miniscule as ours there's not a lot to do, so every high school event is significant. Even if you're not interested in the latest wrestling match, it makes for a real destination – a good excuse to get out of the house to hang out with friends. Our high school has only three hundred students - about seventy five in each grade. Hardwick and the surrounding area have a population of about five thousand people, but not many actually live in the town. We are about an hour from Worcester, the only big city anywhere near, and also the location of the closest theater and mall. Turning sixteen is a major milestone here in nowhere Massachusetts, because it means we are finally able to drive to Worcester.

Mr. Stanley's tone started to change, signaling that first hour was almost over. The assignment surprised nobody. "Please turn in your answers to the odd numbered questions at the end of chapter 23 tomorrow morning, class."

I pondered his wooden face. What was he thinking? Did he daydream through the entire hour just like us, able to recite his lectures from memory? The bell rang, and I felt my coffee kicking in. Time to wake up, see my friends and get to a more interesting class. The glazed eyes in the room blinked, and all the zombies came to life to shuffle out of the room.

I dropped my paper coffee cup in the recycle bin on my way out the door and edged into the crowded hall. I stopped at my locker and traded my Econ book for my Chemistry book, then slowly made my way down the hall. The Chem lab is located in the senior hall, one of four halls that branches off the main area of the school where the office, gym and cafeteria are located. Our lockers are in our class halls, but rooms are grouped according to subject, so it's not possible to avoid any particular hall. Walking down the senior hall meant walking past the senior boys hanging around their lockers. As I approached, one looked up at me and smiled a sly grin, Jeff, my boyfriend.

"What's up Meggie?" he asked. I smiled at the handsome face, and we touched hands as I walked by. Though he was never concerned with being late to class, since teachers tended to give the student body president a lot of leeway, I was.

Jeff and I had started dating when I was a sophomore and he was a junior. Jeff had a reputation for dating girls for a short time, and then dumping them and moving on to the next one, at least until I came along. He was charming and good looking, popular and liked by guys, girls and adults alike, and unfortunately he knew that. He was captain of the football team and editor and chief of the school newspaper. He fit in comfortably with every crowd, whether it was the cool kids, the athletes, the geeks or even the partiers. Obviously I noticed him around school - who wouldn't - but hadn't known he had noticed me until out of the blue he asked me to Prom my sophomore year.

I had felt like Cinderella with Prince Charming asking her to the ball. I was a plain and insignificant sophomore, and he was the most popular guy in his class with everything going for him. I fell for him hard and saw him every chance I could, though he was always busy with sports, his friends and the newspaper, as well as with working on his parent's farm. My parents liked him, but my mom said I was too young to be so serious about anyone. She was right to worry, but I never would have admitted that to her.

At the start of this school year, Jeff broke my heart when he told me he wanted to date other girls, even though that shouldn't have been any big surprise given his history. Then it became clear it wasn't other girls - it was Shawna Martinez, built like a 25 year old Dallas Cowboys Cheerleader. I cried for two months. I was inconsolable, spending all my time in my room listening to sad music. I knew my parents were worried, but I couldn't pretend everything was normal. After weeks of moping, I started to come out of it a little bit and showed the tiniest interest in a boy named Ryan who was in my Spanish class. He caught my attention with his clever pick up line.

"Hey Meg, did you get run over by a bus?"

We became friends.

As I was coming back to life, hanging out with Ryan and my girl friends, Jeff decided we should date again. Shawna had dumped him for a college guy, the ultimate insult for a high school boy. I knew it was a bad idea, but my heart overruled my more logical head. Jeff was fine with us being apart while I was miserable, but the combination of him being dumped and someone showing interest in me was too much for him. He decided we truly belonged together. I don't know what I was thinking, maybe it was that I liked the feeling of claiming him as *my* boyfriend, when everyone wanted him, like he was a prize or some sort of measure of my worth. I liked being a couple. That was my reasoning the first time anyway. Now we'd played the getting back together game a few times as he'd discovered new girls he was interested in, and I wasn't sure what I felt. Maybe just bored. From the outside it may have looked like he was my boyfriend, but I never knew exactly where I stood with him. It would be nice if one day he didn't know where he stood with me.

Why did I put up with this? What was it about him? What was it about me? Besides being totally hot, Jeff had that irresistible bad boy streak. There's something exciting about a little danger I guess. In good weather he wore a leather jacket and rode a motorcycle to school, which only re-enforced his image. Jeff had a mischievous glint in his chocolate eyes, and a swagger that just screamed self confidence. He was muscular from the work he did on his family's farm and playing football, basketball and baseball. In short, he was everything we shallow high school girls want in a guy.

Still lost in thought, I walked past the "nothing in this room is safe for human consumption" sign on the Chemistry lab door, and took my seat at the table toward the back that I shared with Brad. Brad had been the unofficial class clown since we were in seventh grade, when he discovered his path to popularity. He was the kid who could guzzle root beer and shoot milk out his nose. Brad learned quickly that he won friends and admiration when he made jokes at the expense of himself or teachers, rather than other kids. In middle school, he would stick a pencil in his nose and see how long the teachers would tolerate it. They would usually take the adult attitude of "ignore it and it will go away" until the class got too out of control and they had to do something about it. What was funny about it was that he did it with every teacher, every semester. With each new class, we would all anticipate the pencil gag, stupid though it was.

Brad was not my first choice for a lab partner, but seats were assigned, and I could have done worse. He was smart, but with the joking came a laid back attitude about most things, including school work. I ended up doing most of the work when we had assignments. I knew team and partner assignments were supposed to teach us what it was like in the real world, but it was still annoying when the choice was to do the bulk of the work myself or get a bad grade.

As class started, I turned toward the front. I noticed him right away. In the first row, the only place with empty seats, sat a new guy. His hair was longer than boys around Hardwick usually wore it, and it looked sun streaked. He also looked a bit tan - unheard of in Hardwick in the winter time. He was alone at his two person lab table, because until he arrived, we had an even number of students in the class.

In our small town it was highly unusual to get new students, especially in the middle of a school year. I felt a wave of sympathy – I would have hated to be the object of everyone's curiosity as he was now. At the same time, I was part of the problem – gawking at him like everyone else. His arrival was none of our business, but what else did we have to focus on? The normal quiet conversations were missing as we all waited for an explanation. It wasn't every day a surfer dude was planted into your New England high school. He had to feel our eyes assessing the back of his head.

Mr. Witt galloped in and said in an annoying cheerful voice, "Hi guys, ready for another fun filled day of Chemistry?"

We humored him and gave a collective groan. I think he secretly liked this game. We pretended we thought he was a total geek, but he was one of our favorite teachers, as teachers go.

"I assume you all noticed we have a new student today."

Seriously? I thought.

"This is Andy Garrett. His family just moved here from California."

Bingo again, obviously California.

"Today, we're going to consider gas laws," Mr. Witt said.

That's it? Though Mr. Witt was trying to get our attention, we were more interested in knowing more about the new guy. I studied him. He had long legs, was fairly tall, and I could see he had an athletic build. Maybe a basketball player.

"Who can tell me how gas laws impact our daily lives?" Mr. Witt looked expectantly around the room.

Blond and gold longish hair past his collar and falling into his eyes.

"Anyone?" he asked.

This was the highlight of our week. Most of us had been in this town all our lives, so I struggled to imagine what it would feel like to be alone at the front of the class without all those connections and our shared history. We didn't all like each other, but there was a certain familiarity in how we all knew everything about each other.

Sara Morseman broke her arm in sixth grade and we all helped write her assignments. Matt Larson had always been able to do more pull ups than anyone. Rob Anderson's parents divorced when we were in the eighth grade, and now he lived with his dad and ran wild. Kelsey Rogers and Jennifer Shepherd had been best friends since the fourth grade. I could tell you the life history of anyone in class.

It soon became obvious nobody was going to give us any more information about this Andy guy, and finally Mr. Witt got us focused on Chemistry.

Andy was in my third period History class also. Again he was forced to sit near the front, because the rest of us had already claimed all the good seats. A new kid would know he couldn't just sit anywhere he wanted without offending someone. *Everyone* was watching him. Kelsey was giggling like an idiot to get his attention. Why did boys fall for that? Could she be any less subtle?

Why did I care?

Kelsey has always been the girl every guy would kill to date. I'd seen so many boys make fools of themselves over her. This new guy wouldn't be any different. If she set her sights on him it would be all over, and it appeared she was considering the idea. Who could resist her long sleek shiny hair, her perfect pink baby doll lips, that perfect complexion and those soft brown eyes with their long black mascara coated lashes? I couldn't name any guy who ever had. To top it off, though she was completely unathletic, she had the body - an impossibly small waist, long legs and of course large perky breasts. Her physical attributes were balanced with a lack of brains and personality, but if anything, guys saw that as a plus.

Kelsey was a cheerleader of course, but not a good one. She couldn't do any tumbling and often got out of step, but nobody seemed to care. She'd just claps her hands and yell, and swish her little skirt. It was so annoying how all the guys would fall for her batting eye lashes hook line and sinker. Andy was a goner and didn't even know it. He would soon enough.

Andy would never notice someone like me with Kelsey around. Girls like Kelsey wouldn't be acting like idiots unless it worked, right? I told myself I was interested just because I was bored, but a nagging feeling in my stomach told me that probably wasn't entirely true. This guy was really cute and different. I wondered if all people were just shallow enough to care only about looks. Maybe in high school we were. After all, what if he was a total jerk? Besides, I reminded myself, I was the last one who should be looking, since I was back on again with Jeff.

Kayla Martinson, Rachel Simpson and Emilee Jansen are my best friends. When we were in grade school, we loved to chase the boys on the playground. When we caught them, we sat on them. Jennifer and Kelsey were too mature to chase boys. They played calm games and waited for boys to notice them. To our disappointment, their hard-to-get strategy worked. Boys have *always* noticed them.

This time would be no different – I could see Kelsey and Jennifer watching Andy and whispering. They planned to reel him in like a fish. He politely returned their smiles, unsure of what to make of them. Nick Meyers shook his head in sympathy. He'd been one of Kelsey's targets and knew this game. When she turned on that charm, it was hard to resist. Even I could see that. She was just as charming to me at times, when she wanted something. Luckily for Andy, they only had a few opportunities to get his attention during class. Couldn't they even let him settle in for a few days? Apparently not. Finally, the bell rang and it was lunch time.

We filed out and headed to the cafeteria. We can leave campus, but we usually don't, since there's almost nowhere to go, and we are only given thirty five minutes. I took the broccoli cheese soup and plunked down in my usual chair next to Kayla and across from Rachel and Emilee. The soup wasn't bad. A little bland, but not bad. Andy sat alone at the end of a table full of guys. They weren't unfriendly to him, but weren't friendly either - just carrying on their familiar routines. I tried not to watch him, but couldn't help it. Kelsey and Jennifer were busy holding court at their own table, so Andy was at least allowed to eat in peace.

"What do you think of the new guy?" Rachel asked. "Is he hot or what?"

"Hot like California," said Kayla.

"He's in my first period class. Did you see his eyes?" asked Emilee, looking at me.

"I didn't," I answered. "I don't think anyone except Kelsey got close enough to look, poor guy."

Rachel laughed, "I know, don't you just feel sorry for him? I hope he can take care of himself."

"Wouldn't it be great if he wasn't interested?" I asked.

"Yeah, but what are the chances of that? He's a guy, right?" Emilee observed.

We all laughed.

"Yeah he certainly is, and not like any from around here," I said quietly.

"Maybe we'll get lucky and he's gay," joked Kayla. "Then she'd be embarrassed."

"Or maybe," Rachel said, "he might notice one of us. Except you, Megan, you have Jeff."

"Yeah," I said absently. I was not thinking about Jeff.

I was a little disappointed Andy wasn't in my Journalism or Business Law classes that afternoon. I wondered what he was taking, and then I wondered why I wondered. After school it was snowing again. I sighed and pulled on my mittens, hoping I wouldn't have to scrape my windows. I trudged to the parking lot and was thankful there was no new ice.

I thought about Andy as I drove home, wondering what he thought of his first day and the snow. And his new classmates.

As I opened the door to my house, Max, our border collie, leaped at me with joy. After enduring a full minute of licking, I wiped my face and continued into the house.

"Hi Mom," I said, seeing her in her office grading papers.

"Hi Pumpkin, anything interesting happen in school?"

"Actually yes," I replied. "There's a new kid named Andy who moved here from California."

"I bet this is a shocking change for him!"

"I guess it would be," I replied. "Snow, ice, cold and a small town where everybody already knows everybody. Like, he was sitting all alone at lunch. Nobody was mean to him, but nobody included him either."

"Is he cute?" She would be thrilled if I dated other people, even though she liked Jeff.

"Sure," I said casually, not knowing what else I wanted to say on that subject for the moment.

She turned to look at me as I paused in the doorway. "That must be the family that just moved into the old Bruce house when Mr. Miller passed on. I wonder if they knew Richard Miller, or if his estate just sold the house when he died." She paused. "Well, I hope it's not too hard an adjustment for them. This sure isn't California." She shrugged and looked back toward her stack of fourth grade math papers.

No, it certainly isn't, I thought.

2 DISTRACTIONS

Thursday at lunch we discussed our new favorite topic over salads and soup of the day, vegetable beef. “Do you think Andy will go to the dance?” Emilee mused.

I snorted. “I don’t know, but I think if I were new I’d avoid it at all costs. Can you imagine anything more uncomfortable than going to a school dance where you didn’t know anyone?”

Rachel, more outgoing than the rest of us, chimed in. “Maybe it would be a good place to get to know some people, don’t you think?”

I shuddered. “Maybe,” I ventured. “But wouldn’t a decision to go end up being a decision to get to know piranha woman? He might not be ready for that, and you know she’d be on him like white on bread.”

Kayla laughed. “Yeah, it would be a lot more comfortable if you had friends to hang out with. That’s the part that would be hard for me, just standing around waiting for a guy to ask me to dance, or even worse, getting up the guts to ask a guy to dance, all without having anyone to talk to. I'd avoid it until I at least knew a few people."

Over the last few days I'd spent more time watching and thinking about Andy than I wanted to admit. He continued to keep to himself for the most part, but not in a rude or unfriendly way. Maybe next week would be more comfortable for him, as some of his new classmates started to lose interest. He didn't seem terribly concerned with being alone.

By Friday it had to be obvious to Andy that Kelsey was throwing herself at him. Classic Kelsey. We were quietly sitting back and observing. The interesting part was anticipating how Andy would react. We fully expected him to fall for her, but would it be quick or would she have to work for it? It was like watching the state champion volleyball team playing a match against a freshman team. The end was a given, but it was still fun to watch the game - to see exactly what strategies they would use, whether the underdog would score any points, and to participate in the drama. In the same way, we were all highly interested in the drama playing out between Kelsey and Andy, though we tried not to be obvious about it.

As I took my seat next to Brad in Chemistry, my gaze quickly went to the front of the room to make sure Andy was sitting there. He was. Why did I care? I didn't want to think about why. I was just happy to see him there.

Today he looked just like you'd picture the ideal California guy. There were things about him that continued to set him apart from the other guys. It was mostly in the way he dressed. His clothes were more loose and baggy, in kind of a skateboarder/beach bum sort of way. He didn't look sloppy, just casual and easy going. His hair looked like clean shiny straw with layers of different shades of blonde. He had a wide smile with perfect white teeth, though I hadn't seen it much. Even under his baggy jeans and loose t-shirt I could see that his shoulders were broad, his waist narrow, and his chest and arms muscular. He walked like an athlete, like he was well coordinated and strong but didn't need to show it. He hadn't gone out and instantly joined the track or baseball teams, so he must have been into different sports. Looking at him, you would just assume he could easily shoot a basket, throw a football, or run a 5k if he wanted to.

He seemed a little shy, but I guess I would seem that way too if I was shoved into a group of strangers. None of my friends had talked to him, but some of the guys he sat by had talked with him a little. And of course Kelsey and Jennifer asked him stupid questions every chance they could get.

Next to me, Stacy Harris dropped her Calculus book on the floor, jolting me out of my Andy daydream. We all turned to look, and Stacy's face went from pink to red to hidden beneath the table as she scooped up her things. I turned to the front to avoid embarrassing her further, and saw Andy's movie star face. I stared at him like an idiot. He was turned around with a look of hesitant curiosity on his face, no different than how the rest of us were looking in Stacy's general direction. As I glanced from Stacy to him, what *was* different was instantly imprinted in my mind. His eyes were stunning. A person could get lost in those eyes. I'd never seen a shade of blue like that. I thought my green eyes were unique, but Andy's eyes made me catch my breath. For a minute, I lost track of everything else going on in the room.

Blue eyes with blonde hair have always been considered beautiful I suppose, but usually when someone is describing a blue-eyed blonde they are referring to an attractive woman. The combination in Andy was just as striking. "Blue" was a completely inadequate description of Andy's eyes though. That one word would never do them justice, and I could see that even from ten feet away. Andy's were the most intense, deep blue I had ever seen. I guess up to that moment, I had thought eyes that color could only be made with colored contact lenses. I wondered if that could be the case here, but doubted it. Andy's eyes were not blue like the ocean, not like the sky, not like anything I could describe. I would call the color a jewel tone, but there is no jewel like that. Sapphire is too dark; blue topaz and aquamarine are too light. Cobalt?

Andy's eyes also had depth to them. In that moment I was openly staring at him. I felt drawn to him. I wondered if he had that impact on everyone who looked at him or just me. Or just girls? I was fascinated by my own reaction. Eyes are the window into every person, but this was the first time I'd seen someone and known instantly there was much more there than what I could see on the surface. I suddenly desperately wanted to know what was below the surface. What are you thinking? I asked myself, and realized I had no answer.

I became aware that the class was returning to order as everyone turned back to face Mr. Witt. I couldn't stop thinking about the glimpse I had gotten of Andy's eyes and the perfect face that went with them. I really wanted to get a closer look. I had never thought that guys could be beautiful, but I couldn't think of any better word to describe how Andy looked to me. "But Jeff…" said a little voice in my mind.

For the first time in a very long time, I thought of Jeff and my heart didn't flutter. A realization popped into my head. It occurred to me that there were other guys on the planet, and that maybe life was not meant to be all about chasing one who sat back and enjoyed letting me chase him without putting any effort into chasing me back. This tiny thought was a major revelation because I had been so wrapped up in Jeff for so long. Maybe he didn't have all the power in our relationship after all.

As the bell rang, I glanced toward Andy again. To my surprise, he glanced back. A slight smile flicked across his face, and I swear I saw a light in his eyes. I smiled slightly and turned away quickly, embarrassed that I had been watching him.

At lunch, Jeff stopped by our table. "See you at 6:30?" He asked.

"Sure," I returned absently. Tonight was the basketball game and dance. I imagined that in big high schools in big cities only some of the kids would go to the dances, depending on their social groups. Others might instead hang out at an arcade or go to the movies or a mall. We didn't have those options, so almost all the kids went to the dances. I wondered if Andy would be there tonight. Surely Kelsey would have made sure he knew about the game and the dance, especially since she would be wearing her cute cheerleading outfit.

After school the halls were loud and excitement was in the air, typical of a Friday afternoon. Everyone was in a rush to leave, and the parking lot was jammed with cars heading toward the exits. At home I fed Max, ate dinner, changed my clothes and then re-did my makeup and touched up my hair. Jeff was at the door promptly at 6:30.

"Megan, Jeff is here," my mom called.

I came down the stairs and found them chatting like old friends.

"You have a fourth grader who is saying swear words in class?" Jeff asked.

"Yes, and he is not getting the point that his behavior is not ok. I wonder what his home life must be like," my mom mused.

"Man, I could never deal with little kids," Jeff said.

"It can be a challenge. How's the paper going?" my mom asked.

"Oh, just great. We have good writing skills on our staff this year." Jeff looked up and saw me. "Hi Meg!"

"Hi," I returned.

"Well good luck with that kid Mrs. Burke," he said to my mom as we were leaving.

"Thanks Jeff. I'll see you kids later," she smiled.

He certainly knew how to charm parents - I had to give him that. In the driveway he opened the door on his side of his big farm truck, and I climbed up and crawled past the driver's side to the middle.

"Hey Meg," he said, and kissed me quickly on the cheek.

"Hey," I returned. I felt strangely distracted, but he was too busy talking about himself to notice. We were off to see and be seen. Jeff got a lot of satisfaction from the way he was treated around school. He was like a celebrity - the town's shining star, the kid every parent would be proud of. He definitely had an ego. All that and a bag of chips, that's what they say, right? He certainly thought life was all about him.

Jeff went to change into his uniform, and I took my usual spot in the student section next to Kayla.

She lit up when she saw me. “Hey girl!”

“Hey to you too,” I returned. “Do you know if Rachel and Emilee are coming?”

“Emilee is, but I think Rachel had a date with a new guy she met from Ware. Kyle, I think his name is. Did you come with Jeff?”

“Yes, and he’ll be out there.” I gestured to the gym floor.

I glanced across the gym and saw a lot of my friend’s parents on the other side, where I was sure mine would soon be, along with my brothers. In front of the students stood the six varsity cheerleaders in their red, white and black uniforms. They were the picture of American high school girls - the cool ones, not the geeks or misfits. They had perfect hair with perfect bows, perfect makeup and perfect bodies. You could see on their faces they knew everyone was watching them, and they loved every minute of it. Sometimes I wished I had the courage to try out for cheerleader, but usually I was thankful I wasn’t part of that group.

Kelsey and Jennifer looked like their perfect selves in their short swishy skirts. In the front row of the bleachers sat the grade school girls who idolized the cheerleaders with stars in their eyes. One even had on a little cheerleading costume and miniature pom poms. Every guy in the gym was stealing glances at the cheerleaders, though they would never admit they weren’t watching the game.

I didn't have any interest in basketball, but I enjoyed watching the people at the games. The cheerleaders, the band – you couldn't help but feel proud of your school when everyone got excited and cheered for the team. For me though, the best part was seeing who was together and of course who was not together. Kelsey didn't have a boyfriend at the moment, which obviously left her free to pursue Andy. Jennifer's boyfriend Pat was sitting with the other guys looking smug and cool. I could see he felt it was a great compliment to himself that he had Jennifer, in the way he would glance at her and then laugh with the other guys. She was returning his looks with big sappy smiles.

After scanning the entire gym at least nine or ten times, I decided Andy wasn't there. I felt a little tug of satisfaction in knowing that would piss Kelsey off.

Kayla looked at me knowingly. "He's not here, huh?"

"Who?" I asked.

"Oh come on Meg, it's me," said Kayla.

"Ok, you're right," I admitted. "No, I don't see him anywhere. Do you?"

"No, but here comes Emilee."

The three of us watched a little of the game, but mostly we talked and laughed about the cheerleaders and the latest gossip around school. I wasn't even embarrassed that I wouldn't be able to describe any of Jeff's great plays to him. I didn't pretend to be here to watch basketball.

After the game some of the kids snuck out to the parking lot to guzzle a beer or two, but most of us filed into the dance. My thoughts were on Andy, when I should have been enjoying the fact that I was with the man of the hour after another victorious basketball game. Somehow it seemed shallow and unimportant at the moment, and I wasn't enjoying myself like I normally would at a dance. I was secretly happy Andy wasn't here. I didn't want to watch him falling for Kelsey. A tiny voice in my head whispered, "Or for him to see me with Jeff." That was what was bothering me. I was jealous. How stupid though. I didn't have any right to think about him like that. As a matter of fact, I had less right than most, considering I was here with my boyfriend.

As the dance was winding down, we got into Jeff's truck as was our routine, and took off to be alone. We parked on a country road and kissed for a while. I was surprised to find my heart wasn't really in it, after I had looked forward to the dance all week. Jeff started to become more aggressive and I backed off, also our normal routine.

He asked, "What's wrong?"

It's not that I didn't find him attractive, I did. In fact I found him very attractive, and that in itself was the problem. There was a reason I held him off. He knew where my limits were, but didn't understand why, and I refused to tell him, in our familiar pattern. Something was shifting inside me. This did not seem like the right time to have deep philosophical thoughts, but it occurred to me for the first time that maybe my ultimate dream was different than being with Jeff.

"Nothing, I'm just tired today."

Jeff dropped me off at my house with a kiss on the cheek, and I knew he was going out to party with his friends. I didn't approve, but he had never had a curfew like mine, and he didn't see why my curfew should have any impact on him. I didn't have any good argument for that, and listened to his truck drive away as I locked the door behind me.

3 FOALS

June, 1867- Allie

That rooster was crowing again, spoiling my dream of galloping through the meadow on my sleek black horse. That feeling of freedom rapidly left me as I awoke to find myself in my bed with the first light of dawn just beginning to come through the open window. I could hear the sound of iron against iron as my mother moved pans on the cook stove while making breakfast downstairs. The rooster was honest – it was time to rise. I could not bear the thought of dragging myself out of my comfortable bed with its feather stuffed mattress and fluffy feather and down quilt, but I knew I must.

It had only been two days ago that school had ended for the summer, and with that ending went most of the excitement in my life. For me, school had ended forever. I suppose I was fortunate I had been permitted to attend school as long as I had. Not many girls made it all the way through tenth grade. Some of my friends were even married already. I was not ready for my childhood to end, but here it was. The last scrap of childhood I could cling to was now receding. Suddenly life and adulthood were upon me. Today it would only mean a full load of work on our farm, but soon life would become even more serious, with marriage and a family. I just wanted to play with my dolls and be ten again with no cares in the world.

Alright, I was moving now. The lovely sounds of birds singing outside my window gave me a bit of vigor for the day. The entire earth was alive out there, green and colorful with blooming flowers. I paused for a moment before closing the window against the heat of the coming day. I could smell the woods and feel the humidity in the air. I reluctantly pushed the window down and drew the heavy curtain. I pulled my house dress over my head and slipped my feet into my shoes. I pulled my hair into a tight bun at the back of my head while descending the stairs to the kitchen. Mother, Father and my elder brother John were already seated at the table. John and Father were dressed for a day of working outside, just like every other day except Sunday.

I went to the basin of water sitting in its place on the table by the window, dipped a washing cloth into it, and swiped it around my face. John's first duty every morning was to pump enough water for us to wash with and for Mother to cook with, and bring it into the house. I was thankful it was not my chore, because I would have had to rise even earlier, and full wooden buckets of water were quite heavy. The day promised to be hot and uncomfortable, even though it was only five thirty in the morning. Maybe Mother would assign me some work in the cellar, which would be the only cool place to be found on our farm. Summer in central

Massachusetts could be so unpleasant during the heat of the day. Heat and bugs did not make me happy.

"Good morning Allison," Father said.

"Good morning Father," I replied.

I took my plate from the table in the dining room and walked into the kitchen. As I approached, the heat from the cook stove engulfed me like I had ventured into the hot sun of the day, and I felt moisture break out on my face. I hastily spooned the remaining two fried eggs from the frying pan onto my plate, and retreated to the dining room where I took my place beside my brother. I poured fresh milk from the pitcher into my glass, took a piece of toasted bread from a serving plate in the center of the table, and then pondered my food. There was nothing to anticipate today, and the thought saddened me. It was going to be a day filled with chores, with many more days just like it to follow.

Father watched me pushing my eggs around my plate for a moment. "I have something for you," he said.

I looked up at him with interest. "Really?"

"Yes, well, I know you are sad that school is over. I thought you might enjoy a new writing project."

I was sad that school had ended, yes, but I wasn't so sure I was going to miss writing. I would miss learning new subjects certainly, but mostly I was longing to socialize with my friends. Now we had all gone our separate ways and would not often see each other. No more games in the school yard and no more lively discussions about government or history. On a daily basis we had imagined ourselves in faraway places and conversed about the world. I regarded my father, not knowing what to think. I hadn't noticed the little wrapped package sitting on the table, but now he was pushing it toward me. Mother watched with a small smile.

I couldn't remember the last time I had received a gift. Christmas I suppose. I smiled at Father and he smiled back. I carefully tore the tissue paper off the small package. It was a book, but there was no title on the cover. I was puzzled.

"It's a diary," Mother said. "You can write your private journal in it, and some day it will be amusing for you to read your thoughts from when you were seventeen in Hardwick Massachusetts, in 1867."

I smiled at them both, touched by the gift. It would be nice to have a place to write what I really thought about things - a place to be completely candid. "Thank you," I said to Father. "It is a very thoughtful gift." I considered how I would get started.

John put his dishes by the basin and went out the back door to attend to his duties. His most important one, besides getting water for Mother, was feeding all the animals in the morning and evening. With several cows, a few hogs, a flock of chickens and about thirty horses, it was a significant responsibility. Father soon trailed John out the door, setting off for the fields. Mostly we grew hay and corn to feed our animals. Mother would begin her day by baking the bread for the week. That was a very unpleasant task in the summer, since the stove made the kitchen so unbearably hot. My first duty was to wash all the breakfast dishes, which I did as quickly as possible so that I could escape the stifling kitchen. Then I was to gather the eggs.

"Allison, when you are done with the dishes and eggs, you can work on weeding the garden," Mother instructed me.

I despised weeding. It was boring, hot and tiring. But so were all my other duties.

"Put on a sun bonnet," Mother added.

"Yes ma'am." I replied.

I rubbed the dishes with a wet rag and soap in the first basin of water, then rinsed them in a clean basin of water, then wiped them dry and returned them to the cupboard. Then I heaved the dirty water out to the back porch and dumped it a few feet outside the door, leaving the basin in the sun to dry. I pulled my bonnet off its peg by the door and plunked it on my head. Then I secured my favorite long nail, to be used to help pry weeds out of the ground, and placed it in my pocket. Last, I found my egg gathering basket.

After going down the back steps, my first stop was the outhouse. Our house had an indoor privy, a luxury most people don't have, but we only used it when it was cold outdoors. During those times we were quite thankful for it. Each spring Father would shovel a wagon load of dirt down the holes so the house would not smell bad. The outdoor privy however, smelled like a normal privy. From a young age I had learned to hold my breath the entire time I was in there, and mostly didn't notice the odor. I quickly did my business and exited, taking a nice deep breath as I hastened away from the little building.

I retrieved my basket from where I had left it on the grass, and walked to the chicken coop built next to the barn. The hens were out of the henhouse in the fenced chicken yard, pecking at food John had given them. That was good, because they were sometimes hostile when I tried to take their eggs while they were on their nests. I unlatched the wooden door into the coop and proceeded into the smelly nesting area. Once per week John had to muck it out and fill it with fresh straw, one of his most unpleasant chores. It was mildly enjoyable to gather the eggs because it was like finding treasure, even though the treasure was always the same. Today was a productive day for the hens, ten eggs. I carefully laid them in the basket and let myself out of the henhouse. I took the basket to the kitchen and put it on the shelf.

I dreaded the next several hours, and it felt like rocks were chained to my feet as I plodded slowly to the garden. In the summer, the garden was a never ending task. If it wasn't weeding it was picking. If it wasn't picking it was fetching water for plants that were too dry. I knew I shouldn't complain, because that patch of dirt provided a great deal of food for us. Still, it was torture to take care of. Mother made preserves from our harvest and we ate them all winter. There were beans, peas, potatoes, onions, greens, tomatoes, cabbage, carrots and beets. There were also blueberries, raspberries, strawberries and currants. Every single one of those plants had to be cared for.

I settled in the dirt at the end of the row of beans. I had to pull out every plant that wasn't a bean all the way down the row. As I started to weed in the early morning sun, my thoughts drifted. Was this all there was to life? Would I be weeding gardens all my days? It had to be more interesting to live in a city. Nothing interesting ever happened in our small town. Going to school was probably the last meaningful thing I would ever do. Now I would have a life of pulling weeds and baking bread. There were no other choices. A tear escaped my eye and rolled down my cheek.

My thoughts turned to Jeremy as I made my way down the row. He was the boy I was promised to marry. I did not love him. I wasn't sure how to feel about that, but it wasn't really important. It was just the way of things. I had known Jeremy Hunter all my life. He lived on a farm situated five miles from ours, and would someday take it over from his father. He was two years older than I and had stopped attending school at sixteen to work on his family's farm. Some of my friends thought he was handsome, and I supposed he was. He was very serious though, and we'd never had much of a conversation. When we had agreed to marry, it was because we were doing what was expected of us. Our parents were very pleased with the arrangement. At my age, it was one of those things that needed to be settled by now, and so it was. I would marry soon just like all the other girls in their late teens.

I glared at the beans. Is this how it would be, my life? Instead of weeding Mother's garden I would weed Jeremy's garden. My garden I suppose. Was that supposed to content me? It did the opposite. A lifetime of drudgery lay ahead of me. I felt as if more weight were being added onto an invisible anchor pulling me down. I could see by observing Mother what married life would entail. Her existence was for the purpose of working to take care of her family. She toiled in a hot kitchen in the heat of the summer. She labored from sun up to sun down. She didn't seem to object, but I couldn't imagine anything more saddening. After several hours of weeding, I needed a rest. I made my way to the house to get a drink of water and to check with Mother to see if anything else needed doing.

"How is your weeding progressing?" Mother inquired.

"Fine. I've finished the beans and am working on the corn." I scooped water from the clean water basin into a cup and drank thirstily.

"Please pick enough greens for dinner and bring them in so I can get them cooking. Then get an onion from the cellar for me."

"Yes, Mother." I picked a basket of greens, made sure there were no insects on them and returned to the house. I noticed my fingernails were stained slightly green from weeding. I'd have to scrub them well. I was relieved to go to the cellar for an onion from last fall's harvest. It was a frightening place at night, but interesting and relatively cool during the day. I descended the steps off the kitchen until my feet touched on the dirt floor. The air smelled musty and damp. My eyes had to adjust to the darkness because I hadn't brought a lantern. The only light came from two small windows at the top of the far wall and the stairway behind me. The onions and potatoes were stored in piles in the nearest corner to the steps. I went to the onion pile and selected one. Standing there, I noticed an unpleasant smell straight away. There was likely a rotten potato in the pile. It always seemed to be the one at the bottom. One must get the rotten ones out or the whole pile would go bad. I wondered if I should stay and sort through the pile, but decided against it.

As I slowly climbed, I could feel the temperature rising with each step. The baking bread made the kitchen even hotter than outdoors.

"Thank you Allie," Mother said, as I placed the onion on the counter.

I turned to go back to the garden.

“Allison?”

I turned around. “Yes Mother?”

“You seem sad, is everything alright?”

I knew there was no candid response I could give, but was torn because I could see she really cared. I wanted to throw myself in her arms to be comforted like a child. How could I tell her I didn’t want this life, her life? I knew as well as she did that there were no alternatives. What good could come of making her feel badly?

“I miss school,” I offered.

“I know my dear. Let’s go into town tomorrow. I need to purchase some flour and sugar.”

“Yes Mother, that would be pleasant.” It would be nice to get away from chores for a few hours, but would do nothing to solve the real problem - the course of the balance of my life.

“Why don’t you weed until dinner, and then after dinner we will spend the afternoon sewing. It will be terribly hot by then. You can work on your quilt. Then we’ll prepare a roasted chicken for supper. Won’t that be good?”

“Yes ma’am.” Chicken with mashed potatoes was one of my favorite meals. I knew how to prepare it too. Jeremy would probably like it when I cooked it for him.

As the sun blazed even hotter, I traversed from the corn to the peas, noticing there were already some ripe pods. I cracked one open every now and again as I moved along, and ate the sweet crunchy peas within. I loved uncooked peas. As I was finishing weeding the beets, Mother called us in for dinner, our noontime meal. I hung my bonnet on its peg and left my nail on its shelf. I washed my hands, scrubbing hard around my fingernails. Then I took a loaf of freshly baked bread and sliced it, placing the pieces into a basket lined with a napkin. I carried that and a dish of strawberry preserves to the table.

Father and John came into the kitchen and washed their hands. They were dirty and sweaty. The house was cooler than outdoors, but not much. At least we were shaded from the sun. Father said grace, and we began to eat. The fresh bread with butter and preserves was delicious, as always. Mother did make the most wonderful strawberry preserves.

"The foals are growing and getting much stronger," Father said, looking at me.

I smiled. We had eight foals, all born during April, and they were the most precious little creatures I could imagine. They seemed to be made mostly of legs. "And their mothers?" I asked.

"All taking very good care of their babies. Why don't you walk out with me after we eat and have a look?" asked Father. Mother nodded and smiled. They both knew how I loved our foals. My father raised Morgan horses. They were hard working, sturdy and muscular, but also beautiful. Men came all the way from Boston to purchase them. The civil war cavalry had wanted as many as Father would sell, but he was reluctant to sell them for that use, because so many horses were injured or killed at war. He did sell some to high ranking officers however. Father was also known for helping other men with training problems, and sometimes men boarded their horses with us so Father could fix whatever was displeasing about them. Father simply had a way of communicating with the animals. Horses were the main business of our farm.

Father relaxed at the table while I finished washing up the dinner dishes. Then together we walked out past the barn and down the dirt road. The foals and their mothers were in one of the further pastures today. They would be moved from pasture to pasture, depending on which had the most grass for them to eat. Between them and the milk cows, it only took them a few days to trim down the grass in any pasture.

We arrived at the edge of the stone wall, and I carefully climbed the steps to the top and sat. Father settled next to me. This pasture held ten mares and eight foals. Our stallion and other horses were in another field, away from the babies. The mares stood about thirty yards from us, grazing in a small group while their foals napped on the ground close to their mothers. I had hoped to see them frolicking about, but it was too hot for that. I didn't blame them for wanting to nap. They were adorable. I loved how the mothers never ventured far from their babies. Maybe I would feel that way about my babies some day.

"They are so sweet Father."

"I know Allie. Every single one is special to me."

"To me also," I said.

He continued, "And you are even more special to me. I'm very proud of you. You have grown into a beautiful young woman, it seems like overnight."

It was very unusual for him to voice anything like that. "Thank you Father."

He gave me a brief hug.

4 HORSE TRADING

June, 1867- Allie

After watching the horses with Father, I walked slowly up the dirt road toward the house. At the edge of the stone wall that surrounded one of the closer pastures, I veered off into the woods and followed the wall a short distance. Soon I came to my special place. There was a large oak tree at the edge of the woods here, where Father had hung a swing when I had been but a small child. Mother used to bring me here to play, but hadn't in years. She thought I had outgrown the swing, which was true, but it was still a special place to me when I wanted to think or be alone.

There was a welcoming cool shade beneath the oak, and I sat on my swing looking about the pasture and distant hills, enjoying the few moments without responsibilities. The peacefulness of the place always gave me comfort. I could hear the sounds of birds and insects, but nothing else. There were tiny pink wildflowers in the grass arranged around my swing and trailing into the woods. I breathed in the smell of the woods as I swung slowly back and forth. After a short while, I realized I needed to return, because Mother would be wondering after me.

Mother and I spent the early afternoon sewing and sipping lemonade. She was stitching a new shirt for Father and I was mending one of my housedresses and working on my patchwork quilt. Though I was already a skilled seamstress, I was practicing tiny perfect embroidery stitches. The quilt blocks were various shapes and colors, depending on the scraps of fabric I could gather at any given time. Most were familiar scenes of my life. The quilt was only about one fourth completed, and each block seemed to take hours, because I wanted them all to be perfect.

Mother inquired, “What do you think about marrying in the late autumn, maybe around harvest time? Then we would have an abundance of wonderful food for the celebration.”

I didn’t want to discuss this subject, and wasn’t sure when I would want to. Wasn’t I supposed to be excited about getting married? I knew some of my dearest friends were excited about their upcoming marriages. Why, Janie was not only married already, but pregnant with her first child. She certainly seemed content. She and Samuel Patterson had been promised since eighth grade. They had always fancied each other, and Janie had been elated to marry. All I could think was that when I said ‘I do’ I would be conceding to myself and the world to be a farmer’s wife living a life of drudgery. My stomach twisted. Mother’s gaze was upon me, waiting for an answer.

“Yes, that would make sense,” I said quietly.

She smiled. “Good. We need to start planning. You and Jeremy must decide on the right date. Maybe you can approach him after church.”

“Yes.” I paused, considering whether to ask what I really wanted to know. “Are you happy Mother?”

“Whatever do you mean Allie? Of course I am. I have a wonderful husband and two perfect children. We have plenty of everything we need. What more could I desire?”

I don’t know,” I replied. “I was just wondering.”

“Did I say something that gave you the impression I wasn’t?’ she asked.

“No Mother, I was just wondering if you were doing what you wanted with your life.”

She pondered that for a moment. “What else would I do Allie? It’s a very complete life your father has made for us.”

I could see she was puzzled by the conversation. I knew our family was much better off than hers had been when she was a child. My father’s family had resided in this very house and raised livestock just as we were doing, though not as prosperously. They had four children, which meant more mouths to feed, but also more people to do the work. The previous generation, the original Bruce family, had eight children, and had owned much more of the surrounding land than we did today. Our farmhouse was the largest around, with five bedrooms and both a front and back staircase. It was nearly one hundred years old, but still sturdy and well taken care of. Someday John would own it and manage the horse farm.

“You’ll speak with Jeremy then?” Mother asked.

We both knew Jeremy was waiting for me to confirm the date for our wedding. I knew Mother couldn't understand why I was hesitating. I wasn't sure I could either.

"Yes," I said again.

"Allie, I believe we can afford to sew you a special wedding dress. That is part of why I want to confirm the date, so we can make the dress appropriate for the season. You know, whether it should have long sleeves or short, details such as that," Mother said.

I could see she was quite excited about the dress. I knew it was an extra expense to purchase the fabric and would mean a great deal of work for her. I truly hadn't expected to have a dress just for the wedding, and it seemed like an extravagance. I was touched that she was willing to do it.

"Mother, that is so nice. Thank you," I said warmly.

She continued, not wanting to make a fuss, "and the July 4th celebration is coming."

"Yes, that will be pleasant," I replied absently as I stitched.

In the late afternoon we folded our projects and stored them, and got to work preparing supper. John had killed a chicken, and Mother prepared it to roast and put it in the oven. I took charge of the potatoes, peeling them, boiling them and then mashing them. Mother basted the chicken and made gravy from the drippings. The roasted chicken turned out just as delicious as I had anticipated.

After saying grace, Father started the conversation. "John and I were in town this afternoon. There are always new faces these days. So many people are starting new lives after the war. Many have been displaced from wherever they came from, or needed to come north to find work. The whole economy in the south has been devastated. We met a Wayne Collins, seemed a decent sort. He'd been in the war. He's going to come out and see our horses. He needs a few good ones to take out west."

Mother was proud of Father's reputation with our horses, "He's certainly looking for quality horses in the right place," she said.

Father smiled at her.

John spoke. "He was interesting. Fought in the war, but didn't want to discuss much about it. No different than most I suppose. He's entering the cargo business, providing supplies to western territories. There's probably good money in that."

"Won't that be dangerous?" Mother inquired.

"Probably so," Father replied.

I could barely imagine a life out west. It was no place for a respectable woman, I was certain. All those territories were a man's world. Still, I wondered what it would be like to have a new adventure every day. Probably worth considerable danger.

My life was the opposite of dangerous. Everything about it was predictable. We all did what was expected of us, and our lives played out in a familiar pattern – birth, school, church on Sundays, marriage and death all in our little town of Hardwick. And there was plenty of work for everyone to do every day. We weren't touched much by the outside world.

I washed the supper dishes and stored them, read from the bible, wished my parents goodnight, and then mounted the stairs to my room. It was a pleasant place, with a pretty wood floor under my mother's handmade rug and a big window overlooking one of the pastures. There was a walk through closet to the next room, which we only used for storage. My bed had a soft feather mattress with a lightweight summer quilt my mother had made when I was a child. I drew open my window, and after the heat of the day the cool breeze was most welcome. I burrowed under my quilt, feeling safe and secure in the house I grew up in.

Morning came too quickly, as always. Today though, John would drive us into town in the wagon and wait for us while we did our errands. Sometimes we walked the distance to town, but today would be too hot, and we would not have wanted to carry our purchases all that long way home.

At breakfast Mother regarded me. “I saw that the first beans need picking and the carrots need to be thinned.”

I nodded. After finishing the dishes, I took my bonnet and nail, picked up a basket and made my way toward the garden. The carrots were easy to pull, and my nail stayed in my apron pocket. Then I picked a half basket of beans. I took them in the house where I washed them and cut them into bite size lengths. Mother boiled them and we ate them for our noontime dinner, along with leftover chicken and more fresh bread.

After dinner, John went out to hitch up the horses, Bess and Clover. When he drove the wagon around to the front door, Mother and I stepped out to meet him. Bess was my favorite horse, and on rare occasions I was permitted to ride her. She was gentle and sweet. I stroked her soft nose. “Hey sweetie, how are you?” She gave me a nudge.

The ride into town was hot and dusty. When we got there we drank water from the pump and then splashed a little on our faces. The horses drank greedily from the trough.

"I'd like to walk around the common a little, is that alright Mother?" I asked.

"Yes Allie. Come and meet us at the store when you are finished," she replied.

Mother and John entered the general store, while I wandered across the common, staying in the shady areas as much as possible. The common had beautiful old oak trees around it. I supposed they could tell a story. The grass was soft, because we weren't far enough into summer yet for it to have turned brown. I walked past the cemetery with its little white fence surrounding the grave stones. Then I walked past the open door of the church, and noticed how the light looked pretty streaming through the stained glass window and reflecting on the polished wood floor. I waved at Reverend Halvorson as he looked up from sweeping the stops. When I arrived at the general store, Mother was conversing with Janie's mother.

"Hello Allison," she greeted me.

"Hello Mrs. Wallace," I replied politely.

"You are looking well dear. Have you seen Janie recently?"

"No ma'am, not in a while. I know she is going to have a baby of course. How is she?" I could see Mrs. Wallace was excited to respond.

"Oh, she couldn't be better. She's a little uncomfortable in the heat. She would be pleased if you would stop by to visit."

"I will soon, I promise," I replied. That would be something to anticipate. I truly liked Janie and had known her since we were children. Maybe she could reassure me about this whole marriage idea.

"And presently you will be married and having your own children," gushed Mrs. Wallace.

My mother smiled at her.

"Yes," I agreed flatly.

John hoisted the sacks of flour and sugar to the wagon and Mother carried a folded length of fabric she had purchased. She handed me a small package.

"I purchased these for you."

I looked in the little sack. There were five small cards of colored embroidery thread – blue, white, orange, yellow and red. They would be wonderful additions to my quilt. "Thank you Mother, these are beautiful," I exclaimed.

"You are welcome Allie. I'm so glad you like them," she replied with her warm smile.

Bess and Clover were anxious to go. They were always much more enthused about pulling the wagon home than going anywhere away from home. The ride was at a brisk horse pace and didn't take long. The wildflowers in the woods were bright and colorful growing in the shade of the trees and bushes. I felt a sense of contentment about getting home, as I imagined the horses did. How would I feel about going to my new home? I pushed that thought from my mind.

We prepared a supper of ham and greens. Father gave the blessing and we passed the food. Then he said, "John, in the morning let's put the geldings and young mares in the house pasture, since Mr. Collins will be coming to view them. Let's have bridles and saddles ready also, in case he wants to ride any of them."

The house pasture was what it sounded like, the one closed to our house – the one I could observe from my bedroom window. I loved when the horses were there. They were beautiful and majestic, and I could watch them for hours if I were given the time. The best time was when the foals were in that pasture.

"Allie, can you help John polish the saddles in the morning?" Father asked.

It was one of my favorite chores. I glanced at Mother, who nodded, and I nodded also. It was always good to have guests, because it meant a change of routine and that Mother would make iced tea to serve, one of my favorites when I added a little sugar.

After supper I read from the bible. Then I started my diary. The easy part was entering my name in it. The difficult part was pondering anything else to say. Maybe tomorrow would bring something noteworthy, I mused.

In the morning I followed John out to the barn after breakfast. He presented me with a rag and the saddle soap, and pointed to the two saddles he wanted cleaned. I didn't need any further instruction on how to do this work. John retreated to feed the animals and I started in on the saddles, wiping away the dust and dirt and polishing the smooth leather to a shine. The smell of the soap made me happy, for it was another familiar smell of home. I presumed Mr. Collins would be impressed at how smartly this horse farm was run.

Reluctantly, I left the barn with is nice smells of clean hay and saddle soap, and found my mother in the garden.

"Allie?" she called as she saw me.

"Yes Mother?"

“I think we might have a spoiled potato, can you sort them? Then bring up eight or so, to mash for dinner. If you could peel them, we’ll get them cooking.”

“Yes ma’am,” I replied. The cool of the cellar would be a respite from the heat, but there weren’t many odors worse than rotten potatoes. I made my way down the steps and settled on the floor next to the potato pile. At least it was summer, which meant the pile was much smaller than it could have been. We only had another few months worth of potatoes in the pile.

“Hello potatoes,” I said. I laughed at my silliness. I began a new pile right next to the current one, as I scrutinized each one. Sure enough, toward the bottom I found two rotten ones – white and smelly. I placed them in my basket, carried them up the steps and tossed them outdoors on the waste pile. Then I returned to the cellar and selected eight nice looking potatoes and carried them upstairs to the kitchen. I scrubbed each one, and then peeled them with a paring knife. I put them in a pot of water and set them on the cook stove to boil, adding more wood to the fire.

When Father and John came in for dinner they took extra time cleaning up, and after dinner they both changed into fresh clean shirts. Mother and I washed the dishes, and then we all arranged ourselves in the parlor as if that were what we did after our midday meal every day. Nobody wanted to get started on any chores since we were anticipating company.

Shortly, out the front window, we saw a man ride up on a horse. Father and John went to the door, while Mother and I remained in the parlor. Father let the man in, and the man removed his hat and followed Father into the parlor, where Father presented us.

"Mr. Collins, this is my wife, and my daughter Allison."

I gazed on him in surprise. This man was not much older than my brother. I had been expecting someone much older and much less interesting. I couldn't help but notice he was very attractive. He had straw colored hair that almost touched his shoulders, pale blue eyes the color of a cornflower, and broad shoulders.

"Pleased to meet you Mrs. Bruce," he said to Mother. Then he turned to me and his mouth bent up in a crooked smile. Something about his smile felt personal, like it was especially warm just for me. But that was silly. His eyes twinkled and he said, "and you too, Miss Bruce."

I nodded, dumbstruck. What an idiot he must think me.

"May I offer you some iced tea?" Mother asked.

"Oh thank you ma'am. Not now, but I'd appreciate some after we look at your horses."

"That would be fine," Mother said.

Mr. Collins followed Father out the door. I couldn't help but watch as they left. He seemed very self assured in the way he walked. He was as tall as Father, but more slim. I surmised he wasn't more than twenty two or twenty three years old. What was his life like?

The men went to the pasture. I dusted everything in the entire house and then swept the floors. Every now and again I looked out toward the pasture, and was amazed at how they could talk so long about horses. Sometimes they would point at one or another. At one instance I saw Mr. Collins running his hands over one of the geldings. Finally they all came back to the house, and they were talking with each other as if they were old friends. They took chairs on the porch next to the pots of bright red geraniums, where Mother served them iced tea in tall glasses. The men removed their hats and conversed some more, as if none of them had work to do or any place else to be. I would have liked to have joined them, but of course that was not proper. I did steal peeks at Mr. Collins however. He was quite handsome. There was a manner of confidence about him, and he seemed quite charming. Finally he shook hands with Father and John, then untied his horse and rode away.

At supper Mother and I were anxious to know how the meeting had gone. Father teased us by saying nothing. Finally Mother inquired, "Well?"

"Yes?" he teased her.

"How did it go with Mr. Collins?" she asked, slightly annoyed.

"Very well actually. He is probably going to purchase two, maybe three. He needs good reliable horses to take out west with him. He said he'd never seen better."

"Well, I'm sure that's true," Mother said.

"He needs to consider which will best suit his purposes for a few days, and think about the cost. There are no bad choices. Of course he likes the same ones best that I like best."

"Yes, but you know you can't keep all of them dear."

"I know. We're in the business of raising and selling horses, but even so, I'm attached to every one."

She smiled at him. I could see the love between them. Were these moments of love worth the drudgery of their lives? Possibly so. Was I looking at myself in thirty years?

Would I love my husband like my parents loved each other? I hoped so, but I wasn't certain.

Sunday dawned like any other day, but after the animals were attended to, we didn't have to do any more chores besides cooking and washing the dishes. After breakfast we dressed in our best Sunday clothes. Unfortunately, my best was a winter dress that still fit. It had long sleeves and a high collar, which made it quite uncomfortable when the heat was stifling. I put it on, added a sun bonnet, and we assembled in the parlor. John brought the wagon around, and then Father helped Mother and me up onto our seats. He sat up front with John. We drove to the beautiful little white church. The windows were open, and though it was only mid-morning, it was already quite hot inside.

We took our usual family place in the second row on the right hand side. All the families always sat in the same places, and any visitors sat in the open places that remained toward the rear. I said a short prayer, and then rested quietly on the bench between Mother and John. I glanced to the left and saw Jeremy sitting with his family. He smiled at me, and I smiled back quickly and returned my gaze to the front. Soon I forgot that I was trying not to move and turned around to see who else was in church. I noticed Mr. Collins standing in the back, looking quite dashing in a pale blue shirt that matched his eyes and brown trousers. He nodded ever so slightly as my eye caught his. I felt myself blushing. He must think me a bored child.

After church I avoided talking to Jeremy, even though Mother seemed to linger so I would have ample time. I made my way outside and stood under a tree, fanning myself with my bonnet. It was just too hot to deal with any problems. Finally Mother finished conversing with the other women, and we were able to leave. I could feel her gaze upon me, but pretended not to notice.

At home we changed into regular clothes, and Mother set out a light dinner of bread and jam with cold ham. After dinner, we were free to do whatever we pleased until it was time to cook supper. Father cleaned his guns, Mother embroidered, and John went outdoors to go riding. I read a little, then went to observe the foals and visit my swing, and then worked on my quilt. I was excited about using the new threads Mother had purchased, and planned out a Fourth of July themed square. It wouldn't be a flag because I wasn't patient enough to sew that many stars, but it would have the same colors and a few stars. Each star was considerable work, but I could see they were going to look quite pleasing.

I helped Mother prepare a supper of pork roast with mashed potatoes and gravy, beans and bread. We worked in a familiar routine side by side.

"I noticed you didn't talk to Jeremy," she started.

"I was too hot to think about it. I had to escape the church," I replied.

"I see. I hope he didn't think you rude."

"I don't think so. I smiled at him."

She wanted to continue discussing Jeremy. "When are you going to talk to him?"

"Soon Mother, soon. Please don't worry."

"Alright Allie, I won't. I just don't want you to forget your manners. And I want some time to plan the wedding and your dress, once you know the date," she reminded me again.

"I know Mother," I forced myself to smile.

I changed the subject. "What did you think of the music at church today?" Mother really enjoyed music.

"It was lovely. We are so lucky one of the women plays the piano."

"Yes," I agreed. "She must practice a lot."

"I'm sure she does, to be so accomplished. When will you go to visit Janie?"

"I don't know. Probably after the July 4th picnic. Or maybe she will be there."

"Yes, after would be good, we have a lot to do over the next several days." We always brought much more food than our family could possibly eat, and Mother was known for having the best pies in the country. I was sure she wouldn't disappoint. We had early raspberries and blueberries, and Mother was letting them ripen until the very last minute so they would be as sweet and juicy as possible. I was a little surprised she wasn't making me stand guard over them all day to keep any birds away. The annual picnic was important to everyone. For Mother and all the women, it was a chance to show off their cooking skills. For me it would be a chance to socialize with my friends.

5 HOT OPPORTUNITY

Monday in chemistry class, Kelsey was flirting with Andy again. He looked slightly uncomfortable, but who wouldn't be in the presence of the most beautiful girl in school? She giggled as she leaned over the table toward him, her shiny hair falling forward. Was it only obvious to me that her shirt was too tight and she was pushing her chest in front of his face? I didn't know how to feel. On one hand, I wished I had the guts, well, and the natural assets, to act like her, but on the other, her behavior seemed so superficial. Was he responding? I couldn't really tell without getting up and walking over there. Out of the question of course. I wondered if I was the only person in the room who felt a need to rescue him.

What was I thinking though? Didn't I already have a boyfriend?

Wednesday morning as I was getting out of my car, I saw Andy pulling into the parking lot in a Toyota Prius. I snickered, because that's exactly what people from Hardwick would imagine someone from California would drive. It's not that we don't care about the environment in Massachusetts; we just aren't rabid about it like Californians seem to be. I wondered why Andy was driving slowly toward the corner of the parking lot furthest from the building, but as he stepped on the brake, the car slid for about ten feet on the ice. Ah, that's a good reason to park out there. I bet nobody ever taught him to drive in snow.

As he got out of the car and glanced toward me, I looked away guiltily. It *was* a little funny, but I didn't want to make him feel bad. Snow driving was just something kids around here took for granted. I turned away quickly and walked into the building.

Econ passed slowly as usual, and then it was time for second period Chemistry. I wondered why Mr. Witt was always so cheerful. Could anyone really care about Chemistry that much? I guess I knew the answer. It was not that he cared about Chemistry; it was that he cared about kids. He talked to us like we were adults, and acted like we were much more responsible than we really were. He was excited when we understood difficult concepts, and wanted us to succeed. I guess most teachers would want us to succeed, but most didn't seem to care much whether their class was interesting or not, just whether we passed the tests.

"We're going to talk about Hund's Rule today."

The class groaned, as Mr. Witt expected. He grinned at us, then turned and drew five boxes on the board, and put an x in the fourth box.

"Guys, pretend you walked into the bathroom and here are the urinals," he said, pointing to the boxes. "The one with the x in it is occupied, and the rest are empty. How do you choose which urinal you are going to use?"

Mr. Witt looked at us expectantly. Were we supposed to answer that? Clearly he had everyone's attention. The boys were weighing whether or not to answer, though their faces showed they knew the answer. The girls looked more confused. What kind of answer could there be to that question?

Tyler raised his hand tentatively. "You have to pick the one farthest away from the one that's being used, so the first one."

"Exactly!" pronounced Mr. Witt. He then erased the x, and put an "x" in boxes one and three. Pointing at the boxes he asked, "Now if people were already using the first and third urinals, which would you choose if you walked into this bathroom?" He looked around the room making eye contact with the boys.

In unison, the class yelled, "The last one!"

"Yes again!" Mr. Witt said. "Why?"

"Well," ventured Matt, "it's because you would be invading someone's privacy if you stood right next to him when there was all that empty space in the rest of the bathroom."

"It's socially unacceptable," added Stacy.

"It's uncomfortable both for the person already there and for the person just arriving," commented Sara.

"You're all right," said Mr. Witt.

"Now what if you go into the bathroom and urinals one, three and four are occupied? He drew the x's. Is it ok to use the second or fifth one?"

"Yes!" we yelled.

"Why?" he returned.

"Because then you have no choice, so nobody thinks you're weird," said Brad.

"That's exactly right," smiled Mr. Witt. "That is why I call Hund's Rule the urinal rule. Remember how we've been talking about how electrons fill orbitals, and surround the nucleus? The idea is that if you are electrons filling orbitals, you can only go to a space where you wouldn't be making one area too crowded and leaving another too empty. In other words, the electrons have to be as evenly distributed as possible, so they are exerting as close to the same amount of energy on each other to remain in their positions. Everything must remain as balanced as possible. There is order to where each new joining electron will choose to go."

The classroom erupted in debate. Not about electrons or orbitals, but about the best methods for choosing urinals or bathroom stalls, and all the factors that could lead to a different decision, for instance a bathroom emergency or a broken urinal. The decision process for the boys was simple, as Mr. Witt had illustrated. For the girls though, it was a little different. The girls agreed the criteria should be first, whether the stall had a door, second, whether the stall was clean, and third, whether there was toilet paper. Last was whether there were other people nearby or not. The boys were surprised to find that the issue of stall choice was important to girls, figuring with walls and a door on both sides of the toilet, it shouldn't matter much which stall you got.

"Electrons go through the same sort of "decision" process in choosing how to occupy orbitals," Mr. Witt went on.

It was safe to say we would not forget Hund's Rule.

As we were walking out after our energetic classroom debate, I noticed Andy walking next to me. He glanced over and asked, "Do girls really care whether the next stall is occupied? I mean, bathroom stalls are much more private than urinals."

He talked to me. I froze for a second, and then replied, "Yeah," I paused, "unless one of the toilets hasn't been flushed."

He smiled and walked away. I could feel Kelsey's glare, and as I turned to look she looked away quickly. I smiled to myself.

The next day Mr. Witt gave us Bunsen burners, scales and little metal trays with a blue substance in them. I thought he was smarter than that, but apparently not. Each burner was a small glass jar filled with liquid paraffin. Each jar had a screw on metal top with a hole in the middle, and a piece of white cotton rope pushed through the lid into the liquid below. When Mr. Witt turned his back, Brad grabbed our burner, turned it upside down, and drew a huge squiggle across our lab table with the liquid paraffin. I shook my head and rolled my eyes.

"Now what's the first thing we need to do, even before I explain the experiment?" Mr. Witt asked.

"Safety glasses," we groaned, and we all put on our dorky glasses.

"Good. Now in your trays is a hydrated molecule. Who can tell me what that means?"

Stacy raised her hand and said, "It's a substance that has water attached to it."

"Yes!" said Mr. Witt. "What we are going to do is first weigh the substance in the tray as it is. Then, we'll heat it up so that the water evaporates, leaving only the remaining chemical. We will then weigh the remaining chemical, and by comparing how much it weighed with the water and then without the water, we will be able to determine what the formula is. Go ahead and start by weighing your substance," instructed Mr. Witt. "Then you can light the burners and hold the tray about an inch over the flame to heat up your substances for about one minute."

I weighed the tray with the blue substance and wrote down the number.

Brad lit our burner, and also lit the line he had squiggled on the table. The squiggle lit up in the same way you see a line of gunpowder burning in the movies. It was kind of fascinating. Everyone gasped. Though the flame went out quickly, Brad obviously would not be allowed to get away with it. I could see in his devilish grin that he knew that, but considered it worth it anyway. He had a reputation to maintain after all. Mr. Witt had him out the door and on the way to the office in an instant, but he knew better than to leave us unattended with miniature fires on our tables. As he came back into the room, we all made an effort to be serious and focus on our lab work, not knowing what his mood would be. Mr. Witt acted as if nothing had happened, until he said words that froze me.

"Andy, would you please join Megan at her table? This lab is really best done in two person teams, so Chris and Mike can go on without you, and you can finish up with Megan."

Andy picked up his notebook and walked around the tables toward me. As he passed Kelsey, she smiled her million dollar smile at him and he smiled back. Why did that bother me? I didn't know, but it did. As he walked past her toward me she turned, following his motion, and gave me a quick warning look as if to say, "watch yourself, he's mine." I got the message loud and clear. As he lowered his lean body into the chair next to mine, I could feel my palms getting sweaty. Get a grip, I told myself.

"Do you want to hold the burner and I'll hold the tray?" he asked. "I see you already got the first measurement."

"Ok."

Is that all I could muster, ok? Lame.

When the water had obviously cooked off, I blew out the burner. He put the little tray on the scale and read off the numbers as I wrote them on our piece of paper. He nodded his head in approval, his shaggy hair falling around his face and looking like it needed my fingers in it.

Why would I think such a thought? My boyfriend would be waiting for me after class. I looked up at Andy. Those dark blue eyes. They were looking right into mine. I could fall into them.

He asked, "Do we compare to the chart to see what it is?"

I saw a light in his eyes as they studied me seriously. The gaze was a little too intent, but I couldn't break away. Was I some kind of weak fool? Close up I could see his perfect white teeth set in an impossibly beautiful smile. I could only hope I didn't look as stupid and dumbstruck as I felt. I wondered if he knew he had this impact on people. If he did, he didn't seem to be conscious of it.

"Uh, I think so," I stammered.

"Please turn in your lab results as you leave," instructed Mr. Witt.

I gathered my things.

"Thanks for letting me join you," Andy said.

"You're welcome."

Mentally I kicked myself again. You're welcome? Is that all I could think of? Like I had any say in whether he joined me or not? Like I wasn't the one who got the gift? I wished I had been allowed time to come up with a more intelligent response. But then, why did I want to flirt with him anyway? Why did I find myself pondering such questions so often lately?

Walking into the hall, I saw my boyfriend of the last year deeply engrossed in conversation with a sophomore named Julie who was looking at him with puppy dog eyes and a big drooly puppy dog look. I'd seen it a million times. I didn't feel jealous, just annoyed. Jeff didn't even try to hide the fact that he was flirting with her. If it were me, at least I'd have the decency to pretend it didn't happen or to feel guilty about it. He did neither. I walked on to History, where I was able to spend the next hour secretly observing Andy.

At lunch Kayla asked, "Why is Jennifer giving you dirty looks?"

"She is?" I responded.

"Well, just small ones," Kayla replied.

"Probably because Andy sat next to me in class today," I offered with a smug smile.

"Oh I get it, she's defending Kelsey," said Rachel.

"It's not like I did anything wrong," I said quietly. "First, Kelsey doesn't own him, but even if she did, all we did was a stupid Chemistry assignment."

"Yeah, but I think they want you to understand that Andy is taken," said Emilee.

"Whatever," I said.

"Was he nice?" asked Rachel.

"Very," I said.

"What else?" Kayla asked.

"What do you mean?" I replied.

"Well, did he flirt with you or anything?" asked Kayla.

"No, he was just nice. He did smile at me." I realized how stupid I sounded.

"You think he's hot, don't you?" asked Emilee.

"Well yeah, but don't you guys too?" I replied.

"Oh definitely," Rachel said, and they all nodded in agreement.

Very hot, I thought. Too hot. I found myself looking forward to Chemistry the next day. Would Brad be back?

He wasn't. My heart lifted in anticipation of what I hoped that would mean. I also hoped Brad wasn't in too much trouble. Maybe his punishment was only for the rest of this week, which really meant just yesterday and today since it was now Friday. Right before the bell rang, I heard the soft low voice right beside me.

"Mind if I join you again today?"

Did he ask me if I minded?

"No," I said, and nodded toward the empty chair. Is that all I could say? No? Pitiful. Lame. Idiotic. I wondered if he thought so too.

I found it very difficult to pay attention with him sitting next to me. He seemed unaffected in any way, though he noticed every time Kelsey turned around to glance at him. I could tell by the slight way he shifted in his seat, almost as if he were embarrassed by the glances and was trying to duck from them. I was actually impressed by how her body language communicated extreme warmth to him and in the next instant hostility to me.

The bell rang too quickly and I was sad to give up my place next to Andy. Today's class had been mostly lecture so we hadn't talked, but I had spent the entire hour enjoying how it felt to have him sitting next to me where I was able to see his every move and observe him in what I hoped was not an obvious manner. We exchanged a quick smile as we got up to walk out. In the hall I saw Jeff engrossed in flirting with another sophomore girl.

As I closed the distance between us he asked, "Hey, are we going out tonight?"

"I don't think so," I replied.

"Are you ok Megan?"

"Yes, I just have some things to do."

I could tell he was annoyed. On a normal Friday night I would be hanging out with Jeff, or at a party, or doing something with my friends. Tonight though, none of that seemed appealing. I felt like I had a big problem to solve, without knowing what the problem was. My mom and dad were thrilled to have me there watching a movie with them, and Max sat with his head on my lap as I stroked the soft fur under his chin. There's nothing like a dog. Loyal to the end, uncomplicated, wanting what is best for you and loving you no matter what. Why couldn't people be like that?

My thoughts drifted to Jeff. And then to Andy. Now was a good time for some honesty with myself. Why had I been so sure at one point that Jeff made me happy, but now I was filled with doubt? What had changed so much? I thought about it all weekend.

Monday morning arrived with a dry parking lot at school. Spring was indeed coming. Andy pulled in right behind me, parked, and walked toward me as I leaned over to get my coffee out of my cup holder.

"Hey," he said.

"Hi," I replied. "You did better today." I nodded toward his car in its space.

He blushed slightly, knowing exactly what I was talking about. I felt a little bad for having said it, but then he flashed me a shy but brilliant smile.

"See you in class, huh?"

"Yeah," I smiled.

Later as we were walking into the Chemistry lab, I saw Kelsey ahead of me and Andy ahead of her. She took a couple of quick steps, bumped into him, and exclaimed, "Oh, sorry!"

Obviously she was not sorry at all. I felt a flash of annoyance, and then looked toward my seat and was disappointed to see Brad was back. I felt guilty for feeling disappointed, but I had hoped I would be "stuck" with Andy again. Brad was cheerful as always, as if nothing had happened, and Andy was back in his front row seat. Andy seemed to be having casual conversations with Chris and Mike, so I felt glad he wasn't so alone. I loved watching him interact with them. There's something about how guys can be so easy going with each other, as if they had known each other all their lives. He laughed casually and said something I couldn't hear.

Mr. Witt went right into it. "Ok guys, next week is our test. Today we'll review."

Collective groans echoed around the room. It was hard to concentrate. Chemistry formulas, periodic table, how could that compare to the gorgeous creature sitting in the front row? I wondered if this was what they meant about how boys are always distracted by having girls around. I sure felt distracted. But not by all the boys, only by one of them. By the end of the period, we were all good and brain dead. The bell rang, and we were eager to leave. I turned to the door, and heard a soft low voice in my ear. "Do you want to study for the test together?"

My face must have shown the shock I felt, because as I turned toward Andy, he looked like he might have regretted asking.

"Yeah, that would be great," I said. What was I thinking? Like that was going to go over well with my *boyfriend.* Now what was I going to do?

"Do you want to come to my house on Sunday?" he asked.

"Yeah, that works," I said. "I get off work at 2:00."

"I live..." he started.

"I know," I interrupted. "This is too small a town not to know where everyone lives. You moved into the Bruce house."

"Right, I did. Ok, so I'll see you a little after two on Sunday."

I wanted to scream with excitement, but managed to contain myself. Then the reality of what I had agreed to hit me. Now what? There's no way I can NOT do this.

As I sat down at the lunch table Emilee said, "So?"

I looked up. “What?”

“You know what,” said Rachel. “Tell us!”

“About what?” I asked.

Kayla said, “You know how fast text messages travel, you know, Stacy just kind of mentioned to Lindsay that you and Andy were talking, and, you know.”

I didn’t know what to tell them. The truth I guess. I looked at their three expectant faces and broke into a silly grin. “He asked me to study for our test with him.”

“What about Jeff?” asked Rachel.

“I know. I don’t know.” I paused. “I know.”

“Well, glad that’s settled,” laughed Emilee.

“Yeah hardly, right?” I said.

“You lucky dog,” said Kayla, obviously not concerned about Jeff.

“Jeff has been kind of an asshole lately anyway, hasn’t he?” asked Rachel.

“I don’t know. In some ways I guess,” I said. I felt like I should be defending Jeff, but at the same time I knew I didn’t want to. I wanted my friends support for the pain I was going to have to go through next.

“Are you going to tell him?” asked Kayla.

“I need to think about it, but I’m not sure what there is to tell. Andy and I are only going to study together. It doesn’t mean we’re dating. Still, I wouldn’t think Jeff would be happy about that. I think I am going to tell him I want to see other people for a while. I guess that’s the truth. I don’t have to tell him which other people.”

“Oh, he’s not going to like that one bit. I bet nobody has ever broken up with Jeff,” said Rachel.

I smiled weakly.

6 ENDINGS

Over the next few days, my head lined up with my heart on what I already knew I had to do. It was just so scary. I'd never ended a relationship. And what if I was making the wrong decision? I felt so paralyzed.

"You're doing the right thing," Kayla assured me. "Jeff doesn't treat you well. He's dumped you several times, and he's always flirting with somebody or other."

"Why didn't you ever say that before?" I asked.

"I think I did, but you didn't seem like you wanted to hear it," she replied.

"I'm sorry Kay."

"No worries, I'm just glad that for whatever reason, you're seeing other possibilities. Jeff's hot, but that doesn't mean he can treat you any way he wants. You deserve better."

"Thanks Kayla, you're a good friend."

"It'll be hard, but you'll be fine Meg."

"I know, you're right. I just wish it were over with."

"Be strong," she encouraged.

It was time. Besides being the right thing to do, I was not going to play any games with Andy, and wanted to be able to tell him honestly that I didn't have a boyfriend. That is, if he asked. I didn't want to even consider that he might only be looking to study with someone and nothing more. Of course Kelsey was still in his face every chance she got. I couldn't think of any reason he wouldn't be interested in her. No matter what Andy's intentions were though, I was not going to play games with Jeff either, testing the waters while still holding on to him, even though he was constantly doing that to me. As I walked out of Business Law, I saw Jeff by his locker with some of his friends. I took a deep breath. Now or never. As I walked up to him, he gave me his devilish grin, like we shared in some amazing secret. My heart clenched. That grin had always melted me. I steeled myself.

"Can we go for a drive after school?" I asked. "I want to talk to you. We haven't talked in a while." I felt like I was stammering.

"You need help with your Business Law homework?" he joked. We both knew Business Law was not his thing.

Despite myself, I laughed. "No, I'm doing fine in there. Ok?"

"Sure Meggie," he replied. "Meet me at my truck after school."

There it was. I was committed now.

I sat through my last class filled with dread. I had no idea what the teacher was saying and didn't care. All I cared about was that this horrible feeling end. It almost felt like those times when Jeff had broken up with me, like I was starting to mourn a loss. I thought about how silly that seemed, because it was me taking the action here. Still, Jeff and I had some good times, so it was probably natural that I would have some regrets. Understanding that logic didn't make it any easier. My stomach was in knots.

After class I fumbled with my locker. I slowly put my books on the top shelf and then took out my coat. I made my way to the parking lot and saw that Jeff was already waiting for me in his truck, stereo blaring. He was oblivious to the fact that something was wrong. I climbed in on the passenger side and kicked the snow off my boots before closing the door.

"Where do you want to go?" he asked. He leaned over and kissed me. Why did he have to be all sweet and charming at this moment? I knew why. That was the magic of Jeff. It always had been.

"We don't have to go anywhere I guess."

"I thought you wanted to go somewhere," he said, puzzled.

"No, I just wanted to talk to you. Can you turn down the music?"

He did, and looked at me. "Ok, talk." He was starting to get uncomfortable. One thing I knew about Jeff was that he did not like complications, and having a serious conversation was definitely a complication.

"I... I think we... I mean I think I want to cool it for a while," I stammered.

His face clouded. Was it anger? "What do you mean? What are you saying?"

"I, just…"

"You just what Megan?"

"I guess I want to be friends for a while, and see how that goes."

"You're breaking up with me?" Jeff asked with surprise.

For a moment I considered his reaction. Insulted? Embarrassed? There was no disappointment or hurt in his expression, only disbelief. He had always taken the lead in every part of our relationship.

"I guess I am," I said slowly.

"What's wrong with you?" he asked.

"What's wrong with me?" The question made me angry, but I couldn't think of anything to say. He went on before I could speak.

"Yeah, you've always been the one who wanted to try to make it work."

"I know, but,"

"Are you cheating on me?" he accused.

"No, of course not, I just want to see how it would go. I think we're growing apart and I just don't feel the same." I wanted to tell him I was also tired of his flirting and ignoring my feelings, but didn't. I didn't want him to apologize or try to fix it.

"I'll tell you how it will go," he snapped. "You'll be really sorry, that's how it will go."

I wondered if he was right. I had cared about him and believed in us for a long time. We had fun together, and I was proud to call him my boyfriend. What was I thinking? And yet, something was missing, I just couldn't think what. I looked into those chocolate eyes that had always held me, and I saw… nothing.

"I'm sorry," I said.

"No, it's fine, have it your way," Jeff spat. He should have been sad and asking me to stay, but he was acting like I had insulted him. Was this how little I had ever mattered to him? After all the tears I had shed when he had broken up with me? That made me angry. I hadn't wanted it to go this way.

"But can't we…"

He cut me off. "No, we can't. You'll be sorry, but you'll find that out for yourself. We're done." His attitude communicated that *he* was breaking up with *me*.

I suddenly felt panicked. I had become so used to having Jeff in my life that it was hard to imagine him not being there. What would people think? That he dumped me? So what if they did?

I felt tears welling in my eyes. Without looking at him, I got out of his truck and shut the door. I walked to my car, got in and mechanically drove almost all the way home. As I turned down our street, I couldn't hold in my emotions any longer. I pulled over in front of a vacant lot. I felt hot tears sliding down my face, and gave into them and sobbed. A tiny bit of me felt a sense of relief, but most of me felt sad, alone, and traumatized.

What if I had just thrown away the guy that was right for me? What if he would have changed? Even as I asked myself those questions, I knew I had done the right thing, but that didn't make it hurt any less right this moment.

7 PARADES

July 1867- Allie

Mother and I spent the next two days preparing food for the picnic - picking berries and vegetables, rolling out dough and baking in the sweltering hot kitchen. I was so weary of cooking by the time the day of the celebration dawned. This reprieve was even better than a Sunday. We would spend the entire day at the common with all the other families, visiting, eating and playing games.

Mother and I loaded all the food into baskets and then carefully placed the baskets into the back of the wagon with blankets tucked around them to hold them firmly in place. Father added some potato sacks to contribute to the sack races. We were all excited. The parade would commence at noon, and then a meal would follow. Families would arrange their food on their blankets, and everyone would share with anyone who came along.

We arrived in ample time to secure a good spot in the shade of a medium sized oak tree. Father and John spread our blankets while I helped Mother carry our baskets from the wagon and arrange them, leaving ample room to sit.

"Alright Allie, you can walk around a bit," Mother told me.

Freedom. The common was filling with people, most of them people I'd been familiar with my entire life. I wandered about, chatting with school friends and sipping lemonade offered to me. Presently it was time for the parade to start, so everyone made their way to their blankets. If everyone were seated, nobody's view would be blocked. It was a good system.

The parade commenced with two decorated wagons followed by a three person drum and fife band. A group of small children trailed with streamers on sticks, and then there was a wagon carrying the mayor. Two more brightly decorated wagons with beautiful horses pulling them brought up the rear. It was a short parade, so it circled the common twice.

After the parade, families gathered on their blankets to eat. Mother and I set out all the food we had brought, and we all ate our fill and more. I sampled Mother's strawberry and apple pies, and both were excellent.

After people had a chance to let their food settle, there were organized sack races, running races and all manner of fun games for the children. The older kids threw balls or tossed bean bags at boards with holes in them, playing corn hole. It was amusing to watch the children compete with each other, especially the boys. Even the young ones were quite aggressive, tumbling over each other to be the best and fastest. In the heat of the day people dozed on their blankets or held quiet conversations. Women cooed over babies, children chased each other and old men played cards. It was unbearably hot, but nobody wanted to be anywhere else. I saw Jeremy at a distance, but he seemed content to be spending time with other young men we were acquainted with. Mrs. Wallace told me Janie had stayed home to nap, since it was plainly too hot for her to be out. I enjoyed simply watching all the people as I sipped lemonade.

The heat finally started to let up a bit, and it was time for supper. All the leftover food from the noon meal was brought out again, and now that everyone had become reacquainted with their neighbors, people were unabashedly sampling each other's food to get something different. I discovered some delicious cold pork and potato salad a few blankets away. Mother and I were content to converse with the other women about food and people, while John and Father were off doing whatever men do – probably discussing crops and horses. And possibly the war.

The musicians had traveled all the way from Worcester to play for the dance. They started to arrange themselves, and I could feel the excitement in the air. A dance was a rare event in our tiny town, though there was usually at least a fiddle player at most wedding celebrations.

The littlest children were sleeping on their family's blankets, and a few families had gone home, but most stayed for the dance, because this was an all day event and a rare chance to socialize. As the band struck up, people were hesitant to dance, but as dusk settled and lanterns were lit, more people worked up the courage. Father pulled Mother out for a dance, and then asked me for the next one. I enjoyed myself twirling in his arms. As we were finishing, Jeremy requested a dance. I could feel Mother's eyes on us, but luckily the music was too loud for any serious conversation. I danced with a few boys from school, and then stood watching the pretty colors of women's skirts twirling by.

An unfamiliar voice said in my ear, "May I have this dance?"

I turned and encountered the pale blue eyes of Wayne Collins. He offered his hand and smiled at me. I'd never seen such life in a face. I couldn't think of anything to say, so I reached out and took his hand. It felt firm and strong, and curiously like a lifeline retrieving me from a fog. He pulled me close to him and I felt the heat of his body. He smelled fresh and clean, like he had just bathed with pleasant smelling soap. Then the music started. I looked into his eyes and saw a fire deep beyond the blue, and the rest of the world slipped away. I could no longer see the other people around us and I couldn't hear the music. I couldn't do anything except stare into his eyes. I stumbled like a clumsy ox, but he caught me and righted me as if nothing had happened. His grip was firm and his movements were smooth, so nobody would have noticed he had been carrying me for a moment. I smiled at him gratefully, and he returned a beautiful white smile. His arms held me steadily, and I knew for certain in that moment there was no place else I was meant to be.

His eyes mesmerized me. It felt as if he were looking deep inside me and knew everything about me. And I wanted him to. I drank in his gaze hungrily. My heart was pounding, and feelings ran through me that I had never even dreamed of. I felt as if the world was shaking, when all we were doing was a slow waltz. It was as if a door had opened.

I blinked, and saw that his eyes held a look of hunger that matched what I was feeling. How could that be? Who was this man? If he could make me feel this way with a simple touch and a glance, what did it mean?

The song ended and I clung to him. I didn't care what anyone thought. I felt as if letting him go would be letting life go. I didn't know I had it in me to feel so strongly about anything. I'd never felt such an attraction in my entire life. He bent and whispered in my ear, "Thank you beautiful lady." I could see he didn't want to let me go either, but propriety demanded it of both of us. We were barely acquainted, and any more than one dance would have raised eyebrows.

My heart ached as he released me. I reluctantly let him go and walked unsteadily back to our blanket. I sat in the near dark against the tree trunk while my heart slowed to a normal pace in my chest. Nobody around me seemed to notice anything was unusual, but I felt as if I were suddenly an entirely different person. It was as if I had just done something outrageous such as taken my dress off in public or stolen candy from a child. I felt everyone must realize by looking at me that something was different, but nobody seemed to notice at all. Nobody even glanced at me. Everyone was consumed in their own lives.

I did not venture near the dancing people again. I couldn't bear the thought of dancing with anyone else now – of having anyone else touch me after Wayne Collins had. I wanted to be alone and think. Wayne. The name echoed in my head. The sound of his voice burned in my memory. He was the most handsome incredible person I had ever encountered. His touch set me on fire in a way I had never dreamed possible. I could not stop thinking about it. I sat lost in my thoughts until it was time for us to pack up and travel home.

"Allie, why are you so quiet? Did you have a pleasant time?" Mother asked. "I saw you dancing with Jeremy."

"Yes Mother, it was lovely, I'm just very tired." I used the normal excuse. "The heat drained all of my energy today."

"I know what you mean," said Father. "It was damn hot today."

Mother glanced at him and raised her eyebrow.

"Very hot, I mean. I think we're all tired," Father added.

When we arrived home I helped unload the remaining food, and Mother and I stored it away while Father and John tended to the horses. I vaguely wondered if our horses had enjoyed socializing with the other horses. Probably so. I was grateful to retreat to my room, and opened the window to the cool night air. I lay on my quilt and thought about Mr. Collins. I fell asleep and dreamed of a handsome man on a horse who came to rescue me from monsters chasing me through the garden. His horse was a white stallion and his face was Wayne Collins. Then he kissed me.

When I awoke in the morning I was terribly disappointed that my dreams had ceased. I fought to keep them fresh in my mind for as long as I could, though their content would have been shocking to Mother and Father. They were the vivid dreams one can't easily forget, and I reviewed them over and over in my mind throughout the morning, savoring the feelings.

We were all tired from our big day yesterday, so we did our least strenuous chores. In the afternoon Mother and I settled down to sew, and I put aside my July 4th block for a time, in order to start a new one. As far as anyone would know it was a scene of mountains, but I knew it to be otherwise. It would be an upside down letter W made of brown fabric on a blue background with a yellow sun. Each piece would be outlined in tiny stitches. W for Wayne. Wayne. Wayne. The quilt of my life would now include Wayne. What if I never saw him again? A stab of pain shot through me.

"I like your idea for mountains Allie," Mother commented as she glanced over.

"Thank you Mother, it just came to me." By late afternoon, the pieces were secured together such that the W was formed. I would never be able to tell anyone what these mountains really represented.

For supper we had leftovers from our picnic food.

"Did you Allie?" asked Father.

I had no idea what he had asked. My mind was a hundred miles away imagining the possibility of being someone other than a farmer's wife. It was not so much that I expected someone like Wayne Collins to rescue me, as it was that I was wondering if there really were other options. But that was silly, there weren't any other options. Mother would be shocked that I was even thinking such thoughts. I realized they were all looking at me.

"I'm sorry, I didn't hear you Father. What did you say?"

"I asked whether you tasted any pies at the picnic that were half as good as your mother's."

"Oh no, not even close."

"Where were you just then?" asked Mother.

I had to think of something. "Oh, I was just thinking about how cute all the children were in the sack races. When little Tommy Norton fell and took his partner down, and then the next two teams fell on top of them, it was so amusing, the big pile of sacks and struggling little boys."

"It *was* amusing," Father agreed with a snort.

I was unusually preoccupied over the next day. My mind was racing a million miles an hour, but there was nobody I could unburden myself to. Not one of them would understand what was distracting me. I was expected to simply plod along in my life, do my chores, plan a wedding, get married, go off and have children and be a farmer's wife. I would socialize with my family at church on Sundays and work hard all week just like everyone else. Was that all there was meant to be?

Sunday I awoke and my mind was no more peaceful. I hoped I would find solace in church. I struggled into my best dress, feeling too hot even though it was still quite early. It would be a relief to come back home and change to cooler clothes. Thankfully, this morning there was a small breeze to keep the day from being completely stifling.

We made our way to the second row, as always. I said a small prayer, asking for peace in my head, and then settled into the bench to wait for the service to start. I looked idly around and saw the familiar faces I had seen all my life. As my gaze wandered to the rear of the church, I saw him. Mr. Collins. I was shocked at the jolt of lightning that traversed my body. My eyes locked on those cornflower blue eyes, and again it was like everyone else disappeared. He held my gaze for but a moment, but it felt as if a lightning bolt traveled from him to me and back again. He winked at me. I turned away and was certain my entire body must be shaking. It felt like an intense physical reaction, from just having seen a set of eyes. I wondered if everyone was staring at me in horror, as if I were convulsing on the floor. They weren't. Nobody even noticed me.

I ached to turn around and stare openly at him, but of course I couldn't. As I tried to listen to Reverend Halvorson, my head gave way to what my heart had been screaming for the past few days. There was more. There was different.

I didn't know how I could accept the life that had been planned for me. It was not my plan. I didn't know if it ever had been. I needed to have a say in this, but I hadn't had one. I hadn't known what to say. Now my eyes had been opened, and I couldn't close them. But what did it mean? What could I possibly do? Even Mr. Collins would have to think me a silly school girl for having such thoughts. As handsome as he was, he was probably accustomed to girls looking at him with doe eyes. He probably hadn't given me a second thought. But whether he had any part in my future or not, his presence had altered my thoughts, my mood, my place in the world and the course of my life. How could I accept the life set before me?

Sunday afternoon I sat sewing with Mother. Did she notice the particular care I was taking with my mountains? If she did, she didn't say. My mind was in turmoil. I wanted to scream. I willed myself to sit silently and sew.

"I noticed you didn't speak to Jeremy today," Mother begin.

I looked at her. This conversation again. "I was just so miserably hot in church again today Mother. I couldn't muster the energy to make my way over to him and then to have a conversation. It seems a private matter, to discuss one's wedding date, but at church there are so many people about. I don't want to discuss it with him in front of everyone."

She nodded. "I can understand that I suppose. But how will you decide a date? Would you like to write a letter? Or perhaps you and I could call on his family? Or we could invite them to supper at our house?"

"Those are all good ideas Mother. Please let me consider them for a while."

"Alright Allie, but we really do need to settle it soon."

"I know Mother." I knew all too well, I thought, as I smoothed my hand over the rays of the sun that hung over the W of my mountains.

Monday started like a normal day. I did chores all morning. After dinner Mother went to work in the garden, while Father and John labored in the fields. I was to do more tasks around the house. The heat of the day was so oppressive that it felt as if it might rain. I took my wooden bucket to the pump and filled it with water, then carried it to the front porch. I would water the geraniums and pinch the dead flowers off so new ones would grow. The potted flowers were quite beautiful, and very important to Mother. They gave our house such a pretty look for anyone who came calling. There were three large half barrels, with eight red geranium plants in each.

I seated myself next to the first barrel and started to pinch off the dead flowers. I glanced up at an unusual sound, and saw a rider making his way up the driveway. It couldn't be. It was. I watched as the tall handsome man approached, sitting like a knight on his steed. He stopped and dismounted before me. The sunlight glinted on his straw colored hair as he removed his hat. In a heartbeat I was lost in those pale blue eyes that looked right through me.

"Afternoon," he said.

I looked up into his face. "Good afternoon," I replied.

"Is your family around?" he asked.

"Mother is out in the garden, and Father and John are working in the fields. Were they expecting you Mr. Collins?"

"I think at some time today, but we didn't settle on a specific time."

He climbed the steps toward me and I could feel my heart pounding as if it would leap from my chest. He took my hand and lifted it to his lips. A shiver ran through me at his touch. "It's very good to see you again Miss Bruce."

"Allie," I croaked.

"Allie." The melody of his voice saying my name was magical. I noticed he was still clasping my hand. I looked at our hands guiltily, and noticed his fingers were long with clean fingernails and rounded tips. His hand was strong, but cradling mine gently. I knew I should remove my hand, but I couldn't command myself to do it. I gazed into his eyes.

"There's something here between us," he said.

I saw myself reflected in his eyes. My future? Everything that mattered? "I know," I replied. I did know. I could feel it.

"This doesn't happen to people every day."

"No, it mustn't," I agreed. I poured out my thoughts. "I have never imagined someone like you. Where have you come from? I mean, why here? Why now?"

He continued to hold my hand as he led me to our porch bench. I continued to let him, knowing my parents would be scandalized. With his free hand, he brushed my hair back from my face and trailed his fingers down my cheek. It sent an unfamiliar ache of longing through my body.

"I'm here because your father has a reputation throughout the north for having the best horses anywhere around. But that's not what you're asking."

I shook my head no. I wasn't concerned with his words. I just thrilled at the sound of his voice. I watched him as he talked.

"I fought in the war."

"So you've seen horrible things," I stated.

"Yes, too numerous. I'm very grateful those times are over and that I survived it with all of my body intact. I am starting a shipping business, to bring supplies out to the western settlements. For that I need good reliable horses. It will be hard work, but there is an immense need for it. People will pay a high price for the goods they cannot make themselves – fine fabrics, tobacco, pots and pans, tools. I believe I can make a successful living at it. I'm sure it will have its share of adventures also."

"It does sound very interesting." I paused. "I am promised to someone," I said, looking down at my lap.

His hand did not release mine. "Do you love him?"

I was shocked at the bluntness of the question. Such things were simply not asked. I looked back into his eyes. I didn't know how to respond other than to speak the truth. "No," I said quietly. "He is simply a boy I have known all my life. He is a good man." A tear escaped my eye. I was mortified.

Mr. Collins gently wiped the tear away. "I am so very drawn to you. I don't even know you, but it is as if there are magnets in our bodies drawing me to you. I have thought about you constantly since I first laid eyes on you."

I couldn't believe I was hearing this. Was he sincere? If he was, it was beyond my imaginations and dreams. I searched his eyes. I knew with a certainty that he meant what he was saying. I wanted to ride off with him on his horse, never looking back. I knew that thought was ridiculous even as I was thinking it.

"Can that be true? I have thought of you a significant amount also."

"Not only can it be true, it is true. I must see you again."

I couldn't stop the words before they fell from my lips. "I want nothing more." Had I really said that? It was entirely improper.

He smiled and squeezed my hand. I had said it.

"But," I started, "how can that possibly happen? Mother and Father would never let me be alone with you."

"I know Allie."

We sat in silence for a moment, knowing even our privacy in this moment would end at any time. I thought furiously. "Mr. Collins?"

"Wayne, to you I am Wayne. Or darling," he added with a crooked smile.

I blushed. "Wayne." I liked the sound of my voice saying his name. I felt ashamed for what I was about to say. "I will meet you tomorrow evening, after supper."

His eyes lit up and he nodded yes. "How? Where?"

I rushed on, before I lost all courage. "I will go to see my friend Janie, who is pregnant. I have been meaning to visit her. Mother will let me go by myself. Meet me just outside town on the road. I will see Janie for a few minutes, but then meet you."

"I will be there Allie. I cannot wait to steal a moment of your time."

I could not believe I had just planned such a thing. I would have to do penance in church. I must be evil and wicked. I couldn't help myself. I was so excited.

"I must tell Father you are here, before we are discovered."

"I know. I just don't want to release you. I will content myself with the knowledge that you will meet me tomorrow."

"As will I," I replied. I regretfully withdrew my hand from his. He remained seated on the porch, while I went to find Mother and Father. I found Mother in the garden and told her we had company. She rushed to the porch to offer him refreshments, while I went to find Father. I located him and John in the field, and they came in right away to attend to Wayne. Mr. Collins. Whoever he was. Who was he?

Wayne passed the next few hours with Father, and Father seemed pleased when he came in to supper. They had agreed on the horses and their prices, and now Mr. Collins only needed to come back with the money.

"Is it settled then?" asked Mother.

"Yes, at a very fair price for both of us," replied Father.

"How many will he take?

"Three. Two geldings and a mare. He's getting his money's worth."

"Of course he is," Mother agreed.

"He'll be back for them in a few days."

"Good," she smiled at him.

I was tormented. I remained silent, though I listened intently to the conversation. I felt as if I were on the edge of a precipice that would decide the course of my entire life. It was probably the biggest fork in the road I would ever encounter. In my head I was screaming in confusion, but my face remained composed, for I had to pretend everything was normal. What if I made the wrong decision? What decision did I even have? The only thing I knew for certain was that more was possible. Different was possible. But what? Wayne hadn't offered me any future. He had only given me a glimpse into his life. He had only made me aware that the touch of a man could electrify me and set my body to longing for him. How could I let that knowledge pass? Was I weak and without morals for even thinking these thoughts?

As I slept, he filled my dreams. Those eyes and that hair, those strong hands that had held mine. In my dreams we waltzed in a meadow. I touched his face as if he belonged to me. We laughed without a care in the world.

8 APPLE PIE

I felt surprisingly better the day after breaking up with Jeff - relieved but a little sad. It was like I had said goodbye to an old friend, but at the same time it felt like a weight had been lifted and I had a fresh outlook on the world. I felt relatively normal, except that my eyes were puffy. After Saturday morning chores of vacuuming, laundry, dusting and washing the dog, I spent four hours studying Chemistry. Pre-studying actually. I was not going to go to Andy's house and look stupid.

My shift at the deli started at 8:00 every Sunday morning. I only worked two days a week during the school year, Wednesday nights and Sundays, but it was enough to keep gas in my car and a little money in my purse for movies and stuff.

The deli was part of a convenience store and gas station. Early on a Sunday it was rare to have customers in the store, and it was kind of peaceful that way. The cashier looked up from the morning paper spread across the counter as I walked in. "Hey Mike," I called.

"Mornin' Megan," he replied, returning his attention to the newspaper.

I made myself a latte and walked through the candy aisle to the back of the store, then past the drink coolers to the deli area. I flipped on the lights and hung my coat on a peg. I put on my green and white striped apron and flicked on the radio. Then I washed my hands. I took tubs of meat and vegetables out of the cooler and filled up all the trays. I wheeled out the slicer and plugged it in, then pulled a giant turkey breast from the cooler. I cut the wrapper off with my sharpest knife, then loaded it into the slicer and started shaving off turkey in paper thin slices. Sometimes they folded into neat accordions as they landed. As the pile grew, I grabbed handfuls of turkey and stuffed them into storage jars. I could never resist eating a few slices as they piled up. Breakfast on Sundays always consisted of freshly sliced meats and usually some melted cheese. And occasionally some tomatoes and sprouts.

After finishing the slicing, I pulled the hot plate out of its drawer, plugged it in, and set it to high. I filled an enormous pot with water and put it on the hot plate to boil. As the water heated, I peeled 30 pounds of potatoes that would eventually become potato salad. I was fast and quite skilled at peeling with a paring knife - I could work as a galley cook for the military. I wondered if military cooks cut themselves as often as I did. The good thing was that the routine of preparing all the food made the time go very quickly. Not a minute after the potatoes were in the water, people started arriving. Sundays were busy because people stopped in to get food for picnic lunches for weekend outings. There were lots of beautiful wilderness areas in this part of

Massachusetts and people around here liked to be out in them, at least when the weather was nice.

A young couple with a baby in a stroller stepped up to the counter.

"May I take your order?" I asked.

Without pausing or looking at her husband, the woman replied. "Two turkeys on wheat, tomatoes, lettuce, pickles, mayo."

"Cheese?"

"Yes, Swiss." It was clear who the boss in that family was.

Velma, my grandmotherly co-worker, arrived at 11:00 to work until closing. That meant my lunch time had arrived, and I made my favorite personal creation. Swiss cheese on a plate, corned beef on top of that, sprouts, tomatoes, and more Swiss cheese on top. All of that nuked for 45 seconds. Perfect. Ah, melted cheese.

My first customer after my break was a regular. I smiled at him as he walked up. "Roast beef and catsup with cucumbers on white, right Mr. Walker?"

"Yes Megan, same as always," he smiled. There was no accounting for taste.

The lunch business always kept us busy, which was why two of us covered those hours. When I glanced at the clock, it was 1:55, five minutes to quitting time. I had forgotten to be nervous about going to Andy's house, but now I felt a sudden wave of panic. This is what I wanted, right? It had better be, I'd already broken up with my boyfriend and pissed off Kelsey and Jennifer. No point in wasting all that effort! Well, the boyfriend part would have happened with or without Andy, but still…

I threw my apron in the hamper, struggled into my down jacket and stood on my tiptoes to look out the front windows, considering whether I needed my boots. Sighing, I put the boots on. There was no fresh snow, but everything was still covered in this morning's slush, including the hood of my car. My Civic wouldn't complain though, it had front wheel drive, and hadn't let me down yet. I slid into the icy seat and noticed I could see my breath. I turned the key and the engine came to life along with the blaring radio. I shivered while I tried to get organized. Books in the back seat? Check. Hair combed? Check. Makeup freshened, light, but not too light? Check. Nothing could be done about the boots, bulky wool sweater and puffy winter coat. I looked like I was headed to a geek convention.

I headed my Civic toward the old Bruce place - out on the highway, and then off into the thick woods on both sides of Flowers Road. I'd never given much thought to that old white farm house that sits tucked into the woods on the right hand side about a mile up the road. It had always been there, just like the old church on the common and countless other buildings around town. Those old places might be interesting to strangers, but when you'd seen them all your life, they weren't very noteworthy. As I drove carefully up the narrow driveway, I looked at the house as if I was seeing it for the first time. It was quite big for an old farmhouse, and a little mysterious looking. It was mid-afternoon, but the sky was covered in dark clouds and the woods added to the lack of light. The house had a lot of windows and most of them looked dark from the outside. I followed the driveway as it circled to the front of the house. I parked as close to the front door as possible, and stepped out into the icy cold air. There was a warm glow of lights in a few of the main floor windows, and the light reflected off the snow outside even though it was still daylight.

Suddenly I was looking at a different scene. Different but not different. It was exactly the same view, but it was summer. The house stood in the bright light of full summer sun. The lawn was green and there were leaves on the trees. The house was freshly painted white and there were three wooden barrels of bright red geraniums on the porch. The heat of the day was oppressive, and I felt a bead of sweat rolling down the small of my back. I blinked and it was all gone. It had felt absolutely real for just a split second. What was that all about? It was as if I had a strong memory of the way the house looked, but I didn't recall ever even standing in front of it before. I was too nervous to think about it and dismissed the whole thing.

I sucked in another deep breath of icy air, crunched through the snow to the door, and knocked on the black painted wood. I waited, wondering if I had knocked loudly enough. As I considered what to do, Andy opened the door.

"Hi Megan!"

"Hi."

The way his eyes met mine made my heart jump and then turn to mush. I pictured him as this incredibly attractive guy, but when I saw him in person, the reality was ten times better. And I had him all to myself. Today he was wearing loose faded jeans, white socks and a faded red UC Santa Clara sweatshirt. There was nothing special about the clothes, but somehow on him, the effect took my breath away. Maybe it wouldn't be any different if he were wearing a simple brown paper bag. No matter what he wore, nobody could fail to notice those eyes, the longish golden hair and that shy smile.

"Come in," he said. That voice.

I walked in and the aroma hit me - a heavenly apple pie smell. I asked, "Is your mom baking?"

"No, I am." He glanced at me to see my reaction, smiled, then laughed at my skeptical expression. I didn't know him well enough to know if he was teasing me, but he had to be.

"You can leave your boots by the door and I'll take your coat," he said.

I shrugged out of my coat and handed it to him. He hung it on a coat rack standing in a corner. Then I kicked off my boots and set them on the mat by the door. I had remembered to wear clean socks without holes. That was a good thing. I looked around. Some houses have names, and this was one of them. The whole town knew this house as the Bruce house, even though it was most recently owned by Robert Miller, who I remembered as a grouchy old man. The house was one of the first houses in this part of the state, and was named for the family who had built it and owned it for decades. Generations.

Racking my brain for something intelligent to say, I blurted, "So this is an old house, huh?" That wasn't it.

"Yeah," he said. "It was built in 1776, the same year we became a nation. Very old."

I didn't usually care about history much, but I'd had no idea it was that old. "Wow," I said. "How did your family come to be here?"

"It's kind of a long story," replied Andy. "Come in and sit down." He led me to the kitchen and pulled out a stool for me. I perched there with my elbows on the counter while he opened the oven door and checked the pie.

I hadn't been sure he was serious about baking until that moment. "You really are baking a pie?"

"Is that a bad thing?" he asked, with just a tinge of embarrassment.

"No, of course not," I replied quickly. "Just unusual. In a good way. In a cool way."

He smiled. I smiled back.

It was warm and cozy in the bright yellow kitchen, and smelled incredibly good.

Andy asked, "Can I get you something to drink?"

"Sure, water would be great."

He took two glasses from the cupboard and filled them with ice and water from the dispenser in the refrigerator door. He handed me a glass, and our hands touched as I took it from him. His fingers were very warm.

I felt an awkward need to say something to break the silence. "Ok, so tell me the story. What brought your family here?"

"Well, Robert Miller, who lived here until he died last year, was married to my grandmother. My mom's mother. She was part of the Bruce family that built this house, and I think it was five or six generations that owned it."

"Wow, I had no idea," I said.

"Grandma died before I was born, cancer, so I never knew her. Robert was her second husband, so he wasn't my real grandfather. He never tried to act like one either, and never wanted any involvement in our lives."

"That's kind of weird, isn't it?" I asked.

"I think so. He must have been lonely the last twenty years of his life, but I wouldn't know, because we never talked to him. It's not that we never tried to talk to him. It was more that he never wanted anything to do with us. My mom says he just stayed around here and kept to himself as long as she knew him. We knew he was getting really old, but our Christmas cards never got returned, so we were pretty sure he was still here. After he died and his lawyer contacted us about the will, we found out he stayed here until the end, but paid someone to come in and help him with food and cleaning."

Andy turned to look in the oven again, closed the door, and then dropped the potholders on the counter. "He had no relatives except us. My grandmother wanted the house to go to us, and he respected her wishes, even though she'd been gone almost twenty years. It was her family's house after all, not his. Still, we were surprised he left it to us. And unprepared. The last thing my parents wanted was to deal with this house and all the stuff in it. They had talked about retiring to New England, since they both grew up in New Hampshire, but not here. Somewhere closer to the ocean and in a bigger city. Then my dad got a great job offer from Boston General Hospital, and the timing just seemed right to move out here. He's mostly teaching residents. Besides that, my sister Samantha is out here going to college in New York. Everything just kind of came together."

He paused and looked directly at me with those Caribbean blue eyes. "My mom is a writer, and she can work from anywhere. She said she wouldn't make us move while I was in high school, and my dad was willing to commute for a while, but I told them it wasn't that big a deal."

"Wow," I said. "It would have been a big deal for me. It would be awful to be the new kid in a tiny town like this and to leave all my friends."

"It's not so terrible, and I knew it was what they wanted to do. I didn't want to be the reason they couldn't. I'll be in college soon, so I won't live with them that much longer anyway. I figured they should get to do what they want. They agreed we would live in this house and get it ready to sell while they figure out where they want to settle permanently. Dad drives into Boston and stays three or four nights a week. He has a little cot in his office at the hospital, and a bathroom with a shower. It's ok for the short term."

I glanced out the window over the kitchen sink. It looked out over the back yard into the woods. Big white flakes were starting to fall. I was perfectly content just to be with Andy and watch him as he talked.

"Do you have brothers or sisters?" Andy asked.

"Yes, two younger brothers, Justin and Nick. They're good kids, but sometimes a pain."

"That's probably what my sister always said about me too," he smiled. "I just can't believe how cold and snowy it is here," Andy said, from closer to my ear than I had expected. "This climate is freaky."

I laughed. "I guess it is, but I've lived here my whole life, so it seems normal to me. What would it be like in California right now?"

"It would probably be warm enough to be at the beach."

With ocean colors that are nothing compared to your eyes, I thought. Those eyes were only a foot away from my face.

"Nice," I said. "I could see how you could miss that."

Andy smiled and turned back to the oven. He brushed his hair away from his eyes with an oven mitt, opened the door, and took out a beautiful pie. He set it gently on a cooling rack on the counter. I couldn't believe I was thinking that a guy took a beautiful pie out of the oven. I couldn't imagine any of the other boys I knew baking, but for Andy it didn't seem strange, it seemed romantic. Unique. Intriguing. And the pie smelled heavenly. I breathed in, "Mmmm."

He smiled at the compliment. "Come on. Let's get started on the books while it cools." He picked up my books, turned to glance at me, and walked toward the table by the window.

I was slightly disappointed we were really going to study. On the other hand, I was glad to be here and realized that I might have been just as disappointed if Andy had not intended to study – it would have seemed deceitful. I sighed. Chemistry wasn't nearly as interesting as hearing about Andy's life.

"Anyway," he said, "we moved out here. We were all kind of shocked when we got to the house. First, it was ridiculously cold the day we got to town, and the heating system in this house is from the 1920s or something. It's terrible at heating so much space. Worse though, we didn't expect the house to be so dirty and full of junk, but maybe it shouldn't have been surprising for an old man living all alone. We had to stay in the hotel the first week, until we could get it clean enough to live in."

"Yuk," I shook my head sympathetically.

"Yeah, and there's only one bathroom that was added in the 1950s or so."

I shook my head slowly. That would definitely be a problem at my house.

He continued, "We've been here about four weeks now, and haven't even begun to go through all the stuff. There's the whole house, plus the entire barn is full. My mom isn't sure what to do with it all. Some of it must be important, historically I mean, but it's going to be a huge job to figure out what might be worth saving. There's no hurry really, so we're just going through it a little bit at a time. I'm making some money selling stuff on eBay and Craig's list. Some of the things we've found are very old and worth something to antiques collectors."

"Wow, it must be interesting," I said.

"It is a little bit." He opened his book. "Enough about me. Were we on chapter twelve?"

"Yeah, I think so. Chemical equations. ABCD method."

"Oh yeah."

We took out our notes and started going through problems. I didn't learn a thing about Chemistry, and was glad I had pre-studied. However, I learned a lot about Andy. He was intelligent, no doubt. After twenty minutes of balancing chemical equations, Andy said, "Stay there."

I watched as he walked across the room into the kitchen, admiring his broad shoulders and looking unabashedly at his butt. A girl can look, right? He looked way good in his jeans. Andy got a tub of vanilla ice cream out of the freezer and set it on the counter, cut two slices of warm apple pie and put them on plates, added a big scoop of vanilla ice cream to each plate, and then brought them to the table. He set one down in front of me with a shy smile. Then he spun on his heel and sauntered back into the kitchen where he filled two small glasses with ice cold milk, and brought them over to the table. He plunked into the chair and looked at me expectantly.

I was touched. No boy I'd ever known would cook for a girl. I sliced off a small bite with my fork and put it in my mouth carefully, so as not to get food in my teeth. As the flavor of fresh apples filled my mouth, I looked at him in genuine surprise and smiled. It was seriously one of the best pieces of apple pie I had ever eaten. He looked like a puppy that had just fetched a ball. He was so innocently pleased with himself. I just wanted to hug him and fall into those blue eyes.

As I was getting the very last crumb onto my fork, a woman who was obviously his mom pranced into the room. "Something smells good," she said. She did not look like the moms I was used to. She was the right age to be a mom and everything, but she looked strong enough to chop a cord of wood. Not in a bulky way - in a fit way. She had on black yoga pants and a blue tank top over a very lean body. She moved with a grace that reminded me of her son's gait.

"Hi honey," she said, as she walked over to him and kissed his cheek. "This must be Megan."

"Yeah Mom, meet Megan. Megan, this is my mom, Stacy."

"It's very nice to meet you Mrs. Garrett," I said. "You have a very interesting house, and a beautiful kitchen."

"Please call me Stacy, Megan. Sorry I didn't come down when you arrived, but I was right in the middle of an idea, and had to get it written down before I forgot it. Thank you too. The kitchen is the only part of the house I'm happy with right now. It was so hideous when we got here that we had to have it gutted before we could even use it. The refrigerator wasn't cold, the oven only worked sometimes, and one of the burners on the stove didn't work at all. The sink was cracked and the counters were stained. There was also a layer of grease on the walls. It was really horrible. I'm afraid that when you're old you can't see well you don't realize how dirty things are. Robert might not have even known, but it was unbearable. And unsalvageable. The remodel did turn out nice though." She paused. "Is this normal March weather? I can't believe how cold it is here."

I laughed. "That's what Andy was saying too. Yes, it's normal. It won't last much longer though. I think we've all had enough winter now. I know I'm really looking forward to spring."

"Me too," she replied. "Hopefully it will feel more like home when we can get outside more. Andy, I'm off to class, and then I'm stopping by the grocery store. I'll be home in about an hour and a half." She turned to me. "It was nice to meet you Megan. I'm glad Andy is finding some friends." She was gone as quickly as she had arrived.

Me too, I thought. "Nice to meet you too," I called.

"She seems pretty great," I said to Andy.

"She is. You couldn't ask for a better mom. As you might have guessed, she's very into health, yoga and new age stuff. It's pretty cool I guess. She believes in intuition and getting guidance from the universe. You know - karma and all that."

I could see he really did admire his mom. I didn't think most teenage boys admitted they liked their mothers, so it was kind of nice. We worked on balancing chemical equations some more and I could see he had no need for studying, because it all came very easily to him. So why had he asked me over? I hoped I knew why, but was not ready to assume anything. All too quickly, it was time to go.

"Can I have your cell phone number in case I think of any last minute questions?" I asked.

"Sure, tell me yours."

I recited my cell phone number as he punched it into his phone. Almost instantly my cell phone rang. I giggled, and punched the "end call" button. I quickly edited the caller ID to say "Andy." I could see he was doing the same with my number.

"Thanks," I said. "This was fun. And helpful."

"You're welcome, I'm glad you could come," he returned, as he walked me to the door.

As I pulled on my coat and found my car keys I said, "The pie was great Andy. See you tomorrow."

"Thanks Meg. Yeah, see you tomorrow."

The whole drive home, I racked my brain for reasonable questions I could ask him about our Chemistry homework, as an excuse to communicate with him again. I finally thought of something. I'd work one of the problems we hadn't gotten to, and ask him to confirm the answer. When I got home I struggled through question 43, then texted "#43, did u get 2,3,4,7?"

He texted back, "bingo, u rock"

I smiled and held my phone to my heart.

9 POWER SLIDES

The next morning I dragged myself into the shower and squirted shampoo into my hand. It was way *way* too early. Suddenly it hit me as if the water had gone cold – I had spent the afternoon with Andy yesterday, and soon I would see him again. For the first time in weeks, I was excited about going to school. Suddenly I was happy to be awake. This was *not* an ordinary Monday. Get a grip, I warned myself. You and every other girl are looking forward to seeing him. Nonetheless, I took extra care with my hair and makeup. Fresh snow was starting to fall as I got in my car. "Enough with the snow already," I said to my car, which gave me a sympathetic rumble as the engine came to life. On the way to school, I stopped by the deli, grabbed my latte, and headed off to start my day.

I slid into my seat in Econ just as the bell rang. Ha! Made it again.

"Remember students, Prom is coming and tickets are already on sale. Tomorrow's girls basketball game starts at 4:00. Today's soup is tomato basil."

The hour passed like five hours, as mind numbing as ever and extra difficult because I couldn't wait to get a glimpse of Andy, even if we didn't get a chance to talk. I didn't see him until I got into the Chemistry lab, and he was already seated. He turned to glance around the room as people were shuffling in the door and chatting, and his roving gaze stopped when he saw me. His face changed instantly, breaking into a shy smile. I smiled back, and he turned back to the front. I glanced at Kelsey and saw by the sour look on her face that she had seen the exchange. Her eyes narrowed, and then she looked away quickly as if it hadn't bothered her. I knew her well enough to see that it did though. My phone vibrated in silent mode.

"Gd luck," he had texted.

"u 2," I texted back. I smiled to myself. My day was now complete. I hadn't even bothered to worry about the test.

"All cell phones off please," said Mr. Witt. "It's time for our test."

The test took the whole hour, and though difficult, I thought I had done pretty well. I better have, it would be too embarrassing to tell Andy if I hadn't, and he would probably ask. As we dropped our tests face down in a sloppy pile on Mr. Witt's desk, Andy glanced back at me and smiled, and then left the room. I watched his back side as he left, then hurried to my locker and then History class. Andy sank into his seat at the front of the room right as the bell rang. My phone vibrated.

"did it go ok?" he had written.

"think so, u?" I replied.

"think so 2" he answered.

In the cafeteria line, I got my tomato basil soup and a salad. I noticed Andy was involved in a conversation at a table of guys, and that made me happy. After paying the lunch lady, I performed the noon time ritual by walking to the corner table and sitting down next to Kayla.

"Well?" she enquired.

Emilee and Rachel arrived, right on schedule. They had a little further to walk from their classes than Kayla and I. I looked at their three expectant faces and laughed. "It was good, we studied."

"That's it?" asked Rachel, her look incredulous, waiting for more.

I felt reluctant to give them all the details, even though there was nothing overly interesting about any of it. Somehow it felt like a betrayal of something very private, which might make it less special. I didn't want this brand new relationship analyzed. I didn't even know if it *was* a relationship. I hoped against hope, but didn't even want to admit that to myself. I knew my three best friends only had good intentions, but I didn't want to be today's lunch discussion subject. I knew I had to offer more though, or they wouldn't leave it alone. I guess if I were one of them, I wouldn't have either. What are friends for if not cheap entertainment? I kept the fact that he cooked to myself, but offered, "It was fun, but we really did study the whole time. I only stayed a few hours. He was very polite. Maybe *too* polite." I smiled at them with an expression that communicated a slight frustration.

"Oh," said Kayla, clearly disappointed at the lack of juicy details.

I took the pause as an opportunity to change the subject. "What about you Rachel, didn't you have a date with Kyle this weekend?" Kyle was a guy from Ware, the next town over from Hardwick.

She blushed. "Yes, and it was fabulous. He's *really* hot."

That was easy, I thought, relieved the focus was on someone else.

"What did you guys do?" asked Kayla.

Rachel was happy to tell us. "Oh, it was awesome. He took me to his school's basketball game, and lots of the kids were obviously wondering who I was, because they kept staring at us. Seriously though, there were no other guys there as hot as him. I could see why the girls might have been pissed. I think his ex girlfriend was there too, but he didn't point her out to me. It was fun to be his date. I felt like he had gone outside his school to send a message to his friends that nobody there was good enough. That sounds conceited, doesn't it? I don't mean it that way, but it felt like he was showing me off."

She was clearly pleased with herself. I was hoping the date wasn't just about getting back at people in his school, because Rachel really seemed to like this guy.

She added, "He was totally paying attention to me, and some of the girls were giving me dirty looks. It was kind of fun."

I could relate to the dirty looks part I thought, as Kelsey's expression flashed into my mind.

It continued to snow all day, not unusual for spring in Massachusetts. By the time I finished studying Business Law and went to bed, there were six inches of white fluff on the ground. I set my alarm for five minutes early, knowing I would have to deal with ice in the morning.

Sure enough, Tuesday morning had me scraping my windows. Still, I was cheerful about it, because I couldn't wait to get to school to see Andy. In the last few days, I had discovered a whole new attitude about school. When I got there, I saw him sooner than I expected, as he did an accidental 360 on the packed snow when he tried to park his car. I noticed two sophomore guys pointing and smiling. I felt embarrassed for Andy and an urge to protect him as if he were a little kid being teased. No guy who'd grown up around here would be spinning in the snow unless he was doing it on purpose. Once he had his car safely parked, I walked carefully over to where he was getting out. He looked up at me and blushed, truly embarrassed.

"Need a driving lesson?" I joked.

He laughed. "I guess I do," he said sheepishly. "I've never driven in snow like this – it just never happened in California. I know I look like an idiot."

"Oh, not so much," I laughed. At his smirk I said, "Well ok, I know how you feel, but it's not your fault. Snow driving is just second nature to us, since we practically learned in the snow. There's no reason you should be able to do it well."

He nodded uncertainly.

I wanted to put him at ease. "You can't get around this place unless you can drive in snow though. How about if we meet after school and I'll show you a few tricks my dad taught me?"

I gauged his reaction, hoping I hadn't embarrassed him further.

"Ok," he nodded his head slowly, but he looked a little pained.

"The best place to learn is the grocery store parking lot, because there's plenty of space there," I offered. "Why don't you meet me there after school?"

He was recovering from his embarrassment now, and could see the situation was amusing. "How embarrassing," he smiled. "A girl has to teach me how to drive. It's ok though, I can take it."

I laughed. "Don't worry, I won't tell anyone." Except Kelsey I thought. It would be great if *she* thought he was an idiot and left him alone. Of course I would never do that though.

It was nice to have a plan to meet Andy after school, because it didn't concern me so much that Kelsey was flirting with him like crazy in Chemistry. I knew what she didn't know – he was all mine after school. I smiled to myself with satisfaction.

Even that small satisfaction wasn't enough though, because she was perched on the edge of his table looking at him with her soft brown eyes and giving him an eyeful of her cleavage. I couldn't tell what she was saying, but what guy could avoid noticing that? I had to be careful not to assume too much about him. After all, I had asked him to meet me after school, not the other way around. Maybe he only wanted to be friends, or was only trying to be polite in agreeing to go. At this point, it was not my business how he responded to Kelsey.

I watched him anyway. He wasn't leaning toward her, but wasn't pulling back either. To me it looked like he was simply responding politely, but I didn't know him well enough to say for sure. After all, how could he not be interested in Kelsey? Even I thought she was gorgeous. Still, he might not be shallow enough to fall for looks alone. That hopeful thought made me brighten a little.

At lunch I got a text from Andy, "I'll b a ltl l8, let prk lot clear out"

"no prob" I texted back, knowing it was still very slick out there.

School took forever to end, but finally it was time to head to the parking lot. I threw my books in the back seat and drove to the grocery store. I parked in the far corner, but left the motor running so both the heater and stereo could stay on. Twenty minutes later Andy's car turned into the lot and approached mine creeping very slowly. I giggled to myself. He came to a long slow stop about ten yards from my car. I shut off my engine and got out, walking toward him.

He leaned over and opened the passenger door from the inside, and I got in.

"Pretty funny, huh?" he asked sheepishly.

"Oh, it's not so bad," I said lightly. He looked at me expectantly. I took a breath.

"First, you have to get comfortable with how it feels when your car is out of control," I said. I motioned toward the center of the lot. "Why don't you get us pointed in that direction?"

Andy slowly turned the car around until we were facing the large open space in the parking lot, with only trees on the far side.

"Ok," I said calmly. "Floor it!"

He looked at me with a questioning look, wondering if I was serious.

I nodded. He still looked skeptical. "Ok, just act like you're doing a fast start," I said.

He turned his head to look forward, stepped on the gas, and the wheels instantly lost traction, spinning us sideways. He took his foot off the gas, stomped on the brake and we skidded across six spaces.

He looked at me. "Is that really what you wanted me to do?"

"Yes, did you feel which way the car was going when it started to spin?"

"Yes," he replied uncertainly.

"Ok this time, keep your foot on the gas." He pushed on the gas pedal and we started to spin off to the side. "Now turn the wheel just a little to the left and see what happens."

He did, and the spin changed. He took his foot off the gas and we continued to slide.

"This is fun," he grinned, and shot me a wide white smile.

"Good!" I laughed. "Ok, now stop."

He stopped, feeling the car skid, and turned to face me with expectant deep blue eyes. I was distracted for just a moment. Focus, I reminded myself.

"Ok, now drive slowly forward, then turn suddenly and see what happens."

He pressed slowly on the gas and turned the wheel, and we started to slide. "Cool!" he exclaimed.

"Yeah," I said smiling, trying not to dampen his enthusiasm. "Now see how the car slid the opposite way as you were turning? Try it again. Turn to the left, but as the car slides to the right, gently turn the wheel to the right and see what happens."

He did as I had instructed, and was amazed to see that the car aimed itself back to straight.

"Wow, I never would have thought to do that!"

I laughed. "I know, it's not how you feel like reacting but it works. Try it again."

He did, and was able to control the car better this time.

"Of course sometimes you can't stop a bad slide at all," I said. "But you can at least minimize the effect by knowing what to do."

"Totally Megan, I get it!" He was pleased with himself.

I was pleased too, happy to have shared this new experience with him.

"Thank you. Now I won't look like such a fool!" he exclaimed.

"Oh it's ok," I said. I felt awkward. I knew it was time to go, but I didn't want to leave him. Still, I couldn't think of anything else to show him. His car already had anti-lock brakes. I didn't want to seem condescending by explaining how those worked.

"This was cool of you Megan, really. I'll see you tomorrow at school?"

"Yeah, definitely. I'll be there balancing my equations."

He laughed. "Cool, I'll be looking forward to it."

I smiled, then turned and got out of his car and walked to my own. He said he'd be looking forward to it. I could float on that for a while. I chuckled to myself as I got in my car, and watched as he slowly drove away.

The next day, Wednesday, as the bell ended first hour, my mood lifted at the thought of Chemistry class. Well, not Chemistry class, the person sitting at the front of Chemistry class. I got there before him, and took my seat next to Brad. As Andy came into the room, he walked toward me, paused by my table and said, "Thanks again for yesterday afternoon."

"Sure," I smiled, and he moved on to his seat, walking with the easygoing casual grace of a cheetah. Lean yet strong. Graceful and coordinated. Yes, that described him well. Beautiful, lean, coordinated, strong. Quit daydreaming, I told myself. I looked up.

Kelsey was glaring at me. I couldn't help myself. I smiled sweetly.

That got me a dirty look.

I was the first one to get to our lunch table, with my noodle soup on a tray. Then Jennifer, Kelsey's best friend of course, plunked her tray down next to mine. I wondered what I owed this honor to. I could guess. I was uncomfortable, as if my mom were about to yell at me.

"Hey Megan, how are you?" She asked in her perky cheerleader voice.

"I'm fine," I replied, offering nothing more. I really wanted Rachel, Emilee and Kayla to get there. I waited, while chasing a noodle around the bowl with my spoon. We both knew she was up to something. I was not going to ask.

"So, are you and Jeff going to the Prom?" She asked.

I turned my head to look at her. I could see she was making an effort to act like this was an innocent friendly question, but clearly it wasn't. "I don't think so," I said slowly, and looked back at my soup.

"Why not?" she chirped.

I said to my soup, "I'm just not sure we're into it this year." The real reason was none of her business.

She yammered on cheerfully, acting as if she didn't notice I wasn't holding up my end of the conversation. "Well, Pat and I will be going of course. I think Kelsey will probably go with Andy."

My stomach clenched. "Really? That's nice," I said coolly, still looking toward my tray. Did she know this, or was she just trying to get a reaction from me?

She popped a grape in her mouth. "Yeah."

Finally Emilee, Rachel and Kayla arrived and sat. They exchanged glances with each other. Emilee looked at me from the corner of her eye. I raised my eyebrows and gave her my 'I don't know' expression. Nobody but Jennifer said a word. She didn't seem to notice she was the only one talking.

Jennifer blathered on about dresses and lunch and classes, appearing to be completely comfortable sitting away from her normal crowd. It was a little fascinating. I had to admire her ability to mindlessly socialize. Emilee, Rachel and Kayla were observing her with subtle sideways glances and an occasional nod, but remained silent. I didn't hear much of what Jennifer said. I was too busy stewing about whether Kelsey was going to the Prom with Andy. Of course I had no claim on Andy, but he could have mentioned it if he was dating Kelsey. Why would he ask me to study if he was interested in her? Did he just want to be friends? I realized with certainty that I did not want to be just friends, but I would steel myself and not show him I was hurt if that was all he wanted.

Lunch was almost over, and Jennifer got up and left. “Later guys!” she squeaked happily at us, as if we were all the best of friends. I wondered if that was her normal tone. Did she think we were happy she had joined us?

“What was that all about?” asked Kayla.

“I have a pretty good idea,” I replied. “She wanted to be sure I understood very well that Andy belongs to Kelsey.”

“Does he?” Kayla enquired.

I had a sinking feeling. “I really don’t know.”

Over the next few days I was cool toward Andy, but not cold. I didn’t know what to think or how to act. All I could do was wait for him to make the next move. I couldn’t stop myself from observing his every action. I didn’t see him going out of his way to pay attention to Kelsey, but it was a little hard to tell what he was thinking, because she was giving an all out effort to smother him with attention.

At lunch on Friday, Kelsey made a point of stopping at his table. She put her hand on his shoulder, and every guy at the table turned to look at her. She said something I couldn’t make out, and the whole table laughed. She caught my eye and returned the sweet smile I had given her. I looked away. I probably deserved that.

The weekend came, and I felt depressed. I didn't miss Jeff, but I missed the feeling of knowing where you stood with someone. I realized that was ridiculous though, because I never knew exactly where I stood with Jeff. That realization didn't make me feel any better.

Saturday night Emilee, Kayla and I went to a movie in Worcester. We enjoyed our girls nights out, and tried to keep up with them even if any of us had boyfriends. The movie was a sappy love story, which didn't make me feel any less blue. What if I had made the wrong decision about Jeff? I thought about it. No. Andy or no Andy, it had been the right time to end it with Jeff. It had been an unequal relationship, and I had been the less equal one. I had finally been strong enough to see that. Luckily, my friends didn't press me on why I was so quiet. They probably already knew. Sunday passed quickly because I had agreed to work until 4:00 so Velma could have most of the afternoon to visit with out of town family. I was tired by the time I got home. My feet hurt from standing all day, so after dinner I took a hot bath and went to bed.

Monday roared by in a blur, but Tuesday morning, time suddenly came into sharp focus. I got a text message from Andy.

"r u ok?"

Was I? "y" I replied, not sure whether that was a lie or not.

"u seem upset"

I pondered for a moment. What to say? "no, busy" I replied.

"somthg I want 2 show u, can u go after game Fri?"

My stomach flipped. I didn't know what to make of it. Of course I wanted to spend time with him, I just didn't know what he wanted. I texted back, "ok."

10 JANIE

July 1867- Allie

I could think of nothing aside from meeting him. I was living for the moment I could see his face, look into his eyes and touch him. If it were the last time, it would still be enough. I composed myself as best I could to talk to Mother.

"Mother, I intend to call on Janie after supper this evening. Will that be all right?"

"Oh that's a good idea sweetie. She will appreciate seeing you. I think it will help settle some of your fears about getting married too, when you see how content she is."

"Fears?" I asked, surprised that she had used that word.

"I know you are a little uncertain Allie, it's all right. Everything is going to be fine, you will see."

I hadn't known she had noticed. I felt all the more desperate. She was watching my face. I nodded and smiled, anxious to retreat from her lest I lose all composure. I sat in the garden weeding, as my mind churned. What do I want? What am I hoping for? Why can't I just accept the life in front of me placidly? If it's going to evolve that way anyway, why not embrace it? I had no answers for myself. Maybe meeting Wayne would help me settle everything in my mind. He would talk sense into me. Nobody would ever know there had been anything between us.

I could scarcely behave normally at supper time. I chattered like an idiot school girl, trying to survive through the meal.

"Are you excited to see Janie?" asked Father.

"Oh yes," I gushed, grateful for an excuse for my excitement. "Since she wasn't able to attend the picnic, I am really looking forward to seeing her. Her family said it had simply been too hot for her to be out that day. It will be so good to catch up and to hear how she is doing."

Mother and Father smiled at each other. I did not miss the exchange. They wanted me to want exactly the same life Janie had. It would be so simple. I knew they only wanted me to be happy, but it saddened me all the same. They had no idea what was taking place within me. They couldn't know. They would be shocked. I would never desire to hurt them. I loved them dearly and they loved me. They had given me a good life up to now. How could I even consider the idea of disappointing them? As supper ended, I rose to attend to the dishes.

"Go ahead and go Allie, I will clean up," Mother offered. "I know you have a lengthy walk to Janie's house."

I smiled, eager to be gone. "Thank you Mother, that is very considerate of you." I skipped upstairs to brush my hair. As I came back through the kitchen, Mother presented me with a jar of raspberry preserves.

"Take this to Janie. It is some of our finest."

"She will adore this, thank you Mother." I controlled my pace as I walked out the door. When I lost sight of the house, I picked up my pace almost to a trot. I needed to see Janie quickly and carry on with my real plans. I made my way to her house in record time, a slight sweat clinging to my body. I dabbed at myself with my handkerchief, trying to appear presentable and composed, unlike how I felt.

Janie herself drew open the door, and was very pleased to see me. She accepted the preserves with genuine appreciation, knowing my mother's reputation for cooking. "It's so good to see you Allie, how are you?"

For but a moment, I considered telling her the truth. She had been my closest friend for years, after all. But of course I couldn't. I couldn't make her guilty in my deception of my parents. And I suppose of Jeremy too. I smiled and told her things were fine.

"Have you planned a wedding date?" she inquired.

"No, not yet, though Mother keeps prodding me to."

"Well why do you hesitate?" she asked.

I studied my dear friend. "Did you experience any nervousness about getting married?" I asked.

Her face became serious, as she led me to her parlor. We were seated and she looked at me. "No. I was truly excited to take leave from my parents and embark on my own life."

"Is your life very different now? I mean, now you're doing all the same work but in your own house, right?"

She smiled. "Yes, I suppose one could view it that way. But it means more now. I want so much to care for Sam. I adore him, and it pleases me to care for him. I am so very excited that we are expecting a baby. My life feels very complete. You will feel the same, you'll see."

"Do you think so?" I asked. "What if I don't? I fear I may not. What if I don't feel the same about Jeremy?"

She laughed. "But you will. He is a good man, and so very attractive. What is there not to be happy about? He is mad for you, anyone can see that. He will take good care of you and give you a good life."

I decided that had been enough honesty. "You're likely right. I do not know why I am so nervous. I am struggling to handle it all."

"Just release your worry Allie. It will all be wonderful, you will see. You'll have babies too, and we'll raise our families together and do all the things wives and mothers do. It is a good life, my dear friend."

"It makes me happy to see you so happy Janie," I told her.

"And I am Allie. And you will be too, you'll see."

We chatted a while longer, and I related all I had seen and done at the picnic. Well, almost all. Then I made excuses to leave, telling Janie I was tired. She was disappointed that our visit was short, but I could barely contain myself, I was so anxious to leave. I had a burning desire to see Wayne that I knew would certainly kill me if I didn't indulge it. I hoped Janie didn't think me rude, but I couldn't help it. As I had when I left my house, I broke into a run when I was out of sight of Janie's house. I laughed at myself for being so ridiculous. When I got close to where Wayne would meet me, I slowed in order to catch my breath and dab the sweat off my face.

He was there. I let out a breath in relief because I had worried there was a chance he wouldn't come. He stood by his horse looking like a Greek God. Or a president or a general. He took my hand and clasped me to him in an embrace.

"Let's get away from town," he whispered into my hair.

I nodded. He helped me up onto his horse, and then mounted the saddle in front of me. We rode into the woods not terribly far from my house, but far enough that there was no chance anyone would come upon us. We halted by the creek, where he helped me down. He tied his horse to a small tree, and we strolled hand in hand for a bit beside the gurgling water. At a fallen log we stopped and sat, looking at the water and the flowers all around us. It felt like a private paradise. I turned to look into Wayne's eyes, and he reached up to touch my face. With that lingering touch I closed my eyes, and knew in that moment that if I died right then I would die happy.

We sat by the creek as if we were the only two people in existence. I allowed myself to forget about the time and the possibility anyone could be wondering where I was. Conversation was so easy.

"Why is your family's house so large?" Wayne asked.

"Oh, that goes back to the original family who built it," I replied. "The house is almost a hundred years old."

"Your family takes good care of it. It certainly doesn't look that old."

"Yes, it is important to my father. The house has been in his family all this time. He is the fourth generation of the Bruce family to own it. The house was built around the time of the American Revolution, by his great great grandfather.

That family had eight children and quite a bit of wealth for the time. There are five bedrooms upstairs, and both a front and back staircase. At some time between then and now, an indoor privy was even added."

"An indoor privy? I've never seen one in a residence. That is impressive."

"Well I don't know about that, but it is a comfort in the winter time."

"It must be, especially for women," Wayne smiled.

"Of course I have lived there all my life, and Father has been successful raising horses."

"It seems like a pleasant place to grow up," Wayne said.

"It was I suppose. We have always had everything we needed. Tell me about your plans," I said.

I could hear the excitement in Wayne's voice as he talked about his future. "I made so many acquaintances during the war. My job was to coordinate getting supplies for the troops, which is probably why I am still alive and whole. All those merchants I worked with are just as eager to sell their supplies to the western settlements, since they no longer have the military to provide for. All I have to do is set up relationships with shopkeepers on the other end, and then figure out how best to transport the goods."

"It sounds so very exciting. And well thought out," I said.

"Yes, there is an extreme shortage of goods in the settlements, so everything I can deliver is guaranteed to sell, and at a good price. It's all a matter of high demand and short supply. I am in the right place with the right connections to make it work."

"But won't it be dangerous?" I inquired.

"Maybe a bit." He glanced at the worried expression on my face. "But not terribly. There are many people with an interest in safely getting goods transported west. There are secure shipping routes, and people in the business of ensuring they stay secure. Besides, I can choose the safest routes, and don't have to do business with the less established places unless I choose to."

"Will you?" I asked. "Choose to, I mean."

"I suppose I'll see how things go. I will be quite busy in the beginning just establishing one or two routes. The business will expand as I am successful. What do you think of 'Collins Shipping'?"

I enjoyed the expressions on his face as he talked about his business. He held my hand as we conversed, and the sound of his voice was like warm honey on fresh bread. Essential to life. "It is a lovely name," I replied.

"I believed for a long while that establishing the business would see my life complete," he said slowly.

"And won't it?" I asked.

His hand again moved to my face, and he traced his fingers down my throat. My breath caught, and his touch felt like heaven. I wanted the moment to last forever. He leaned closer, and I could barely contain the feelings that washed over me. I wanted to cling to him, drinking him in. His every feature was perfect, and the smell of him was soap, horse and fresh air. He brought his lips to mine, and kissed me gently. I could see my passion reflected in his eyes. We desired nothing but to be together. I knew this must be how Janie felt about her Sam. It was what she had tried to describe anyway, but I couldn't imagine it when I thought of Jeremy. I knew now it could never be how I would feel about Jeremy. This man positioned in front of me was all I would ever want. I was humbled by it, struck by it. I kissed him back, drinking in his warmth and the scent of him, and craving the feel of his touch. Around us the birds were singing, the water was gurgling in the creek, and everything in my world was right, perfectly right.

"No, I don't regard it that way anymore," he said.

We clung to each other as if we were in a sinking boat, realizing the time was getting on. "You will have to get home," he said.

"I know, but I cannot bear it," I replied.

He smiled and kissed me again. "Nor can I."

His face became troubled, to match my own. We looked at each other with longing. He rose and unsheathed his knife. I had no idea what he was about to do. He secured a length of his hair, sawed it off with the knife and presented it to me. I brought it to my lips, and then tucked it in my pocket, a little piece of Wayne I could take with me. The gesture meant everything to me.

"May I have a tiny piece of yours?" he asked.

"Yes," I said, undoing my bun. I pulled my hair loose, and shook my head. He stepped closer and threaded his fingers through the length of it. He focused on me as if I were the most beautiful race horse he had ever seen. I held up a small lock of my hair, and he cut it off with his knife. Like I had done, he brought it to his lips and then tucked it in his pocket.

With tears in my eyes I followed him back to his horse, where he helped me up again. He took me to the road just beyond our house and kissed me goodbye.

"Think of me," he said.

As if that would be any problem, I thought. "Of course," I replied. "And think of me."

"Always," he said.

I didn't know what else to say. It was agony to let him leave, but what choice did either of us possess? I walked slowly home, trying to gather my composure. How could I possibly go on living my life as if it were normal? How could I marry Jeremy, knowing what it felt like to truly be attracted to a man? How could I settle for a life of being a farmer's wife with someone I felt no passion for? How could I do anything other than what was already planned without scandalizing my family? These questions seemed more and more urgent, and try though I might, I could not find any answers.

I gave Mother a brief update on Janie, and retreated to my bedroom as quickly as possible. I had to be alone. Think, Allie. What could I do? No answers came to me as I tossed and turned through the night. Should I run away? Should I refuse to marry Jeremy? What about Wayne? Should I follow him? Would he want me to? Should I join a convent? Did I have any options at all? What would it do to my family if I didn't marry Jeremy? How could I scandalize them in that way?

The mountain and flag blocks were sewed in beside each other. My hand kept making its way to my pocket to stroke the little lock of hair. Each touch filled me with memories of him and also gave me moments of peace. Wayne. I said his name in my mind. I had said his name out loud in the garden this morning. The sound of it was glorious. The path ahead of me was nothing but settling for a joyless life. It would be giving up and accepting something less than. Less than what? Less than true happiness. Was it what most people did? Probably. Or maybe most people didn't know such a thing as the happiness I felt with Wayne existed. My stomach ached.

I entered the house to get some cool water and felt as if I were going to be ill. If only I could stop fretting, even for a few moments. I hastened from the kitchen to the indoor privy just in time to retch down the hole and felt a tiny bit better. I had to gain control of my emotions or I would become a wreck. I was already a wreck. I sat in the privy room and examined the walls, drawing in deep breaths. Since we were not using this room as an outhouse during this season it did not smell unpleasant, and was not a bad place to be alone. It was like a small refuge. I sat a few more moments, thinking of Wayne and composing myself. It was not that I disliked Jeremy, but I knew I would never like him more than a brother or classmate. I could never feel about him the way I felt for Wayne. That was the crux of the matter. Was that acceptable?

I drew in some deep breaths, then returned to the kitchen to wash my mouth out with fresh water. I needed to try to calm myself. Nothing had to be resolved this very day. I decided to create a new quilt block. It would be a blue bird perched on a branch over our creek. The sound of that creek was forever etched in my memory. That log would forever be our log. I fingered the lock of hair and smiled.

The next day Wayne came to get his horses. I felt my heart would leap out of my chest when I saw him ride up.

Mother was seated beside me on the porch, so all I could do was remain still as a statue.

"Good afternoon ladies," he said as he approached.

"Hello Mr. Collins," Mother replied pleasantly.

"Hello," I added, locking my eyes onto him and then forcing myself to avert them downward.

He smiled easily, and climbed the steps up to the porch.

"Could I offer you a cool drink?" asked Mother.

"That would be very nice Mrs. Bruce," replied Wayne, without looking at me.

She turned and entered the house, leaving us alone. He stepped closer. My heart leaped as I took in his face. His expression was tender and longing.

"I can't stand being apart from you," he said.

"Nor I you," I said miserably.

"You must meet me again," he said urgently.

"I don't know how," I replied. "I don't have any other good excuses to go off alone."

"Meet me beyond your house along the road after everyone has retired to bed," he instructed me.

Mother returned with tall glasses of lemonade.

"Your flowers are quite lovely Mrs. Bruce," Wayne said.

"Why thank you. I do think they add a pleasant touch to the porch," Mother replied.

"Indeed they do."

I could not speak. He had requested that I sneak out of my house. Only girls without any morals would do something like that. Or that is what I had believed up to now. I knew I had to see him.

"Run and tell your father Mr. Collins is here," Mother directed me.

I nodded, smiled at them both and left.

As I did chores about the house, I kept an eye on Father and Wayne. Wayne lingered as long as he could, but eventually his three new horses were tied to his saddle horn, my father had received his money, and Wayne was riding away. We had not had any chance to exchange any further words. How could I live without seeing him again? I knew that I must see him, no matter what the consequences. He had no more reason to call at our house. If he did I wouldn't be left alone with him anyway. His business with my father was concluded, and he had no more reason to stay in our town. He had achieved what he came here for.

11 SMALL WAVES

Spring fever was in the air, and as the days were getting warmer, everyone I knew was looking forward to summer. It took forever for Friday to arrive. I didn't get much chance to see Andy during the week, other than watching him from the back of the room in the two classes we shared. We did exchange smiles a few times. I was no longer acting cool toward him, and would just have to accept it if he only wanted to be friends. It was dumb to think I could compete with Kelsey anyway.

Even though we might only be friends, the basketball game couldn't come fast enough. I couldn't imagine what he wanted to show me, but I wanted to spend time with him no matter what it was. At the game I sat with Emilee and Kayla, and halfheartedly kept up with the conversation about people and clothes as I scanned the crowd. By the end of the first quarter, I was convinced Andy wasn't coming and I stopped looking around for him. I couldn't concentrate on anything except the minutes ticking by on the scoreboard. Either he forgot he was meeting me, or he would find me afterward.

"Are you going to the party at the meadow tonight?" Kayla asked. "I think everyone's going since it's the first halfway warm weekend night since fall. Jack Edsal is going." Jack was the boy Kayla had been daydreaming about lately.

"I might be there later. I have something I have to do first," I replied. I hoped I did anyway.

"Ok, cool. Just find us when you get there," Emilee said.

I could see she wanted to ask what I was doing, but she also seemed to sense that I would have told her if I wanted to talk about it. She let it drop, and I was grateful. I don't know why I was feeling so secretive about Andy. I guess because I didn't want to look stupid mooning over him, especially if he was dating Kelsey. Nothing is more embarrassing than a one way crush.

As the game ended, I walked out to the parking lot and headed toward my car. There he was, in jeans and a brown leather jacket, leaning against my car with his hands in his pockets. I noticed his car was parked next to mine. Despite my fears that he wasn't romantically interested in me, I felt a wave of excitement at the thought of spending time with him. I couldn't help it.

"Did we win?" he asked.

"Yes, which was good since it was the last home game."

Andy waited until I was close, and then walked around to the passenger side of his car and opened the door for me. Jeff had never done such a thing. "Don't worry, the roads are dry tonight," he smiled. I laughed. He waited for me to get in, closed the door, and then got in on his side and said, "Thanks for coming. We didn't get to talk much this week."

"I heard you're dating Kelsey," I blurted. Did I just say that? I was a total idiot.

"What?" He looked at me, and his face registered genuine disbelief.

"That's what Jennifer told me," I offered. Now I was feeling really stupid. I looked at my feet and tried to shrink into the seat.

Andy turned, and I could feel him looking at me. I couldn't face him. "I have no interest in Kelsey," he said quietly.

That sent my mind racing. I was an idiot, but suddenly I felt as if a great weight had been lifted. I looked at him cautiously and smiled sheepishly, not knowing what to say. I finally settled on, "oh."

He had a puzzled look on his face. "Do you still want to go with me?" he asked.

"Yes," I replied meekly.

He started the car and we headed out of the parking lot, where he turned onto the highway.

"Where are we going?" I asked after a while.

He replied. "Well, it's a little warmer, the snow has melted, and it's a beautiful evening. There's something I want to show you."

He turned off the highway at the sign that said Quabbin Reservoir, and drove us to the landing where boats were kept in slips along the four docks. Tonight it was deserted, though not in a scary way - just a bunch of boats floating in their spaces and bobbing gently. Thought it was dark, the moon was almost full, casting a soft light on everything. Andy parked the car, got out, and came around to my side to open my door. I shivered a little as I stepped out.

"Are you cold?" he asked.

I replied truthfully, "A little."

He took off his brown leather jacket and laid it on my shoulders. He still had on a thick blue, black and white plaid flannel shirt over a t-shirt. Through my light sweater I could feel his jacket was still warm from the heat of his body, and I snuggled into it.

"Come on," he smiled. I was still thinking about how he had said he wasn't interested in Kelsey. He led me down the last dock and stopped in front of the second boat from the end. It looked like some sort of fast speed boat.

He started to step onto the boat and I asked, "What are you doing?"

"This is my family's boat," he told me.

"Ohh kaaaay," I said uncertainly.

"It's ok, just trust me." He turned and held out his hand.

I let him help me step onto the boat. Andy settled me into the passenger seat, then pulled a key out of his pocket, started the motor, and backed us slowly away from the dock. The boat made a pleasant low chugging noise that sounded very powerful. I smiled, certain our parents would *not* approve. I was surprised at how well we could see. The moon reflected off the water, making it look more like dusk than ten o'clock at night. Andy backed the boat in a slow half circle until we were facing the far shore, and shifted it into a forward gear. We moved slowly across the lake, barely making a wake behind us. It was peaceful, and the only sound was the low chugging of the motor. A cool breeze made by the movement of the boat blew across us. When we were out near the center of the lake, Andy stopped the motor and the boat drifted slowly along. Andy turned to look at me. The moon overhead made a shimmering golden path across the water, right up to the boat. I'd never seen anything as beautiful as the shine on the water and him bathed in the moonlight. I shivered slightly.

"Are you still cold?" he asked softly.

"Just a little," I replied. My shiver was not really because of the cold, but he didn't need to know that. He held out his hand and I took it. He stood and then pulled me to stand in the middle of the boat next to him. He kept my hand in his warm and steady grasp. He looked up at the moon.

"It's beautiful, isn't it?" he whispered.

And it was. It seemed like we were the only two people in the world. The only sound was of waves lapping against the boat. It was as if time were standing still.

"I really wanted to see you again," he said in his soft low voice. "Away from school, I mean."

I angled toward him and smiled, suddenly feeling shy and self conscious. His eyes caught mine, and I was mesmerized by the intensity of his gaze. I could feel myself blushing, and looked down. I felt his fingers gently brushing by my cheek as he pushed my hair away from my face. His fingertips traced along my jawbone, then gently touched my chin and turned my face back toward him. He leaned down toward me and touched his lips to mine, and the world fell away. I froze for an instant, then put my hands on his chest and kissed him back. He pushed me back a little, then traced his way from my ear to my throat with his soft kisses. He pulled me closer with both arms around me, and we stood looking at the moon.

This is how it feels, I realized. I thought I knew what love felt like, but I had been wrong. In wonder at this beautiful creature next to me, I looked up at him. I ran my fingers through his hair as I had been dying to do for weeks. His eyes met mine and he smiled. He put both his hands in my hair, and gently pulled me into another kiss. This time, I felt his tongue lightly licking my lower lip. I opened my mouth a little, and touched his tongue with mine. I was certain I could stay there and just kiss him like this forever. I was not cold anymore. Then I felt myself losing my balance to the left, as the boat floated over a small wave.

"Whoa," I said as I grabbed at him and the boat seat.

"Let's sit down. I'd hate for you to have to explain to your parents why you came home wet. Besides, I'm sure the water is pretty cold," he said. He pulled me toward the bench seat along one side of the boat, where he sat with his back against the side and I sat between his legs with my back against him. He put his arms around me, and we looked out at the moon and the water. I was warm nestled against his chest, and could have stayed there all night.

In my ear he said, "I heard you had a boyfriend. I don't want to put you in an uncomfortable position."

I pondered that for a moment. This was a good time to avoid saying something stupid.

"Maybe from the same place I heard you were dating Kelsey," I said slowly.

"Probably," he agreed.

"I did have a boyfriend until recently. We started off pretty serious, but we had been on again off again for quite a while, and we broke up again not too long ago."

"Why's that?" he asked quietly. "That is, if you don't mind telling me."

"I don't mind. There are a lot of answers to that, I guess. Lately I've realized I might want some different things." I remembered my promise to myself that I would be completely honest with Andy, no games. "The simple part of the answer is that I felt myself feeling attracted to someone else. It's not just that simple though. I knew that if I felt attracted to someone else, something had to be missing in what I had with Jeff. He'd hurt me many times, and I realized there was meant to be more to a relationship than what we had. I was starting to see him and us in a different light, and didn't like what I was seeing. Maybe it was me changing more than him."

He was silent as he absorbed that.

"Was that TMI?" I asked timidly. Good job Meg, you scared him away with heavy relationship stuff already, I thought.

"No not at all. It's very well thought out."

"Anyway no, I don't have a boyfriend. And I have to say," I snuggled against him, "I'm glad."

He paused a moment. "Someone else?"

I laughed. "Yes, but I didn't know if he liked me."

"Who's the lucky guy?" he wanted to know.

"Well," I replied, "you may not know him. He's new in school. Just moved here from California."

He hugged me tighter and nuzzled into my neck. I felt goose bumps down my spine. It was heavenly being in his arms. I sighed a deep breath of contentment.

"What about you, did you leave a girlfriend in California?" I asked.

"No. I dated, but there was never anyone serious."

I stated the obvious. “Well, I’m sure you had plenty of dates.”

“A few,” he conceded.

“What about Kelsey though? She seems totally into in you.”

He turned my face toward him, saw my serious look, and laughed. “Don’t you find her just a little scary?” he asked.

“Me? Well, I never thought of it that way.” I considered what he had said. “She is pretty aggressive I guess.”

He gave a quick laugh. “That’s an understatement. She’s good looking and all, but she and everyone else knows it. I bet she’s pretty much used to getting what she wants.”

“Yes, and she clearly wants you,” I told him.

“That’s flattering I guess, but she’s just not attractive to me at all.”

I felt a new wave of joy. Was it really possible he liked me? I pondered that. Why did I find it so surprising? Maybe some guys did care about more than just looks. The possibilities ran through my head. That would mean an entire shift in the social structure my friends and I had known for so long. We sat in comfortable silence for a while, looking at the moon.

“So is your family planning to stay a while?” I just needed to know before it was too late and my heart got broken. What was I thinking? It was already too late.

“I really don’t know. We have a lot of work to get the house in shape to sell. Every now and then my mom thinks she might want to fix it up and stay, but the time and money that would take would be enormous. They haven’t decided if they even like it here.”

"What do you think of it here?" I asked.

"There's one thing I really like a lot here," he said quietly.

I grinned.

He continued. "Ok, there's the obvious, it seems pretty cold. People are friendly, but not overly outgoing. That's ok, because I'm kind of a loner anyway. I have enough to keep me busy, and I understand everyone already has established friends. They seem to be lifelong friends in a lot of cases. Moving to a small town toward the end of your junior year can't be viewed as a good social strategy."

"We're not so bad. We're just used to the way things are. Is that why you didn't come to the basketball game?"

"Yeah, mostly. My dad was home for dinner too, and I hadn't seen him all week so I wanted to spend some time with him."

"You won't think it's cold when summer comes," I said. "Are you going to get a job or go out for any sports? You seem like you'd be athletic."

He shifted a little and ran his fingers through my hair, which sent another shiver down my spine. I twisted so I could lie against him and tuck my head up next to his. He smelled clean and fresh, like the night air.

"I kind of have a job. I'll have to show you. My family is going to Boston tomorrow and staying until Sunday evening - Mom wants to get reacquainted with the city, and I've barely spent any time there, so we have to do all the touristy stuff. Maybe you could come over next Saturday, and I'll show you the rest of the house and what I'm doing. You'll be shocked. The amount of *stuff* in this house and barn is unbelievable. It's like nobody threw anything away for two hundred years. There are seriously five or ten of every piece of junk you can imagine. Some of it is great stuff, but a lot of it is simply junk. My parents said I could keep half of whatever I can make selling it. I've sold a little on eBay and Craig's list so far, and I'll probably also sell some things locally. We could just auction it all, but we kind of want to go through everything in case there are treasures or family history we would want to save. Mom has already found a few things she wants to keep."

"Sounds like a big project," I said.

"It is. As to the other part of your question," he continued, "I played a little basketball in California, but I'm not sure I want to play anymore. I do love sports, but my favorite right now is water skiing. That's a large part of why we have this boat. I don't know how much you know about boats, so I'm sorry if you already know this, but it's a ski boat, not a fishing boat. I've been in some competitions, and want to stay with it. I haven't looked into whether that sort of thing even exists around here though. If it does, the season would have to be a lot shorter than in California."

I'd heard an invitation to Andy's house next Saturday. My heart gave a happy leap. Get a grip girl, I told myself for the millionth time. You have no idea where this is going yet. "I'd love to come over again and see the place."

"Good, it's a date," he said. "Tell me about your job."

"Well, there's not that much to tell," I started. "When I turned sixteen, I really wanted a car. Any car. You can see why that would be important around here, right? My parents were ok with the idea, but said I would have to help pay for it. I got the job at the deli that summer, and worked full time. The deli has been great, really. Free food and lattes, and decent pay. When school started again, they agreed to allow me to work only on Wednesday nights and Sundays. It's just enough to keep me in gas money, with a little left over."

"That's cool," he said. We sat in comfortable silence for a few minutes. "There was one other thing I wanted to bring you here for."

"What?" I asked. Nothing could make the night more perfect than it already was.

He pushed me away and turned me around to face him. I was getting used to the way his eyes would lock on mine, and there was nothing else I would rather look at. "Would you go to the Prom with me?"

I was stunned.

He asked me! Me.

"Yes!" I squealed.

12 GIRL TIME

I slowly cracked open an eye and confronted my alarm clock. Ten o'clock in the morning, still a reasonable time to be in bed. I snuggled under my down comforter and snoozed a while longer, basking in happiness. Was last night just the most amazing dream I'd ever had, or was it real? I played the details over and over in my mind. The way his eyes were dark in the moonlight, the feel of his hair, the way his body felt solid and strong against mine, the reflections on the water, the swaying of the boat, the warmth of his chest as I lay against him. It had been more romantic than any love scene in any movie I'd ever seen.

Finally I got up. I was reasonably sure my friends would be awake - it was past eleven anyway, so I started texting them.

"he askd me 2 prom" to Kayla.

She responded instantly, "Andy?"

"y" I returned.

"omg, sweet, go 2 Worc 2 day 2 shop?" she returned.

"y" I returned.

"b there 1"

"k" I answered.

I quickly texted Rachel and Emilee, and they were just as excited. Rachel told me Kyle was taking her to our Prom. All the more reason to be happy.

I floated down the stairs to search for some food, and found my mom making lunch for my brothers.

"Mornin' sleepyhead. What time did you get home last night?"

"About midnight."

"What were you doing?" she asked.

"Oh, after the game I was with that new guy I studied with last week, Andy."

"I see. Is he a nice boy?"

"Yes definitely," I said with a big smile.

"What did you guys do?" she wanted to know.

I hopped up to sit on the counter. "Mom, it was the most romantic thing ever. We took his family's boat out in the moonlight on Quabbin reservoir."

"In the dark?" she asked, as if I were insane. "That doesn't sound like a very good idea."

"It was full moon, and we could see really well," I said a little defensively.

"You're not going to get right back into a serious relationship, are you?"

"What do you mean mom?"

"Well, I'd just like to see you spending more time with your friends instead of always having a boyfriend, that's all. You just need some time to recover." She set two bowls of macaroni and cheese down in front of my brothers.

"Mom, I broke up with Jeff, he didn't break up with me."

"I know honey. I just don't want to see you get hurt."

"Andy's different than the guys around here Mom."

"What does that mean?"

"I don't know. I just mean he's really really nice. He has manners and integrity. He's not the type that would cheat on his girlfriend. He doesn't play games, he says things like they are."

"Well, I'm certainly glad for that. He sounds great Megs, just be careful, and don't let any boy make you act like someone you're not."

"I know Mom," I said as I jumped off the counter. I opened the refrigerator door. Nothing looked appealing. I grabbed a vanilla yogurt and turned toward the counter. I glanced at Nick, the older of my two brothers, who was going to be in high school next year. He gave me a quick sympathetic smile. I winked at him.

"Are we going to get to meet this boy soon?" my mom asked over her shoulder, as she finished putting dishes in the dishwasher.

"Yes," I said. "He asked me to the Prom." I couldn't keep the excitement out of my voice.

She turned quickly to face me, with a huge smile on her face. "Really honey? That's great! I had assumed you wouldn't be going this year. Does that mean we're going shopping?"

"Oh, I'd hoped you'd ask!"

"Great, we'll drive in to Boston on a Saturday in a few weeks and hit all the best stores, just the two of us."

"Thanks Mom, that sounds fun." It did. We hadn't spent time together like that in ages.

"What is Andy going to wear?"

"I don't know. We didn't talk about details, just that we'll go together. That's all I care about anyway. Mom, you're really going to like him."

"I'm sure I will honey."

"Kayla and I are going shopping this afternoon in Worcester. The summer clothes are out in the stores now. Aren't you just so sick of snow?"

She laughed. "I sure am. I guess it *is* time to start thinking about summer clothes. You know what? Let me give you a little money."

"Thanks Mom."

Kayla arrived at 1:15, just as I finished dressing.

"Bye Mom, back around dinner time!"

"Bye sweetie, be careful."

"We will." I smiled knowingly at Kayla, and we danced out the door.

Kayla had her mom's Toyota SUV. I jumped into the passenger side, and we were off. I couldn't stop smiling, thinking about Andy.

"You look so happy!" Kayla said.

"I *am* so happy. I'm afraid I really like this guy."

"I can see that. He's really hot, but what's he like? What did you two do last night? I didn't even know you were meeting him. You never made it to the party. You wanted to keep him to yourself? Details!"

"Well, I wasn't sure until last night how he felt about me. I really thought he liked Kelsey. I didn't want to ask him to come to the party when I didn't even know whether he liked me or just wanted to be friends. He just told me he wanted to show me something, so I didn't know what to expect."

"Well, what did he show you? Was it naughty?" She grinned.

"No, of course not!" I said, with pretend shock.

"Oh, that's too bad."

I laughed. "It was totally the most romantic thing that has ever happened to me in my entire life. It was totally unbelievable."

"Tell me!" she demanded.

"Well, I got in his car, and he still hadn't told me what we were doing. I didn't know what to think. But we drove out to Quabbin reservoir."

"Quabbin reservoir? I don't get it. Why?"

"Yes, and parked at the boat docks. His family keeps a boat there."

"But it was dark," Kayla said.

"Yes, but there was almost a full moon, and you could see really well once your eyes adjusted."

"Well why the boat docks? Why drive all the way out there?"

"We actually got in the boat, and he drove us out into the middle of the lake. It was so beautiful out there. The moon was shining on the water and we stopped the motor and looked at the stars, and he kissed me like I've never been kissed before."

"Wow, that does sound awesome. He kisses better than Jeff?"

"Oh Kayla, there's no comparison. He was gentle, and he moved slowly. He touched my face and ran his fingers through my hair. He smelled really good too. He wasn't slobbery or anything like that. He acted like he really knew what he was doing. It was sweet though, we didn't just make out - we talked for a few hours while we sat looking at the moon. He's a lot more mature than most of the guys around here. And different from them." I sighed, re-living the feelings.

"I'm so jealous Megs. Why don't I ever find a guy like that?"

"Honestly Kayla, I think most guys just aren't like that at least until they're in college. Maybe later. Most guys our age have no maturity. But you're going to meet a great guy. You're way too special not to. And way too pretty!"

She smiled. "I hope you're right. So he asked you to the Prom out there, huh?"

"Yes, toward the end. Until we got out there, I really thought he was going with Kelsey. I was stupid to believe Jennifer. He's not interested in Kelsey at all, can you believe it?"

"Well, if he's like you say, then yes, I believe it. It's about time someone with more going on than hormones put her in her place. That's what you mean by different isn't it? He sees beyond her great looks and cares that there's no brain in that pretty head."

"He didn't say it that way, but yes, I think that's the gist of it. He's interested in more than just good looks. Thank God!" I added.

"Oh Megan, you're gorgeous."

"Oh please Kayla. I'm girl next door all the way."

"Well maybe, but you have this great light in your eyes. Like looking at you, it's obvious you're intelligent and full of life."

"Really? That's a nice thing to say."

"It's only the truth. Well what else about him? Why did they move here?"

"Oh, his mom inherited that old Bruce house, and his dad got a job in Boston. He's a doctor."

"Why would they want to live here, when Boston is almost two hours away?"

"I don't think they do want to live here, long term. They're trying to decide what to do with the house."

"So he might move away?"

"I guess so. I don't want to think about that. I don't think he knows either way. It did sound like his parents care about his opinion though. He's the only kid left at home. His older sister is in college already."

"Wow. I'm happy for you Meg."

"Thank you. I'm happy too. I don't know what this means. I didn't mean to jump right into having a boyfriend again, if he is my boyfriend, but I can't think about anything except him."

"You've got it bad girl! You were just smothered with Jeff, and didn't even know it. Now the real thing has come along and smacked you in the face. So to speak."

I grinned sheepishly. "Yeah, maybe that's it. He's just very different and special."

We sat in silence for a few miles while I daydreamed about Andy and watched the scenery going by. The first hints of green were starting to show in the woods.

"Do you realize it's going to be summer soon? I just can't believe how fast time is moving," said Kayla.

"I know. We really have to get going with those college applications and gearing up for senior year. Time is flying. Where are you thinking you want to go these days Kay?"

"I still don't know really. Nowhere far away. I've decided that. I mean, I want to be a decent way away from my parents of course, but not necessarily out of state. I'm still thinking business I think, but I'm not totally sure. If I just go somewhere reasonably big, I could always switch majors. I think psychology is really interesting too. What about you?"

"I don't know either. I feel like there's a lot of pressure to decide though. I think for now, we should just get accepted a few places, and then we'll still have some time to decide."

"Makes sense to me. I need a place with cute guys!"

I laughed. "Of course that's important! Seriously, I think the most important thing is to study something you really enjoy, so you can get a job you really like."

"Yeah, it's just hard to know what that is. Do you know there are girls in our class who believe they're just going to go marry rich guys and shop or lay by a pool all day?"

"Like who?" I asked.

"Oh, I've heard some of the girls in my English class talking like that, Shayla and Jenna. Just where do they suppose they're going to go find rich guys? I mean sure, we'd all like that, but come on. How do you not have a backup plan?"

"I know. That's pretty hard to believe," I replied. "And I'm not even sure I *would* like it."

We were pulling into the mall parking lot. The drive had gone quickly.

"Ok, shorts, tops and swimsuits, right?" asked Kayla.

"Right!" I confirmed. We were on a mission.

The first store we went in had tons of cute stuff. We each grabbed about fifteen things to try on, and headed to the dressing rooms. We got side by side rooms, and carried on our conversation over the wall.

"Ick," said Kayla.

"Which one?" I asked.

"Oh, these maroon shorts make my butt look huge. And my skin look really white."

"I doubt it could be that bad Kayla, but our skin *is* really white. It's like we've been hibernating all winter. We're pasty white!"

I heard snickering from a dressing room across the hall.

I said, "You have to try to ignore that. We'll get tan soon. Try on a swimsuit."

"Ok, you too."

I struggled into a light blue and white plaid bikini. I *was* white. "Are you ready?" I asked.

"I guess so," she said.

"Ok, let's see." We both stepped into the hall, and burst into laughter as we saw we had on the same swimsuit. "Well aren't we the dork twins?" I asked. "Actually Kay, I think it looks better on you."

"I do kind of like this one. Are you sure you don't mind?" she asked.

"No, not at all. It's not that great on me. It's better for your shape. Let's try another one though."

We each put on another swimsuit and stepped into the hall again.

"I liked the first one better on you," I said. "I don't like this one on me either though. I'll try another one."

We continued to try on clothes and model them for each other.

"Does your family have summer plans?" I asked over the wall.

"I think we're going to my grandma's for a week, in Michigan, but other than that I need to find a job. What about you?"

"I'll work full time at the deli again. I don't think we're going anywhere. The boys are in football and basketball camps, and playing summer league baseball, so it's kind of hard to get away. They're going to be really good athletes by the time they get to high school."

"Ok, look at this."

"Hang on." I threw on another pair of shorts and stepped into the hall. "I like that top, but not the shorts. The shorts are too poofy."

"That's what I thought too. But I like those shorts you have on."

"Me too, actually."

We stepped back into our rooms, just about done with our piles.

"Well, what are you getting?" I asked.

"That first swimsuit and two of these tops. What about you?"

"I like two of the shorts, and one top. I do need to find a swimsuit though, so let's keep shopping. Are you done?"

"Yes, two seconds."

We paid for our purchases and moved on to the next store. Nothing like a good shopping trip to top off a great date the night before.

"Oh Megan, I forgot to even ask if you wanted to look at Prom dresses, do you?"

"Oh no, my mom is going to take me to Boston for that."

We went into the next store, allowed ourselves to be sprayed with perfume samples, and repeated our process - picking out shorts, swimsuits and summer tops. I found a great pink bikini with silver trim, and two more tops. I was done. Kayla found some great shorts, and we were good to go.

"Let's get ice cream," suggested Kayla.

"Sounds good to me."

I got chocolate fudge brownie and Kayla got peach. We sat in the food court and as we watched the people walking by we made up stories about them. I cocked my head to the left. "Kayla, an alien space ship came down from the sky, scooped up that girl, and tagged her with that band on her ear so they can trace her."

Kayla glanced at the Goth girl walking past. "Which band? She has *everything* pierced."

I snorted. "Yeah, maybe it was a lot of aliens."

"Meg look at that one," Kayla whispered and rolled her eyes towards the guy. "He's practicing reading his book while walking, in preparation for his cross country walking fund raising trip for save the pansies. How many books can he read while walking across the United States?"

I looked over. He was an overweight middle aged man in jeans and a too tight yellow polo shirt stretched over a large belly. Kayla was right. He was shuffling along slowly, reading a book. "Why wouldn't he just sit down somewhere? Does he think he's getting some exercise?"

"Oh look at those cute guys!" she exclaimed, and looked over my shoulder.

Casually, I turned around to look. They were cute, but not compared to Andy. They were looking at us too. I gave Kayla a look that said "really?"

She locked eyes with me. "I know, I can see it on your face - not compared to Andy, right?" She laughed. "I repeat - you've got it bad girl."

"I know Kayla. I didn't mean to, but it just happened. I really like him."

"Well, he's going to love that rockin new swimsuit!"

"I hope so," I giggled.

"I told my mom I'd be home for dinner, so we'd better get going," said Kayla.

"I know, I did too. This was fun."

We chatted all the way home, and Kayla dropped me off just in time for dinner.

Monday morning I couldn't wait to get to school to see Andy, after having thought about him all weekend. I was disappointed that I didn't see him in the parking lot. I went to boring Econ, and took my seat. I was thrilled when my cell phone vibrated. It had to be him.

"missd u" he'd written.

I felt giddy with excitement. "missd u2, how was wknd?" I returned.

"great history in Bstn"

"y, a must c" I replied.

"y, lking fwd to c u"

"me 2" I replied.

As I sat down to wait for Emilee, Rachel and Kayla at our lunch table, I replayed the events of the morning in my head. Chemistry class had been so satisfying. Kelsey had strutted into the room in high heels, tight jeans, and a tight t-shirt over a lacy cami. She had red hot lips, fluffy hair, and was oozing confidence and sex appeal. She'd glanced from side to side to see guys and girls alike staring as she strode across the room like a runway model. I felt her confidence growing as she took in the looks of admiration, until suddenly a look of disbelief washed across her face. She had strutted past Andy, trying to look casual, and he hadn't even turned his head toward her. It was like he hadn't even seen her. I had been shocked myself, then immensely pleased. He'd glanced at me, our eyes had met, and he had flashed me his California smile. She'd seen it too. As she rounded my lab table she had said under her breath, "Don't you already have a boyfriend?"

My phone vibrated, startling me out of my daydream. The text message said, "fav food?"

"cheese, u?" I typed, and hit send, back to Andy.

"ice cream," came the reply.

Lunch time arrived and the girls arrived and settled in their usual places.

Emilee said, "Tell us all about it!"

I told them as much detail as I was willing to share about my date with Andy, which was pretty much all the same stuff I had told Kayla on Saturday. Kayla reminded me of key points as I described my date on Quabbin reservoir.

"So," Rachel said, "it looks like you two are an item, huh?"

"I guess we are," I said. I broke into a grin. Then I squealed in excitement. Like true friends, they squealed with me.

As lunch was ending he texted again. "fav movie?" This went on throughout the day. I learned he liked green, ducks, the Lord of the Rings movies, and skittles.

"Lunch tmrw?" he sent.

"y" I returned.

Lunch Tuesday couldn't arrive fast enough.

I waited in line for my soup of the day, chicken with rice, and a small salad, and then headed over to our usual lunch table. I sat on the opposite end today, away from my regular spot, knowing Andy would arrive soon. Emilee, Rachel and Kayla arrived and took their places, and smiled at me with understanding. Andy came up soon after and sat across from me.

"Hey, soup huh?"

"Yeah, pretty much every day – soup and salad. Boring, huh?"

"Oh I don't know. It's cafeteria food after all." He picked up his cheeseburger and took a bite. I picked at my food, nervous about eating in front of him. "Not hungry?" he asked.

"Oh not so much," I answered.

"Ok, what was your family's best vacation?" he asked, and then took another bite. He didn't seem nervous about eating in front of me.

I thought for a moment. "Disneyworld? Yes, Disneyworld. Have you been there?"

"Yes. No childhood is complete without it, right?"

"That's what they say," I said. "What was your favorite ride?"

"It had to be space mountain. Or the mine train. What was yours?"

"I guess splash mountain," I mused.

"Yeah, that's a great one too."

As lunch was ending, I saw Kelsey approaching. Andy had his back to her, but I could see her over his shoulder. She had a smug look on her face. She sat down next to him, very close. She looked me in the eye, like she was daring me to say something. I smiled confidently at her. Andy looked distinctly uncomfortable.

"Hi Andy," she chirped.

"Hi Kelsey," he returned, and took a gulp of water.

"Hi Megan, how's your boyfriend?" Kelsey asked me.

I almost felt bad for her. She had no idea what an idiot she looked like. I hoped Andy didn't think I was being too presumptuous, but I looked from Kelsey to Andy, then back at Kelsey and said, "He's absolutely great."

Andy smiled in amusement and rolled his eyes, leaning away from her slightly.

Kelsey looked a little puzzled, then a little uncomfortable. "Well, I just wanted to say hi. See you in class," she said to Andy.

He nodded, and we watched her leave.

"I'm absolutely great?" Andy asked me, with a twinkle in his liquid blue eyes.

Oh yes, I thought to myself. “She was just trying to make me mad. Is it ok if I think of you as my boyfriend?”

“I’d be honored,” replied Andy softly.

13 A BUTTON

July 1867 – Allie

I made my best effort to behave normally. I engaged in conversation through supper, read a little from the bible afterwards, and retired to bed early. I could not continue to be two people – one I displayed on the outside and one I felt on the inside. One way or another, this would have to cease and cease soon. I wrote in my diary, blew out my lantern, and then lay in my bed watching the pale moon moving slowly across the sky. I listened to the sounds of my parents moving around downstairs and the creaking of the old house around me as it too settled for the night. A cool breeze blew in through the window as I waited.

I heard John going to bed, and not much later I heard Mother and Father making their last rounds of the house and climbing the stairs. I could not believe I was about to sneak out. I felt full of sin and guilt, but knew there was no alternative. I felt I would die a painful death of longing if I didn't meet Wayne. I waited until the house had been silent for half an hour, then slowly crept across the floor to my door and opened it a crack. No light came from anywhere. I inched the door open, squeezed into the hall, and then inched the door closed. Still there was silence. I made for the back stairway, the one closest to my room.

I eased down the steps one by one, skipping the third step from the bottom because I knew it squeaked. At the landing I asked myself for the millionth time what I was doing. Resigned to my plan, I moved silently through the kitchen to the back door. I unlatched the lock and ever so slowly eased the door open. I let myself out into the night, noticing that the crickets didn't change their rhythm. I moved to the barn and circled to the rear, where I could then move through the woods to the road without being as careful. The almost full moon made it reasonably easy to find my way.

I arrived at the road and looked around. Nobody was in sight so I stepped out of the woods. I turned to my right and set off along the road, away from town and toward the woods behind our pasture and stone wall. When I arrived at the far side of the stone wall, Wayne was there waiting, sitting on my very own swing. I noticed the shining dots from lightning bugs all about him, twinkling as if they were protecting an angel. I ran to him and he rose as I threw myself into his arms. I clung to him with urgency, since we both knew he was leaving soon. His lips crushed onto mine, and I felt a passion I had never imagined flooding through the center of my body. I felt weak, but he held me in his firm grip. I felt I would die if he didn't continue to kiss me, and I pulled myself tight against him hungrily. Finally I had to take a breath.

"This is my swing," I said. "It's where I come when I need to think or want to be alone. My father hung it for me when I was but a small child."

"It's a wonderful place," he said. "Did you notice the fireflies?"

"Around here, we call them lightning bugs. Yes, I thought it was perfect that they are here tonight. They make the woods appear so lovely."

"Yes, they do. It's perfect. How long do you have?" he asked.

"Quite long probably, everyone is asleep. They would never imagine I would attempt such a thing as to sneak out. Or that I would have any reason to desire to."

"Of course not, you're a good girl," he said, stroking my cheek.

"I don't feel like a good girl. I feel I'm doing something terribly improper. I couldn't restrain myself. Did you know I would come?"

"I would have waited here all night hoping you would." He paused. "No, I didn't know, but I prayed you would."

I had to inquire, but dreaded the answer. "When are you departing?"

"I was intent on leaving in two days. My plans might change a little, but I have commitments in the west in a little more than a week. I am establishing my first route, and have already arranged meetings with shopkeepers along the way."

"Will you reside in one place?" I asked.

"I believe I will settle somewhere along the route, and anticipate quickly hiring additional help to do the hauling. They will have to be people I can trust with my new horses of course," he smiled. "I will also have to be in the East frequently to maintain relationships with manufacturers."

"So you will return."

"Yes, from time to time."

He pulled me close again, and we kissed passionately, desperately. I pressed myself against him, knowing this was all I desired in the entire world. He grasped my hands and placed them on his chest. I felt his strong muscles underneath, and felt a tingling in my own body I had never experienced before. Yearnings of a sort. He placed his hands on my breasts, gently, which no man had ever done. I had never even been kissed before Wayne, let alone like this. I wanted him to touch me, and I felt guilty about that, but also anxious for him to continue. His mouth closed on mine again, and I felt his tongue pushing inside my mouth. I allowed him to do what he wanted. I had never known a kiss could be like this – warm and wet and so intimate.

"Allie, you make me want to take you right here. You are so beautiful."

I was fairly certain I understood what he meant by that. He was the most handsome man I had ever seen. I didn't know how to respond.

He continued in a low husky voice. "I will not of course, I would never do anything to upset you or dishonor you."

"What if I desired you to?" I asked timidly.

He sighed. "Even then. I would never do anything you would regret. Though obviously I asked you to meet me here and I know it is not proper. I felt you could make your own decision, and if we never met again you could still forgive yourself.

He held me close and we stood in silence for a few moments. It was all too overwhelming to take in. How would this end? "What will we do?" I asked against his chest.

"We must be together," he replied. "You have to come with me."

"What do you mean?" I stammered.

"I mean you must come with me. Marry me. Be my wife. Share your life with me."

I couldn't believe what I was hearing. No words could sound sweeter, yet how could I possibly do what he was requesting? "My family wouldn't understand. They could never forgive me. Or you. They believe I am going to marry Jeremy."

"You cannot live your life for the will of others. To satisfy what others want. What about you? What do you want?"

That was easy. "I want you. I want to be with you. But I barely even know you. How can I feel so certain?"

"People don't feel like this every day. You know you were meant to be with me, as I know it about you. Tell me I am mistaken," he insisted with urgency.

"I cannot. I've never experienced anything at all like this."

"Nor have I. That's how I know we are meant to be together."

"What do I do?" I asked again.

His eyes shone in the moonlight. "You must come with me."

"What do I tell my family?"

"The truth. Tell them you love me. Tell them your life is with me." He paused and gazed deep into my eyes. "I love you. I want to share my life with you."

It was all too much. It was happening so quickly. A decision here and now would dictate the course of my life. How could we know for a fact that we loved each other so quickly, so completely? But we did. I knew it and he knew it. I now understood what my life was supposed to be.

He continued, "I had planned to depart in two days. I can delay a week and we can hold a wedding with your family. Please say you will." He got down on one knee. "Allison Bruce, will you marry me? I have no ring to give you tonight, but I offer you this as a placeholder until I can get a proper one." He pressed a brass button into my hand.

This chance at happiness would be worth all the trouble we would stir.

"Yes Wayne Collins, I will marry you." I was ecstatically giddy with excitement. "What is it?" I asked, indicating the button.

"It is a button from my military uniform. If it were light you could make out the impression on it. It is an eagle holding a shield on its chest. It is very precious to me, because it reminds me that I served my country with honor."

"I treasure it," I assured him.

"I can speak with your father tomorrow and ask his permission," Wayne said.

Fear stabbed through me. "He will be angry. He will say we do not know you and that it is wrong to break my plans with Jeremy. And Mother will be very upset also. What if Father wants to harm you?"

"Your father is a good man and I believe after his initial anger he will understand that I am sincere. That we are sincere. I do not want to do anything to dishonor you. I want to ask your father for his blessing. I should have done that before I asked you, but I didn't know for certain you would accept. I didn't want to cause a scene if it were a course of action you were not interested in. But for you, I am willing to endure any pain required for us to be joined."

"I will have to think of something to tell Jeremy. He will be so upset."

"Yes, and I feel regret for that. He is a decent sort. But you don't love him."

"No."

"And never will."

"No."

"So it's not the proper fate for you. Even your mother will have to concede that. She does want you to be happy, right?"

"Yes of course, but she would never dream I would consider leaving Hardwick. And now all of a sudden I will be leaving in a week."

"But we'll be back frequently."

"That would be wonderful. Oh Wayne. I can't believe this is all coming to pass."

"I can't either Allie. I didn't come here looking for you or even thinking about women. You took my breath away from the moment I laid eyes upon you, and suddenly my plans weren't complete without you. It was as if I looked at you and saw a piece of myself I didn't know was missing. I didn't know such a feeling was even possible. If you insisted, I would stay and try to make a living as a farmer."

"You would give up all your dreams for me?"

"I would. You matter more than any of it. I can feel that is true to the core of my being."

I pondered. "I would never ask it of you. I do not want to be a farmer's wife. I want to be your wife, and be with you whatever you are doing."

"So it is settled then, I will speak with your father."

"Yes, but give me a day to consider how best to approach them."

"Fair enough my lady. My future wife. How does it sound, Allison Collins? Mrs. Wayne Collins?"

"It sounds like a symphony of words. I love you. I'm afraid of how everyone will react."

"I know, but as I said, we can't live our lives for them. They will all recover from it. We are destined to be together."

"I know."

"It will be alright, you'll see. Trust me," he said.

"I do. I trust you with all my heart."

"Good my love. We will have a beautiful life together. I will come calling the day after tomorrow to speak to your father. Go now, dream of me."

"I will Wayne, I love you."

"And I love you."

14 EXPLORING

Andy and I spent the rest of the week texting and eating lunch together. Though school had never been so interesting, I couldn't wait for Saturday to arrive so I could spend some real time with him.

Saturday morning I ate my breakfast and hurried through my chores – vacuuming, dusting and watering the plants.

"Where are you off to today?" my mom asked.

"I'm going to Andy's house. He's going to show me around, and then we're going to study."

"I'd love to know what that house looks like inside. It has quite a history."

"I'll tell you if I see anything interesting. See you later Mom, love you."

"Bye sweetie."

My tires crunched on the gravel as I steered my car up Andy's driveway. I turned off the engine, got out and walked to the door. I knocked, feeling stupid for feeling nervous. I felt just as excited to see him now as I did every single time, and wondered if that would ever change. As the door opened and I saw him standing there, I felt like I was melting inside. He had the most beautiful wide smile. And his eyes sparkled as he looked at me.

"Right on time," he said, smiling. "Did you bring your books?"

I groaned. "Yeah, I did."

"Well, throw them on the table there," he indicated an end table in the hall, "and let me take you on the grand tour. Leave your jacket on. We'll go outside first. You just won't believe this."

"What?" I asked.

"You'll see. You'll see why I won't have time for a job any time soon."

I dropped my books on the table and noticed there was a strange pole with a silver knob on the end, leaning against the door jamb of the coat closet. It was about three feet tall, and about the circumference of a toilet paper tube. I couldn't think what it could be.

"What's that?" I asked, pointing at the stick.

"Oh, that's kind of cool," Andy said as he picked it up. "Take a look." He handed me the pole.

It was a heavy, made of some kind of solid dark colored polished wood. I examined the knob on the top. Embossed on it was, "Hardwick's Oldest Citizen."

"Oh, I remember reading about this," I exclaimed. "It was your grandfather's cane, right?"

"Yes. You read about it? Is it one of those small town things?"

"Yes, I guess it is. It was in the paper. Mr. Miller was the oldest man in town. He turned one hundred and four right before he died, didn't he?"

"Yes that's right," Andy said. "Pretty amazing, huh?"

"Yeah, that's like so old. Cool. Now what do you do with it?"

"Well, my mom says we should give it back to the city, so they can give it to whoever is now the oldest. Like it should pass around or something."

"Yeah, that would be cool," I replied, gently setting the cane back where it had been resting.

Andy grabbed a plaid farm jacket off the coat rack and threw it on, then led me back out the door. We rounded the corner of the house, and from there we had a view across the pasture to the woods on the other side. I could see the stone wall stretching away from the side of the house for a few hundred yards all the way to the woods where it ended. As I gazed out toward the trees along the edge of the pasture, I imagined the continuation of the stone wall running along, just this side of the woods. I had a vivid picture in my mind of three horses grazing on very green grass. I blinked, and knew before I even looked that there was no wall along the edge of the woods, no horses, and the grass was still brown from winter. I couldn't understand why I would imagine it any other way. It was freaky. I suddenly remembered a similar thing had happened the first time I had come, when I had seen the red geraniums on the front porch for just a moment. I couldn't get this latest picture out of my mind.

I asked hesitantly, "Do you have horses?"

"Oh no," he said. "Nobody has kept horses here in seventy or eighty years. There isn't a fence around the pasture now. I guess at one time this was a horse farm, but that was in the 1800s and early 1900s. There are some things in the barn that would have been used with horses. That's what I want to show you. You just won't believe how much stuff is in this barn and how old some of it is."

"I really enjoyed the last thing you asked to show me," I teased.

He glanced at me with a grin. "Me too, most definitely." Then he pulled me to him and kissed me. Warmth flooded my body.

We continued toward the enormous barn that stood behind the house, picking our way through the patches of ice along the gravel path. It looked like a story book barn. The front had wide double doors that would open outward, though these didn't look like they had moved in a long time. Above the doors was a hayloft door with a criss cross of boards on it. From the roof just above the hayloft door, there was some sort of metal loop hanging right above the hayloft door, which would be a place to put a pulley. The barn had peeling white paint over faded grey boards. It had certainly seen better days. I wondered if it was safe to go inside, because it looked a little rickety. Andy led me to a door at the back. It had a window that was too dirty to see through and a rusty knob. He felt above the door frame for a key, put it in the rusty lock and turned it, then opened the door and disappeared inside. I peered into the doorway and saw hazy darkness.

"It's ok Meg, you're eyes will adjust."

I cautiously stepped in, and the air smelled dusty. I blinked as my eyes focused, and saw that everywhere there were piles of stuff. I hadn't been in many barns, but the ones I had been in always had a large open area in the center. Not so this one. There was floor to ceiling stuff everywhere I looked.

"Look at this." He walked over to the wall, excited to show me. We stood looking at a collection of gardening and farming tools hanging from old nails. That would be expected in a barn, but the quantity of tools was enough to outfit an entire hardware store. "Why would anyone have twelve pitch forks?" he asked.

I counted. Sure enough, hanging on the wall were twelve pitchforks. They seemed to be all different ages, all different sizes. Short wooden handles, long wooden handles, a plastic handle, three tines, four tines, tines worn down to nubs. I bet some were actually a hundred years old. It was beyond me. Why *would* anyone keep all those pitchforks?

"When was the last time this was a farm?" I asked.

"I think it's been over thirty years, but I don't know," Andy replied.

"Why would you keep the broken ones?" I asked, gesturing toward the wall.

"I sure don't know," said Andy, "but I remember my mom saying that Mr. Miller liked to fix things. What she meant was that he wouldn't throw anything away, because he thought he could fix it or find some use for it.

Making our way toward the front of the barn, we came to a corner where there were old carts and wagons. Five wheelbarrows - two with missing wheels, one with a broken handle. Some kind of small cart that looked like you might hitch it to a horse. Leather straps and buckles were everywhere. In another corner was an area that looked like some sort of workshop. There was a peg board nailed to the wall, with every kind of tool imaginable hanging from it. Eight hammers. Twenty three hand saws. There were rusty cans full of bolts, screws and bent nails. Everything was covered with a layer of dirt, and many things were rusty.

There were also items we couldn't identify. I found a tool that looked like a giant corkscrew. It was a metal pole, about two feet long. The top half of the metal was smooth and round, but the bottom half was spiraled. On the top, forming a letter T of the whole thing, was a wooden handle that would allow you to grip on both sides and twist it into something. "What do you suppose they drilled with that?" I asked.

"I have no idea, and that's the challenge of it," Andy commented. "It might actually be rare and worth something, but I won't know until I research it on the internet. There could be hidden treasures here, I just don't know."

We moved further along the wall. "Here's one I researched. What do you think this is?" He pointed to a metal object leaning against the wall. It was shaped like two big iron fish hooks, each about two feet high, with mean looking prongs on the end, facing each other. They were held together at the top by a few loops of chain.

"For hanging something up?" I questioned.

"That's close," Andy replied. "It's a log dragger. When they cut down a tree and made a log, they attached this to the end of it – these hooks go into the wood. Then they chained it to a horse or ox or something, and dragged it to wherever they were taking it."

"But that had to be a really long time ago, that anyone would do that," I said.

"Yeah, like in the 1800s. I have that one on eBay right now."

Against another wall was an enormous assortment of cans, bottles and other containers. Most of the labels were gone, so it would have been impossible to identify their contents. It looked like there were old bags of fertilizer, rotten grain, and wood chips. There was a wooden box about the size of a shoe box sitting by itself on a board with a nail sticking up out of it. The box was weathered and looked extremely fragile. I crouched down next to it and peered at the faded lettering.

"Arsenic?" I squeaked. "Isn't that really dangerous? Where does someone even get arsenic?"

"Hell if I know. I told you this was crazy. I found that under a whole bunch of other broken boxes and bits of metal."

I pulled out my cell phone and took a picture of the box. I had an urge to run my fingers over the top of the box, but realized instantly that was the last thing on earth I wanted to do. It would probably kill me or something. Why would I even consider touching it?

"Did you wear gloves when you moved it?" I asked.

"Yes, and I was really glad I had them once I saw what the wording on the box said," Andy replied.

"It just gives me chills," I said. "Isn't this what they always murdered people with, in the old movies?"

"Yeah I think so," he replied.

We spent about an hour in the barn because there was just so much to see. The lawnmower collection would have been a good representation of the history of lawn mowers. Someone must care about that. The assortment included a scythe, a push mower with a bent blade, two gas mowers, a mowing attachment for a tractor, three riding mowers and a little electric mower with a cord. One of the riding mowers looked new enough that it might even work. Unbelievable. Every last horse stall, cubby, shelf and corner was full of amazing junk, all of it filthy. The hayloft was just as full.

I felt grubby even though I had barely touched anything.

Andy was ready to go. "Let's go wash our hands – you have to see the inside of the house. It's just as amazing." That was hard to imagine, but it was great being on this adventure with Andy.

Andy guided me out the back door of the barn, and we circled around toward the house, walking through the brown grass of the yard. We walked up the stone path to the back door of the house, which opened onto an enclosed porch connected to the kitchen. We left our shoes on the porch, and then went to the kitchen sink and scrubbed our arms with soap up to our elbows. Andy tossed me a dish towel and winked at me.

"Ready to see the inside now? It has some interesting features too."

He took my hand, and at that moment, I didn't care about the house. His touch gave me goose bumps. I was thankful that he couldn't see that. I followed him down one of the two hallways leading away from the kitchen. At the base of a stairway was a closed door.

"Can you guess what's behind this door?"

"Brooms, twenty of them?" I guessed.

He laughed. "Nice. That was actually a very good guess, but no. You probably couldn't guess this." He opened the door and I peered in. It was a little room the size of a typical bathroom. The only thing in the room was a bench built into the wall, with three holes about the size of Frisbees in it. I looked at him, puzzled.

"Potato storage?"

"It's an indoor outhouse! Can you believe it?" Andy exclaimed.

"An indoor outhouse?" I repeated. I'd never heard of such a thing, but then, I'd never considered it either.

"Yeah, it was the ultimate luxury a hundred years ago. With the winters around here, it makes perfect sense, doesn't it?

"I guess it does," I offered. "But why three holes? Do you think people would use them at the same time?"

"I don't know," he replied seriously. "Maybe kids would. Or maybe they didn't care about privacy as much as we do. Or maybe everyone had their own designated holes."

I snickered.

"Have you ever made out in an outhouse?" His eyes glinted mischievously as he asked me the question.

I didn't have to think about that one. "I can't say I have. They don't tend to be my favorite places. I have to admit though, this one doesn't smell bad, and I don't see any flies."

"Yeah, it hasn't been used as an outhouse since the 1930s or something. And then they filled it up with dirt and concrete. I think it's mostly been a storage room since then."

He pulled me into the little room and closed the door. Dim light came in through a tiny window covered with a frilly white curtain. We were shut in an outhouse together. I wasn't so sure this was romantic. He gently backed me against the wall opposite the bench, and placed his hands on the wall, one on each side of my shoulders. About two inches from my face he said, "Would you like to make out in an outhouse?"

Maybe it was romantic after all. How many people would say yes to that question? He smelled fresh and clean, and he looked deep into my eyes with his liquid blue ones. Just like that I was putty. Oh, to have that power over the opposite sex. I wondered if he had any idea of his effect on me. I hoped not. I tried to stay cool.

"If we must," I teased.

"We must," he whispered, as he leaned toward me and kissed my neck.

I put both my hands in his hair, and burrowed my fingers in. My heart fluttered and I sucked in my breath, hopefully quietly, as his lips grazed my collarbone. Then he raised his head and held my gaze for a few seconds, and touched his lips lightly to mine. I moved my arms around his neck and pulled him closer, pressing my lips back against his more firmly. The kiss turned wet and delicious, and time stood still as we kissed in the indoor outhouse. As that thought ran through my head, I giggled.

He whispered in my hair, "What's so funny?"

"It's just that we're kissing in the toilet room."

He laughed, and then we were both laughing.

"You're right," he said. "We can find somewhere better to kiss."

He smiled, took my hand, and led me back out into the hallway toward the stairs.

"Hi Megan!" Andy's mom called from the kitchen.

I could feel myself turning ten shades of red. I was sure she knew I had just been kissing her son. What would she think? I was mortified.

"Hi Mrs. Garrett," I called back meekly.

Andy pulled me up the stairs, snickering. I shoved him in the shoulder. At the top of the stairs, a hallway ran along the whole length of the upper floor to a window above a staircase on the other side that led down.

"Another staircase?" I asked.

"Yeah, it has a front and a back staircase. There are five bedrooms up here, which is huge for a house this old. When it was built it was ultra modern and luxurious.

We went into the first bedroom on the right. It was a decent sized room, decorated with old fashioned vertical striped wallpaper with roses on it. There was an old iron bed with a faded pink bedspread on it, and boxes were stacked everywhere, including on the bed and dresser.

"Look at this," Andy motioned.

He disappeared into the closet, and I followed, pushing aside the clothes and edging along the wall. We came out the other side into the next bedroom over.

"This is my room," Andy told me.

"Wow, for a moment I thought we were trying to go to Narnia."

He smiled. "It totally wouldn't surprise me if this house had a secret passage or something, but nope, in this case it's just my room."

It was clean, that was the first thing I noticed with relief. There was a double bed with a puffy quilt that looked home made. Fluffy pillows, a polished wood dresser, a desk with a computer on it and an office chair. It was comfortable and peaceful. The large windows looked out over the back pasture and the woods beyond. It felt secure.

"We'll come back here in a minute, but there are two more places you have to see first."

We left through the door out to the hall instead of back through the closet. Half way down the hall Andy opened another door on the opposite side of the hall. Behind it was a narrow wooden stairway leading up. He started up the steps and I followed him. As we got to the top, Andy grabbed a string to turn on the bare bulb in the ceiling. It was a very large attic that ran the length of the roof, with old furniture stacked along the walls and a variety of other odd things stacked everywhere, just like we had seen in the barn. There was an old sewing machine, a broken lamp, shoe boxes, files, books, spools of thread, decorations, framed pictures, a baby's rocking horse, glass bottles, a bird cage, and several things I couldn't identify.

"Wow," I shook my head. "It's pretty amazing. I wonder how anyone ever found anything they were looking for in all this. I see now how this will keep you very busy."

"You should come back and help me explore up here. I bet there's some cool stuff. I haven't even begun up here. Look at this."

He walked to a nearby dresser and motioned toward a large coffee can on top. He picked it up and handed it to me. I almost dropped it because I hadn't expected the weight of it. I held it against my body, took the plastic lid off, and saw that it was completely full of old skeleton keys, some of them quite detailed in their design, and in every shape and size imaginable. Dark metal, bright metal, brass, dirty and clean.

"Wow, they're amazing. And beautiful. What do they go to?" I asked.

"Not even the first clue," he replied.

"These would have to be worth something to someone," I said. "Even if only for artistic purposes."

"I think so, but what if they go to something around here? I can't get rid of them until I go through everything and make sure I don't need them for something. I wouldn't be at all surprised if some of them go to furniture or who knows what in this place."

"Good point," I agreed. "This is an attic like you'd read about in a book – where kids find amazing adventures, and there are treasures and magic. We just need a few strategically placed shafts of sunlight and some magic dust, and we'd be set."

He turned to face me, and the blue in his eyes shone as if liquid. "You already are a ray of sunlight. We don't need anything else."

I touched his face, feeling the smooth skin and running my fingers from his cheek down to his chin. He took my hand, placed my palm over his mouth and kissed it, his eyes never leaving mine. It was as if I felt warmth moving up my arm. I never knew palms were so sensitive. Without letting go of my hand, he pulled me to him, turned me so my back was against his chest, and put his arms around me.

"It is a storybook attic," he whispered against my neck. "Will you dance with me?"

We swayed slowly to the invisible music, for just a moment. The feeling of him pressed against my back made me want to pin him against a wall. Yes indeed, this was an amazing house. It was an even more amazing guy.

I glanced at a dresser by the doorway to the stairs. It was a square piece, about chest high, in some kind of dark wood, with brass handles. For a split second, it seemed to shine in the dim light as if it were new and polished, rather than old and covered with dust. I could imagine a small box on top of it, sitting on a delicate crocheted doily. I blinked and saw that it was just a dusty dresser.

Andy's low voice broke into my thoughts. "I want to show you the basement too."

"We usually call it a cellar around here," I said. That got a smile.

"Yeah, it's like people here speak a foreign language or something. Supper? Dinner? Who knows?"

We picked our way back down the steps, and then down the hall to the staircase opposite the one we had come up. We clomped down the stairs to the main floor, and continued around the corner of the hall. There was yet another staircase that led down.

"It seems like there are staircases around every corner," I said.

"I know. It really is a big house."

Andy led me down to the bottom step and opened the old white door there. It squeaked on its hinges. We stepped onto concrete, into a room that smelled damp and musty. Again he pulled a string attached to an overhead light. The cellar was large and had support posts every six feet or so. The ceiling was very low, and I could touch it if I stood on my tiptoes. It was dark and a little scary down there. An enormous iron boiler stood in one corner. Scattered throughout the rest of the space were shelves, a clothes line, old canning jars, a hand cranked washing machine, kitchen tools, brooms, and all kinds of other stuff I didn't recognize. It was also cold.

Andy glanced at me. "We don't have to look around here; it's just more of the same. I just wanted you to see the unbelievable amount of stuff. How about we go somewhere cleaner?"

"Yes, and warmer," I said, a little relieved to leave the cellar.

"And we should do some studying, don't you think?"

My heart sank a little. I had hoped not. I'd be perfectly content to just kiss Andy for the rest of the day. Maybe not such a good idea with his mom in the house though. We climbed back up the stairs to Andy's room. We sat on his bed with our backs against the wall, and talked about Chemistry and History a little half heartedly.

"Why are we studying, again?" I was only sort of teasing.

"Ok, ok." He closed his book and set it on the bed stand, then rolled over off the bed onto his feet and padded across the room and pressed 'play' on his cd player.

"Sweet!" I said with satisfaction, as soft music filled the room.

He returned to his position beside me, and we held hands as we listened to the music.

"Believe me, the last thing I want to do is study when you're here, but I'd sure rather study with you than without you, and it's something we both need to do, so we might as well do it together. I want to get to know you, and all about you. I want to talk about our school subjects and how you feel about them, but also about your thoughts, feelings and dreams. I have big dreams," he said softly.

I turned my head toward him. "Tell me," I whispered, not knowing what to expect.

"I've always wanted to be a doctor." He looked at me, to see what my reaction would be.

"That's great!" I said. "I'm so jealous of people who know exactly what they want to do. I know I want to make a difference in the world, but I don't know how. I want to do something meaningful and special, but I have no idea what. Why a doctor? What kind of doctor?"

"I want to be a plastic surgeon."

I looked at him quizzically. Did he dream of going to Hollywood and making tons of money working on the stars?

He absently ran his fingers up my arm. "When I was in grade school, one of my best friends was in an accident, and was severely burned over 60% of his body. He was just a kid. It was a car crash, and his babysitter was driving. She was injured too, but not as bad. After that, he was scarred. He had a lot of surgeries on his face, but never looked normal again. I got used to it." He paused and took a deep breath. "He was exactly the same normal kid, but looked really different. That wasn't the way most people saw him though. Some people even treated him like he was mentally impaired." He paused and then added, "He had twenty three surgeries. He's still my friend to this day."

I moved closer and Andy put his arm around me. I lay against his chest.

He continued. "Ever since that accident, which was when we were in sixth grade, I have known I wanted to be able to help people like him. Especially the ones who couldn't afford to have twenty three surgeries. My dream is to go to third world countries and help people who can't afford medical care, but I don't know how I'll be able to do that. I'm trying to be realistic – I know it will take me years just to pay off my student loans. Long story short, I need to get good grades and try to get some scholarships."

"That's so awesome that you know exactly what you want to do. I'm proud of you for having a goal like that." I was impressed.

"What about you," Andy asked, "are you thinking about colleges? Do you know what you want to study?"

"I have so many interests. I guess that's what makes it difficult. I want to do something creative, but I also want to be able to take care of myself and make enough money to live comfortably. I'm interested in Business, Psychology, Journalism, Art and Science. I don't know how to choose among those things though. I like them all. I could see paths in any of those areas. It stresses me out when I think about it. I know I'm going to have to make some decisions soon."

"Yes and no. You know, even if you get a certain degree, it doesn't mean that sets your career for life."

"I guess that's true," I ventured. "Still, I don't want to be wishy washy about it."

"What do your parents do?" Andy asked.

"Well, we've lived in Hardwick all my life. My dad is an insurance agent. My mom is a teacher, which has been great because she could be home at the right times with me and my two younger brothers."

"How old are your brothers?"

"Fourteen and twelve," I replied. "They're good kids. They're both really into sports - the typical stuff, football, basketball, baseball and soccer. They're just the best of friends. I think you'd like them. Why don't you come over one day after school next week and have dinner with us? My mom is pretty curious about you."

"Oh no," he said in pretend shock. "You've told her about me?"

"Oh yes," I smiled. "So it's a date?"

"Cool," Andy said.

I asked, "What about your sister, what's she like?"

"She's cool. We're pretty close. She's a freshman in college at NYU studying pre-law. That's another reason my parents wanted to move out here. They thought she was awfully far from California. She's very busy with classes, so I don't talk to her much. She'll be home for the summer though, so you'll get to meet her then. You two will get along great."

"Does she look like you?"

"You mean scruffy and baggy?"

"Oh yeah right," I said. "I bet she's beautiful."

"She is pretty. We look a little bit alike. She has blue eyes and blondish hair like me." He paused. "How about you stay for dinner tonight? I promised my parents I'd watch a movie with them, one they rented, but they'd love to have you too. What do you think, too dorky?"

"No, not at all, that would be great. Let me call my mom."

I called, and she said it was fine, but also asked when she could meet the mysterious Andy.

"Soon Mom, I promise. As a matter of fact, he just agreed to come have dinner with us next week."

"Oh good. Just let me know when. Honey, don't stay too late."

"I won't Mom, thanks, bye."

"Let's go ask my mom how much time we have before dinner."

He stood and offered me his hand. I took it, and he pulled me from the bed. We tromped down the stairs to the kitchen, where Mrs. Garrett was rolling dough on the counter.

"Oh Meg, you're going to love this," Andy said. "It's her homemade pizza. Thin crust, homemade sauce, and lots of cheese."

"Mom, do you mind if Meg stays for dinner?" Andy asked.

"Of course not, that would be great! You're dad just called, and he'll be here in about fifteen minutes. He'd love to meet her too."

15 ARSENIC

There's usually nothing good about a Monday at school, but I was excited because it was another chance to see Andy. There was no sign of him in the parking lot or halls, and since I was trotting to get to class on time, it was my own fault if I missed an opportunity to see his brilliant smile. As I scooted in the door and sunk into my chair in first period Econ, my phone vibrated. I fished it from my pocket and shoved it under the desk in front of me.

The message read, "sold 4 irons"

"Cool" I texted back, and then "irons?"

"clothes irons"

"funny" I replied.

"11111" he returned.

"?" I texted.

"means I'm thinking of u"

A warm feeling ran through me. "11111 2" I replied.

First hour lasted as long as it usually takes me to shovel snow from the driveway, in other words, forever. If I hadn't been dreaming up romantic fantasies involving Andy and trying to think of clever flirty things to say to him, Mr. Stanley's tone would have lulled me into putting my head on my desk. Better kids than I were giving in to the boredom today. Finally the bell freed us from our torture.

I let out a small sigh of disappointment when I saw I had beaten Andy to Chemistry. I glanced around the room with little interest, got a slight frown from Kelsey, and then opened my book. I turned to look again, and suddenly he was there by my side, bending down next to me. I breathed in his clean smell, and fought not to touch his face. Mr. Witt probably wouldn't understand. Though his beautiful face was now very familiar, it still took my breath away when I saw him up close. It was like everyone else in the room had faded into the background.

"Why do I always beat you here?" I asked.

"My first hour is twice as far as yours," he said in the silky voice reserved only for me.

"Ok, that's true," I conceded.

"Did you save those pictures of the arsenic box?" he asked.

"Yeah. I didn't know what you meant by "irons" in your message. It could have been golf clubs, branding irons, who knows?"

"Yeah. We probably have all those somewhere, too. Actually, now that you mention it, I think I saw a branding iron with two B's facing each other – not the straight edge facing each other, but with the loops slightly overlapping each other. I don't know where that went." He thought for a moment. "It'll turn up I guess. Let's go ask Mr. Witt if we can see him about something after school, and see what he thinks about the arsenic."

I pushed my chair back and stood, "Ok, let's."

I followed Andy to the front of the room where Mr. Witt was shuffling his papers around at his podium. I noticed the other students watching us, just in case we were about to do something interesting. I think we disappointed them. Mr. Witt looked up at us as we approached, over the top of his reading glasses.

"We found something interesting," Andy said.

"Oh? What?" asked Mr. Witt.

"Well," I said, "we took pictures of it. Can we show you after school? We were wondering if you could explain it to us."

"It's a mystery thing?" asked Mr. Witt.

"Not really, it's just too much to explain right now," replied Andy.

"Sure, I'd be happy to talk to you guys after school. I'll be right here grading papers," said Mr. Witt.

"Ok, we'll be back," I told him.

Andy and I smiled at each other over our shared secret, and went to our respective desks. Kelsey had seen the whole thing, but was acting as if it didn't concern her. Maybe it didn't.

Lunch was my opportunity to catch up with my friends on the happenings of the weekend.

"Jack asked me to the Prom!" Kayla squealed.

"That's awesome!" I said enthusiastically.

Kayla continued, "And Kyle is taking Rachel, so now we just need to find Emilee a date."

"Oh no," Emilee protested quickly.

"Any ideas?" Rachel asked, looking at Emilee.

"I'm ok with not going, really," said Emilee. "Besides, there's still next year too, right? Junior/senior Prom - two opportunities, right?"

"Maybe you could just go with someone as a friend," I offered. "What about someone like Brad?"

"That might be fun I guess," said Emilee. "Is he dating anyone?"

"I don't think so. You know we're lab partners in Chemistry, and he's never said anything about any girl. Want me to suggest it?"

"I don't know," said Emilee.

"Well think about it," said Rachel. "Meg knows him really well."

"What's your dress like Rachel?" asked Kayla.

"Oh I love it," Rachel replied. "It's a light pink satin, form fitting, and it flares a little below the knee. It's strapless."

"Wow, I can't wait to see it. It will look stunning with your dark hair," said Kayla. "What about you Meg?"

"My mom and I are going shopping in a few weeks, in Boston."

"We're probably going this weekend to look for mine," said Kayla. "Remember we have to get flowers ordered, and stuff like that."

We talked about Prom all through lunch. Emilee didn't seem to mind, but I wondered whether it bummed her out.

After school, Andy met me at my locker. I wanted to jump into his arms and wrap my legs around his middle. Instead I shoved my hands in my pockets. We weaved our way down the crowded halls to Mr. Witt's room.

Our teacher looked up as we entered. "What've you got?"

I went around the corner of his desk to stand next to him, opened my phone, and retrieved the pictures of the arsenic box. I held the phone out to him.

"Arsenic? Interesting. Where did you see this?"

Andy replied, "It's in the barn of the house my family just moved into. Why would anyone have a big box of arsenic?"

"How big is it?" asked Mr. Witt. It was difficult to tell from the picture.

Andy held out his hands and spaced them about eight inches apart. "About like a shoe box," he said as he motioned.

"Wow," said Mr. Witt. "You can't buy it like that anymore. The box looks really old, would that seem right?"

"Yeah," said Andy. "Everything in the barn is really old, some of it from the 1800s. Do you think they did something bad with it? Didn't people use arsenic to murder people?"

"No, I really don't think it was for a bad purpose. Since you two are so young, you might find this hard to believe, but it used to be that you could readily buy all kinds of things we would consider very dangerous today. Nobody would have thought anything of having something like this box of arsenic on a farm. Arsenic was a very common poison, used to kill all kinds of things, just like we might use bug spray or weed killer these days."

"That makes sense," Andy said. "Our house was a working farm for decades."

Mr. Witt went on, "Yes, farmers would actually take granules of arsenic and add some water, and then pour it on insects on their crops, or an ant hill or a wasp nest. Or maybe use it to poison raccoons bothering their chickens, or wolves attacking their livestock. They didn't have all the environmental safety regulations we have these days, and would sell relatively dangerous chemicals to anyone. Part of it was, they didn't realize how harmful some of these things were back at the turn of the century, or even into the 1940s and 1950s."

"What should we do with it?" asked Andy.

"Well that's a very good question," replied Mr. Witt. "Do you know if there is actually still something in the box? First, you should just make sure it has something in it. If it is as old as it appears, it could have long since been used up."

"We didn't want to touch it," I said.

"If there is something in it, it should be disposed of by someone familiar with hazardous waste. We have someone who comes to the school a few times a year to help us with chemical disposal, so maybe we could have him come out to your house and grab that too, while he's at it."

"That's a good idea," said Andy, "and I bet there are more things like it."

"I'm sure he'd be happy to help you out," said Mr. Witt. "You should make sure nobody gets into it, and you shouldn't try to do anything with it yourself. It's not the kind of thing you should just put in the trash, it could be fairly harmful to the environment."

"We'll check it out and let you know if we need help disposing of it," said Andy. "Thank you."

We turned to leave, and I said to Andy, "Well, I guess it wasn't such a mystery. I was worried we'd hear there were only bad reasons someone would have had it."

"Me too. I'll walk you to your car."

We walked back to my locker, where I picked up my coat and books. Then we stopped at Andy's locker, where he did the same. The halls were empty now, and I enjoyed having him to myself. We pushed out through the doors into the cold, and Andy's warm hand closed around mine. His touch sent tingles up my arm and through my body. I didn't want to think of anything but him. At my car he opened my door for me. He leaned in to give me a soft kiss, but then it turned into a firm kiss that told me he was thinking of me as much as I was of him. Though it was only about forty degrees, I wasn't the least bit cold. I was in heaven. He let me go reluctantly, and turned toward his car.

"I'll be looking forward to seeing you tomorrow," he said.

"Me too," I replied, as I turned to get in my car.

"He's pretty amazing, isn't he?" I said to my car once I was inside. My car responded by chugging to life and blaring the radio at me.

Max greeted me at the door with lots of happy wiggling and licks all over my face. My dad always reminded me that Max used that same tongue to lick his butt, but how could I not allow Max to lick me? I guess it hadn't hurt me yet. I did tuck my lips into my mouth when he licked my face though. I ruffled his thick fur, and went into the kitchen.

"Hi Mom," I said.

"Hi honey, how was your day?"

"Good. People are starting to get really anxious for spring and for the school year to end. We showed Mr. Witt some pictures of a big box of arsenic we found in Andy's barn the other day."

"Arsenic? Goodness, what was that doing there?"

"We don't know, but Mr. Witt said that farmers used to use it like an all purpose poison to kill pests. It looked seriously old."

"That's a little scary Meg. I'm glad you asked somebody about it. Speaking of Andy though, I'm making your favorite meat loaf for dinner tomorrow night. Do you want to invite Andy over? We'd really like to meet the guy we've been hearing so much about."

"Do you promise not to be embarrassing?" I asked, turning toward her as I closed the refrigerator door.

"What do you mean?" she asked innocently.

"Well, like you can't say, 'oh you're the guy we've been hearing so much about' ok? Or 'I see why Megan thinks you're so cute' or anything like that."

"Yes, I get it Meg. Of course we won't try to be embarrassing, but you know your brothers."

"Yeah Mom, that's what I'm afraid of."

"Oh, they'll be fine. They'll just be goofy."

I rolled my eyes at her and went to my room and grabbed my phone. I texted Andy. "11111"

A minute later a reply came back. "11111 2"

I smiled happily to myself and sent, "can u come 2 dinner 2 morrow?"

"with ur family?" he replied.

"yes mom wants u 2 come, wants 2 meet u"

"yes"

I did a little leap onto my bed. "u can come home with me after school"

"k" he replied.

"c u 2morrow" I sent.

The next morning I stuffed my down jacket into my locker, and then dug around in the bottom until I found my Econ book. I leaned down to pick up the coffee cup I had set on the floor and closed the locker door, all in one motion. As I started to straighten, I was startled by a person standing there, where there had been nobody just a moment ago. I jumped, almost spilling my coffee. It was Jennifer, leaning against the next locker. I instantly felt stupid for having jumped, but it had been an instinctive reaction.

"Hi Megan," she said evenly.

"Hi Jennifer," I replied in the same tone.

"Are you going to the Prom with Andy?"

I hesitated, searching for a clever reply. I couldn't think of anything - too early in the morning, so I went for the simple truth. "Yes."

"Does Jeff know?" she asked, clearly hoping it would be a problem.

"I don't know and I don't care," I returned, feeling very defensive. "What difference does it make to you?" I looked her in the eyes.

She suddenly looked a little embarrassed, but said nothing. She did an abrupt turn and flounced away, her high heels clicking on the polished floor.

Emilee scooted over. "What was that all about?"

"I don't know. I think she thinks my personal life is her business. The hot news of the day is that I'm going to the

Prom with Andy. It was only a matter of time until that got out."

"Oh, I bet Kelsey just found out and is pissed at you," said Emilee.

"Maybe, but she didn't have any claim on him. He was totally not interested in her."

"Oh I know, but I don't think she ever got that part."

"That's just because he's been so nice about it," I said.

"Don't let it bother you Meg, they'll get over it, and she'll be on to her next kill."

I gave her a wry smile.

At the lunch table Andy sat next to me, while my friends settled in their usual places. He spoke in a low voice. "Why do you think Kelsey was giving me dirty looks in class this morning?"

Rachel, Emilee and Kayla pretended not to be listening.

I replied in an equally low voice. "I think she just found out that we're going to the Prom."

Andy gave me a blank look.

"She wanted you to ask her," I informed him.

"But I never gave her the slightest impression I was interested in her."

"That doesn't matter. She's never found a guy she couldn't get if she wanted him."

"Girls are so hard to understand sometimes," he said.

Rachel, Emilee and Kayla smiled at each other knowingly.

I changed the subject. "So how about you meet me in the parking lot after school, and you can follow me to my house?"

"Ok," he nodded.

Rachel asked, "Andy's coming over to your house?"

"Yeah, do you feel sorry for him? I just hope my brothers aren't too embarrassing."

Andy flashed me a 'what did I get myself into' look.

Emilee leaned across me and said to Andy, "Oh don't worry, they're not that bad. Her brothers are adorable, and they'll think you're great."

He smiled at her.

"It's kind of embarrassing," I said to my friends, "but they really want to meet him, especially since we're going to the Prom and we've been studying together."

"Yeah, might as well get it over with," said Kayla.

16 CHANGING SEASONS

July 1867- Allie

I awoke giddy with excitement and yet stricken with panic over what I would say to my parents and Jeremy. And Janie and everyone else I was acquainted with. What manner of girl falls in love with a stranger and rides off into the sunset with him after only a scarce few weeks? They would all think I had lost my mind at best. I wondered what they would think of Wayne. It's not like he was a rich old man stealing a young stupid girl. He wasn't more than a few years older than me, and just starting out. We'd make our way together.

I suddenly wondered if last night had all been a dream. I snatched the dress I had worn off the chair and thrust my hand in the pocket, withdrawing the small hard disc. I carefully examined the button in the light, running my finger over the polished brass. Sure enough, there was the eagle Wayne had described. It was beautiful and shiny. I pressed it to my lips and kissed it, then held it to my heart. I pulled on a fresh housedress and tucked the button safely in my inside pocket.

I did my chores with a newfound energy. I wondered who would perform these duties once I had departed, since that would be only a short time hence. I supposed Mother and Father had to have been planning for my leaving, since they believed I was marrying soon anyway. I studied them as we ate our dinner. They did not know anything had changed. Why would they? I felt strangely calm for the first time in days. A decision had been made. There was peace in that. Now we had only to implement it. Father and John rode to town after dinner, while Mother and I performed our afternoon duties and progressed on our sewing. It permitted me time to work on my creek block, but also to consider what I would say to all of them. Wayne was correct. The direct truth would be the best approach. I would allow him do most of the speaking. He would call tomorrow, and I would be grateful when the conversation was over.

Father and John arrived home shortly before supper. Father came rushing into the kitchen without washing up.

"What is it?" Mother asked.

"Oh it's bad," he replied with a stricken look on his face.

I turned, concerned. He glanced at me and continued.

"It's Mr. Collins. He's dead."

I could not have heard him correctly. It was impossible. He had just been kissing me a few hours ago.

"What?" Mother asked. "Dead?"

"Dead. Killed," he looked at us with a grim face.

"Mr. Collins?" I asked.

"Yes sweetie."

I sunk to the floor and laid my face in my hands. I heard a whimpering sound escape my lips as if it were coming from a wounded animal.

"Allie?" Mother called.

"I didn't realize she would take it so severely," I heard my father say.

"Allie?"

I looked up. "What happened?" I choked out.

Father eyed me with worry, and then explained. "Nobody knows for certain. Several witnesses at the pub late last night stated they saw Mr. Collins riding through town and saw two men on horses following behind him calling him by name and demanding that he give "it" to them. The witnesses didn't know what "it" was and Mr. Collins might not have either. The witnesses heard him claim he didn't know what the men were speaking of. Nobody had ever seen the two men before."

I was going to be ill. I ran to the indoor privy and vomited down the hole. Mother followed after me and pressed a damp cloth against my head.

"It is perfectly shocking isn't it? It appears it wasn't random however, so there is not a danger to people such as us. Still, there has not been a murder anywhere around here since before you were born. I suppose with the war and all, people are more prone to violence."

I didn't know what to even respond with. I nodded my head yes. She led me back out to the kitchen, where Father still stood.

Mother asked, "Did the witnesses see him get killed?"

"Oh no, they said when they saw him and the two men he was perfectly alive. They didn't pay particular attention, since the dispute was not their concern. He was found this morning beside the road, stabbed."

"Oh that's so horrible," Mother said. "And the two men?"

"Nowhere to be found and no good descriptions either – they were simply two men on horses on a dark street."

"I don't feel well," I said. I took my wet cloth and retreated upstairs to my bedroom. I crawled into my bed and sobbed for what felt like hours, and then fell asleep.

When I awoke it was evening. My head ached and my eyes felt swollen. I was thirsty. It was hot. Wayne was dead. The thought of it assaulted me like a punch in the stomach. I felt as if I would retch again, but I had no food remaining in my stomach. My perfect dream had turned into the most terrible nightmare I could imagine. And there wasn't a soul I could even confide in. Nobody had known there was anything between Wayne and me, and now it was of no consequence. As far as everyone knew, nothing had changed for me. But everything had changed for me. Nothing could ever return to the way it had been. I pressed the still damp cloth against my face and it felt good.

I crossed to my bureau and removed the little lock of hair from its secret place in the top drawer. I held it to my face as a tear escaped. I pushed my hand to my pocket where the brass button was, removed it, and pressed it to my cheek. These items were the only proof of a story that easily could have been all in my imagination. But it hadn't been. His touch was real. His face was real, his hopes and dreams, and mine along with them, were real. How could I go on?

I descended the stairs and observed that my family had eaten supper. That was comforting, because I didn't want to face them. I secured a hunk of bread and a glass of water, and retreated back up the steps and closed myself in my room. I ate the bread in slow small bites, and then I was crying again. I just couldn't contain the pain.

The next thing I knew, it was dawn and the rooster was crowing. I opened my eyes, and didn't have even a second of peace before the reality of what had happened yesterday assaulted me. I didn't know how I could possibly get up and function. For some reason I realized today would be laundry day, as if that were important. Mother would be looking for any clothes that needed washing. It gave me a purpose anyway.

I fingered the dress I had worn the night I met Wayne, only the night before last, the last time he had touched me. Maybe I should never wash it, but it was just a dress, and one of the few I owned. It would be silly not to wash it. I sniffed it carefully. It didn't retain any scent of him. It only smelled faintly musty from the humidity. It seemed a huge effort to go through the pockets to ensure my handkerchief and anything else I might have collected were removed, but I knew Mother got very annoyed when items such as that were left in the wash. I grasped my soiled handkerchief and pulled it from the pocket. As I tugged, something else fell to the floor with a loud thud.

I looked down and saw that it was a coin. A coin? I picked it up. It was heavy and seemed to be made of silver. It had the year 1861 etched on it. It looked like a half dollar, not that I had seen many. What was it doing in my pocket?

I knew the only possible explanation. Wayne had placed it in my pocket. But why? And why hadn't he confided in me about it or just presented it to me? Suddenly I knew. He was hiding it. He was protecting it. There must be something special about it, but special enough that someone killed him over it? I shuddered at the idea. It couldn't be. Could it? I felt in my heart that I had hit on the answer. This was precisely what those two men had been seeking. He hadn't given it to them because he hadn't had it. He died for nothing. It was pointless. It was only a damned coin.

I passed the next several days moving around in a fog, just trying to understand all that had transpired in the last week. It made no sense. My life had changed completely, and yet as far as anyone was aware, nothing had changed at all. I felt trapped.

As we sat sewing Mother asked, "Are you alright Allie? You seem so shaken by this death."

I didn't know what to reply. How could I describe my heart being ripped out when as far as she was aware, I had scarcely noticed the man and was promised to another? I struggled for words. "I. I just can't imagine such a thing transpiring here in our town. I feel shaken to the core. As if the goodness in the world has been stripped away. As if nothing is safe when I thought everything was safe." I looked at my mother with tears pooling in my eyes.

"I know sweetheart. But you must remember, these people were all strangers in our town who were only passing through. Not the people you have known and loved all your life. They brought big city ways and the ways of the war with them. They are not a part of how we live," she assured me.

"But Mr. Collins was a good man Mother."

"Yes, I believe that is true. Still, we cannot know what all his business dealings were. He may have had dealings with unscrupulous people. The worst in people would have emerged in everyone doing business related to the war. Many people were looking to make a profit from the misery and deaths of others. It is difficult to say what he may have seen in his short life."

She paused while I looked at her and nodded.

"And further," she continued, "he would have been consorting with all sorts of unsavory people in the line of getting supplies to the western outposts. It requires a great deal of courage to enter into that kind of business."

I said nothing, considering what she had said. Courage yes, but also a sense of adventure and a good plan. He would have made a success of it, I knew it. And now it was all gone. Him, his plans, and the life that was in me. For what? Was it that damned coin? I had a plan for that. I would hide it. I would make a map of the location that only I would understand. It would be safe and protected for him, waiting for his return that would never come. Just like me. I would spend the rest of my life waiting for his return that would never come.

I felt a tiny bit better having a purpose. I would honor Wayne's memory in the tiny little ways I could. I spent August and September doing my chores like a walking dead person, and furiously working on my quilt every chance I got. It was the only activity that gave me solace. I made a new square with an eagle on it, though I admit it scarcely appeared like a bird. At least I made the head white, with white thread. Mother complimented it even though it was not a good likeness of a bird. Besides my quilt, my life was dull and pointless. I could see the flowers outside, but I couldn't see their colors. I did my chores, sewed and slept. I overheard Mother and Father conversing about me, worried that I was in such a sad state. I felt bad that they were worried, but I couldn't help myself. I had no life in me. I did not have the energy to pretend to be content or normal.

By November, I had completed my quilt and hidden the damned coin for all eternity. The quilt was a patchwork of my life, such as it was. It covered my bed, and I studied it in the light coming in the window. I crossed to the bed, sat, and gathered the quilt into my arms, hugging it for comfort. It was no substitute for the man I loved or the innocence I had lost. But as I nuzzled my face into the block of the mountains and the eagle, I played the sweet memories in my head of the short time we had spent together. I imagined his smile, his laugh, his golden hair and those cornflower blue eyes.

Mother kept trying to discuss Jeremy and the wedding, but I hadn't been able to talk about it. I finally told her I was simply not ready to deal with it, and that we must wait until spring. She had left it unspoken of for several weeks. How was I to put aside everything I had learned and go back to the path of becoming a farmer's wife? Would it be so terrible? Could I settle for it? I felt as if I would never be happy again, so maybe it didn't matter. My whole world had vanished, and I couldn't grasp life again, search though I might. There were no colors, there were no flavors. I walked slowly down the stairs and found Mother baking in the kitchen. I hugged her and told her I loved her, and went outdoors.

I walked slowly along the stone wall around the pasture to the edge of the woods, where my swing sat still in the cool of the November afternoon. I hugged my coat around myself against the chill in the air. I remembered how Wayne had been sitting there, and how we had laughed and made our plans. I sunk onto the swing and kicked myself slowly back and forth, smiling sadly as tears trickled from my eyes.

As dusk started to settle, I made my way into the dark barn. It was peaceful and quiet because all the animals were out to pasture. I could smell things here, unlike most other places lately. The barn held comforting animal earthy smells. I settled against the wall and studied the dust playing in the last shaft of dim sunlight coming through the hayloft. I pondered the box of arsenic. It was on the dirt floor of the barn about five feet from me, against the wall and away from where the animals were kept. I crawled to the box and ran my hand lightly over the wooden cover. I felt repelled even as I touched it, because I knew it was poison. I wondered if I should just eat a handful of it to end this sadness.

17 THE PARENTS

Andy met me at my locker after school.

"Are you nervous?" I asked.

"No, I'll be fine," he replied.

I knew he would be. He was charming and easy going, and good at making conversation. We walked to our cars.

"Just follow me," I said.

"No worries ma'am," he replied.

I laughed and got in my car. I was nervous. What if they didn't like each other? Well, that was stupid. Who couldn't like Andy? But what if he didn't like them? That was probably stupid too, and really, all that mattered was that he liked me. And he seemed to.

He followed right behind me to my house, and parked on the street in front. I walked down the driveway to meet him at his car. He got out and looked up at our house. "This is a nice house Meg."

"Thanks. It's several hundred years newer than yours."

He laughed. "No complaints about that! I bet your furnace actually heats the house."

"It does," I agreed.

I led him up the walk and opened the door. Max bounded through the doorway and planted both paws on Andy's chest.

"Hello," Andy said to the dog.

Max responded with slobbery kisses, which Andy allowed. Andy ruffled Max's fur, and stepped through the doorway.

"Get down!" I said to Max. Max got down and grinned happily at us, tail wagging like crazy.

"I'm sorry," I said. "Did he get you dirty? Do you need a washcloth?"

"No. I love dogs," Andy said. "We had a great yellow lab up until a few years ago, Max. Everyone should have dogs. My parents will probably get another one soon."

I was glad he took that so well.

"Mom, we're home," I yelled.

"Come on in here," she replied.

"Give me your coat," I said to Andy. "I'll hang it right here in the closet."

He gave me his coat and slipped his shoes off. I took his hand, and led him into the kitchen.

My mom looked up from the cutting board, where she was slicing cucumbers for a salad. Her eyes landed on Andy, and she gave him a warm smile. I could see immediately she understood why I thought Andy was so hot. She looked at him almost in an amused way.

"I'm Kelly Burke, and you must be Andy," she said, holding out her hand.

"It's nice to meet you Mrs. Burke," replied Andy.

"You can call me Kelly," she replied. "We are so glad you could come."

"Thank you," said Andy.

I jumped in. "I'm going to show him around the house Mom."

"Ok honey, dinner will be ready around 5:30."

"Ok Mom."

I led Andy through the main floor, showing him the living room, dining room and my parent's office where they each had a desk and computer. It wasn't nearly as interesting as his house. Max followed us as we went, nudging Andy's hand with his nose. We stopped and looked out the window of the dining room into our large back yard. My brothers were out there throwing a football, even though it was quite cold.

"That one is Justin," I said, pointing to the shorter boy, "and that one is Nick." I pointed to the other.

"You have woods behind your house just like we do. It's cool. In California, where we were from anyway, there weren't trees everywhere like this. It was much drier."

"Yeah, the part you haven't seen yet is how the woods are full of bugs in the summer. The trees do give great shade, but that shade helps keep the ground and vegetation moist, and the bugs just love it."

"That's not so good, I guess. But the trees sure make your yard seem a lot more private, even though there are a lot of houses around here," Andy said.

"Yeah, we do like that, and except in the winter, there are a lot of bird sounds. That's nice too. Let me show you the upstairs."

Andy followed me up the stairs, where we peeked in my parents' room and the boy's rooms.

"A fish!" said Andy, as we peered through the piles of clothes and toys on the floor of Justin's room.

"Yes, that's Poppy. His name is Poppy because he is bright orange. He's a beta."

"He's very pretty. Does Justin take care of him?"

"Yes, with reminders from the rest of us of course."

"That figures," Andy said. "I never would have remembered to feed a fish at that age."

"Yeah, it takes all of us to keep him alive I'm afraid." We continued down the hall.

"So this must be your room," he said, as we reached the last door in the hall.

"Yeah, as the oldest, I got the best room. It's a little bigger than the boys' rooms, and it faces the front so I can look out the window and see who is coming or going."

We walked in and Andy stood in the center of the room, turning slowly.

"It's nice," he said. "Colorful. Maybe a little too girly for me," he said teasingly.

"It's much nicer with you in it," I said.

He walked over to my shelves and looked at the pictures of my friends. Then he picked up a few of the cds sitting by the stereo.

"Country?" he asked.

"Some of it's pretty cool," I said.

"No, don't get me wrong, I like it. I just didn't realize you did." He looked through a few more, and then looked up at the higher shelves. "Look at all these stuffed animals."

I was embarrassed. "Yeah, when I was a kid, I really loved stuffed animals. I have gotten rid of a lot of them, but these are the ones that were my very best friends. I'll probably keep them forever."

He held up a zebra. "Who's this?"

I grabbed it and said, "That's Stripey."

Andy looked at me to see whether I was joking. I looked back, expressionless, and wondered what he was thinking. He snickered. I was mortified for a moment, but then I realized it was kind of funny and smiled.

"Ok, I know Stripey isn't very original," I said. "But I was only five when I named her."

"I think it's sweet," said Andy. "Let me guess, is this Mooey?' He held up my stuffed cow.

"No, Bessie," I said in a very serious voice.

We looked at each other and tried to keep straight faces. I couldn't do it, and soon we were both grinning like idiots.

"Ok, maybe we better stop there," he said.

"You think I'm a dork, don't you?"

"No, I think the reminders of your childhood in your room are very special. I'd never get rid of them either."

He put Bessie back on the shelf and crossed the room to me. He looked into my eyes, and mine locked onto his. Time stood still. I continued to focus on his eyes as he slowly leaned in and softly placed his lips on mine. I inhaled, loving the smell of him. I closed my eyes and kissed him back. I burrowed my fingers in his hair, and pulled him closer to me.

I heard the door close downstairs, and the sounds of my parents voices as they talked to each other in the kitchen. It jolted me back to reality. I let Andy go, still in wonder that such a perfect creature wanted to kiss me as much as I wanted to kiss him. I thought of him as some kind of wild animal, who by some miracle was tame enough for me to touch when nobody else could. That was how it felt, since he had ignored Kelsey's attention and somehow focused on me. I wondered for a moment if he was going to come to his senses and discover that there really wasn't much special about me. Unlike me, everything about him was special. I pushed that thought from my mind, determined to just enjoy the moment.

"I guess I can't sit here mauling you, in case someone from my family walks in. Do you want to see last year's yearbook?" I asked.

"Sure. You can maul me later," he said, and winked at me.

Oh, but I will, I thought. I wanted to touch him with an intensity that I'd never felt. Maybe it was how drug addicts felt about drugs. I just couldn't get enough of him. We sat on my bed and I told him stories about the people on the pages.

"I can't believe how well you know them all," he said. "At my old school my class had a thousand kids in it. Even if most stayed the same from year to year, you could never know them all like you guys do. I guess that's probably good and bad, depending on how you look at it."

"I know, right? When you screw up, you don't want everyone in the entire school to know, but there's no way around it. Any bad history stays with you forever. Like with Mike Holman – in grade school once he had a diarrhea accident in his pants. He was teased about it for years.

Finally that stopped, but I guarantee you nobody has forgotten it. What a thing to be branded with, huh?"

"Yeah, that's brutal," said Andy.

"It's like we all assumed roles a long time ago, and even though some of us have grown and changed, those roles still stick with us," I said.

"What do you think your image is?" Andy asked.

"That's an interesting question. Maybe I should ask you – what does it look like my image is?"

"Well," Andy thought a moment. "You don't seem to realize that guys look at you. You seem even keeled. You don't seem to get upset about much. You seem to know who you are. You have close friends who seem like they would stick by you. And you were dating the most popular guy in school until very recently."

"Wow," I said. "I totally don't believe guys look at me. Guys look at girls like Jennifer and Kelsey."

"That's true, they do look at girls like Jennifer and Kelsey, but they look at you too. It's like, hmm. How can I say this? Like you can admire a great painting of a beautiful horse, but it's nothing compared to seeing a live horse running in a pasture."

I looked at him, considering that.

"I mean," Andy explained, "sure, every guy wants to look at Jennifer and Kelsey, but there's nothing more to them than being good to look at. You have more depth and substance. You are a whole person."

He was embarrassed. He looked at his hands. I was incredibly touched. He was too sincere for this to be only an attempt to flatter me.

"Thank you," I said quietly. "That has to be one of the nicest things anyone has ever said to me. I'm touched that you see me that way."

The blue eyes looked into mine. They were warm and liquid, and I wanted to fall into them. My mom's voice shocked me back to the present.

"Meg!" she yelled. "Dinner is ready."

"Ok Mom, coming," I called back.

I turned to Andy. "Are you ready? Are you nervous?"

"I'm fine. Let's go."

And he was fine. I was impressed. I took his hand, and we walked downstairs. I led him to the dining room and showed him where he would sit. He didn't sit though. I sat in my chair next to his, watching him, a little curious. When my dad came into the room, I understood. Andy took a step toward him.

"Hi Mr. Burke, I'm Andy," he said, and held out his hand.

"Hi Andy, I'm Scott. It's great to meet you."

Andy said, "It's great to meet you too sir."

My dad sat down, and still Andy stood. My brothers came in and slumped into their chairs, and I introduced them to Andy. My mom came in then, bringing the meatloaf. She placed it on the table, and as she sat in her chair, then Andy sat too. She smiled at him, acknowledging that he had waited for her. I smiled at him too. My dad led us in a blessing, and then my mom started to pass food around the table.

"This looks great Mrs. Burke," Andy said with enthusiasm.

"Well, I hope you like it. This meatloaf recipe is one of Megan's favorites," she said.

My dad asked, "So Andy, you came from California?"

"Yes, we moved into the old Bruce house. I guess everyone in town knows the house, right?"

"Yes, we're a very small town. That house is certainly a part of the town's history, as one of the very first built in the area. Is your family part of the Bruce family?"

"Yes," Andy replied. "My grandmother, who was married to Robert Miller, was a descendent of the family."

"Ok, well that makes sense," my dad said. "We never did see the house go up for sale or anything. What does your dad do?"

"He's a doctor. He works at Boston General, mostly teaching residents. The job opportunity came up just after we inherited the house. I think originally they were just going to sell the house, but then it seemed to make sense to come here. Dad stays at the hospital three or four days in a row, and then comes back here for a few days. They are trying to decide what to do with the house and where to live long term, but they don't want to rush the decision. We all hate having him gone for days at a time, but it's only temporary."

"That is an interesting problem," said my mom. "It certainly doesn't seem like you could commute to Boston long term, it's just too far."

"Yeah, we think so too. I think they want to consider where they want to retire, and what sort of place they want to live in once I am gone to college, since that's so soon. That's why they're taking their time about the decision. I don't think my dad is ready to retire anytime soon, so they will probably settle on some place closer to Boston. There's a lot to be done in getting the house in any sort of shape to sell. It's completely full of stuff, some junk and some not."

"Andy's selling some of the antiques and other stuff on eBay and Craig's list," I said.

"Well that sounds interesting," my mom said. "Is there a lot to sell?"

"It's pretty unbelievable Mrs. Burke," Andy said. "The place is like a rundown museum, isn't it Meg? There's just stuff everywhere. And it isn't all trash, but it's like the people who lived there since the house was built never threw anything away. I'm finding all kinds of things from the 1800s."

"It sounds fascinating," my mom said.

"It is Mom," I said. "I thought all that old stuff would be boring, but some of it is pretty amazing. It's like a mystery just to figure out what some of it is."

"What do you do for a living Mr. Burke?" asked Andy.

"I sell insurance. You know, auto, home, farm. I've been at it for thirty years. I went into business with my dad and just sort of ended up staying with it. My dad had built up a good clientele long ago, and those people have been like family to us ever since."

Andy turned to Nick. "So you'll be in high school with us next year, are you looking forward to that?"

"Yeah, I guess. I'm kinda tired of middle school."

"I don't blame you," Andy said. "It gets old. I hear you're a pretty good football player, will you keep up with it in high school?"

"Oh yeah, I really like it." Nick was visibly pleased at the attention from this older boy.

"Me too," said Justin. "I love football."

"Well, the high school will be very lucky to have both of you," said Andy. "Megan says you're great basketball and baseball players too – the Burke's will rule at sports for years, huh?"

"That's the plan," said Nick.

"Well, I'll go to every one of your games next year," said Andy.

Nick beamed.

"And mine?" asked Justin.

"I'd love to see some of yours too," said Andy. "Mrs. Burke, Megan is right, this meatloaf is fantastic. What's the secret?"

"It has those French fried onions in it," she said. "Other than that, it's pretty ordinary meatloaf."

"Well, it's excellent," Andy told her.

By the end of dinner, I could see my whole family was entranced with Andy, just as I was. I was so proud of him, and relieved that it had gone well. I had been silly to worry about it.

When dinner was over, Andy offered to help my mom clean up.

"You're definitely not *my* child," she laughed. "No, you kids go on."

Andy helped clear the table anyway, and then thanked my mom for the great dinner. She beamed at him.

He turned to me. "It was great to be here Meg. I gotta get going, I told my mom I'd be home at a reasonable time, and I still have some chores and homework to do."

"I'm so glad you came. You did just great," I said.

"Thank you, but I really liked them. It was easy."

I really liked *him.* That was what was easy. I walked him to the door, and handed him his coat.

"Bye," he said, and gave me a quick kiss on the lips.

"Bye," I said back.

Wednesday school flew by, and then I worked my shift at the deli. Andy came by to say hello, but didn't stay long because he didn't want to get me in trouble with my boss. I was touched that he wanted to see me.

Thursday morning my heart leaped with happiness when my phone vibrated. I knew it was him.

"tell u ltr, found smthng else"

"?" I texted back.

"11111, c u soon"

That had to be good enough for now. I would see him soon. I made it through Econ, but just barely. I had been at serious risk of falling asleep and sleeping all the way through Chemistry, like in one of those nightmares where you missed a test or something. Maybe the bell would've woken me. I made it to Chemistry and settled into my seat, waiting for the moment he would come in the room.

"I found something interesting," said a soft low voice in my ear. He had leaned in close to me as he walked slowly past me to his seat. I watched him all the way, feeling like a drooling puppy looking at a juicy steak.

"?" I texted.

"lunch" was the reply.

Finally lunch came. I plunked my tray down across from his, sat down, and stared at him expectantly. For a second he pretended to go about eating his pizza, then looked up and laughed.

"I found an old safe, at the back of a closet in the attic, under piles and piles of other stuff. It has an old fashioned padlock on it, like it would open with one of those skeleton keys. Do you want to come over after school and help me go through the keys to see if one fits? If we have to, we can probably saw through the metal, but I hate to do that if one of the keys works. You never know what could be in there."

"Yeah, I'd love to," I said enthusiastically. I didn't care what we were going to do, I was just happy to be invited to spend time with him.

18 PRIVATE THOUGHTS

After school I followed Andy to his house, in my car. Walking up to the door, I glanced out at the fields, and thought about how perfect it would be if there were a huge tree off beyond the stone wall, with a swing hanging from one of the branches. It was not so much that I imagined it; it was like I saw it. But then I didn't. There was just something strange about this place. I dismissed the whole thought as I turned to meet Andy coming from his car. I didn't care whether we were going to mop the floors or chop wood, I was just happy to be with him.

We shrugged out of our coats and shoes, said hello to Andy's mom, and then padded up the back stairs to Andy's room. It was such a peaceful place, quiet and cozy, with afternoon light coming in the window and casting a soft light on everything. Andy picked up his ipod and ipod dock, and then led me up the stairs to the attic. It was just as cluttered and dusty as before, but I could see some things had been moved around since the last time I had been here.

"You've been busy," I said.

He pressed the "play" button and turned to me. "Yeah, I'm waiting until it gets warmer and there's more daylight to tackle the barn. I did a lot up here last night after I saw you at the deli. Here, look at this."

He pulled me toward the back of the attic, where the safe stood just outside a closet. It looked like it was made of cast iron. It was about two feet high and maybe two feet wide. As Andy had described, there was a sturdy but old looking padlock with a keyhole in it holding the door firmly closed.

"How funny," I said. "How old fashioned."

"I know, I just keep finding surprise after surprise around here. Here's the bucket of keys," he said, dumping them on the floor in front of the safe.

We sat on the floor and stared at the pile of keys, then looked at each other and laughed.

I picked up an intricately detailed skeleton key and turned it over in my palm. "Some of these keys are really beautiful. At least someone gathered them all together. What if they were scattered throughout the house? It could be like a giant treasure hunt."

"I'm not that patient," Andy said. "I would just find a way to cut the lock off. It's really not the end of the world if we don't find the key, but it would be cool to have a working old fashioned padlock like this. I hate to destroy it, and it might be fun if we actually find the right key."

"Oh I think so too, so let's just try."

With that, we took turns trying keys in the lock, moving the ones that didn't work to a new pile.

After about thirty keys, I was looking through the pile for more likely candidates.

Andy said, "I found it!" He held up a medium sized silver skeleton key.

"You did?"

"No, not really, it was just getting quiet in here."

"I know, that's because I'm using my full concentration," I joked.

I tried my next dark grey key. It slid in and turned in the lock.

"*I* found it!" Silence. "No really!" I showed him.

"You did!" he said excitedly.

I worked the lock as he watched expectantly. I pushed him over, laughing. The lock opened, and I carefully eased it off the loop of metal holding the latch closed. I looked at Andy, thinking he should be the one to open the door.

He looked back at me, then tentatively took the handle and pulled. The door opened with little effort. Inside were a small book that was obviously very old and a manila folder containing some papers.

"I guess it's not a hidden treasure," he said.

Andy picked up the book and turned it over in his hands several times. It had a dark brown cover that seemed to be made of very thick card board, or compressed paper. There was nothing printed or written on the cover. He opened it gingerly, and we could see the pages were yellow and brittle. The faded words on the pages were hand written in tiny but neat cursive. At the top of the first page was written, "Allie Bruce."

"It's a diary," I said. "Do you know who Allie Bruce is?"

"No idea," he replied, "but she must be my relative. The last Bruce who lived here was my grandmother, the one who was married to Robert Miller of course, who just died. Her name was Elizabeth. Let's take this stuff to my room and look at it in some decent light."

He carefully closed the book and handed it to me. He picked up the folder; then led the way back down the stairs to his room. He laid the folder on his desk, and then sat in his desk chair.

"You can sit here." He patted his lap.

I gladly sat where he suggested, with a twinge of worry that he might think I was too heavy. He didn't seem to notice my weight at all. He swiveled the chair sideways and flicked on his desk reading lamp. I carefully opened the book. It was very fragile. There were not many pages with writing, so we decided to read it.

The Diary of Allison Bruce

My name is Allison Bruce. Allie to my friends and family. This is a private diary. It is June of 1867. I am seventeen years old.

June 25, 1867, Tuesday

Today I sewed on my quilt. It's a story of sorts, representing pictures of my life. I don't think anyone realizes that, for it looks very much like anyone else's sampler, with kitchen and barnyard scenes. Today I embroidered a silver water pitcher onto a burgundy background. That is a bit dull. I am promised to Jeremy Hunter. He has good prospects for the future and will take over his family farm in a few years. He will be a good provider. He is courteous and strong, and the men around town respect him. I wonder what marriage will be like. It is a little frightening.

June 27, 1867, Thursday

Father and John, my older brother, were conversing about a stranger who arrived in town. Mr. Wayne Collins. It seems he's only passing through on his way out west. He's not a farmer. He is coming to our house to possibly purchase a horse or two. The geraniums are blooming a bright red. I have added two geranium blocks to my quilt. Embroidered bright red flowers with deep green stems on yellow backgrounds. As long as I live I will not forget how the real ones appear in their pots outside our house. I love flowers. Bright red geraniums are my image of home and family.

June 28, 1867, Friday

Mr. Collins called at our house this afternoon to look at our horses. We have some of the best horses in the county. Father is very proud of them. They are beautiful animals. I was surprised to find he is only twenty two years old. From what I heard my father and brother saying, I expected someone much older. He is going to purchase two of our horses. The men were outside conversing about horses for hours. Boring. They came in to have iced tea, and Mother and I were introduced. Of course we didn't linger, we both had chores to do.

June 30, 1867, Sunday

I like Sundays because we do only the essential chores. We drove to church this morning, Father, Mother, John and

I. We sat in our usual pew. I noticed Jeremy glancing at me several times. It was so very hot in there. I was quite miserable in my long sleeved dress. Mr. Collins was there too, in the back row. I wonder how long he is staying in town. He is quite striking in appearance. He seems a bit of a rogue. I wonder if I could make a quilt square that looks like our house. I think I will try.

July 1, 1867, Monday

Hardwick will have a 4th of July party and dance. This is one of the highlights of our summer, along with the harvest festival in September. Mother and I will be baking all day, the day before. We will take a picnic of more food than can possibly be eaten. It is such fun. I am working on a flag square for my quilt. Each little star is quite time consuming to make. The square is a white background, with red strips sewn on. It is some of my best work, with tiny perfect stitches. I am making the stars blue, and each is hand stitched, on top of the stripes. It is not arranged like the flag because that would be too many stars to make, but it has all the right colors and elements. I think it very pretty.

July 3, 1867, Wednesday

Today I stitched more stars. Well, mostly I peeled and cooked potatoes. Tomorrow is the big day. I know mother will get compliments on her food. She does make the best pies in all of Hardwick.

July 4, 1867, Thursday

This diary can no longer be about mundane things. My life is about mundane things, at least as far as everyone else knows. I have been raised to do what is expected of me, and to all accounts, that is exactly what I am doing. Here in my words my true heart will speak, only for me.

July 5, 1867, Friday

Yesterday my life changed forever. Did anyone notice? I didn't know such feelings were possible. It started ordinary enough. All the families arrived on the common and spread their blankets under the canopies of the trees. Children played games all day. The women gathered to converse about babies and food, and the men gathered and talked about livestock and hunting. Normal and ordinary. My school mates and I updated each other on our lives. Janie Wallace is married already. Everyone ate and ate and ate. A parade marched around the common. Two times, because it was so small. The children had a sack race. After supper a band set up in preparation for the dance. Some of the littlest children slept on their family blankets, and a few were taken home to bed, but most of the town stayed for the festivities. As the music started, people began to dance. I danced with Jeremy, with Father, and with Stanley Irwin. Then Wayne Collins asked me to dance. There was nothing improper about that of course, so I accepted. He took me into his arms for a waltz. It was as if I were struck by lightning. As if an electric shock ran through me. I looked into his eyes, and everyone around us disappeared. I stumbled, and he caught me. It was as if in looking at him, I was looking at life. I felt like I was awakening from a dream. I can't explain it. I knew in an instant he was meant for me. But how could that be? His eyes never left mine and they mesmerized me. There was a true depth in them and I felt I could see into his soul. I have never considered such things. It is as if I have been awakened from a long sleep. As if a path were shifting underneath my very feet. I thought everyone around me must have heard my heart beating. To my utter amazement, I could see he felt it too. He was as drawn to me as I to him. To most people, this never happens. I don't know what it means.

July 6, 1867, Saturday

Today I am making a quilt block with two mountains on it, and a sun over them both. It looks like scenery, but the mountains form an upside down W. Wayne, the name sounds magical on my lips.

July 7, 1867, Sunday

Wayne attended church this morning again. It took all my willpower not to stare at him and cause a scene. I am afraid. Now that I know there is more, there is different, I am not sure I can accept the life set in front of me.

July 8, 1867, Monday

He came over to call on Father about his horses today. When he arrived, Mother was behind the house in the garden, and Father and John were out in the fields. We were alone. He rode up on his horse, with the sunlight behind him and glinting off his straw colored wavy hair. His blue eyes shone only for me as he stopped and dismounted. He came to me as I waited on the porch. He took my hand, and it sent a shiver through me. "There's something here," he said. I replied that I knew that to be true. He told me he had fought in the war, had seen great and terrible things, and was going west to start a transportation business, bringing supplies out to the settlements. It would be a difficult life, but also one filled with adventure. I looked guiltily at his hand. I should not have been holding it, but I couldn't let it go. His fingers were long and rounded on the ends, warm and gentle. I looked in his eyes and saw my future, impossible though that could be. I told him I am promised to someone. He said he must see me again. It is so very wrong to want to see him, but with all my heart I must do it. I am tormented. I know I am on a precipice that will decide the course of my life. I cannot turn the wrong way. A thing learned cannot be unlearned.

July 9, 1867, Tuesday

I took a terrible risk tonight. I told Mother I was going to visit Janie to share her exciting news of her pregnancy. It is not a long walk to town, and I have been allowed to go by myself since I was sixteen. Almost a year now. I did go see Janie, but I only stayed a half hour. I met Wayne just outside town. He helped me up on his horse behind him, and we rode into the woods. We stopped by a creek and walked a little, and we sat on a log. We did not speak many words, but we held hands. He reached up to brush my hair to the side, and I thought that with that touch I could die happy. The sun was setting, the creek was gurgling, the birds were singing. It was as if all of nature and the two of us were meant to be. As if none of the rest of the world existed. He spoke of his future with an excitement in his voice. It sounded like a grand adventure. He turned to me, touched my cheek with his fingertips, then ran his fingertips down my throat. I looked in his eyes and saw a fire there, a passion there. He slowly moved toward me and his soft lips touched mine. I could not stop him. I didn't want to stop him. All I wanted was for the moment to go on forever. Time stood still as passion washed over me. All too quickly, he took me back to the road so I could walk home. Before I reluctantly let him go, he took out his knife and cut off a lock of his hair for me. I tucked it in my pocket. What will I do? How can I go on living as if my life were normal? It is not normal. How can I be satisfied to marry Jeremy and be a farmer's wife? How could I do anything else without scandalizing my family?

July 11, 1867, Thursday

My mountains quilt block is complete and sewn in next to my flag. The two do go together. They both belong to Wayne. Wayne Wayne. I love the sound of it. I love the way it looks in writing. I don't know what to do. My life is already set out in front of me. I never thought of it as settling, it is no different than what all girls my age do. But I see it now, it is settling. It is boring, it is mundane, and I could never feel a passion for Jeremy. I didn't know there were such feelings, but now that I do, how can I live without them? Mother wants to start planning the wedding. My stomach aches when I consider it. I am making a block that is a creek with a bird. The sound of the creek and the birds is forever etched in my mind. I am using tiny perfect stitches.

July 13, 1867, Saturday

He is departing soon. He has his horses, and has gathered his provisions. He has made his business contacts and knows where he is setting off for. I had to see him again. I am a sinner, but I snuck out of the house in the middle of the night to see him. Mother would disown me. He was waiting for me out beyond the stone wall. As I ran to him, he gathered me in his arms with an urgency and panic. He held me close, and I knew I was in the only place in the world where I belong. I asked him what we will do. He told me I must come with him. I said my family would never understand. He said I could not live my life for the will of others. His kiss brought feelings through the center of my body that I hadn't imagined were possible. Like I would die unless he kissed me more. I agreed to go with him. To marry him. He gave me a button from his uniform coat to keep until he can get me a proper ring. It has an eagle on it. I can barely admit it even here, in my private diary. I did. I know it is the only right thing, and I know nothing else matters. They won't understand. We are telling them in two days. I have until then to decide what to say. I am almost eighteen. Old enough to make a decision like this. Many of my friends are married already. I cannot live the passionless life that has been set out for me. I must determine a way to tell them, though it may break Mothers heart.

September 19, 1867, Thursday

Everything is dying as winter approaches. He's dead. Everything inside me is dead. All the colors are gone. Though it is only September, I cannot see the colors of the flowers. Maybe they are already dead. How can I pretend to go on, when my whole world has been turned upside down and drained of life? I know now what he died for, but I don't know why. How could this thing have been worth his life? And my life. I found it in my pocket today. He must have slipped it in there the last time I saw him. Why would he do it? Did he know they were looking for him? It means nothing to me. All I want is him, and that will never be. I will hide it. I will make a map. I will never speak of it again. I don't understand. The only reason it matters is because it mattered to him, and to honor him, I will make sure it is safe, forever. It and my eternal love will be hidden and never spoken of again.

November 20, 1867, Wednesday

The gospel teaches us there is always some good in everything. How could there be any good in this? Some chances only come once in a lifetime. Mine was here and gone, I know that now. I will settle for the mundane things, I have no choice. I have nothing left to write about. Goodbye diary.

A tear rolled down my cheek, and I brushed it away, embarrassed.

"It's just so sad," I sniffed. "To feel so trapped and hopeless, with no options."

"Yeah, I wonder who she was," Andy said softly.

The red geraniums – she had described them just as I had imagined them. What could that mean?

Andy opened the file folder. On top was a hand written letter in blue ink on yellow legal paper. It was old, but not old like the diary.

From Gilbert Bruce, to my heirs. June, 1945.

There has been a mystery that I spent a great deal of time trying to solve during my life time. My life is not over at

75 years by any means, but I have come to accept that the mystery will never be solved. Still, I'd like to explain it so my work and our family story will not be lost to the world when I am gone.

A family diary has been passed down. That of Allison Bruce, my aunt, known to me as Allie Hunter. Her brother John Bruce, was of course my father. Allison died in 1923, and in her personal items was her diary. To the best of my knowledge, no one had ever seen it until she died.

In the diary she spoke of a man who had passed through town, just after the civil war. In researching the man and the town at the time, I found that the town might not have paid any attention at all, except that he was murdered, which is very significant in a town this size. The murder has always been an unsolved mystery in the history of Hardwick. There is no record that the sheriff or any of the newspapers of the time had any idea why he was killed. News accounts from the time only say people were quite worried about it at the time, since a murderer was on the loose, but then there was nothing new about the story after a few weeks, and it was never mentioned again in any documents I could find.

Aunt Allie's diary said he was killed because of an object. I wondered if we could figure out what the object was, and perhaps solve the mystery. Allie referred to a map she had made which would reveal the object's location, but in all the years I have searched this house and through her personal items, I never found a map.

I also researched Wayne Collins. From what little I could find, he was born in upstate New York, and went to fight in the civil war around the time he was seventeen. He was an officer of some sort for the Union, but seemed to have some dealings with the leaders of the confederacy also. I was not able to determine whether he defected to the south, or was a spy of some sort, or whether there was some other explanation for why he was associated with the south. It is clear that he was involved in the business of supply to the troops and various garrisons.

I have never been able to determine what the object is that Allie refers to. My best guess is some sort of artifact from the war. I have spent many years searching this house, the barn and the grounds for the object. I have become convinced that if it could have been found, I would have found it. I have moved every board and searched every corner of the entire house. I have traversed the wall and removed all loose stones, and even looked in the outhouses, indoor and out. I also looked in the church and in the cemetery. In short, there is no stone I have left unturned. I fear the object, whatever it might be, is lost forever. Unfortunately, the knowledge of its whereabouts was lost with Allie.

"Unbelievable," Andy murmured.

"So she did marry Jeremy after all," I said.

We pondered in silence. Andy thumbed through the other papers. There were a few old clippings, but nothing remarkable. The last few papers in the folder were old copies of deeds and legal papers related to the house and surrounding property.

I wrapped my arms around Andy's neck, since I was still sitting on his lap, and glanced around the room, lost in thought. Andy said nothing, and I knew he was thinking about Allie too. My eyes landed on Andy's clock. "Oh no," I exclaimed. "I have to go. I promised my mom I would be home for dinner. What are you going to do with this stuff?"

"I don't know. Why don't you give it some thought and help me decide? What if we could figure it out?"

"After all this time, and after someone already tried? Maybe," I said doubtfully. "Maybe we should do some looking ourselves, with fresh eyes."

"That might be fun. Come on. I'll walk you to your car," said Andy.

We walked down the stairs and out to my car. Andy kissed me quickly, and then opened my door for me. I could get used to this.

"Thanks," I said.

"No problem. I'll see you in school tomorrow."

As I drove away, I missed Andy already. I thought about Allie the whole way home. Her story was so incredibly sad. A hundred and some years ago, it would have felt so hopeless. Women had so few options. Not that it wouldn't feel horrible today, but I wouldn't have felt so trapped. At least I wouldn't have married the wrong guy.

That night I dreamed of mysterious men and horses.

19 THE BIG CITY

Saturday I had a hot date. Well ok, it was with my mom. She's one of my best friends, though I don't know if I could admit that to my high school friends. Mom and I were planning to drive to Boston to spend the day shopping for my Prom dress, and there was nobody I'd rather share the experience with. Since I was a little girl, we had made shopping trips special times for just the two of us. I felt like a princess who had been asked to the ball by the handsome prince, and my mom was almost as excited as I was.

My mom packed a bag of snacks and drinks and set it in the back seat of the car. We ate a quick breakfast and headed out. We spent the next two hours yakking about everything. Life, love and the pursuit of happiness, as she would say.

"Do you miss Jeff at all?" she asked.

"I really don't Mom, I don't know why. I guess I feel like I should. I'm kind of embarrassed that I don't."

"Oh I don't know, I think you worked up to letting him go for a very long time, and I think you were ready. You just didn't know it."

"That's probably true," I replied. "It's like, now that I know Andy, my relationship with Jeff seems like it was a grade school game or something, like I didn't know what a mature relationship was about, I just thought I did. It also seems like it was a long long time ago."

"You can never tell someone their relationship is wrong, they just have to figure it out on their own. You know you never would have listened if I had tried to tell you that, right?"

"Yeah, you're right. It's funny how that works."

"What's so different about Andy? I mean, why is *he* different?" she asked.

"I can tell you, but it sounds corny."

"Just try me," she said.

"Ok. Well, he's good. Noble. He has good intentions toward people and the planet. I mean, just the fact that he even thinks about those things is different. What seventeen year old boys think about those things?"

"Like what things?"

"Like people starving and women being mistreated in other countries."

"That *is* unusual for a teenage boy," she agreed.

"And he's truly a good person. He wants to make a difference in the world. He wants to be a doctor. Not to make a lot of money, but to help people who can't afford medical care in third world countries. I just can't imagine Jeff or any other guy I know thinking like that."

"Sounds like he has goals then."

"Yes goals, and plans. He's been working toward these same goals for years. It's not just a whim or something he said to sound important. He's totally sincere about it. He talks with his parents like it's a given. I admire and respect him. I can't imagine saying that about any other guy my age."

"So it's more than just good looks, huh?" She giggled.

"It is," I replied. "Of course I noticed his looks. Who wouldn't? Every girl in school did. But he didn't immediately fall into the popular crowd or eat up the attention. It's like he doesn't realize the impact he has on people. He's almost shy."

"I'm glad you're seeing beyond looks and status. I mean, Jeff is very attractive and charming and all, but he doesn't have much depth. In other words, he's a normal teenage boy. I never would have said that to you when you were dating him, but I'm glad you're seeing glimpses of the difference between a man and a boy. I mean, how it takes a lot more than just looks."

"It's funny you say that Mom, because my friends and I criticize the boys for the same reasons. "Like they look at Jennifer and Kelsey, and they're all ga ga because those girls are so gorgeous, but my friends and I know they're pretty brainless. We've just been waiting all these years for the time when the guys would realize that and look for something more. I guess we girls can be just as bad at being superficial."

"Well, that's all part of growing up. You just wait and see - when you go to your ten year reunion, you'll be shocked at what some of the 'ugly ducklings' have turned into. You'll see they were the real catches, but people judged them by how they looked in high school. And the same with the popular kids - in ten years you'll see a lot of them have been tripped up by the realities of life, when they ran into situations where they couldn't cruise by on their good looks and charm. The real world can be pretty shocking to them."

"I never thought about it that way. I guess I just assumed people like Jeff and Kelsey would always have it easy."

"I don't mean to discount looks and charm. They are very lucky to have them. But often when you can get by so easy, you don't learn how to work hard for anything, and you get passed up by people who did."

I thought about that for a moment. "I wonder if that's part of Andy's deal. He's never thought of himself as good looking, even though girls stop and stare at him. He just doesn't seem to get that. Maybe his mom is part of that – she's very new age. They fit right into that California stereo type. It's that he cares about real issues and substance, not just the popularity contest."

"You know what Meg? Some guys, and girls too – to be fair, never get there. They never get past the popularity contest. Life is very tough for them when the good looks fade."

"Maybe Andy just bloomed early. He almost seems like a thirty year old in a seventeen year old body sometimes. He makes me think about issues I had never considered before. I mean about the world and stuff.'

"I think that's wonderful Meg."

"And you know what? I think part of why I think he's so gorgeous is that there is wisdom behind his eyes. I see a depth in there and goodness in his face. Is that too corny mushy?"

She glanced at me and smiled. "No, I understand what you're saying. It's definitely ok to feel that way about someone. I think one of the most important things in a relationship is to have respect for who the other person is. There's so much more than just physical attraction. Once the newness of that wears off, you have to like who the person is. It's great for me to be able to have this kind of conversation with you Meg. I'm very proud of the person you've become."

"Thanks Mom." We drove in silence for a few minutes. "You know, I really like him. I know it hasn't been very long, but I think I might love him. I feel so much more for him than I ever felt for Jeff. Like he represents what is good in the world. I know he can't be perfect, but he seems like an angel to me."

"You do seem smitten my daughter," she laughed.

"Yes 'smitten' is a good word for it," I returned. "That I am."

We drove in silence for a while. I thought of Allie's diary.

"Andy and I found something really cool at his house."

"What's that?"

"Well, you know he's been going through all the stuff in the house, right? I mean you wouldn't believe the amount of stuff packed in every corner over there."

"Yes, right."

"Well, he found this old safe, and it had a lock on it. An old fashioned lock with a key hole in the center. We found this big bucket of old skeleton keys, and one opened the lock."

"Wow, that's pretty amazing."

"Yeah, but the amazing part was what was in the safe. It was this old diary, written by one of his relatives in 1867. It was this little cardboard bound book, with very fragile pages."

"You mean it was authentic? Wow, that must be very important to their family."

"It probably will be. I don't know if he has even told his mom about it yet. Probably so. But it was this way sad story. This girl who wrote the diary was seventeen or eighteen years old, and she was engaged to a local farm boy."

"She wrote that in the diary? What's sad about that?"

"Well, it didn't start sad, but then she meets this mysterious stranger."

"Are you sure it wasn't a book someone was writing? It sounds like a romance novel."

"Yeah Mom, it was definitely a diary. Anyway, she falls madly deeply in love with this stranger, and she was actually going to run away with him, which would have caused a scandal for her family."

"Wow that *is* interesting."

"Yes, and she had decided to do it, and then there was nothing written for a few months. It turns out he died before they could run away. He was murdered."

"Murdered?"

"Yeah, and of course she was very upset, but she couldn't tell anyone, because she was still engaged to this farmer, and nobody knew she had fallen in love with this mystery man."

"All that was in the diary?"

"Yeah, and it was like she lost all hope after that. She finished the story in just a few sentences, and that was it. She just wrote that she had nothing else to write about. Her one and only chance at life had come and gone, or something like that. It was really pretty short."

"That *is* sad.'

"It was. It made me cry to read her words. And then, we found some papers written by someone who was her nephew or something, and he had found the diary and was researching her in the 1940s. The diary said the mysterious man left something with her, but it didn't say what. The nephew thought it was some kind of artifact from the civil war, and was looking for it, but never found it. It also sounded like she did end up marrying the farmer, but the nephew didn't say anything else about her or them. He had mainly been focused on the possibility that a civil war treasure might be hidden on the property. Maybe we could figure that out."

"It would be interesting to know more about her. I wonder if you could even work it into a school project somehow."

"Oh yeah great Mom," I said with mock sarcasm.

"Well, it would be an interesting History or English paper, since it would be a true story."

"Yeah, I guess. Andy should get first dibs on it though."

She smiled. "Yeah, I suppose that's fair. Is that all there was in the safe?"

"There were also some papers about the house – tax stuff and copies of legal papers."

"Is Andy having luck selling things on eBay?" she asked.

"Yeah, here and there. Mostly on Craig's list. It's a lot of work cleaning this old stuff up, figuring out what it even is some of the time, and then taking pictures and posting them.

He gets to keep the money for college, so that's what he'll be working on all summer. There's that much stuff, decades worth of stuff. And his parents will pay him to help clean up the place – you know, painting, weeding, mowing, fixing stuff. It'll be just like a full time job."

"Sounds like he'll be busy. Do you have your summer plans worked out with the deli yet?"

"Yeah, it's no problem. They definitely want me to work full time."

"That's good honey. What are you thinking about college these days?"

"That I'm going," I replied.

"Well of course you're going," she said, "but it's time to start narrowing the decision about *where* you're going."

"I know, I know. I'm thinking about it, I really am. I don't think I want to go far away."

"Well, there are some great choices that aren't that far, like Boston College, U Mass, Boston University, and even Worcester State. Any of those would be great."

"I know Mom."

The time flew by as we caught up with each other like old friends. I realized we hadn't spent time together like this in a long time, and I missed it. With a twinge of sadness, I realized that my chances to spend time like this would soon be coming to an end, as I went off to college and started my own separate life. I knew she was feeling that too. We both wanted to hold on to those familiar ties a little bit longer.

We found a parking spot at the mall and went in. There were so many stores selling evening gowns that we didn't know where to start. We defaulted to normal shopping protocol and started to circle the mall clockwise, hitting each store as we went. After spending an hour in the first two stores, where I tried on seven dresses, we stopped for gyros at the food court.

"I kind of liked the red satin one," my mom said. "It was pretty dramatic though."

"Me too, but I didn't love it."

"Well, we'll keep it in mind," she said.

We watched the people walking by, and it was obvious we were in the city, because people were dressed so much more formally than we were used to. It was fascinating to see the business women in their high heels and suits, and sometimes in fashionable boots. The only boots we were used to seeing were snow boots. They walked with a purpose and looked like they were on their way to something important. Maybe someday that would be me.

At the first store after lunch, we scored. I saw a dress I liked immediately, but still tried on eight others for the fun of it, and to make sure. I tried on "the" dress last, hoping against hope that it would look as good on me as it did on the hanger. It was a form fitting stretchy black fabric, with tiny gold sparkles woven in. It was sleeveless, with a halter cut top, and floor length. The shoulder straps were about an inch wide, and right below the neck line on each side, attached to each strap, was a little gold half moon. It was simple but elegant, and fit me perfectly. It reminded me of my moonlit boat ride with Andy. I swear I saw a tear in my mom's eye.

"You've turned into a woman on me sweetie," she said a little sadly.

"This is the one Mom."

"I think so too, it's perfect. Only you don't have any shoes to go with it, so we better find some." She winked. Cool.

We settled on a pair of high heeled black strappy sandals, impossible to walk in of course. Perfect. Last, we found some dangly crystal earrings. I felt totally spoiled, and grateful my mom was willing to pay for it all.

"Can we shop for anything for you Mom?"

"No honey, this day is all about you. It's been really fun just being with you. I know how special this Prom is, and I wanted to share in it. Do you have any idea how much I love you, and how proud I am of the young lady you've become?"

"Thanks Mom. Yeah I think I know you like me. I love you too."

We drove home feeling tired but happy.

"got my dress" I texted Andy.

"cool, want 2 c" he returned.

"no way :)" I typed back. "surprise"

"can't wait 2 c u" he replied.

"me 2" I finished.

20 PROM

Prom Saturday finally arrived. Rachel, Kayla and I met at noon to do each other's nails.

"What's Kyle wearing?" I asked Rachel.

"A black suit with a black shirt and a silver tie. That's what he told me anyway. That will look good with my dark blue dress. Where are you guys going to dinner?" Rachel asked.

Kayla replied, "We're actually leaving at 4:30 and going to Worcester, to a seafood place."

"And we're going to Worcester to a steak place," Rachel added.

"What about you and Andy?" Kayla asked me.

"I don't know, he won't tell me."

"Ooh that's romantic," said Rachel.

"I know," I giggled. "I can't wait to see him dressed up. I think he rented a tux. He wouldn't tell me that either."

"I think Jack rented a tux too," said Kayla. "They're all going to look so good. Well, so are we though. You wanted this darker shade of red on your nails, right?"

"Yes, my dress is black, so I think red is good," I replied. "I love your dress too Kay, the peach color goes so well with your skin. Jack won't know what hit him - he'll be drooling over you."

"Oh yeah I'm sure," Kayla replied. "But that would be nice," she added. You know the rest of us get jealous about how Andy drools over you on a daily basis."

"I can't wait to see everyone dressed up," added Rachel. "Your nails look perfect," she told Kayla.

"Drools over me?" I asked. "I'm the one drooling over him. Do you really see it that way?" I was intrigued.

"Well duh," said Rachel. Kayla laughed.

The thought of Andy drooling over me made me feel giddy. Also embarrassed. I said seriously, "Well, Kyle definitely seems pretty into you too Rachel."

"Yeah, I think so," she said. "You know though, you never want to assume too much."

We worked ourselves into a state of excitement talking about our dates and how everyone looked, and when our nails were dry I went home to continue getting ready. That wasn't the end of girl time though. We kept each other well informed of our progress and about our anticipation of the big night via text message. My mom helped me do my eye makeup with glitter on my eyelids. Then we curled my hair and piled it loosely on top of my head, which made the crystal earrings really stand out. The end result was pretty good, if I do say so myself. I looked in the mirror and saw what looked like a twenty year old woman, not an awkward seventeen year old. I looked a little pretty, and desperately hoped Andy would think so too. I paced around the house nervously while my mom stalked me like a Hollywood paparazzi taking pictures.

"Look," I said, "let me just pose a few times, and then stop, ok?"

"But you look so beautiful honey," she said apologetically.

"Ok, I'm going to stand by the fireplace, and then in the back yard by the tree, but then we're done." I said firmly.

She nodded with resignation, then added, "And some of you and Andy when he gets here."

"Yes, right," I conceded.

It was a beautiful spring evening, just barely warm enough that I didn't shiver outside in my sleeveless gown. It was almost six o'clock as we came back into the house after pictures by the spruce tree, and I knew Andy would arrive at any moment. My stomach was all in knots. Get a grip, I told myself for the twentieth time. I realized that I couldn't be at the door looking like I was waiting anxiously, so I went upstairs to wait anxiously in private. As I reached the end of the hall, I heard the doorbell ring. I froze. I heard my parent's voices as they let him in and told him he looked nice. And then my mom yelled up the stairs, "Andy's here sweetie."

I took a deep breath. Then it occurred to me I needed to let it out. I breathed out, and started carefully down the stairs in my too high heels, gathering the bottom of my dress so that I wouldn't trip on it. He stood in the entryway looking like a movie star, in a black tuxedo with a white shirt and a black bow tie. He took my breath away. I could tell my mom thought he looked amazing too, as she chatted casually with him. His shaggy hair was somehow perfect and his blue eyes shone with appreciation as he turned to look at me. That was all I wanted for this day, and as if I had earned an A on a test, relief flooded through me. I was no longer nervous, only excited.

"Megan you look stunning," he said. My mom beamed. Andy stared at me for a moment, and then opened the box he was carrying, which I had hardly noticed. It was a beautiful wrist corsage, with baby's breath and tiny red roses. He slipped it over my hand. I held his hand, moved both our hands to my face, and inhaled deeply. The scent was heavenly. I moved our hands to his face, and he smelled the flowers too, and smiled.

It was then that I noticed the pin in his lapel. It was a half moon, the same as the two on the straps of my dress. "Where did that come from?" I asked in surprise. "I didn't tell you what I was wearing."

"I know," he replied. "Your mom gave it to me."

"It's perfect!" I exclaimed. I turned to her, "Thank you."

She smiled. "You're welcome honey."

"Ok guys, it's time for pictures," my dad announced as he came into the hall.

It started out ok. One or two would have been bearable, but they insisted on fifteen, in various poses in the house and in the back yard. I was mortified. Andy followed me dutifully around and flashed his beautiful white teeth in an amazing smile each time it was requested. Finally we were allowed to leave. My parents stood at the door and watched as Andy helped me into the car. I waved to them as we were leaving. I knew Andy had dinner plans, but he had refused to tell me what they were.

"Where are we going?" I asked. "Did you make reservations somewhere?"

"Somewhere very exclusive," he said. "You really look amazing Megs."

"Thank you," I said, feeling a little shy all of a sudden.

We crossed town, and in a few moments we were pulling up the tree lined driveway of Andy's house. He parked.

"Do you need to pick up something here?" I asked.

"No, this is where we're having dinner."

"Really? Is your mom cooking for us?"

"Yes really, and no, I'm cooking for us."

"You are?"

"I am. I sent my parents away. They went to dinner and a movie in Worcester. We're alone."

He came around to my side of the car, opened the door for me and helped me out. Then he led me into the house and into the kitchen. The first order of business was a delicious long kiss.

"Ok, I've got to do a few things now," he said as he gently pulled away. "You sit here." He motioned to the stool at the kitchen island where I had sat the day he was baking the apple pie. I perched there and admired him. He removed his jacket and laid it carefully on a chair. I noticed how nicely his slacks fit his slim hips and long legs. He went to the table and lit the candles he had placed there. The table was set with a red tablecloth, expensive looking china and beautifully polished silverware. He returned to me, kissed me softly, and then lit a thick white vanilla scented candle that was sitting in front of me on the island.

I was enjoying watching his every move. Next, Andy went to the stereo and pressed play, and Nat King Cole started to sing. He reached for a bottle of red wine that was sitting on the counter, pulled the cork out with a corkscrew, opened it, and poured a little in two sparkling wine glasses. He handed me one, held his to mine, and said, "to us" as he clinked his glass lightly against mine and looked deep into my eyes. We sipped, and the warmth and flavor ran through me. The candlelight made the wine a beautiful deep red color and the flames reflected in the glasses. It felt like a scene from a movie.

"Do you parents know we're drinking wine?" I asked.

"Not exactly," he said, and smiled guiltily at me. "Are you going to tell them?"

I smiled. "Maybe not."

"We're only having a little," he explained. "They would not want me offering any kind of alcohol to you, but they do allow me to drink a little wine with them with dinner sometimes. In any case, I thought the occasion warranted it."

I smiled and took a sip. It was good. Even if it hadn't been, it was very romantic. I couldn't wait to tell my friends. They would be as impressed as I was.

Andy put a little plate in front of me and poured olive oil and balsamic vinegar onto it. Then he put a basket of fresh bread next to the mixture. He tore off a small piece of bread, dipped it in the mixture, and placed it lightly in my mouth, tracing my lips with his finger as he left the bread there. It was delicious, but the most delicious part was his touch. I shivered.

"Are you cold?" he asked.

"No, no, not at all," I said. He was beautiful. All I wanted was to smother him with kisses, to be wrapped in his arms and to touch his incredible body.

"Let me make sure you're very warm," he said quietly, and moved even closer.

He stood looking down at me with smoldering blue eyes. He leaned slowly down, a sexy smile on his face, and kissed me. Softly at first, and then more intensely. I could never get enough of this. I ran my fingers through his hair, and savored the warmth of his lips on mine. He smiled as he pulled away.

"No," I said in protest.

"Don't worry, there's more where that came from," he assured me.

He turned to the refrigerator and took out a spinach, bacon and raspberry salad he had made and took it to the table. Then he turned on the oven to broil steaks and asparagus. He set a pan on the stove and added sliced mushrooms and butter to sauté. Soon the kitchen smelled wonderful.

"I can't believe you're cooking like this," I said. "I sure couldn't have done it."

"I wanted to cook for you. It was the most special dinner I could think of Meg. And I wanted us to be alone."

"Thank you. This is incredibly special."

"So are you. Come," he said. He took my hand and led me to the table, where he pulled out my chair and got me settled. Then he brought our plates, with perfectly broiled steaks, asparagus and the mushrooms. He sat down with me and made another toast.

"To the most beautiful girl going to the Prom."

I felt myself blushing. "Ah," I said, "and to the handsomest guy."

We clinked our glasses lightly and sipped. I cut into my steak and took my first bite as he watched. I was honestly impressed. "I'm serious Andy, this is the best steak I've ever had. How did you learn to do this?"

"Oh, my dad taught me. It's one of his specialties. My mom loves his steaks, so I was hoping you would too."

"I absolutely do," I said with great enthusiasm.

"Good, I'm so glad," he said.

"I was thinking about Allie's diary," I said, as I cut my next bite. "Isn't it weird that she lived right here in this house over a hundred years ago?"

"I know. It's interesting to think about. So much has changed in that time, but it's still the same house. It was a sad story, wasn't it?"

"It was. It makes me want to help her or something. I mean the person she was at the time anyway."

"I know what you mean. I think the mystery of whatever she had is interesting too. Do you think it was something from the war?"

I took another bite of steak and thought for a moment as I chewed. "I guess I don't know why not. It seems as good a guess as any. It was just so long ago. I wonder if you'll run across any other really interesting things as you go through the house."

"It wouldn't surprise me," he replied.

I finished every last bite of my dinner. It was too good not to. I hoped Andy took it as a compliment, rather than thinking I was a pig. We took our dishes to the kitchen. I excused myself to go to the bathroom to make sure there was no food in my teeth. In the bathroom, I glanced in the mirror and didn't recognize myself for a second. My cheeks were flushed, my hair and makeup were still perfectly in place, and I looked truly happy. I smiled at myself, and then realized all I wanted to do was get back to that beautiful creature waiting for me.

It was dark in the house except for the candlelight. For just a moment I imagined a fire in the fireplace and I could have sworn I smelled fresh wood burning, but then it was gone. I walked past the living room toward the dining room. Andy waited for me there, and swept me into his arms as I came through the doorway. We danced slowly to the soft music. He held me close against him and buried his face in my hair. I felt with absolute certainty that I wanted him to be mine and nobody else's, forever. He was everything I could want. The truth was, he was everything any girl could want. He looked like a male model dressed in his tux with his blue eyes shining and his silky hair glinting in the candle light. He smelled heavenly – clean and fresh, and he was the perfect gentleman.

"Are you ready for dessert?" he asked.

"Is it you?" I joked.

"Not this time, but I think you'll like it anyway. I made it myself."

I could see he wanted to please me. And he was succeeding. I could get used to this princess treatment. What he didn't know though, was that I was happy just to be with him. We could have been eating bread and butter, and I still would have been deliriously happy. He led me back to the kitchen and sat me on my stool. He brought out two little dishes of crème Brule, and fed me tiny bites with a small spoon. It was heavenly, of course.

"Are you sure you don't want to be a chef instead of a doctor?" I asked.

"I do love to cook. Well, it's not so much that I love to cook, but I love to cook for you. I think good food makes people feel happy and cared for. It's something to remember for the time when I actually get to go to a poor country as a surgeon. Part of the experience for the patients should be some really good food. Healthy food of course."

"That's a great idea," I said enthusiastically. We finished our dessert, every last smidgen. "You cook better than anyone I've ever met our age, male or female. Or maybe better than anyone I've met period. I can't wait to tell my mom."

"Your mom?"

"Yeah, she'll be really impressed."

"She won't think I'm weird?" Andy asked.

"No, she'll think you're pretty amazing."

"That's good, because I want her to like me." He took our dishes to the sink, washed and dried his hands and then turned and took his jacket from the chair and put it on. "It's about time to go Megs. I can't wait to show you off. You'll knock all the guys off their feet, and I'll be thinking, yeah, but she's with me."

I blushed. "Oh yeah right. It's all the girls who are going to be jealous of me. Everyone who will be there has seen me a million times. You're the new mysterious gorgeous one. I'll be surprised if Kelsey doesn't push me in a fountain or something, and then try to steal you."

He laughed his beautiful laugh. "But I don't want to be stolen, especially not by her. She still scares me."

I was delighted at his reassurance. “I don’t blame you I guess, she still scares me too. I mean, she’s never had any trouble getting any boy she wanted no matter who was in the way. You might be the very first.”

“I’ll take that as a compliment. Here’s your coat.”

He helped me into my coat, offered me his arm, and walked me to the passenger side of his car. He settled me in, got in on his side, and we drove away from the house. At school, he parked, came around to my side, helped me out of the car, and again offered me his arm. I shrugged out of my coat and left it in the car even though it was cold. It simply did not match my dress. I reached out and gladly took his arm, because my new shoes were unbelievably difficult to walk in. Also, I wanted to hold onto him so that all the world could see that he was with me.

The gym had been transformed into a New York City scene with a silhouette of the skyline all along one wall and twinkling lights hung all over the ceiling with sliver and black streamers flowing down. The tables had silver and black helium balloons tied on ribbons in the centers. Everyone looked so grown up in their formal gowns, suits and tuxedos. Very quickly I spotted Rachel and Kayla and their dates.

“Meg!” squealed Kayla. She wobbled up to us. “Don’t you guys look awesome?”

“Thanks Kay, you look beautiful too,” I replied. And she did. They all did.

It seemed like everyone in school was in the gym. I was enjoying seeing everyone so dressed up. Then I saw them. “Oh my God,” I said.

“What?” asked Kayla.

"What?" asked Andy.

"Look over there," I nodded with my head ever so slightly.

Kayla casually looked in the direction I had indicated. Andy was not quite so discrete. Kayla turned back to me and burst out laughing. I snickered along with her, and soon Andy was laughing quietly too. We were looking at two people who got exactly what they deserved. No doubt they were the best looking couple in the gym, Jeff in a black tuxedo and Kelsey in a bright red form fitting gown, but they looked perfectly miserable. Jeff was staring at his feet as if there was something very interesting on his shoe. Kelsey was busy having a conversation with Jennifer as she glanced at me briefly and gave me a dismissive look, and then stared at Andy for as long as politeness would allow. I bet she had to work to keep her jaw from dropping.

I had to admit Jeff looked great, as always, but he and Kelsey clearly weren't interested in being there with each other. They probably just wanted to show off their respective trophy dates and have an attractive partner in their senior Prom pictures. Kelsey had looked at Andy like she wanted to sink her teeth into him, but I was pretty sure Andy hadn't even noticed, because he was still looking at me as if I were the only girl in the room. I smiled to myself with satisfaction.

Jeff looked up and caught my glance, and instantly the expression on his face turned from misery into a smug kind of look, as he slid closer to Kelsey and put his arm around her. She turned to him, and he led her out to the dance floor. I smiled at him right before he looked away, and said a silent thankful prayer that I was not with him.

Andy and I danced and danced, and I never let him out of my sight. We chatted with my friends and their dates, and Andy and Kyle found they had something in common, since neither of them knew many people at the dance very well - at least not the way the rest of us all knew each other. Rachel and I were thrilled that they were comfortable with each other, because we could double date in the future.

All too soon the dance was ending and it was time to leave. It had been a magical evening. As we walked out of the gym we all gathered our shoes from the various corners we had tossed them in. I carried mine by the straps, just like the rest of the girls. When we got to the parking lot, Andy scooped me up in his arms and carried me to the car. I laughed with delight as I threw my arms around his neck. Spring was in the air, and though it was chilly, it wasn't nearly as cold as it had been the last few weeks.

"Do you want to go park by the creek for a few minutes?" asked Andy.

"Yes, I still have a little time."

He tucked me into the car, and then drove us to the dirt road near his house. We parked at the end of the road by the creek. Andy got an old blanket out of the back of his car, and spread it on the grass. He thought of everything. He wrapped a flannel shirt he kept in his car around my shoulders.

"We won't stay long. I just wanted to have you to myself for the last few minutes of the evening," said Andy.

I was touched. Everything he had done all evening had been so attentive and romantic. Somehow he knew exactly all the right things to say and do.

Then I saw the little dots of light. They were perfect for the evening. “Look, the first lighting bugs of the season,” I told Andy and pointed. “Don’t they make everything look magical?”

“I thought they were called fireflies,” he said. “Yes, they are pretty. I wonder why they light up. It’s probably a mating thing. We didn’t have any in California, but I’ve seen them a few times in places like this. Do they bite?”

“No, they aren’t pests like mosquitoes.”

We stood on the blanket next to the noisy creek, and danced a slow dance to the sounds of gurgling water. I felt like I could melt into him. He put his hands to my neck and lightly ran his finger tips down my throat. I could feel the warmth where he touched me. I touched his chest, and felt his firm body beneath his crisp white shirt. He lightly ran his fingertips down my chest, tracing the curves as he went. With a sudden rush of feeling, I wanted more. I wanted to touch his bare skin under his shirt. I pulled him close and we kissed with a matched sense of urgency.

Before either of us wanted the night to end, Andy was kissing me goodnight on my doorstep. It had been a fantasy Prom night, one I would never forget.

21 ANTIQUES

I was getting into the habit of spending Saturdays at Andy's house. It felt homey, but more importantly, I couldn't get enough of Andy. Besides that, his house had an endless supply of things to do, with places to explore and all the cleaning and organizing he was working on. Today I was going to help him sort through more of the things in the attic. Andy hoped to make some real progress in identifying items to sell. His summer job was like an ongoing adventure, not work, and I was happy to be a part of it.

I stopped at the deli and got two lattes. I drove to the Bruce place, and noticed the grasses and bushes in the woods were green with new growth. There were little clumps of wildflowers here and there. Spring was finally underway. I parked and then stood on the front porch looking out across the pasture past the stone wall, as I waited for someone to come to the door. A clear vision of a creek with a small meadow beside it flashed into my mind, and in an instant it was gone. The place I had imagined was very similar to the place Andy and I had gone after the Prom, only how it would look in daylight.

Vivid images were popping into my head almost every time I was in or around Andy's house, and it was starting to freak me out, in an interesting and strange sort of way. The images were like vivid memories, but I knew they were not my memories. I knew that the memories in my head were images of this house and this land, but I had never been in the house or seen the surrounding land prior to meeting Andy. I wondered if this happened to anyone else who came here. Maybe it was just that Allie's story was very compelling, and I had been spending a lot of time thinking about her life and feelings. Maybe that was all it was - imagining what it must have looked like and felt like to her when she lived here. The part that was weird was that the images were so real for the brief moments they were in my head.

"Hi there," he said, opening the door.

I smiled and handed him the latte. His free arm shot out and grabbed mine, and he hauled me against him, almost spilling both our drinks. I squealed and threw my free arm around him as he spun me around.

"Hi Megan," Andy's mom called from the kitchen.

"Hi Mrs. Garrett," I called with a twinge of guilt in my voice. What must she think of some girl hanging all over her son? I hoped she wasn't too offended. I wanted her to like me.

Andy saw my discomfort and snickered, and then dragged me up the stairs to his room. He pulled me through the doorway and gave me a delicious kiss.

"Ready to go upstairs?"

"Sure," I said.

"I think there are some old clothes and things like that, maybe blankets or sheets, and we should decide what to do with them. Why in the world would anyone still have this stuff? I don't know if they're worth anything, but at a minimum, they should go to the Salvation Army or something."

I followed him up the stairs, and then we stood in the attic trying to decide where to begin. It was overwhelming. We sipped our lattes. It almost felt like we were some young married couple settling into a new home we had bought. At least those were *my* fantasies.

"Hey, I've got one for you," Andy said, gesturing. "Look at this. What do you think it is?"

The game started. He held up an iron rod about two feet long. On one end was a ring, like you would use to hang the thing from a hook. On the other end, the rod was attached to a round metal dish, about 3 inches deep with a tightly fitting metal lid on it. The lid had a little knob in the middle. The dish was about the size of a dessert plate.

"You already know, don't you?" I asked.

He nodded yes, with smiling eyes.

"Ok, let's see," I pondered, playing along with the game. "What could you do with that? Is it a popcorn popper?"

"No."

"A decoration?"

"No."

"For cooking over a fire?"

"No."

"For hitting your boyfriend over the head? I give up. How do you know?"

"I had to research it on the internet. It's a bed warmer. I think you warmed coals or rocks or something in a fire, then put them inside, and then slipped it into a bed. Pretty funny, huh? I think it's from the late 1800s. Someone will want it, so I'm going to put it on eBay with the next group of stuff."

"It is kind of cool," I said. "Some of this stuff is actually kind of interesting."

"I know what you mean, but if we tried to explain it to our friends, they'd think we were geeks. You kind of have to see it to understand."

"Maybe not, if they knew you were also making money from this stuff. I think that's pretty cool. And I'm having fun sharing these discoveries with you. Just think, I could be home helping my mom plant her garden instead," I said with sarcasm in my voice. Gardening was one of my least favorite chores.

"Well, I'm glad you're not, it is great having you here." He pointed to a corner. "That pile over there is trash for sure, so you can put anything that's clearly trash there. I made a big pile of just pure junk in the barn, and I'll add it to that. I'll have to take it all to the landfill one of these days. Do you want to see what's in that dresser, while I pull some of these boxes out of the closet?"

"Sure," I said. "It looks like an antique. I wonder if they would have called it a chest of drawers. Or maybe a highboy."

Andy looked at me and raised his eyebrows, and then turned and disappeared into the closet.

I opened the top drawer of the dresser. I seemed to be full of old clothes, most of them in pretty bad shape. There was nothing remarkable about them. Old off brand jeans that were faded and threadbare, some men's shirts that had seen better days or were just plain ugly, and a few folded up dresses that I would guess would be called house dresses. Totally 'I love Lucy.' Maybe someone in poverty would want them, but that was about it. I looked at each item, and put all but the worst of them in a pile to be given to charity. Toward the bottom of the drawer I found a faded yellow baby gown.

"Ooh," I said softly to myself.

"What?" asked Andy, poking his head out of the closet.

"It's a little baby gown. Look at the careful stitching on it. Someone put a lot of work into this. There are no tags, so I bet it's handmade. Can you imagine what kind of story it could tell about the lives it touched? I seems like it should be kept and taken care of, but that's kind of silly when we have no idea whether it was even special to anyone. It's almost like you can feel it must have been special just by touching it though." I studied the gown for a moment. "Do you believe in good and bad vibes? I mean, I don't know, about good feelings and bad feelings lingering around places or things?"

"I guess so," Andy replied. "I've never really thought about it much. It makes sense though. I know my mom totally believes in karma, all things being related and stuff like that."

"I do too. Sometimes you can just feel things, and there's no good explanation for it. Sometimes you know things, and there's no reason you should know them. This little gown has good vibes. I wonder if a museum would be interested in it. Maybe it's not even that old, but it looks old. We should ask the little museum in town."

"That's a good idea Meg. We might want to make a pile of things like that - that seem too special to sell, or not appropriate to give away, but yet might have some historic value. At least we should talk to someone about it. Do you want to go into town later and see if anyone at the museum would be interested?"

He smiled at me, and I momentarily forgot what I was doing as I looked into those blue eyes.

"What? Oh, yeah, that would be cool," I said.

I put the little gown aside and continued looking through the drawer. The only other interesting thing in the top drawer was an old ladies hat. I could see it must have been very fancy at one time, but it was hopelessly crushed. It was a faded light blue, and had the remains of feathers that must have been colorful at one time, but were now brownish gray and crumbly. I put it in the pile of possible museum items anyway, and stacked the rest of the clothes in the giveaway pile. The Salvation Army could decide whether they were worth keeping or not. They all smelled old and musty, so maybe charity wouldn't even want them. It was worth a try though.

The next drawer held more clothes, and also dish towels. Some looked very old and were hand embroidered. They were faded to yellow, but might have been pretty at one time. Most of them though, were not remarkable in any way – just basic old dish towels, some stained. What were they thinking, keeping stuff like that? At least they could have been made into rags or something, rather than being stuffed in a drawer for decades. I put some of the yellowed embroidered towels in the museum pile, and the rest in the giveaway pile.

I heard a loud bang from inside the closet.

"Andy?" I asked.

"Spider," he replied.

I shuddered and went back to what I was doing, but more cautiously aware of anything creepy that might jump out. I moved on to the bottom drawer. Inside was a large old tattered shirt box. I took it out of the drawer and set it on top of the dresser. I took the lid off, and inside was something wrapped in yellowed tissue paper that disintegrated as I pushed it to the side.

"Look at this!" I said to Andy, as I stared into the box.

Andy crawled out of the closet, covered in dust. He pushed his hair out of his eyes with the back of one hand, wiped his hands on his pants, and walked over to peer in the box. The box held a thin quilt that had been carefully folded and then wrapped in the delicate tissue paper. It wasn't particularly attractive, but it was clearly very old and extremely fragile, and looked like it would crumble like the tissue paper if I touched it. The quilt was made of random sized pieces of fabric stitched together with random colors of thread in tiny little stitches. I took it out and carefully laid it flat on a clean section of the floor. It was about four feet by five feet. We studied it. There were places where the thread was missing and the fabric was ripped, and it looked like it could easily come apart if anyone tugged on two separate corners. It looked like the colors of the pieces had once been bright, but they all looked muted and faded now.

"Wow, it must be ancient," said Andy.

At that instant I had a flash of the same quilt lying on a bed, but with no missing threads or tears in it. The colors were bright and the quilt was clean, and it seemed like the center focus of the bed, even though it wasn't as big as the blanket underneath. The vision was gone in an instant. I shook my head like I was trying to shake off a leaf that had landed in my hair. Then I knew with certainty what we were looking at.

"Andy, this is Allie's quilt," I said quietly.

He paused. "I bet you're right. I'm seeing some of the squares she described. That one done with red stripes and blue stars probably was not originally on yellow fabric. I bet that yellow used to be white. And here's the one of the mountains that form an upside down W. Unbelievable. I wonder why it's in this house."

"Look at all these squares, each one has a picture," I said. "They must have all had meaning to her. It's amazing. This is a piece of your family history, from a hundred and fifty years ago. Can you imagine? She was making this at the time of the civil war. It's very special. Look at this square," I pointed. "This has to be a picture of this house."

"It is, you're right," said Andy.

"Did you tell your mom about the diary?" I asked.

"No, I wanted to keep it as our secret for a while."

"Uh oh, I did mention it to my mom," I said.

"That's ok; it's not a big deal. I just wanted to think about it for a while."

We were silent for a moment. "Maybe it's a good time for a break," I said. "Are you hungry?"

"Yeah, I am a little," said Andy.

"What should we do with this?" I mused.

"Let's leave it here while we get some food," Andy replied.

"Let's go to the deli and get some sandwiches," I suggested. "Then we can stop by the museum and find out who we can talk to about your antiques. We can tell them about this too." I indicated the quilt.

Carefully I picked up the baby dress and we took it down the stairs with us. We went straight to the bathroom, where we scrubbed all the way to our elbows. I still felt dusty, but much better.

We showed Andy's mom the baby dress.

"Oh it's precious," she exclaimed. "Look at the tiny buttons."

"I know, isn't it so sweet?" I asked.

"Mom, we're going to go get some lunch and then ask at the Hardwick museum if they can tell us anything about the dress," Andy said.

"That sounds good sweetie," she replied.

I laid the little dress carefully on the back seat of Andy's car, and he drove us to the deli. Inside he followed me through the store to the back. I went behind the counter while he waited in front of it.

"Hi Sandy," I said to my co-worker. "Mind if I make a few sandwiches?"

"No, not at all Meg. That would be great actually, I'm kind of busy."

"What do you want Andy?" I asked him.

"Oh, I don't know. Turkey? With Swiss on a roll of some sort?"

"Sure. Mayo? Mustard?"

"Yeah, both," he replied.

I made perfect thick sandwiches for us and wrapped them up. We grabbed a couple of cokes from the cooler and packed them all in a bag at the front. Joe, the front clerk, charged it to my tab. With my employee discount of fifty percent, it didn't cost much.

"It's so nice outside that we should eat out here somewhere," I said. "Let's go over to the common."

"Sounds good," Andy replied. He drove us the mile or so to the common and parked under a big tree. He got his old blanket out of the back of his car, and I grabbed our bag from the deli. I was beginning to really like that blanket.

"Good thinking," I said, pointing at the blanket.

"Never know when you might need it," he said, winking at me.

I had some good ideas on that subject, but maybe now was not the right time. Andy spread the blanket on the grass under one of the biggest trees on the common, a giant oak. I sat, and then took out our sandwiches and drinks, handing him his.

"I wonder how they arranged Allie's Fourth of July picnic," I pondered. I pointed to the west. "I bet all the games and races happened in that area. And maybe the dance would have been where one of the buildings is now, just off the common. I can easily imagine an old fashioned scene here."

"Yeah, me too." Andy chewed thoughtfully. "Think about it, these trees wouldn't have been nearly this big, but some of them were probably here. I bet they have stories to tell."

"This is such a peaceful beautiful place," I said.

"It is. These sandwiches are great, by the way."

"Well thank you kind sir. It's our own little almost June picnic."

"Does the town still do a July fourth celebration?" Andy asked.

"Yes, actually. There is a little parade that circles the common, and then families picnic in the park. Most years we have fireworks, but a few years we haven't, because of city budget issues or something. There's never been a dance since I can remember."

We finished eating and put our trash in a can at the edge of the common. Then we walked across the green grass to the museum on the other side. I glanced toward the cemetery, and realized Andy had never seen it.

"This may sound weird," I said, "but the old cemetery is pretty cool. Want to take a look?"

"Ok, sure," Andy replied enthusiastically.

We pushed through the rusted iron gate.

"Wow, it looks just like a haunted cemetery you would see in a movie," Andy exclaimed as he looked around. "All the headstones are falling over, and older than the hills. 'R.I.P." it says. It's so gothic. Yeesh."

I looked around and imagined seeing it for the first time. It *was* like a scene out of a movie, except that it was real. The ground was uneven, probably because some areas settled over time and others were pushed up by tree roots. The headstones were crooked and broken, and many were weathered to the point they could no longer be read.

"Look Meg, this one is from 1810!" Andy called from a few yards away.

"I know, it's crazy isn't it?"

He stopped in front of another row. "Here's an entire family, who all died within eight years of each other, in the mid-1800s. And here's a baby. Wow, this is amazing. I wonder if any of the Bruce family is here."

"I don't know, but I would think so," I said. "This cemetery was used up until about world war two, so there should be." I started to look, and was instinctively drawn to the north eastern corner of the plot. Sure enough, there they were. Roger Bruce, Margaret Bruce, Stanley Bruce and more – all meaningless names. And off to the left I found her. A small weathered white marble headstone read, 'Allison Hunter, March 23 1850 – June 17 1923, beloved wife and mother.' I sat and ran my finger along her name, and felt warmth resonating through me. "Andy?"

He looked up, saw my face, and started toward me. He reached me and put his hand on my shoulder, looking silently at the grave stone.

"Here they are, huh?" he said quietly, looking toward the Bruce headstones. "It's so weird to think these are my relatives. I don't know a thing about them."

"Yeah, it's like you want to feel something, but don't know what to feel, right?"

"Yeah, exactly."

In a somber mood now, we got the dress from the car and walked to the museum. It had once been a church sitting next to the cemetery, but had been converted. We pushed open the heavy wooden door and went inside. It was cool and slightly musty inside.

"Hi Megan."

I looked toward the older lady sitting at the desk. It was Mrs. Marshall, one of my dad's clients.

"Hi Mrs. Marshall, I didn't know you worked here," I said.

"Oh yes, I volunteer here on Saturdays," she replied. "What brings you two young people in here?"

"This is Andy Garrett. His family lives in Robert Miller's house, the Bruce place."

"Hi Andy, it's nice to meet you," said Mrs. Marshall.

"Well," I said to Mrs. Marshall, "we were wondering if you could tell us who we could talk to about some antiques we've been finding at Andy's house. We found this baby dress for instance."

"Oh can I see it? I bet there are all sorts of fascinating things about that house."

"Yes ma'am, there are," said Andy.

I smiled at his politeness.

"My, this does look old. I wish I could tell you something about it, but I can't. I certainly can give you some names though," said Mrs. Marshall. "On Mondays and Wednesdays, Mrs. Lowenstein works. She has been here over twenty years, and has an incredible depth of knowledge about this area, the history of the town, and antiques. Also, there's Ralph Majors, at the antiquarian society in Worcester. He is a wealth of knowledge, and they have many historical documents there that relate to Hardwick. I would suggest you'd do well starting with either one of them. What else have you found?"

"Well, there are lots of antiques, but we've also found an old quilt and a diary," said Andy.

"That does sound intriguing," she replied. "Good luck."

"Well, thank you very much," I said, and turned to go. Andy followed me. We walked slowly down the aisle, looking at some of the antiques on display.

“Maybe when school gets out, we can look into this stuff some more,” said Andy.

“Yeah, if we feel like it. It could be entertaining.”

22 WATER SPORTS

The last two weeks of school flew by. We had finals, the seniors graduated, and all of a sudden it was summer. I started a full time schedule at the deli, and Andy continued to do a lot of work around his house - cleaning, sorting, painting, repairing, etc. We were spending as much time together as we could.

Andy's sister Samantha came home from college and moved into the room across the hall from him. I was nervous about meeting her because I knew she and Andy were close. What if she didn't like me? I arrived at their house about noon on the first Saturday she was home, and Andy met me at the door.

"Hey Megs, I can't wait for you to meet Sam!" We had a delicious kiss and then he pulled me into the kitchen. I saw a beautiful blonde girl, taller than me, with blue eyes a little paler than Andy's. She smiled at me.

"You must be Megan, I've heard so much about you! I'm Sam." She reached out to hug me and I glanced at Andy, wondering what she had heard.

"I'm very happy to meet you Sam, Andy's told me a lot about you too. It's wonderful that you have such a close relationship." I sounded so formal. We hugged, and something about her manner put me at ease. "So you're studying law?" I asked.

"Yes, pre-law at this point. Pretty boring so far. Have you lived here long?"

"Oh yes, all my life. It's a pretty small town, huh?"

"Yeah it's tiny, especially compared to New York City," she agreed. "Are you guys just bored out of your skulls nonstop? And this house! It's such a dump! I hope you won't mind me hanging out with you sometimes. What can you do for fun around here?"

"I know," I said. "I have a job that keeps me pretty busy, and I've been spending a lot of time here. People go to Worcester to shop, go to movies, and stuff like that. During the school year the high school events are pretty well attended, probably because there's nothing else to do. People do a lot of outdoorsy stuff too I guess."

"Well, I'm taking two on-line classes and will be visiting some of my school friends over the summer. Mom wants to take me to her yoga classes and stuff too, and said we should do some hiking. And of course there's always the boat." She winked at Andy. "Anyway, Mom and I are off to do some shopping, but I think we'll be home by dinner time. See you both later, and again, very nice to meet you Megan!"

"Nice to meet you too," I said, as she went up the stairs.

"She definitely liked you," Andy told me.

"Why do you say that? How can you tell?"

"It was the way she looked at you. She's usually very protective of me and suspicious of girls who like me, but she didn't act that way at all with you. Maybe that's because she already knows how I feel about you."

I turned and put my arms around him, looking up into those crystal blue eyes. "Which is?"

He backed me up against the kitchen sink until I was pressed between it and him. Then he locked his eyes on mine, put a hand on each side of my face, and slowly leaned in. I could feel the emotion in his kiss, and I didn't need any spoken answer.

With the arrival of hot weather, Andy was excited to take me water skiing. I agreed to go out with him and his parents the first Saturday in June, though I was very nervous about making a fool of myself. It would be Andy's first time water skiing in Massachusetts.

That Saturday morning I arrived at Andy's house to find him loading life jackets and towels into the SUV. I had on my new bikini under a new pair of shorts and a matching top. I had packed my beach towel, sunscreen and sunglasses in a big tote bag.

"Hi Meg," he said quickly and gave me a peck on the lips. "Ready to go?"

"Yeah," I replied. "Is Sam coming?"

"No, she wanted to sleep in and wasn't interested in getting in a cold lake yet. She'll come with us some time though."

I was relieved – one less person to make a fool of myself in front of, if I had to try water skiing. I wanted her to think I was cool, not an idiot. Andy and I scrambled into the back seat while his mom and dad got in the front. We drove to Quabbin reservoir. I didn't mention to them that Andy and I had been here before or that I'd seen their boat before.

"Do kids come here a lot in the summer Meg?" asked Andy's mom.

"Yeah they do, and families too, since there isn't a pool in town or anywhere near. Sometimes my mom drives us to Worcester to go to the pool, but that's an all day excursion."

"Do you see many water skiers?" asked Andy's dad.

"Not really," I replied. "I didn't really realize it was much of a sport."

Andy snorted and squeezed my hand.

"I can see there probably aren't many serious slalom skiers here," said Mr. Garrett. "See how our boat looks different than most of these Meg? It makes a smoother wake than most boats, and has a very precise speedometer. I don't know what Andy told you about competition, but it involves skiing through a set of buoys, back and forth across the boat's wake at a very precise speed. If you successfully make it through the course at that speed, then you do it again at two miles an hour faster. It goes that way until you reach 38 miles per hour, and then they start shortening the rope on each loop. They keep doing loops until there's only one person remaining."

"Like how they eliminate people in high jumping," Andy said.

"Wow, I had no idea," I said.

Andy squeezed my hand again, and smiled at me.

"Have you ever water skied?" Mr. Garrett asked me.

"No. It looks kind of scary," I replied.

"Well, we'll give it a try today," he said. "You can swim, right?"

"Yes." I looked uneasily at Andy.

"You might really like it Meg," Andy assured me.

“Have you ever snow skied?” Mr. Garrett asked.

“A few times,” I admitted.

“Well, it’s a little similar, but not entirely.”

I nodded. We packed everything onto the boat and climbed in. Andy’s parents sat in the front two seats and Andy and I sat in the back two. Mr. Garrett started the engine and we chugged out into the lake. I couldn’t stop thinking about the last time I’d been in this boat. I realized I was smiling and looked at Andy self consciously. I could see he knew what I’d been thinking, because he put his finger to his lips and smiled. There were very few other boats out, and none like the one we were in. Once we were out of sight of the marina, Mr. Garrett slowed the boat and turned to Andy. “Ready?”

“Me first?” asked Andy.

“Definitely, show us how it’s done,” Mr. Garrett said proudly.

Andy opened a compartment in the floor of the boat and took out a single water ski with two boots on it. He also pulled out a green life vest. I sat in my seat and tried to stay out of the way, as did Mrs. Garrett in the front.

Though we had been seeing each other for a while, I was unprepared for what happened next. Andy kicked off his shoes, and then took off his shirt. I stared, grateful that his parents were behind me and couldn’t see me gaping at him. His body was beautiful. There was no other way to describe it. It looked just like it felt from the outside of his clothes. His chest had firm sleek muscles. His shoulders were broad, his waist was narrow, and he looked slightly tan. I had seen his arms of course, but without his shirt on I could see how well defined his biceps were. He looked like a Calvin Klein commercial. Andy looked up at me from where he was adjusting the ski, saw me gaping at him and winked. I blushed. I was positive he had no idea how good he looked. I think he misinterpreted my staring as interest in the process of water skiing.

"Can you hand this to me once I get in the water?" He pointed to the ski.

"Uh, ok."

"You just have to be careful not to knock it against the boat."

"Ok," I said uncertainly.

Andy took a long looped rope out of the storage compartment and clipped the end to a metal loop attached to the boat. He threw the handle on the other end and the rest of the rope out behind the boat into the water. Then he put on the life vest and fastened the buckles, and put on gloves.

"Here goes," he said, as he stepped onto the platform at the back of the boat. From there, he dropped into the water.

"Woo, that's cold!" he said.

"Maybe I won't go," said Mrs. Garrett. "I hate cold water."

"Ok, Meg, hand me the ski please," said Andy.

It was heavier than I expected. I carefully stepped to the back of the boat and onto the platform, and slid the ski into the water. Andy took it from me, paddled toward the rope and grabbed the handle, and then worked his feet into the boots. Mr. Garrett started slowly moving the boat away from Andy, until the rope became taut.

"Ok!" he yelled.

I pitched forward as Mr. Garrett gunned the boat, but caught myself and stayed in my seat. Andy popped out of the water effortlessly and glided gracefully on the water behind the boat. I could hear the sound of the motor steady as we maintained a constant speed. That was when Andy started to really ski. He went wide out to the left and then cut sharply back to the right, his elbow touching the water as he leaned in to turn. He sliced across the boat wake and did the same thing on the other side. He continued like that, back and forth, making sharp cuts as he turned. I was amazed by how effortless it all seemed, similar to how an Olympic gymnast makes it look like flipping through the air is just second nature.

"Do you get a picture of how it works?" Mrs. Garrett asked. "If you just imagine a buoy at the furthest point of every turn, that is what a competition looks like."

"I think I get it," I replied. "So he's pretty good, isn't he?"

"Yes, he is. He's been doing this a long time. Of course we have no idea what to expect out here, but I would suspect it's not nearly as big a sport as it is on the west coast, so he'll probably do well."

I felt a sense of pride. Then Andy fell in behind the boat again, and suddenly he threw the rope up into the air and slid slowly into the water.

"He's down!" said Mrs. Garrett to her husband.

Mr. Garrett cut the motor and we circled back around to Andy. He handed the ski to his mom and then climbed up onto the platform. He grinned his beautiful smile.

"That was awesome! I've been away from it too long!"

"You didn't lose a thing either," said Mr. Garrett.

"Like riding a bike I guess," replied Andy.

He climbed into the boat and took off the ski vest. He stepped toward me and threw his arms around me, planting a big wet kiss on my mouth. He got me soaked, but I didn't care. I was thrilled to feel the length of his nearly naked body against mine, even though he was cold and wet.

"What did you think?" he asked.

"You looked so graceful," I replied. "I admit I don't have much to compare it to, but what you just did can't be easy."

He smiled. "Just like anything, it takes a lot of practice."

He pulled away from me and wrapped himself in a towel. "The water's glass Dad, are you going to go?"

"Sure, I'll give it a go," replied Mr. Garrett.

Andy's mom gunned the motor. Mr. Garrett was a good skier too, but not like Andy. He did nice turns, but didn't lean over nearly as far. He finished and we picked him up as we had Andy.

"Ready to go again son?" he asked.

"Yup, I am," replied Andy. "You'll see," he said to me. "Your arms get tired and you have to stop for a while, but then you can't wait to go again."

Andy was skiing beautifully, but suddenly was tumbling through the air. Mrs. Garrett yelled from the back seat, "He's down!"

I looked at Mr. Garrett.

"Is he ok?" I asked anxiously.

"Oh yeah he's fine, he just caught an edge. Or maybe he hit a stick or something. It happens a lot."

When we get close to Andy, Mrs. Garrett yelled, "are you coming out or going some more?" asked Mrs. Garrett.

"Coming out, I need a rest," replied Andy.

As Andy climbed over the side into the boat, I saw that he had a small cut on his leg.

"What happened?" I asked, pointing to the cut.

"Oh that's nothing, just banged it on the ski as I came out of it." Water skiers fall all the time. That just goes with the territory." He wrapped his towel around himself and gave me a big hug. "You going Mom?"

"I don't know, how cold is it?" she asked.

"Oh don't be a wimp Mom, you can do it," replied Andy.

Mrs. Garrett skied. She looked pretty and graceful too. Then Andy went again.

He swam up to the platform and climbed onto the edge. "Are you ready Megan?"

"Me?" I asked.

"Yes, you," he replied. "Don't you want to give it a try? It's really fun. You can try it on two skis, that's the best way to get started. You said you can swim, right?"

"Yes," I said uncertainly.

"Wanna try?" he asked again.

I felt like I had no choice. I didn't want to look like a big baby, and even Mrs. Garrett had gotten into the cold water. "Ok," I said.

Mrs. Garrett dried out the life vest with a towel so it wouldn't be so cold when I put it on. I took off my shorts and shirt, and stood self consciously in my bikini. Maybe I should have worn something more conservative since his parents were coming. What had I been thinking? They didn't seem to notice, but I could see Andy noticed. He stole a sideways glance at me, and then whistled.

"Andy!" said his mom.

"Sorry Mom, she looks good."

She laughed. I looked at him and he winked. I was mortified. Mrs. Garrett helped me into the vest and showed me how to buckle it. I felt like a clumsy dork. Mr. Garrett found a set of two skis in the storage compartment and handed them one by one to Andy. I climbed onto the platform and sat next to him.

"Ok, first we'll put your skis on, while we're still out of the water," he said.

"Ok," I said meekly.

"It's going to be fun, you'll see. Turn and put your legs across my lap."

I did, and felt even more awkward.

"We'll put the left ski on first, so put your foot here." He indicated the boot of the ski. "And wiggle your foot into there."

I was sure I'd done more awkward things in my life, but I couldn't think what they were. Finally the left ski was on. Andy lowered it and my foot carefully into the water so my left leg was down and my right was still draped across his lap. Dork. Then he helped me get the right ski on in the same way. Finally, I was sitting on the platform with both feet dangling into the water.

"Ok, now you have to get in," Andy said.

I looked at him. "Just slide in?" I asked.

"Yes, just slide in."

I pushed myself over the edge, felt the shock of the cold and became a big tangled mess of skis in the water. It was completely embarrassing, and I couldn't figure out how I was supposed to be positioned. Andy jumped in after me and wrestled me around like I was a fighting octopus. Finally he had me settled with my back to him and my skis out in front of me with the tips coming out of the water.

"Throw us the rope Mom," he called.

She did and Andy handed it to me. I held it uncertainly.

"Ok, this is important. You need to hold on to this really tight, or the boat will pull it out of your hands."

"Ok," I said.

"Now put the rope between the two skis. When the boat starts to pull, you'll just stay leaned back like this. Keep your knees a little bent, but not more bent than they are now, and let the boat pull you on top of the water. Then just hold the rope and let the boat pull you."

"Ok," I said again. It sounded easy, but I was doubtful.

"Dad, give her just a little pull," yelled Andy.

Andy was still attached to my back and had his mouth right next to my ear. "Now hang on and he's going to move the boat just a little so you can see what it's going to feel like."

The boat started to move. It was very difficult to hang on or stay straight. Suddenly I was flipped sideways and my skis flailed out behind me, even though we were barely moving. There was no dignity in this at all. The boat stopped. I felt like an idiot.

"That's ok, that's ok," Andy said, as he swam the five feet between us. "See, you still have the rope – that's good." He untangled me and put me back into the crouched position facing the boat. "Ok, this time we'll just try it for real."

I looked at him, not knowing what to say. "I'm not sure," I started.

"You'll be fine, just give it a try," he said patiently. "I'll be right here with you."

When I was situated again, with the rope between my legs and a firm grip on the handle, Andy checked my position.

"Ok, straighten your arms, and then it won't feel like such a hard jerk," he said.

I obeyed.

"Hang on, ok? Just relax and let it pull you. Just stay in this exact same position until you're on top of the water, and then you can stand up. Lean back."

I nodded.

"Ok!" he yelled.

The rope jerked out of my hands.

"Oops," I said.

"That's ok, now you know what it's going to feel like," said Andy. "We'll just try it again."

"Ok." I was getting cold. "I'm sorry for keeping you out here in this cold water."

"It's nothing Meg, you're worth it. I want you to experience this."

I felt warmed by his words, and grateful he was being so nice. The boat circled us and Andy grabbed the rope as it went by. He gave me the handle.

"Wait a minute, let's try this," he said. He took the handle back from me and gave me one of his gloves. "Put this on."

It was big, but I did as he said. He tightened it with the Velcro strap and helped me put the other one on.

"Now try gripping the handle," he instructed.

I did, and I could see that the gloves would help me hang on.

"Thanks," I said.

"Ok, here we go again," he replied. He got behind me, got me back into the right position, and the boat tightened the rope between us.

"Hang on tight, and keep yourself exactly in this position," he said in my ear. "Ok!" he yelled.

The boat pulled hard and I remained frozen in my position. To my utter astonishment, it pulled me out of the water. For a yard I was skiing, then I leaned forward and the boat pulled me forward over my skis. I hit the water hard and let go of the rope. I got water up my nose, but I wasn't entirely disappointed because I knew I had almost done it.

"Yard sale!" yelled Andy, as he swam up to me. "Good job! That was great for a first try. Can you give it one more try?" he asked.

I coughed at him and rearranged my swimsuit under the water.

"You didn't lose your bottoms, did you?" he asked with mock hope.

"No, they just aren't exactly where they're supposed to be," I replied. "I feel like such a dork."

"Oh no, you're not at all. You got on top of the water, and most people don't get that far this quick."

"Really?" I asked.

"Really," he replied. "Let's get your skis back on. My mom and dad had to do this for me. It seems like a long time ago now."

We wrestled my feet back into the skis again, and then he got me back into position. I was determined not to make him keep going through this – I was going to get up and ski this time.

"Are you ready?" he asked.

“Um hm.” I replied.

“Ok!” he yelled.

The boat pulled and I was determined. Suddenly I was on top of the water. I stayed exactly in position and the boat pulled me. I was skiing! It was actually fun. I wondered what it would take to go outside the boat wake, and leaned a little to my right. I started to move out toward the right. As I crossed the wake, I got one leg stuck on each side, lost my balance, and toppled into the water.

“Are you ok?” Mrs. Garrett yelled, as the boat approached.

“Yes,” I called. “Only embarrassed.”

“You did better than any beginner I’ve ever seen,” said Mrs. Garrett.

“Thanks,” I said with a small smile, certain she was only being nice.

I pushed the skis in front of me to the boat and she took them from me. I climbed onto the platform and then into the boat, where I took off the wet vest and wrapped up in my towel. By then Mrs. Garrett had coiled up the rope, so we drove back to where Andy was still waiting in the water.

As we got close he yelled, “That was great Meg!”

I couldn’t believe he would sit there in that cold water, just to help me learn to ski. He climbed onto the boat with no complaints whatsoever, but I could see his entire body was covered in goose bumps. Mrs. Garrett handed him his towel, and we huddled together shivering.

After lunch we all skied a little more, even me without Andy in the water. By mid-afternoon, we were all exhausted from the skiing and the hot sun, and we called it a day.

Two days later Andy and I took the boat out ourselves. The day was perfect, about 85 degrees, sunny, cloudless, peaceful and quiet. We found a nice sandy cove along the far shore and pulled up there. We laid out our blanket and beach towels, and arranged our things around us. Before long we were plenty warm, and started shedding clothes. I knew what Andy would look like in his shorts, but still couldn't wait to see. This time, I didn't have to hide my gaze or act like I wasn't noticing. He took his shirt off casually, and the sight of him made me suck in my breath. Corny, but he reminded me of the statute of David we had studied. Perfect smooth muscles over a taut stomach - beautiful. I took off my swimsuit cover up and could see he noticed me just as I had noticed him. We had the whole beach to ourselves. It felt private and romantic, yet not in the way it had when we were alone here at night. Now we were in bright daylight and in view of anyone who might come by.

"Do you have any idea how good you look?" I asked.

"I was just about to ask you the same thing," he replied.

He took my hand and placed it on his chest. I could feel the warmth and softness of his skin, pulled over tight muscles. I wanted to pet him. So I did. I lightly stroked my fingers over the muscles in his chest. His eyes stayed locked on mine and I could see something smoldering there. Then, I took his hand and placed it on my chest. He traced my curves, through my swimsuit top, in the same way. I felt warmth and tingling throughout my entire body. We kissed, gently and then more urgently. I'd never wanted anything more than I wanted his touch.

"We better put some sunscreen on," he said. "Here." He handed me the bottle.

I smiled, only too happy to have this job. I squeezed the bottle, squirting lotion into my hand, rubbed my hands together, and then covered Andy's chest. He sat unmoving, and then turned his back to me. I repeated the process on his back, loving that I was the one touching him. Then he took the bottle from me and did the same to me, while I sat motionless. It was heavenly how he touched me softly, as he ran his fingers over my body. It ended all too quickly though, and we each did our own legs.

We laid down on the towels, just soaking up the warm sun.

"Megan, were you and Jeff intimate? You know, it doesn't matter of course, I was just wondering."

I rolled over to my side and looked at him. "Intimate?"

"You know."

"Yeah, I know what you're asking," I said. "It's funny." I glanced at him, and he looked like he was waiting to be punched in the gut. "It's funny, because everyone assumes we were, because we were together so long."

"Were you?"

"No."

"Really?" He rolled to his side.

"Yeah, really. It was like this big game. But we were playing two different games. Before we started dating, Jeff had a reputation for dating people until they had sex, and then he'd dump them. I decided the only way to keep him was to refuse to have sex with him. It's not that I wouldn't, if I loved someone, but with him, I knew if I ever did that would be the end of it."

I looked at him, and his face was expressionless.

I went on, "I mean, I'm not sure I wanted to anyway, because it didn't seem right with him for some reason, but even so, I refused to even consider it. Of course I never told him that. He thought I was just old fashioned and prudish. I let him believe that. I'm sure he would have been pissed if I had told him the real reason. And now, truthfully, I'm glad I never did. Pretty weird, huh?"

"No, not at all. And I wouldn't be disappointed if you had slept with him." He paused. "Well yes I would. I would feel jealous that he had been that close to you, but I wouldn't blame you. That would have been none of my business."

I replied slowly, stumbling over my words, but knowing what I wanted to say was important. "I would never want you to think badly of me, but at the same time, I will always tell you the truth, even if it's unpleasant. I don't want to play games with you, so even if you decide you don't like me, I will tell you the truth."

"How could I ever decide that?" he asked. "There's no way. You're not like anyone I've ever met."

I was afraid to ask him about his past girlfriends. I don't know why, I guess I just didn't want to know. The thought of him with someone else made me insanely jealous. So I didn't. I wasn't ready to hear it. I changed the subject.

"Wanna get wet?" I dared.

"I'm perfectly willing to get in cold water to ski, but to swim? I don't know."

"Ok you big chicken, let's see who's the bravest."

With that, I got up and started wading into the water. It was just as icy cold as it had been a few days ago, he was right. I couldn't back down now though.

“Go ahead, I’m watching,” he said from the shore, amusement in his voice.

Now I had to, it was a matter of pride. I went ahead and plunged in, and screamed at the top of my lungs. I paddled around for a minute, and then scrambled out onto the shore, where he wrapped me in a big towel and held me close.

Time flew by as we talked about everything under the sun. Our families, our futures, people we knew, and world events. I had never had this experience with a boy. Different, but in a good way. This guy was quickly becoming my best friend.

23 OLD THINGS AND NEW THINGS

I was sitting on a riding lawn mower in the barn admiring a bare chested Andy piling up pieces of scrap metal in a corner. I would never get tired of this view. The barn doors were open and sun was streaming in. I imagined myself living here in a time when they kept horses. A nice country life. It seemed kind of Anne of Green Gablesish. Black stallionish. It would have been fun to be a horse person.

"Meg?"

I was startled out of my daydream, "huh?"

"Where were you just now? I was talking to you," said Andy.

"Just daydreaming. This must have been quite the place in its day, when it was a horse farm."

"Yeah, I know. I think about that sometimes too. I was thinking we should go visit the antiquarian society tomorrow, does that sound too boring? You know, ask about the quilt and the baby dress, and maybe a few other things."

"No, that doesn't sound too boring, let's do it. Do you need help with that stuff?"

"This old car bumper - yes, can you come grab the other end? Let's put it in the back of the truck. We're almost ready for another run to the dump. Another half hour, and it'll be full and we can go."

We lugged the bumper out to the truck, made a few more trips from the barn, and then Andy found his shirt and put it on. I liked going to the dump. It was fascinating to see what people threw away. Once Andy had pulled up to the side of the pit where the garbage went, I helped him hurl the scrap metal into the pit with the old washers and dryers, branches and just plain trash.

When we got back in the truck I glanced at the clock on the dashboard. "Oh, I didn't realize it was getting so late. I need to leave for work when we get back. What are you going to do?" I asked.

"Oh I'll probably do one more load, then swing by and see you."

"Good plan," I said with a grin.

The antiquarian society was in Worcester, so we grabbed a few cokes for the drive, and some of the cds from Andy's room. We took the quilt, the diary, the baby dress and some old looking china we had found in the cellar. Andy had called the day before and made an appointment with Ralph Majors, the person the lady at the Hardwick museum had referred us to.

Andy and I had become completely comfortable with each other, and settled into easy conversation in the car. We were in Worcester before we knew it. Andy parked the car, and as always, came around to my side to open my door as I was getting out. He opened the door to the back seat and handed me the quilt and the baby dress, while he took the diary and a plate and a dish from the china set. We carried our strange assortment up the steep steps of the old building. It was like an old library, very somber, quiet and serious. Maybe it used to be a court house. It did not seem like a fun place. I guess the business of preserving history is not meant to be fun.

At the reception desk sat a stern looking woman who must have been in her seventies or so. I wondered whether she had ever found anything amusing. It didn't appear so. She was exactly the stereotype of a librarian; uptight, stuffy, conservatively dressed, thin, with a face made up of severe angles. Her gray hair was even pinned in a tight bun. I wondered for a moment whether she was dressed as a character, but decided she wasn't. She looked at us over reading glasses perched on her thin nose, as if we were lost children with sticky fingers who clearly had no business touching any books.

"Yes?" she asked doubtfully, as if she already knew we were in the wrong place.

"Is Mr. Majors here please?" asked Andy. "We have an appointment."

"Your name?" She focused a humorless gaze on Andy.

"Andy Garrett. And Megan Burke."

She looked skeptical, but picked up a black phone and pushed a button. Someone on the other end must have answered, because she said, "there's an Andy Garrett and a Megan Burke here to see you. They say they have an appointment?"

The question in her voice made it clear she could not believe we really had an appointment. I shifted uncomfortably from one foot to the other. Andy stood quietly and smiled pleasantly at her. She carefully laid the phone back on its receiver without saying anything and stood.

“Follow me please,” she said stiffly.

She led us to an office on the second floor, where she knocked on the door.

“It’s open Mrs. Evans,” came a voice from inside.

Mrs. Evans stepped aside so we could file past her into the office. The inside of the office was different from the parts of the building we had seen so far. Bright sunlight shone through the window, plants were arranged on the windowsill, and though it was cluttered, it felt cheerful and comfortable.

The short round man behind the desk stood as Mrs. Evans made her exit. I guessed he was in his fifties. He had on a knit vest over a button up shirt even though it was summer, and looked like an absent minded professor.

“Ralph Majors,” he said, holding out his hand to Andy.

Andy shook his hand, and then Ralph Majors offered his hand to me. I shook it as well.

“Have a seat,” he invited us. “I must say, it’s quite unusual for young people to show any interest in what we do here these days. I was surprised you two wanted to meet with me. Still am. What can I help you with?”

Andy started. “Well, my family moved into a very old house in Hardwick. It’s actually been in our family for generations, but my part of the family wasn’t in close contact with the last generation that lived there. We are finding all kinds of interesting things, and were hoping you could help us better understand some of them. The house was built in 1776, and I swear some of the original possessions are still there. There is an unbelievable amount of junk," he glanced at Mr. Majors. "Stuff I mean, there. The house is full, the barn is full - it's unbelievable. We brought a couple of things we thought were especially interesting to ask your opinion about them."

"I see. Well, what do you have?" Mr. Majors sounded just slightly skeptical.

I laid the quilt on his desk and carefully unfolded it.

Mr. Majors took out a pair of glasses and put them on. He stood and leaned over the quilt, studying each square.

"This looks like a fairly typical example of patchwork from the mid to late 1800s," he said. "It's not terribly unusual." He looked up at us. "Do you know much about life in that time frame?"

"No, not really," I said. "But I've been to old Sturbridge village." Sturbridge village is a replica of what a town would have looked like in the 1800s, with people dressed in period costume and going about their work as if they were really living in that time. Most school children around the area had been there on field trips, but I hadn't paid that much attention to the details. It was cool, and we got to do some crafts, but I didn't remember much about quilts. It had been sixth grade after all.

"Well, you have to remember that for most people, everything made of cloth was handmade. For that reason, girls learned sewing skills from a very young age. It was very common for girls to graduate from simple doll dresses and embroidered handkerchiefs to making a sampler quilt like this one. Usually they were made from scraps of cloth left over from clothes their mothers made, or from flour bags, or things like that. The main purpose was to teach them sewing skills, but it would also be a usable quilt. Usually the blocks were blank, or were made into common pictures like you see here on your quilt. Do you have specific questions about this one?"

"Not really about the quilt itself," said Andy. "But we were wondering why someone would make it. More whether it would be unusual for someone to make it – what their family would think of it. The other thing is, we found a diary also, and it describes this quilt."

"Now that *is* interesting," said Mr. Majors. "Did you bring it, and may I see it?"

"Yes," Andy replied, handing him the worn little book.

"Fascinating," exclaimed Mr. Majors. He didn't read the words, but carefully turned the pages to look at the writing. "This does make the quilt a treasure. I would think your family would want to keep it as an heirloom. Is this person a relation of yours?"

"Yes," replied Andy. "An Aunt many generations back."

"That is very special indeed. Have you read the entire diary?"

"Yes. She describes some of the blocks of the quilt."

"Well, as you can see," said Mr. Majors, "the diary is very fragile, and will certainly deteriorate more over time. If there's ever a time when your family would like to donate such an item, our society would love to have it, and we would preserve it and store it. For now though, you should carefully copy the pages or write out what they say, before they fade too much to be legible. That way, you will always have a record."

"That's a good idea," I said. I wondered if Andy would say any more about the diary or the quilt, but sensed that he didn't want to talk about what Allie had written, at least not right now. I carefully folded the quilt and put it on the chair beside me. I then laid the baby dress on the desk.

"Ah, a baby gown," said Mr. Majors.

"Can you tell us anything about it?" I asked. "We have no idea whether it was ever special to anyone, but it looks old."

"Yes I agree," said Mr. Majors. I would estimate this was made in the early 1900s, maybe around 1910. I say that because of the style of the buttons and the texture of the fabric. Just like today, yellow could have been for a boy or a girl. It's in relatively good shape. What are you planning to do with it?"

"I don't know," replied Andy. "It seems kind of silly to keep it, when we have no idea who owned it or why they kept it. We were thinking we might donate it to a museum, if a museum would want it."

"A museum would definitely welcome the donation," said Mr. Majors. "As a matter of fact, we would be honored to display it in our museum, and again, would make preservation efforts."

"I think that would be nice," said Andy. "Could we give it to you on loan?"

"Most certainly," said Mr. Majors. "We'll put a note card with it saying your family has provided it on loan. You could leave it today if you like, and I'd be happy to give you a receipt."

Andy glanced at me. "Yeah, let's do that."

I nodded my head. "That would be cool Andy," I said.

"Is there anything else?" asked Mr. Majors.

"One last thing," I said. "We brought a few pieces from a set of china we found." I put the plate and dish on his desk.

Mr. Majors examined them one at a time, noted the wording printed on the base of each, and then looked up. "These probably date from the 1960s, and were manufactured in great quantities at that time. You would have found them in many households. Unfortunately, they're not worth much from an historical perspective or a financial one."

"Oh that's ok, we're not disappointed," Andy said. "We just wanted to know."

"I must say it warms my heart to see young people interested in items like this."

"Yeah, it is kind of interesting, especially since it all belonged to my family over time. Thank you for your time Mr. Majors," said Andy.

"You're most welcome kids. If you have more questions, please feel free to ask. Do you want to leave the dress then?"

"Yes," said Andy. Andy left his contact information and shared a little more about the house and his family history. Then we said goodbye to Mr. Majors and left.

Mrs. Evans eyed us suspiciously as we walked past her out the large front doors into the sunshine.

"Well," I said, "that was more interesting than I thought it would be."

"It was. It's kind of a shame more people aren't interested in that historical stuff, but at the same time, I couldn't deal with it all day," said Andy. "I sure didn't want to tell him I'm selling antiques on eBay. That might break his heart."

"I know what you mean. I got the impression you didn't want to tell him about Allie's story either."

"I don't know why exactly," he replied. "It just seems personal for some reason. Like we still need to process it more before we tell anyone. Also, if my mom wants to write something about it, we wouldn't want to steal her thunder."

"Yeah, I understand. It does feel like an unfinished story," I replied.

We drove through and got cheeseburgers and ate them on the trip back to Hardwick.

There was something I wanted to tell Andy, but I didn't know how to start. Finally I just said what I was thinking. "You're going to think this is stupid, but I've been wanting to tell you about it."

"Nothing you ever say is stupid Meg."

"Ok, but it's kind of weird."

"Weird how?"

"Well, most of the times I'm at your house, I have these vivid images of scenes around your house, only with slight differences." That didn't even sound to me like it made sense.

"What do you mean?"

"Well, it's like I'm picturing things I'm seeing through someone else's eyes, at different points in time. I think it's maybe through Allie's eyes, in her time." I looked at him.

He glanced from the road to me. "Well like what?"

"Well, like I had this flash of these beautiful sleek horses grazing in a very green field, back in April or so when everything was still very brown. And for a second, when I looked at the dresser in the attic, it was all polished and new. Am I losing it?"

"No, of course not. I don't know what to say though. Are you imagining how it would look, or is it different than that?"

"It doesn't feel like imagining, it's more like knowing. It's like recalling a memory. Like they are scenes I've been in before, not new things I'm just picturing."

"Wow, that is weird. Is it scary?"

"No, it hasn't been. It's like each memory comes with really warm feelings of safety and home and comfort. They're so vivid though. The first few times it happened, it really startled me. It even happened the very first day I came over." I paused. "And then I kind of got used to it. What do you think?"

He glanced sideways at me again. "Well, you know who raised me, right? I've grown up thinking nothing is out of the realm of possibility, you know that. Why not, you know? You're a feeling person, why wouldn't you pick up on past good memories of the place?"

He always knew the right thing to say. "Thanks, I was afraid it would freak you out."

"No." We drove in silence for a moment, eating the last of our fries. "Did you ever get one of these images of something interesting?"

"I don't know if you'd say they were interesting or not. The impressions were always of the exact same view I was looking at, but in different colors or with different details. So not really different views, but maybe different feelings or emotions about the same views. If that makes sense. Like for example, there was that old rotting saddle in the barn. I knew exactly what it looked like when it was new, and I could feel what it was like to rub saddle soap into the leather. I could even smell it. But I've never done anything like that in my life. It was so real though. And like, I've never had any big interest in horses, but it was like I could feel a wave of love for some horses that were nearby."

"You should tell my mom about this. It sounds really cool."

"I might at some point, but for now it feels kind of personal. And kind of embarrassing. But I wanted you to know it was happening. It seems important."

"You mean important that I know?"

"Yeah, I guess. Like it's part of us and your house, and all that. I don't know. I just wanted you to know."

"Well, thanks for telling me. You can tell me anything you know."

That evening as it was getting dark, we were in Andy's room listening to music and talking. There was a beautiful pool of moonlight reflected on the polished wood floor from the window.

"It's perfect, isn't it?" I asked.

"What?"

"The way the moonlight is coming in the window, soft music is playing, and your parents and sister are gone."

"Yeah, it is."

I crossed the room to where he was sorting through a stack of cds. He turned to look at me and I backed him up slowly until he was against the wall. He stood watching me, and I was stunned by how perfect his features were in the moonlight. His eyes were curious. I turned my face up to his and kissed him softly. I touched his face, ran my fingers through his hair, and our kisses became more urgent. I pressed my body against his and could feel how lean and strong he was. I ran my hands down his chest, put my arms around his waist, and pulled his hips against mine. I kissed him deeply, feeling the inside of his warm wet mouth with my tongue, and pulled him as close as I could get him.

He stopped me and held me back a few inches. "Where did that come from? What was that?"

"What do you mean?" I asked, not knowing quite how to respond.

His eyes were suddenly serious, and at the same time liquid blue with feeling.

"Meg, if you lead me there I will follow you." He paused and looked at me. I knew enough to know I was seeing desire in his eyes. I felt relieved because that was the same thing I was feeling. "But I will go there with you because I belong with you, I know that. This may sound funny coming from a guy and all, but I mean that for always. If you take us there, I want to know you belong to me too."

I couldn't believe what I was hearing. It was exactly what I wanted to hear, but more than I could have hoped for. He did feel the same about me as I felt about him. Then another portion of what he was saying hit me. Was he saying he had never had sex with anyone? I stammered, "you've never…?"

"No," he said softly.

"I just assumed…" I trailed off.

"No. It means a lot to me. It means forever to me. I will give you that if you ask." And he said more slowly, almost shyly, "I love you." He paused and looked at me. I was overwhelmed. "Before you take us there, I need you to understand you hold my heart in your hands. You can crush me if you choose. It has to mean forever to you too, or I can't take it."

His eyes reflected a slight fear of rejection, mixed with a smoldering and utmost seriousness.

"I know we're both having strong feelings tonight," he continued, "but we don't have to rush into this. You know I want you, I'm telling you I do, but I want you to be completely sure, and I don't want you to decide that right this minute."

"I love you too Andy, with my whole heart." I said, and I meant it like I'd never meant anything in my life. I realized he was right though, we didn't have to rush into anything. "I do want to go there with you Andy, and I do mean forever, but you're right, there's no need to rush either. We can have a lot of fun working up to it."

"That we can," he replied, as he ran his hands slowly down over my breasts.

24 FIREWORKS

For the hundredth time, I was examining the quilt. Something about it mesmerized me. Being in Andy's house, walking in the pasture and through the woods, holding the quilt; it was like I could feel Allie's presence, and a kinship to who she was. Was I just fascinated with her story, or was it more? My heart ached for what she must have gone though. I imagined that she must have felt about Wayne Collins the way I felt about Andy, and I couldn't stand the thought of being kept away from Andy. He meant everything to me. I wanted to be with him forever, and I knew Allie must have felt the same about Wayne. I would have made the same decision she had - I would sacrifice everything to be with Andy because I knew for certain that something was missing without him. But knowing that and acting on it would be a lot easier for me. In her time, running away with someone would have been completely scandalous and unacceptable, making their love all the more amazing.

I studied the squares of the quilt and imagined myself as Allie. I looked at the pictures on the fabric, and almost felt like I had made them myself. Strange though it seemed, I knew I was feeling what she must have been feeling. I couldn't take my eyes from the block of a tree with a swing hanging from its branches. I knew it was special, but I couldn't figure out why. The tree had to be out behind the stone wall - I could picture it there. Andy and I had walked all around in those woods and there was no swing, but I knew where it had to be. Only it wasn't. But maybe it had been.

"Andy!" I said excitedly.

"What?" he asked, looking up from his computer, a little alarmed.

"Let's go outside, I just had a thought."

"Uh oh, it's dangerous when you're thinking," he joked. "These old pots are doing great on Craig's List."

"Very funny," I said. "And good about the pots. I just want to look at something."

"Ok, let's go," he agreed.

I appreciated how he just went along with me, no matter how insane I must have seemed. We walked in the baking sun along the outside of the stone wall to what once would have been the corner of the wall, but where today it ended. The day was hot and humid, typical for summer in Hardwick. We were damp before we got to the edge of the woods.

"I know this wall turned off in that direction," I said, pointing. "I can just see it." I led Andy along the path in my mind that would have been the wall, against the largest of the trees. Where I felt the wall had to end I stopped. "There was a tree swing here Andy. I can see it in my mind perfectly."

Andy looked around and replied gently. "But there isn't a tree right here that would have been strong enough to hold one."

"Allie made other quilt blocks that represent real things, so why wouldn't that swing have been real?"

"Maybe it was," he replied, "but maybe it wasn't here. Why do you think it should be right here?"

"I don't know, it's just where I picture it." I walked around the area, and noticed there was a slight depression off to one side. I stood in the depression and started kicking at the ground. Then I bent down and dug with my hands, getting dirt under my fingernails. Sweat ran down my back from the effort and the heat. I found what I was looking for a few inches down in the soft ground.

"This is it Andy," I said excitedly. "There is a large stump buried here. This is the tree that had the swing, I know it is."

He walked over and helped me dig. "You're right. This *is* an old stump Meg. It sure could have been your tree."

"She loved this place, it drew her here. I think it was her private place to think."

He looked at me, and I knew I sounded crazy. He was being very sweet about it though.

"I know, there's no way I can know that. I just feel it. It makes sense to me. The images I keep telling you about are hers, they have to be."

We pondered the hole.

"Do you think I've lost my mind?" I asked.

"No," he replied slowly. "Living with my mom, I could never discount anyone's intuition. But why you? Why now?"

"I don't know," I admitted. "Maybe I'm the first person who has come along who can relate to her. Standing here, I can just imagine how it looked to her, and the picture is as real in my mind as what is really here. The swing would have hung over that spot that has a little less growth than the rest of the area. It makes me happy somehow to picture it, like I'm honoring her memory or something."

Andy considered that a moment. "This is a very peaceful place. I think if there were a wall blocking it from the view of the house, and a nice swing to sit on, I would have come here," he offered.

"What do you think happened to her?" I asked.

"I don't know. It was so long ago. She was probably never the same after Wayne died. I wouldn't be, if I lost you."

How was it he always knew the right thing to say? I put my arms around his neck and pressed my lips to his, then we held hands as we walked slowly back toward the house. It was time for me to go to work again.

I was finishing up the roast beef on rye with catsup for my regular customer Pat Simmons, when Andy walked up to the counter. I smiled at him past Mr. Simmons, finished squirting the catsup, wrapped up the sandwich, and handed it over. "There you are, your usual. Have a great day," I said.

"Thanks Megan, looks good."

"Hey there," said Andy.

"Hi! What a nice surprise to see you!"

"Do you realize this Saturday is the 4th of July?" Andy asked. "It's only two days away."

"Wow, it is, isn't it? Is your family going to the park?"

"Yeah we are, is yours?"

"Yeah, we are too. It's a Hardwick tradition. My dad likes to see all his clients in public, and it's nice to see everyone from school."

"Have you been going to the picnic your whole life?" Andy asked.

"I guess I have. You make it sound so small town. I guess it is small town," I added with a smile.

"It is, but it's kind of cool. I've never lived anywhere with traditions like that. Do you want to watch the fireworks together?"

"Absolutely," I said, knowing I didn't need any real fireworks when I had him.

"Good, I'm looking forward to it. Can I have a sandwich?" Andy asked.

"Of course, I make the best sandwiches in town!" I told him. I made him what had become his usual - turkey with Swiss, sprouts, tomatoes and mustard on a wheat roll, as he watched. I wrapped it and took it to the counter, where I leaned forward for a kiss. Andy grinned, and leaned in. He stopped an inch from my face, looked deep into my eyes, and ever so slowly moved in to finish the kiss. I always thought it sounded stupid when people said something made them go weak in the knees, but now I could relate. I finally pulled away, and held out the sandwich. He took it with a sly smile.

"I hope you don't treat all your customers so nicely," he teased.

"Only the very best one," I assured him.

He grinned. "See you soon." He turned and walked away, and I watched his cute little butt as he went.

Picnic day arrived, and as I helped my mom pack food into a cooler, I thought about how it wasn't that much different than what Allie had described herself doing with her mother on this day 150 years ago, in her diary.

"Meg, how are you and Andy doing? You are sure spending a lot of time together."

"I know Mom. We're doing great. He's my best friend. We're having a lot of fun working on cleaning out his house and making discoveries."

"Ok. Well you know I trust you to know what you're doing, but I was hoping you wouldn't get so serious about someone again so soon. Don't neglect your girlfriends, ok?"

"I know Mom. This is just different. It's a whole different kind of serious than I ever had with Jeff. It feels very right."

"I know. I love you sweetie."

"I know Mom. I love you too."

My family arrived at the picnic around three o'clock, and my brothers instantly ran off to play soccer with their friends. I spotted Kayla, and walked over to her. Her face lit up when she saw me.

"Hi Meg! Where's Andy? Are you still together? When did you get here? How is your summer going?"

I thought for a minute. "He'll be here. Yes. Just now. Great and busy. Did I answer all your questions?" I took a deep breath as if the effort had exhausted me. "What about you, what have you been up to?"

"Oh, just working at the grocery store, mostly bagging. I've spent some time with Rachel and Em, but mostly just working and helping out around home. So you're still with Andy, huh?"

I blushed. “Most definitely. This is for real Kayla. He is everything I could ever want in a guy. Does that sound too corny? It’s really how I feel. He’s like nobody I’ve ever met.”

Kayla looked at me. “Oh girl, you’ve got it bad.”

I smiled. “I know. I won’t even deny it.”

“You’re happy though?” she asked.

“Very.”

“Can you believe we’re seniors now? Remember when it seemed so far away? I’ve been spending a lot of time filling out applications for colleges. I think I’m narrowing to teaching. What do you think?”

“Kayla you’d be a great teacher. You have such a way with kids. You know my little brothers adore you.”

“I think I would really enjoy it. What about you, have you made any decisions about school?”

“Well, I wouldn’t tell my parents this, but I am sort of waiting to see what Andy is doing. Not that I would follow him just anywhere, but I really haven’t decided exactly what I want to do, and I am really serious about a long term relationship with him. I don’t want to be the type of girl that follows a guy around of course. I don’t ever want to be dependent on someone. I mean, I’ll be serious about school and everything, but I am not going to pretend it doesn’t matter what he does either. It does matter, a lot. I want to do whatever I can to make sure we can make it.”

Kayla considered that. “I know what you mean about parents. They don’t like to hear about serious relationships, and heaven forbid sex, or drinking, or any other adult stuff. I think it’s hard for them to see us grow up.”

“I know,” I said. “I know. I’m going to go see if my parents have broken out the food yet. Want to come?”

“I’ll be over later. I’ve gotta check on my parents too. You know, can’t leave them unsupervised for too long,” she joked.

“I’m sure I’ll see you later then,” I replied, and turned back toward our blanket. As I approached our blanket, I got a pleasant surprise. My mom was sitting cross legged on the blanket, talking with Andy and Samantha. Andy was sitting with his back against the tree we had spread our blanket under. They all looked entirely comfortable with each other. Andy and his sister just had a way of being at ease with anyone. As I walked up the three of them continued talking like old friends.

Andy’s eyes lit up when he saw me. He had such an ability to simply melt me on the spot. I hoped my mom couldn’t see what jelly he made of me. I leaned down and kissed him quickly, and then sat next to him.

“I think India is a possibility.” Andy was obviously continuing the conversation. “They have deformities because they can’t afford medical care, just like any other poor country, but people also have deformities their own families have inflicted on them so they will be more pitiful beggars. I would really like to help people like that.”

My mom replied. “You know it will take a great deal of bravery, right? I mean, it’ll be very heartbreaking and emotional. And overwhelming.”

“Oh Andy’s up for it,” Samantha said. “I could never do it though, it would be too depressing. I wouldn’t mind helping homeless people with legal issues and stuff like that, but dealing with the kind of poverty they have in third world nations – that's a whole different thing. No matter how many you helped, the line of others waiting for help would never end."

"I know," Andy replied. "I think I would have to meet regularly with a psychologist to stay balanced. But you know that story about the starfish, right?"

"I don't," I stated. We all turned our faces to him.

"Well, it's something like this. An old man is walking on the beach, and a big storm had washed starfish up all over the beach. He comes upon a little boy who is grabbing the starfish and throwing them back in the ocean. The old man tells the little boy that he couldn't possibly make a difference, since there are thousands on the beach. The little boy tosses one back into the ocean and says, 'it made a difference to that one.' That's how I feel – of course I can't change the world, but I want to make a difference to some of the world."

My mom's face glowed. She would never question what I saw in Andy. I looked at Samantha and could see she was proud of her little brother, even though she also wanted to tease him. She punched him in the arm.

"I do think it would be very rewarding Andy," my mom said. "And I think it's highly unusual for someone your age to be thinking about that kind of career."

Andy was clearly embarrassed. He was usually quite modest about his plans and his intelligence. He changed the subject.

"Meg, I saw some of the guys from school setting up a volleyball court over on the other side of the common. Did I tell you I like volleyball?"

At 5'11" and being from California, I was not surprised. "No you didn't tell me, but I guess I should have figured you would. You're probably good, aren't you?"

"Well, not too bad," he replied.

"And you?" I asked Samantha.

"Well maybe," she conceded. She was a good 5'8."

"Let's go," I said, watching Andy's beautiful smile spread across his face.

As we approached the volleyball court, we were spotted instantly. Matt called out, "we'll take Andy!" He must have figured it the same way I did – the California beach bum kid had to be good.

"Who's the chick?" Mitch Rollins asked me in a whisper, looking at Samantha.

"Andy's sister Samantha," I said quickly.

"Sam will be on our side too," Andy told his team. They were only too happy to allow her based on her looks and size alone. Samantha was clearly enjoying being ogled by all the high school boys. Andy took off his shirt and joined in the game. I openly stared at his smooth tan chest with his nicely defined muscles, that little trail of hair leading down from his belly button, and those well formed biceps and blonde shaggy hair. He was a perfect California beach kid. He did not disappoint anyone either – his first hit slammed onto the grass on the other side. I spotted Emilee sitting on the other side of the court, and walked over to her and plunked down.

"He's gorgeous Meg," she said.

"I know. It still amazes me," I replied.

"And he only looks at you. Is that his sister? She looks just like him. Gorgeous."

I smiled. "Yes. She's actually nice too. Who are you here with?"

"Scott Watterson. We've gone on a few dates. I kind of like him."

"A guy? That's great! Yeah, Scott is cute. I remember him, but I don't know him very well. He's two years older than us, right?"

"Yeah," she replied. "He's at UMass."

"What do your parents think about you dating a college guy?" I asked.

"They're not thrilled. But they also understand there aren't many guys around here, and I've told them I understand he's going back to school and everything."

"So you're going to try not to get serious with him?" I asked.

"In my head that's true," she replied. "But my heart says differently. He's so much more mature than the guys our age. Most of them anyway," she said while looking at Andy.

"I know what you mean. Still, be careful. How serious are you?"

She gave me a solemn look.

"Oh," I said. Her look had said it all. "So you…"

"Yeah. We've been together," she said. "Do you think less of me?"

"No of course not Em. I just don't want you to get hurt. I think it's ok if you found the right person and you love him. It's a special gift."

"Thanks Megan. I don't want to have any regrets about it. Even if our relationship doesn't go anywhere, he is special, and our time together has been wonderful. Have you and Andy?"

I blushed. I would prefer not to talk about this, but it was one of those things you had to be honest about with your friends. "No, but I think we will. He's actually a little old fashioned about it."

"Oh Meg, is there anything that's not perfect about him?" Emilee exclaimed.

I beamed. "Nope, haven't found anything."

As the volleyball game ended, a sweaty Andy plopped down next to me. "Water," he croaked. "Hi Emilee." He flashed her a perfect white smile.

"I'm going to check on Mom and Dad," said Samantha, barely looking sweaty.

"Cool," Andy replied to her.

I could see Emilee wasn't immune to Andy's charm in the way she returned his smile. I winked at her. "Let's go find some water," I said to Andy. I stood and held out my hand. Andy gave me his, and I pulled him to his feet.

After a dinner of fried chicken, potato salad and baked beans, we hung out and watched some of the older people playing badminton. As it started to grow dark, people strategically placed their blankets so as best to see the fireworks.

Andy said, "Let's go find a spot as far away from both sets of parents as possible."

"Absolutely," I replied. "Do you think we should ask Sam to go with us?"

"No, she's busy with my mom. Besides, my mom is loving all this time with her only daughter. Don't take that away from them," he said in a mock serious voice. I could see he wanted to be alone with me, and was secretly very pleased.

We crossed to the far side of the common and found a nice spot a little hidden in the trees. A clear view of the fireworks was not our primary goal. Obviously a lot of the people our age had the same thing in mind. We laid our blanket down and sprawled on it, watching the darkening sky. I wished time would stand still. I felt perfectly at peace and relaxed laying there with my head on Andy's stomach. As it got dark, we moved closer and closer. We lay pressed against each other kissing and finding ways to touch each other's bodies that couldn't be seen by the people around us. The nearest people were about twenty feet away, and in the dark we knew they couldn't see much. As we touched each other on the outside of our clothes, I knew there was nothing better in the entire world than feeling his body against mine. In a more private place, what we were doing would have gone a lot farther. In a way, it made it safer to tease each other with promises of what could be, knowing that the promises couldn't be fulfilled this night. I couldn't think of any better word to describe it than 'delicious.'

As the fireworks started, my body was feeling just as much on fire as the incredible explosions in the sky. I never wanted the night to end, but I also knew we had our whole lives to continue the story. I turned and laid my head on Andy's chest as we both lay on our backs looking at the sky. The fireworks brought back memories of my childhood, and I remembered how magical they had always seemed. Tonight they were more magical than ever.

25 RUSTY NAILS

The next day found me at Andy's house again. There was something I just loved about being there. Him of course, but also the feel of the place. As I sat on his bed waiting for him to finish his latest transactions on Craig's List, I held the quilt, touching the decaying fabric and thinking about Allie. Suddenly it hit me like cold water. Then I felt stupid for not having thought of it before.

"Oh my God," I said out loud.

"What Meg?" asked Andy, a little alarmed.

"I get it. It's a map. It's *the* map." The quilt was sitting on my lap as I looked up at him.

"What is, the quilt?"

"Yes." My words spilled out. "If Allie wanted to keep everything about Wayne secret, it was a great way to express her thoughts, tell her story, and make a record of the location of the object. Nobody would have understood that the quilt had more meaning than just an ordinary patchwork project. Even when your great great whatever he was researched it later, a man of his generation would have thought it was just a dumb quilt and wouldn't have given it a second thought. I understand why she did it that way. It kept her from feeling like she was crazy and it was more private even than writing it in a diary. She didn't want to keep it all bottled inside her. The quilt was real and she could touch it - it would have been a reminder and memento when she couldn't share any of the story with anyone, probably for her entire life."

"So how do we read the map then?" asked Andy.

"The story is right here in the pictures." I gestured toward my lap. "It's so obvious now that I'm thinking about it this way. Whatever she hid is in sight of where the swing was, against where the wall would have been. See this block that shows a stone wall?" I pointed. "It has a reddish stone at the bottom among the black and gray ones that make up the rest of the wall. I bet it used to be a brighter red, but faded over time. See how it's faintly heart shaped? I bet there never was a real red stone in the wall. The red stone is just an indicator of a place in the wall. It's meant to show where along the wall she hid something. In the picture, over the top of the wall you can see the hill. That hill is the same view we saw when we stood where the swing would have been."

"It all makes sense. Meg, we have to look for it!" Andy was getting excited now.

"I know. I think the possibilities are that it was hidden behind a stone in the wall, in which case someone would have found it when they moved the stones, or that it was buried close by and maybe still is buried there. We can't just go out there and dig everywhere though." I thought for a minute. "I mean we could, but that could take a really long time. Do you think we could rent a metal detector? If this thing was an object someone put in her pocket, maybe it was metal. A metal detector would work then, right?"

"Yeah, that's a great idea. I knew you were the smart one," Andy said.

I was excited now. "There's an equipment rental shop in town. Let's go see what it takes to rent one," I said.

We drove to ABC Rents It, trying hard to contain our excitement as we walked in the door.

"Hi Mr. Nelson," I said to the little man behind the counter. "Remember me? Megan? Scott Burke's daughter?"

"Yes of course, hello Megan. What can I do for you two today?" replied Mr. Nelson.

I looked at Andy, and then back at Mr. Nelson. "We want to rent a metal detector."

Mr. Nelson's face dropped a little and he looked slightly uncomfortable. "I see. Are either of you eighteen?"

"No," I replied, looking at him expectantly.

"Well, I'm truly sorry, but renting equipment requires a legal adult to sign a rental contract, and I also need a credit card to secure it with. Maybe one of your parents can help out. We do have two metal detectors available right now." He saw the disappointment in my face and added, "Not that you would damage it, but we need an adult to be responsible in case anything goes wrong, and to assume any liabilities if you get hurt."

"We understand," said Andy. "Thank you."

"Yes thank you," I added.

We turned and slowly walked out of the shop.

"What's our plan B?" I asked.

"I think my mom will help us," he replied. "But I don't want to tell her the whole story yet, in case we're totally wrong."

"Yeah, I feel pretty certain about it, but even if I'm completely right and the quilt is a map, that doesn't mean there's still something buried out there. I don't want to sound insane to your mom, at least until there is a way to prove I really know what I'm talking about. I don't want her to feel like she has to humor me, while thinking I'm an idiot."

"She'd never think you're an idiot, but it *is* pretty weird how you figured this all out."

"How we did, you mean," I said.

"Yeah, but mostly you. All the same, if anyone would understand, it would be her. There has to be a reason you've been having these images popping into your head. She would puzzle over it at first, but then she'd say it was supposed to happen and wouldn't be surprised at all. If it does work out, we'll tell her the whole story. She'll love it. It totally matches with her concept of how life works."

"Let's just tell your mom that we keep finding interesting stuff all over the property. That's the truth. Remember the horse bit we found sticking out of the field? It might actually be interesting to see what else is buried around there. Then, if we find something, we'll tell her. At least I won't feel so stupid that way. Do you think I'm crazy?"

"No," replied Andy. "And my mom won't either. But I understand how you feel, so we'll just wait and see what we find."

As we drove up to the house, we saw Mrs. Garrett dressed in her workout clothes, planting flowers along the path leading up to the house. I hoped I was as energetic when I reached her age. Not that she was so old, but she was always doing something.

"They're very pretty Mrs. Garrett," I said, gesturing to the planted flowers.

"Thank you Megan, I thought so when I saw them, and knew this was the perfect place for them. What are you two up to this beautiful day?" She sat back on her haunches and looked up at us.

"We had an interesting idea Mom, and we need your help with it," said Andy.

"Oh? What is it?" she asked.

"Well, we found a rusty horse bit in the field, and it got us to thinking that there might be all kinds of interesting things buried around here. We want to rent a metal detector and check it out."

"That does sound interesting," she said. "I bet you're right, because people have lived right here for over two hundred years."

"But the thing is," Andy continued, "the rental shop won't rent to us because we're not adults. We were just there. So we need an adult to rent it for us."

"And you want me to help with that?" she asked.

"Yes, would you?" Andy asked.

"Sure. It could be cool. I'll tell you what. I only have two more flowers to plant, which will take about five minutes. If you'd run in and get my purse and car keys, we can go do it now and be back before I need to leave for my yoga class."

"Thank you Mom, that would be great," said Andy, grinning at me.

"Always happy to help with learning opportunities," she smiled. "You guys should be sure to look very carefully all around the barn. There could be lots of things around there. I bet you find lots of rusty nails and stuff like that, but you never know."

"That's a good idea Mom. We'll look there and around the house. We want to look out in the fields too," Andy added.

"That was fast," said Mr. Nelson with a smile, as the three of us entered his shop. He disappeared into the back room, and returned with a metal detector. It looked like a weed whacker. He showed us how to turn it on and off, and how it beeped when it was waved over anything metallic. It looked pretty easy. Andy's mom signed the contract and gave him her credit card. We promised to return the machine by the next day at noon, and Andy carried it out to the car and loaded it into the trunk. Mrs. Garrett drove us back to their house while Andy and I sat in the back seat and giggled like excited school kids.

As we got out of the car Mrs. Garrett said, "Have fun you two. Do you have on sunscreen?"

"Yes Mom," replied Andy.

"Let me know if you find anything interesting," she said over her shoulder as she walked toward the house.

We put the metal detector in a wheelbarrow along with a couple of shovels.

"Do you want to go out there right away?" asked Andy.

"Yes. I can't stand the suspense," I replied.

"I know. Me either. That was a dumb question," said Andy.

We headed into the field and picked our way across it to where the stone wall would have been. I went to stand in the indentation where I pictured the swing. The moment of truth had arrived and I was suddenly nervous. What if I was entirely wrong about all of this? I knew I would be very disappointed, even though nothing would have changed. I tried not to think about it, and at the same time hoped that if I was wrong, Andy wouldn't think I was an idiot.

I turned to face the hills, looking in the direction of where the wall would have been. It still felt very right. Andy watched me, and I nodded hopefully at him.

Andy shouldered the metal detector and turned it on. He started walking in a grid pattern, all around where I thought the wall would have been. I picked out a shovel and watched him walking back and forth. Very quickly, the metal detector beeped. Andy stopped. I pushed the shovel into the ground and dug up a chunk of dirt, and then scattered it over the ground. I crumbled the dirt though my fingers and found the metallic object - a rusty nail.

"Well," Andy said, "we know it works."

I noticed the blue of his eyes and the shine in his hair. "You know, there really could be cool stuff all over this place, even if we don't find whatever it is we're looking for," I said.

We found six more nails all in the same area and tossed them in our wheelbarrow. Andy examined one more closely. He had a cute smudge on his nose.

"This might actually be cool," he said.

I gave him a skeptical look, not sure whether he was serious or only trying to preserve my feelings.

"No really," he said. "I think these might be old fashioned handmade nails. That would make them at least a little bit special."

He was such a good sport.

"Let's go over there," I pointed. "Closer to the woods."

I followed as he walked slowly in the direction I had pointed, swinging the metal detector back and forth. I glanced past him, and had a vivid image of the stone wall. It was as if I could actually see it, and then it was gone. I felt in my heart we were getting close to something important.

As Andy came within about two feet of the imaginary wall, the metal detector beeped. I threw the extra shovel on the ground and started to dig.

Nothing.

Andy picked up the other shovel and dug with me.

Nothing.

I sifted through the pile of dirt with my hands, in case there was something really small setting off the metal detector.

Nothing.

"Try the metal detector again," I suggested.

"Ok," he said, picking it up and turning it on.

He ran the metal detector over the hole we had dug, and it made a clear beeping sound. I dug some more, adding to my pile of dirt. Andy dug too, and as he pushed the shovel into the ground, it stopped against something solid. I looked in the hole, and saw something dark colored. A rock? Something metallic?

We carefully moved the dirt away from the object, and saw that it was a small wooden box. We dug carefully around the sides of it and pulled it out of the hole, placing it on our dirt pile. The wood was decayed and the box appeared quite fragile.

We stared at the box in disbelief.

"What if this is really it?" I asked.

"It has to be," said Andy.

The clasp was completely rusted over, so Andy wrenched the top of the little box sideways, and the lid broke off. Inside was something wrapped in shards of what must have been fabric.

"Go ahead," Andy said.

I took a deep breath. I pulled the strips of fabric apart, and found a large single coin. I felt utter disbelief, even though it made perfect sense. It had to be Allie's coin. There was no other explanation. Andy and I stared at each other in amazement.

The silver coin was heavy in my hand. I turned it over and examined it. It was not like any coin I had ever seen. One side had a person sitting on something and looking off to the side, with the year 1861 stamped on the bottom. The other side had something that looked like a shield with stars and stripes on it and a little tree on top. It said 'Confederate States of America' across the top, and Half Dol. on the bottom. I dropped it into Andy's hand.

"I just don't believe this," he said.

I looked up into his crystal blue eyes, which were filled with wonder. "I don't either. I mean, I saw it so clearly in the quilt and in my mind, but for it to really be true blows my mind. I think we found it, after all this time."

"It's heavy," he said, as he turned it over. "You know what?"

"No, what?"

"Nobody else ever would have found it Meg. Nobody would have figured out the quilt was the map, or put that together with the story in the diary."

I couldn't help but think about Allie. "I wonder why she never went back for it. I wonder if she even remembered it when she was old. I bet she did. How could she not have told anyone about it after twenty, thirty or fifty years?" I felt sad for Allie. "What are you going to do with it?" I asked.

"Don't you mean what are 'we' going to do with it?" Andy asked.

"Well, it's your family's heirloom, not mine," I replied.

"Yes, but you are a key part of the story. Without you, it would have stayed lost forever. It's our treasure, not mine."

I was touched. "Thank you, but your parents might not feel the same way. It has to be valuable."

"Ok, I'll grant you that," Andy said, "but we'll see. Maybe we should sell it, if it's really what we think it is. It's cool and all, but logically it really shouldn't have any sentimental value to our family – Allie lived so many generations ago, and we know almost nothing about her. It has a lot more value in helping to pay for college, or something like that. It has to be real, how could it not be?"

"Yeah, there has to be something good that would come of it, after all the pain it caused Allie," I said.

I had an unreal sort of feeling, like there was still something Allie wanted me to understand. But what?

"I'm sure I'll be able to find out pretty quickly," Andy said. "I know all these web sites so well now."

"Let's go look it up," I said.

Andy hesitated. "Let's let it sink in a bit first Meg. I think we should keep it a secret for a while. The whole story is kind of unreal. Unless we're ready to tell my mom, and I'm not, we need to use the metal detector for at least a while longer. Maybe we'll find something else interesting."

"That makes sense, ok," I said.

I agreed with Andy that we needed to keep the coin secret for a while, though I wasn't sure quite why. We wanted to confirm it was Allie's coin before we told anyone the whole story, but it was more than that. In order for anyone to make sense of how we came to find the coin, we would have to explain the events leading up to it, the diary, the quilt, and the research done by Ellis Bruce. It was a lot to think about. Andy put the coin in his pocket, and I put the pieces of the box and the bits of cloth in the wheelbarrow with the shovels and nails.

We spent the next few hours scouting around the property, mostly by the barn. We didn't find much else interesting, just some scrap iron, bits of unidentifiable metal and more nails. After a few hours we were hot and tired, and were not interested in searching any longer. We left the metal detector by the car and trudged into the house. The coin was in Andy's pocket.

"Did you find anything?" Mrs. Garrett called from the kitchen, as we came through the back door.

We flopped onto the bar stools by the counter. Andy pulled some rusty nails from his pocket and put them on the counter while Mrs. Garrett poured us some lemonade. She was still dressed in her yoga clothes. I gulped thirstily as she gingerly picked up a few nails.

"Hmm," she said.

"They look like old fashioned homemade ones, don't you think?" Andy asked.

"Yes, they certainly could be," she replied. "Not much else, huh?"

"Well," Andy said, "We found other kinds of metal and stuff. It's just way too hot to keep going. We got kind of tired of it."

"I'm glad you tried though, it was a good idea. More for your history project at school next fall, right?" She winked. We groaned in unison.

She laughed and continued. "Are you ready to take the metal detector back to the shop? We can grab some hamburgers on the way back. It's getting close to dinner time anyway. That way I won't have to figure out what to make. Your dad won't be home until tomorrow, so we're on our own anyway," she said to Andy. "Oh wait, supper, right Meg?"

"Yes, it's supper around here," I smiled.

"Nobody in California uses that word," said Andy. "It sounds old fashioned or something."

"Yeah, I guess it does," I agreed.

"Anyway, yeah we're done and we're hungry," Andy told his mom.

I nodded. "Yes, thank you Mrs. Garrett."

When we arrived at the shop Mr. Nelson asked, "Did you kids find anything interesting?"

Andy replied. "We found lots of nails and bits of metal, if you consider that interesting. The metal detector sure found everything metal in sight. The nails might be home made ones."

"Yes, that wouldn't surprise me," said Mr. Nelson. "Too bad you can't program it to find only the good stuff. Some people make a career of searching beaches and parks and for valuable things other people have lost. Me, I think that sounds a bit boring. I mean, how much could you possibly find of value, for all the time you'd spend?"

"Yeah, I know what you mean," Andy said, and winked at me.

We were finally starting to get our energy back after having baked in the sun for so many hours. We collapsed into the car.

"Feeling hungry guys?" asked Mrs. Garrett.

"Starved," I said.

Andy smiled. "Ditto."

We stopped at Friendly's and got cheeseburgers, fries and cokes.

"What are you two doing tonight?" asked Mrs. Garrett.

"Oh, just hanging out at home. I have some stuff to finish up on line," Andy said.

"Sounds good. I have a good book I'm going to finish," said Mrs. Garrett. "Are you guys done?"

"Yes," said Andy, and he started to stack the trash on the tray.

"Thank you for dinner Mrs. Garrett," I said.

"Oh, you're very welcome Meg," she said.

We couldn't wait to get back to Andy's computer. When we got to his house, we immediately went up to his room. Andy googled 'confederate half dollar' and we quickly learned that the National Numismatic Association had one in its collection in New York City. Within a few minutes on their web site, the picture popped up. Andy put the coin on his desk. We looked from it to the picture on the screen. It was a perfect match.

"Unbelievable," said Andy, as he scrolled down.

26 PLANS

"We have to tell my mom. And we have to figure out what it's worth," said Andy. Do you think it's really possible it could be worth a lot?"

"Andy, look at it. It doesn't look worn or anything. There's no way it could be fake – nobody would ever have found it if we hadn't followed clues that nobody else understood. It's been buried for more than a hundred years. We can trace the history to exactly who had it and when. It's a little tarnished, but I bet it will clean up to look as good as new." My mind was spinning a thousand miles an hour. This was so exciting, but yet surreal. It was an incredible treasure, but the money it could bring could be life changing. For someone, anyway. Would it alter our lives? Allie's sorrow popped into my head, as if I had lived it myself. A shiver of dread went through me. This heavy coin had been bad luck for her. "It won't be for us," I said softly.

"What?" asked Andy.

"Huh?" I asked, jolted from my train of thought.

“You said ‘it won’t be for us’ – what did you mean? What won’t be what for us?” Those indigo eyes looked at me quizzically.

I threw myself at him, wrapped my arms around his neck and nuzzled my face into his hair. He pulled me close and kissed my cheek. That feeling of being pressed against him, secure in his arms, was all I needed. My fears melted away. This was a different day and time, and that coin was only an object made of metal. We weren’t facing the kinds of choices Allie had faced. All our options were good ones. I was embarrassed to tell him what I’d been thinking, as if saying it out loud would somehow jinx everything.

“What is it Meg, do you think we shouldn’t tell my mom?”

“No. No, it’s not that.” I paused.

“What then?”

I looked into Andy’s curious and trusting face. I knew when my eyes locked on his that I didn’t want to hide my feelings from him on this or anything, no matter how dumb I might seem. He was my best friend, it was that simple. I took a breath.

“I know it’s stupid,” I said. “But I was just thinking about all the pain this coin caused Allie, and how I didn’t want it to bring us bad luck too. I was trying to tell myself that logically it’s just a thing, and it doesn’t have luck, good or bad. But wouldn’t that mean I would be discounting everything that led us to finding it in the first place? You know, feelings, intuition? A sense of how things are supposed to be?”

"What about this?" Andy mused. "Maybe it's more like we were supposed to find it and have good luck, to make up for all the trouble it brought Allie."

"I like your story better," I admitted. I knew telling him had been the right thing. He hadn't made me feel stupid at all. Even though I felt relief at that, this was all a bit overwhelming. Feelings were welling up inside me, and I struggled to put them into words. "The real truth is," I said slowly, "that no treasure or amount of money or anything else would be worth having you taken away from me." A tear rolled down my cheek. I couldn't believe I was crying. Where was this emotion coming from? Allie's pain felt so real to me. The thought of anything happening to Andy paralyzed me with fear.

"Megan, that's not going to happen to us. It's just a dumb coin. If we get some money for it and we can do good things with it – great. If it's not worth anything or my family wants to keep it or something, then it was just an adventure we shared. We solved a mystery everyone before us failed to solve. That's pretty incredible, don't you think?"

Andy pushed me back a tiny bit and locked his eyes onto mine. I felt myself falling into the crystal blue, and everything seemed ok again. He lowered his face to mine, and a little shiver ran through me as his mouth grazed mine in a gentle kiss. I closed my eyes, drinking in his closeness, his warmth, and the feel of his body against mine. I breathed a sigh of relief as his touch made all the tension go away. Then I wanted more.

I wanted to pull him closer. I felt an urgent need to get him to express physically how he felt about me. I needed him and to know he was mine. I kissed his neck. His skin was soft, but like all of his body, the muscles underneath were firm. I put my hands under his shirt, and moved them slowly up his chest, feeling the heat of his body. It was like touching a living breathing piece of art. A perfect sculpture of a male. The sound he made was exactly what I wanted. It wasn't a groan really, but a low 'don't do this to me – but I love it' kind of sound. He kissed me hard on the lips, and my mouth opened as his did too, as our kiss became even deeper. I felt him stiffen as he pulled away from me.

"What you do to me Meg. I've never felt this way about anyone before. Does everyone in love say that?"

I laughed, delighted with his words. "I don't know. I don't care. I just want to hear you say it again."

"Which part?" he teased.

"Any of it. All of it," I said.

"I never want to be without you Meg. It's that simple. You light me on fire."

I didn't know what to say. He always came up with something that was even more than I hoped for. His words were a precious gift. I could feel my love for him growing by leaps and bounds, just when I couldn't have imagined I could feel any more for him.

"Some time soon," he said, "we should figure out a way to spend some serious time alone."

I knew what he meant. He meant alone in a way we wouldn't want any parents to interrupt. I sighed. "Yeah, your mom and sister are right downstairs, aren't they?" It wasn't really a question, only a statement of fact.

"Yes, and though I love touching you, I really don't want my mom to guess we've been all over each other right under her nose. I don't want to answer any questions about it, and I know she's already curious."

Just the thought of it made me feel embarrassed. "Yeah, I'd be mortified if she brought it up in front of me."

Andy laughed. "Well, I don't think she'd do that. She'd never embarrass you on purpose. But she has no qualms about cornering me once you're gone. And neither will Sam."

"Yeah, my mom would do the same. I wonder what your mom is thinking."

"Probably the truth. They have to have some idea. They were teenagers once."

"I know, but it's kind of weird to think about, isn't it? I can't imagine either one of them ever feeling the way we do, but I suppose they did. Or still do." Yuk. I put that thought out of my head.

"Are you ready to tell her about the coin?" Andy asked.

"Yeah, are you?"

We clomped down the stairs to find Mrs. Garrett and Samantha reading magazines in the living room. They looked up as we came into the room.

"Mom, Megan and I have something we want to talk to you about," Andy said. We stood there fidgeting nervously.

Her face clouded. "Is one of you in trouble?"

"Should I leave?" asked Sam.

"No, no," Andy said quickly. "We just need to get your advice about something. Can you come up to my room? Do you want to come too Sam?"

"Sure," said Mrs. Garrett in a puzzled tone, as she marked her place in her magazine and put it aside. They followed us up the stairs and into Andy's room, where Mrs.

Garrett sat in Andy's desk chair and his sister leaned against the desk. We sat on the bed facing them. Andy's mom was still looking at us like we were going to tell her I was pregnant or something.

"Mom, it's not bad, it's exciting."

She relaxed a little, and looked at Andy. "Ok, what is it? And why couldn't you tell me downstairs?"

Andy took a breath. "Well we wanted to talk here, because there are some things we want to show you. Both of you. I just don't know where to begin." They watched Andy. "Ok. The other day, when we had the metal detector, we found something. We think it's worth a lot of money, but we don't know exactly what to do with it now."

"I don't understand," she started.

"What?" demanded Sam. "Tell us!"

I went to the desk beside her, and put the sock with the coin in it into her hand. She picked up the toe of the sock and the coin dropped into her palm. She slowly turned it over. "It's a coin. You just found this? Where was it, by the barn? What kind of coin is it?" She handed the coin to Andy's mom.

"It looks like a silver dollar almost, but not like one I've ever seen. I think they stopped making those in the fifties or so," said Mrs. Garrett.

I started. "We're almost certain it's a Confederate Half Dollar, and that it's very rare. That is what's stamped on the coin anyway.

"Yes I see it," Mrs. Garrett said as she examined the coin. "But why would we have one buried in our yard? Are you saying somebody lost something as valuable as this, and now you just happened to find it buried in our yard?"

Andy smiled. "It's going to sound like that Mom, but there's more to the story. Ok. So let me back up to the beginning. You know I've been going through all the stuff in the attic, right?"

"Yes, and selling it on eBay and Craig's list."

"And getting really dirty and sweaty," Sam added with a smile.

"Yeah, right. Well, Megan's been helping me too," Andy said.

"Yes, I know," said Mrs. Garrett. "Together you've made a lot of progress on all the junk around here."

Andy continued. "Well, one of the things I found was an old safe. I probably should have told you then, but we had no idea what was in it, and it could have been nothing. At the time I found it, it wasn't any more or less interesting than anything else I'd found. Anyway, Meg and I spent about an hour trying all those old keys on the lock, and we actually found one that worked. I could have cut the lock off, but it was cool that a key worked."

Samantha raised her eyebrows. "Seriously? Why didn't you tell us?" she exclaimed.

Mrs. Garrett asked, "Was there something in the safe? Not the coin though, right? You said you found it with the metal detector."

"Right, not the coin. The safe had an old diary and some papers in it," Andy replied.

"An old diary?" his mom repeated.

"Yeah, the diary of your great great great Aunt. Some number of 'greats' anyway. Her name was Allison Bruce. She kept it right after the time of the civil war."

"I can't believe you didn't tell me. This is fascinating. Can I see it?"

"Me too?" added Sam.

"Yeah of course, but the interesting part is that the diary is very short. It's a really sad story, and the diary ends when the story ends. Allison, Allie she was called, secretly fell in love with a guy who came to town even though she was engaged to a local farmer. It seems the guy she was in love with had somehow gotten one of these confederate half dollars and left it with her. Only she didn't know he had left it with her until she found it in her things after he died, and she never said in the diary that it was even a coin. He was killed, but nobody knew specifically why at the time. It just seemed like random violence between people who were not residents of the town to all the townspeople, and freaked everybody out. She made the connection between him being killed and the thing he left with her after she found it. Anyway, she was heartbroken, and she ended the story by saying she would never tell anyone about any of it. It looks like she never did."

"Did you make that up?" Sam asked.

"No, of course not," Andy said a little impatiently.

"You mean she found this coin, knew the man she loved was killed because of it, and kept the secret to herself her whole life? That sounds pretty unbelievable," said Mrs. Garrett.

"I know Mom. You have to read her story. I think she kept it secret because if she had told anyone about it, they would have known she wasn't faithful to the man her family expected her to marry, and we think she went on to marry him. Back in those days, falling in love with someone else would have been completely unacceptable and scandalous. Not that it's acceptable now, but people have options."

"What other information?" asked Mrs. Garrett. "How would you figure out all that now, so many years later? Why didn't someone before you figure it out?"

I continued the story. "We think nobody had any idea about any of this until Allie died. Then, Andy's great great great grandfather, who was Allie's nephew, found the diary. His name was Gilbert Burke. That was in the 1950s some time. When he found it he did a bunch of research on the man who had died and the thing Allie found, and searched for it, but never found it. His notes on the whole thing were in the safe too. Like Andy said, Allie never said in her diary that it was a coin; she just referred to it as the 'thing' that this guy had died for. She didn't seem to ever wonder about it having value. She only hated it because she thought it was the reason he died, and wanted nothing to do with it. She wanted to erase the fact that it ever existed. Allie's diary said she was leaving a map, but Gilbert Burke's notes say he had searched the entire house and never found a map or anything that could be the object she was referring to."

They were looking at us with round fascinated eyes. "So he concluded there was an object, but never found it or a map to lead him to it. So then how could you find it, another seventy years later? Where would you look that he didn't think of?" asked Sam.

"That's where the weird part comes in," Andy said. "Ever since Meg started coming over here, she has been having visions."

"Visions?" Mrs. Garrett questioned.

I was embarrassed even now to talk about this, especially in front of Andy's sister. Though my flashbacks, or visions, or whatever they were had proven to be accurate, it was still weird, even to me. Why me, and why after all this time? I looked at Andy's mom. She was not looking at me like I was an alien. Her face showed only a genuine curiosity. I glanced at her, and then down at my toes, which I observed were still there in my flip flops. I noticed my toenail polish had chipped on my left big toe. Andy put his hand on my knee, and I looked at him. He nodded encouragingly.

I started hesitantly. "Yeah, I think it's happened every time I've come over here. It's not disturbing, but it is kind of freaky. It's like I have very vivid memories of areas in and around your house, but how things look are not exactly like they are now. It's like the same scenes, but like they might have been in a different time and place. I know it sounds really weird, and it took me a long time even to tell Andy. I just couldn't make any sense of it, and it was freaking me out."

Andy took up the story then. "But then not too much later we were going through the clothes in the attic, and we found a box. In the box,"

"Was the map?" Samantha filled in.

"No. Well yes. It was an old quilt. See, in the diary, Allie had talked about a patchwork quilt she was making, and had described some of the blocks. We found the actual quilt, look."

Andy took the quilt out of his bottom drawer, and carefully unfolded it and laid it on the bed.

"This is unbelievable," Mrs. Garrett said. "It's incredible. It's an artifact, a treasure. It's amazing. And you say it's described in the diary?"

"Yes, in a lot of detail."

"It's so random," said Sam. "The pattern and colors I mean. It's not exactly pretty."

I felt defensive for some reason, and wanted to explain. "Yes, we researched it a little. It's called a sampler. Girls would make these as sewing projects to work on their sewing skills. They were often made out of whatever scraps of fabric they could find, rather than planned out in organized colors and patterns."

"And what does this quilt have to do with the coin or the map?" Mrs. Garrett looked up at us.

"That's the weird part," I stammered. "When we found the quilt, the flashes started getting even more intense, and it seemed like some of the pictures in the quilt caused them to happen. I started to feel really strongly that the pictures in the quilt were actual places and things around here, and that they weren't only pictures, but were important. Like they were meaningful to Allie - they were clues. It just hit me one day that the quilt *is* the map. The quilt was a place where she could put reminders that were obvious to her about the man she loved, but nobody else would ever know. I know it sounds stupid, but I just *knew* it was the map. Look at this block – it's the house. And this one, it's the barn. Here are the mountains out to the east. And this swing and this stone wall? They don't exist anymore, but I know where they were. I can see them in my mind. They were in a special place to her."

"To Allie?"

"Yes." I paused. "I know, it sounds crazy. It is crazy, but that's where we looked, and that's where it was. I can't explain it, I really can't, but it's like she wanted us to find it. And we did."

Mrs. Garrett read through the diary as we watched her, and I understood completely when I saw a tear run down her cheek.

I said very softly, "That's how I felt too."

"Let me see Mom," said Sam. Mrs. Garrett moved so that Sam could stand over the diary.

She read the account from her ancestor, and then touched the quilt gently.

"I don't even know what to say," Mrs. Garrett admitted. "It's overwhelming."

"That's why we wanted to tell you Mom," said Andy. "We're not sure what to do now. This is a cool discovery for our family, but if the coin is real, it's probably worth some money. I already did some research on line, and found there's a place called the National Numismatic Association that has one of these. From the pictures, it looks the same."

"This is an amazing story guys. It is an incredible discovery, and I'm glad you told me. I want to know so much more about our family now. I wonder what her life turned out like."

She looked at me. I could see the question in her eyes. I glanced at Sam, who had tears in her eyes now too.

"I... I don't know. I just feel sadness for her. I don't know why I know some things about her life and feelings and not others."

"Megan, the fact that you feel anything is such a gift. It's amazing and special. I think there is so much more going on within all of us than we realize. I completely believe in intuition and getting messages from the universe. I think there was a wrong here that needed to be set right, and it depended on the right person coming along who could be trusted to solve the riddle. There has to be a reason this happened to you."

I felt a little reassured. "The truth is," I said, "I don't have any strong feelings about what happened. I think she loved this house and her life here, but I don't think she went on to any great happiness. I think she lost the one true love of her life and was never the same again. It makes me sad."

"It is sad. Can you believe how rigid the rules were for women back then? I guess for men too, for that matter. But women had so few options. What we take for granted today – our choices, our freedoms – we can be anything we want. Women back then had almost none of those options. It's hard to even imagine."

"It is, it's truly barbaric," added Sam.

We all pondered that for a moment.

"The first thing we should do," said Mrs. Garrett, "is try to verify that this coin is real, and then to figure out what it's worth. Your dad and I meant it when we said you could keep the money you made for college Andy. If this coin is real, it could mean you don't have to take any student loans. Maybe it could even fund your charity work for a few years, if you decide you still want to do that."

I glanced at Andy, and felt a great sense of relief. Andy's mom knew what to do.

I'll make some calls in the morning, and we'll figure out where we go from there," said Mrs. Garrett. She and Sam left to go back downstairs.

I realized my parents would be wondering where I was, so Andy walked me to the front door. I was very tired all of a sudden. It had been an emotionally draining day. Andy opened the door for me, and I glanced out and saw a horse drawn wagon, for just a second. I blinked and it was gone. It stressed me out. I was tired. We had solved the mystery. Why would I still be seeing Allie's memories? Weird. I turned to face Andy, distracted.

"You saw something again, didn't you?" he asked.

"Yeah, I just don't know what it means. Will this just happen any time I'm here?"

"Maybe. Does it scare you?"

"No, it's not disturbing, but I feel like the story isn't over. Like there is still something she would want me to understand. I have no idea what though." I paused. "When I see these images, I can feel how much she loved this place, but there's always a touch of sadness too. It's like there will be sadness until someone understands the whole story. I don't even sound like I'm making sense, do I?" I laughed sheepishly.

"I'm not worried," said Andy. "It will all sort itself out. Everything is happening just as it's supposed to."

He pulled me close, and kissed me long and hard on the lips. My insides turned to putty. Nothing I had ever known had compared to the way I felt about him. I saw why all the greatest stories had to be about love.

When I got home I tumbled into bed exhausted. I feel asleep quickly, and dreamed of an entire afternoon spent on a picnic blanket next to a stream in sunlit woods, with Andy there beside me. The sun glinted through his hair, and he was the image of all things perfect to me. In those moments, the world was right and wonderful, nobody wondered where we were, and we kissed and slowly took each other's clothes off. I felt a sense of disappointment when my alarm interrupted the dream, and I knew that I desperately wanted to repeat that particular dream in real life.

27 POSSIBILITIES

The next day from work, I texted Andy. "?"

"not yet" came the reply.

As I arranged roast beef onto a slice of spongy sourdough bread, I thought about him. Just a year ago I hadn't known Andy. Now I would be willing to sacrifice just about anything if it would make him happy. Without a doubt, he was the most important person in my life. Was that what real love was all about? I had never felt this way before. I cared about him more than I cared about myself. What if this coin could make all his dreams come true? It would be so right. There was nobody more deserving than him. He was going to make a positive impact on the world, and I wanted that for him.

The hours crept by slowly. It was a good thing it didn't take any thought to make a good sandwich, because I would have had to be fired. My mind was miles away from tomatoes and pickles. Finally, it was almost quitting time, 6:00. My phone beeped.

"come over"

"on way" I returned.

I grabbed my purse from the chair in the storage room, flew out into the store, and yelled, "See you tomorrow!" over my shoulder as I pushed through the door into the cool evening air.

Andy opened the door before I knocked, and I could see by his face that he was excited. "Come here you!" He kissed me quickly and pulled me to the kitchen. "Tell her Mom!" he exclaimed.

Mrs. Garrett said, "Well, I don't want anyone to get too excited yet, because we haven't confirmed anything, but, I called the National Numismatic Association and spoke with a Mr. Schneider. I told him we had a coin with a date of 1861 on it that also said 'half dollar' and 'Confederate States of America.' I know he thought I was some kind of nut job at first, but I finally got him to believe I was an adult. After I described the coin to him, he said that if it's real, which he said is highly doubtful; it would be worth over five hundred thousand dollars."

My jaw dropped. "No way!" I said.

"Yes, that's what he said," said Mrs. Garrett. "But he also wanted to be sure I understood that many copies had been made, and that it was just about impossible that we would have the only remaining Confederate half dollar that was unaccounted for." She paused. "But somebody has to have it, right?" She smiled. "Why not you two?"

I threw my arms around Andy and squealed. "Can you imagine? This is amazing! This is awesome!"

"I know, I think I'm in shock," he said against my hair. "I want to try not to get my hopes up, but it's really hard. Everything about how we found it just fits."

I squeezed his hand, and I could feel in my heart that this had to be the authentic coin. I was certain that had to be the reason I felt such a connection with Allie. There *had* to be a reason for it all.

"So we probably need to make a trip to New York to have it authenticated," Mrs. Garrett continued. "And they can probably help us figure out how to sell it, if that's what we want to do. I mean, that would be up to you two," she said.

"Up to us Mom?" Andy asked uncertainly.

"Yes, up to you. You found it sweetie. We said the money you earned cleaning up this house would be your college money and we meant it. This coin is yours, and you have to decide what to do with it."

"I know you said that, but that was before we knew it could be worth that much money," Andy said. "Are you sure?"

"Of course I am. We are. Your father and I discussed it again today after I spoke to Mr. Schneider, and we are exactly on the same page. I would like though, to keep the diary and quilt in our family. I wouldn't mind loaning them to a museum or something, but they are true family heirlooms."

"Mom, I would want to sell it for sure," Andy replied without hesitation. He looked at me.

"Oh yes, no doubt," I said. "You can't pass up on that kind of money, and I'm positive Allie would have wanted some good to finally come of it."

"Ok," said Mrs. Garrett. "I'll contact Mr. Schneider again and make an appointment for us to go to New York. Are you guys hungry?"

"Starved," Andy answered.

After we finished our heaping bowls of beef stroganoff, we slogged up the stairs to Andy's room. "Have you been going through more stuff in the attic?" I asked.

"Yeah, but so much of it just seems like old junk. Some days it really feels like work. I think it's lost some interest for me because we already found the best stuff. Like eating dessert before dinner or something. I guess though, if this coin is really worth that much money, I could look at it differently. I could treat the rest of it more like junk – just look for anything we might want to keep and have a big auction with the rest or donate it or something."

"That's true, you could probably afford to be a lot less careful about it," I said. "Besides, I would think by now you noticed all the good stuff anyway. You've been at it so long."

"Yeah, it is down to just scraps now."

My mind drifted in its usual direction as I looked at the beautiful creature standing by the window. "I see you got some stroganoff on your shirt," I said. "You should take it off."

The corner of his mouth crept up shyly. A glint came into his eyes. He turned to face me, locked his eyes onto mine, reached for the bottom of his t-shirt, and slowly pulled it up to his neck, watching me all the while. Eyes still locked on mine, he pulled it over his head, broke our gaze for just a second, and stood looking at me.

I wondered if he had any idea how he looked. He stood in a pool of golden evening sunlight that glinted off his tousled hair. His skin was tan from time spent outside, and his upper body was muscular like an athlete's, narrowing down to a small waist with faded jeans sitting right below his belly button. A thin line of hair led down from his belly button into his jeans. His expression wasn't tentative, but he didn't look like he understood how he looked either. He stood with his eyes locked on mine, a slight smile on his face.

I couldn't help it, I sucked in my breath. He was beautiful – there was no other word for it. I wanted to run my hands all over his perfect body, but all I could do for the moment was stare. He was far enough from me that I could take it all in while still focusing on his eyes. I said it. "You are beautiful."

"Beautiful?" he asked. "Is that bad? Guys aren't supposed to be beautiful, right?"

I laughed, releasing the tension I felt. "I was just so struck by how you looked standing there. I know it sounds corny, but I can't imagine how any man could look better. You amaze me, and there you are standing there with your shirt off, just because I wanted you to."

I could see I embarrassed him as he turned toward the window with a wry smile. I walked over behind him and placed my fingertips on his shoulders near his neck. I lightly stroked outwards across his shoulders, then down his back. He shivered. I loved the feel of his smooth firm skin and the way it felt to trace the lines of his muscles. He turned to me and pulled me against him into an urgent kiss. His hands found their way under my shirt and felt warm against the bare skin of my back. As we kissed, his hands moved to my belly and slowly up my chest over my bra. And then his fingers were under my bra. I felt like I was on fire, and pressed myself against his body. We continued to touch each other and kiss until we heard Andy's mother coming up the stairs. I had to give her credit for being so cool. She made plenty of stomping noise and walked slowly. She didn't want to catch us in an embarrassing position any more than we wanted to be caught. She was no dummy.

I went to the bed and sat on it, and Andy grabbed a shirt off the floor and hastily pulled it on. He sat at his desk and we gave each other guilty looks. No sooner had we settled than Mrs. Garrett popped her head in the door. "Clean laundry," she said, and placed a stack of neatly folded clothes on the bed beside me.

Andy came into the deli around lunch time the next day, to tell me it was set. On the following Monday, we would drive to New York. Only five days from now we would know whether this coin was real or worth anything. I didn't know if I could contain my excitement that long. I gave him his usual turkey and Swiss and sent him on his way. I didn't have time to talk, since the lunchtime rush was on.

After work I drove to Andy's house, as had become my usual routine. My parents always wondered why we spent so much more time there than at my house. I was the one already out, so stopping by made sense. That was the easy explanation, but there was more to it than that. There was something about that old house and it's grounds that was special to our relationship. There was Allie's presence of course. There were also so many places where we could be alone, unlike at my house. There were the grounds, the paths through the wood, the barn, all the rooms in the house – it was just a different atmosphere.

When Andy opened the door for me, the look on his face told me something was bothering him. He didn't look upset really, just not like himself. "Let's go for a walk," he said.

"What is it?" I asked.

He grabbed a light jacket off the peg and closed the door behind him as he came out. We walked in silence until we got to the dirt road that skirted their property. The air was full of bird sounds, and a light breeze made the temperature perfect. It was peaceful and serene in the forest.

"What is it?" I asked again.

Andy picked up a smooth stone and tossed it into the woods. "Something weird happened today," he said.

I felt a shiver. "What do you mean?"

"Well, some guy called my mom and offered her a hundred thousand dollars for the coin, sight unseen. He wouldn't tell her who he was. She said we were already working with someone, and he hung up. The thing is though; none of us has told anyone we have it, other than my mom telling Mr. Schneider. You haven't said anything, right?"

"No, of course not," I replied.

"I didn't think so. Mom immediately called Mr. Schneider, and he swore he didn't say anything either. It makes me nervous. How could anyone know?"

"I don't know. What does your mom think? Is she freaked out?"

"No, not really I guess. She thinks someone must have heard Mr. Schneider saying something about it. That's the only explanation that makes any sense."

Our conversation drifted onto different subjects. "Let's go down by the creek," I said. "I wonder if this is anywhere near where Allie and Wayne met." I was carefully picking my way along the path. Andy was just walking along, clearly lost in thought. It occurred to me that he didn't know much about these woods. I warned, "I know you haven't lived here that long, but there's all kinds of poison ivy and poison oak in the woods, so we have to be careful. Do you know what it looks like?"

Andy looked at me, uncomprehending for a moment. "No. Poison ivy?"

"Yes, unfortunately. Have you ever gotten into it? It's pretty horrible."

"No, I haven't." He had stopped and was as still as a statue. The look on his face was like something was going to jump out and bite him at any second.

I laughed. "Well let me show you." I went down the path a little more, searching. It didn't take long to find what I was looking for. "Here's some poison ivy," I said. "See how the leaves are grouped in threes, and they're shiny? Don't even get it on your clothes, because it could touch your skin from there. It's just awful. If there's too much by the path we shouldn't even go down to the creek, but the path is pretty wide, so we should be able to avoid touching it. I don't see any poison oak, but I'll show you if I see some."

"I didn't know there was anything dangerous in these woods. I could have gotten into this stuff a lot of times already. I'm glad you told me. What about animals?"

"There's not much to worry about there," I said. "They're more afraid of us than we are of them. We wouldn't want to get close to a porcupine or skunk, and at night there could be bats or raccoons with rabies, but I've never had any trouble with any animals."

We carefully picked our way down to the creek. It was beautiful and peaceful, and there was a nice clearing with a fallen log that made a perfect place to sit. The creek made a pleasant bubbling sound. We sat in silence listening for a while, but then I started to feel the mosquitoes were having too much of a feast on us. "We'll have to use bug spray next time," I said. "Besides, I told my mom I'd be home in time for dinner. Can you come over for dinner tomorrow?" I asked. "My mom is going to kill me if we don't spend some time over there."

We started to walk back to the house.

"Sure, I like your family, and I agree we should spend more time there."

"Yeah I know. It's just that there's no privacy at all there."

"I know, but I don't want your parents thinking I'm stealing all your time, or that we're off doing who knows what that they wouldn't approve of. I want them to like me."

"How could they not like you?" I asked. We both knew though. Andy said it.

"It's not that they wouldn't like me, they might just think we're too serious. They don't want to see you hurt."

We reached my car and Andy opened the door for me, and then put his hand gently on the side of my head, turning my face toward his. He kissed me softly at first, but with a growing intensity. I felt my stomach fluttering. He pulled back, leaving me breathless. I loved being lost in those crystal blue eyes of his.

"I am not going to hurt you though Megan, I promise. Get going," he said with his shy smile.

The next day, right on time, Andy arrived at my house for dinner. As soon as he walked in the door, Nick tackled him. Andy wrestled with him on the floor as Nick squealed with delight.

"Let's go play football!" Nick yelled.

"Ok, ok," said Andy, allowing himself to be pulled out the back door.

"See Mom," I said. "That's part of why we don't spend as much time here. Because when we're here I don't even get to see him."

"I know honey, but look how happy Nick is," she said. "It's good for Andy to get to know all of us. If you really like him so much, we want to know him too. Trust me, you have all the time in the world to be with him. You can share him just a little bit."

"I know Mom." I turned to her. "What do you need me to do?"

She handed me the peeler and pointed to the potatoes. "You're in charge of mashed potatoes, since you're a pro and all."

I didn't mind. As I peeled, I looked out the window into the back yard. Justin had joined them too, and Andy was running around like a little kid, tackling the boys as they screamed with laughter. It *was* kind of cute.

My dad came home from work. "Call the boys in for dinner," my mom said to me.

I went into the back yard and said, "Wash up guys, it's time to eat."

A breathless Andy loped up to me, grabbed me and swung me around, and planted a kiss on my lips. Just as quickly he set me down, and followed my brothers into the house. We all met at the table and piled our plates high with pot roast and potatoes.

"Did you ask your parents about Monday yet Megan?" Andy asked.

"What?" asked my mom.

"Oh Andy and I found an old coin at his house, and Mrs. Garrett is going to drive us to a coin specialist in New York to have him take a look at it. Is that ok?"

"Well sure," said my mom. "You guys have sure been finding some interesting things. Did you just recently find the coin, or has it just been one of the things you have been meaning to look into for a while?"

We looked at each other. Without getting into too much detail about Allie, I told them the story. "And we think it's valuable," I ended.

Andy said, "You know, most of what we have found has been a lot of broken junk, but there have been a few treasures. This coin looks like it might be interesting, so we thought we'd check it out. My mom thought it was interesting too."

"Well it does sound interesting, so let us know how it turns out. I suppose you'll be gone all day Monday."

"Yeah, it's a long drive," I said.

"What electives are you taking next year?" my dad asked Andy, changing the subject.

"I'm taking advanced placement math and advanced chemistry," Andy said.

"Sounds like you're going to be very busy."

"Yes sir. I really need those classes to get into a pre-med program."

I beamed with pride. Andy was a father's dream. And my dream too. He allowed himself to be grilled by my parents on everything about himself for the entire dinner. After a dessert of brownies with ice cream, I walked him to the door.

"You did really well. I'm sorry they asked you non-stop questions. You were barely able to eat your dinner."

"It's all worth it if I get to be with you," Andy said. "Besides, I like them, they're good people."

We kissed quickly, and I blushed as "wooooh oooo" came from the doorway behind Andy.

"Leave Nick," I said gruffly.

Andy laughed. He grabbed me and swung me around, putting me between him and the doorway. He crouched down, made a gun out of his thumb and forefinger, and reached the gun around me to make shooting noises toward the doorway. Nick went shrieking down the hall with delight.

Andy kissed me quickly and left.

28 HIDING PLACES

The next day at work, Friday, I was slicing ham. My cell phone rang with Andy's tone. I knew he wouldn't call me at work unless it was important, so I wiped my hands on a towel and answered my phone. "Hello?"

"Megan someone broke into our house."

"What?" I was in shock. My body went cold with dread and horror. "Are you ok? Are your parents ok?"

"Yeah we're fine, but the whole house was turned upside down." He paused.

It hit me. "They were looking for the coin," I stated.

"We think so."

"Did they find it?"

"No, I had it with me. It was in my car. I drove to Worcester to take a load of stuff to the Salvation Army. I was gone all morning and found the door to the house standing open when I got back. I thought maybe my mom was home, but I looked inside and everything was scattered everywhere. There were no cars there or anything but it was freaky, so I jumped back in my car and called my mom and dad, and my dad called the police. The police just left.

"Did they find anything?" I asked.

"The burglars or the police?"

"Either I guess," I said.

"Well, we can't tell that the burglars took anything, which is why we think they were looking for the coin. The police seemed to think whoever it was got in and out pretty fast. They didn't leave any fingerprints or obvious clues. Getting in was pretty easy, they just broke the glass on the door by the kitchen and reached in and turned the bolt. The police thought the way the house looked indicated that someone was looking for something. Maybe though, the person didn't realize how big the house was. I mean, it could have been hidden in lots of places that would have been difficult to find." He sounded shaken.

"Andy that's so scary. What are you going to do?"

"Well, Dad's coming home from Boston right now, so we should be ok with both of us here with my mom and sister. There's a carpenter and a locksmith here right now, putting in a new kitchen door and upgrading all the locks in the house."

"Do you want to stay at my house?" I asked.

"No, I need to be home with my mom. She's kind of shaken up. So is Sam for that matter. This reinforces her belief that this is a creepy old house."

"I understand," I said. "I don't blame them a bit. I'll come by after work."

"Ok, I'll see you soon," Andy replied.

I went back to slicing, lost in thought. A shiver ran up my spine as I thought of the beautiful old farmhouse being violated. It was just horrible. How could anyone know about the coin? Even if they did, who would break in trying to find it? It must really be worth something. Was this coin going to cause us pain just like it had for Allie? What if someone had hurt Andy or his mom? A tear rolled down my cheek. I couldn't even bear to think about it. Monday couldn't come soon enough, when we would take it to New York. Suddenly I just wanted it out of our lives. I forced myself to think positive thoughts. Andy's dad was on his way home after all. Things would be ok. I concentrated on cleaning the slicer and smiling at the customers as if nothing were wrong.

As quitting time approached, I called my mom. "I'm going over to Andy's house."

"Yes, as usual," she said. I could hear the smile in her voice.

"Mom, someone broke into their house today," I said slowly.

"What? Are they ok? Did they take things? Is it safe to go there?"

"Yes Mom," I said. "They're ok. They can't find that anything was taken. They think someone was looking for that coin we told you about."

She paused. "It's that valuable?"

"We think it is. That's why we're taking it to New York to a specialist. The thing is, we didn't know anyone else knew about it. It could be that the break in was totally unrelated. We just don't know."

"Oh honey, that's just awful. Please invite them to stay with us if they want, especially if Andy's dad isn't home."

"He's probably home by now Mom, he left Boston this morning. But I'll tell them they're welcome anyway."

"Ok honey, just be really careful, ok? I'm worried."

"I am too Mom. I just wanted you to know. I'll call you when I'm leaving there to come home."

"Ok. Please let me know if there's anything we can do. Food maybe?"

"Ok Mom, I will."

I hung up, feeling worse than ever. Somehow I guess I had wanted my mom to make light of it or reassure me, but she hadn't. She sounded as scared as I felt.

I drove to Andy's house, trying to think of what I would say. I wanted to be strong and not fall to pieces in front of Andy. I needed to see him.

When Andy opened the door, I could see the tension in his face. Without a word I went into his arms and we held each other. I felt the tears welling up, and I fought my hardest to keep from crying. I hiccupped once, and he held me closer.

"It's ok Meg, it's going to be ok." He stroked my hair.

With that, I couldn't hold it in. "What if something happened to you or your family?" I sobbed.

"Nothing did. Nothing will. If it's really about the coin, it will be done on Monday. If it's not, then it just had to be random."

After my tears subsided, we went into the kitchen, where Andy's mom was putting clean dishes away and Samantha was sipping tea by the window. At the site of Mrs. Garrett, I wanted to cry again. She looked so stricken. She smiled when she saw me though, and held out her hands. I grasped her hands and said, "I'm so sorry Mrs. Garrett."

"I know Meg, thank you," she replied.

"Are you ok Sam?" I asked.

"Yeah, I guess," she replied slowly. "It's all pretty unsettling."

I nodded, not knowing what else to say. Andy pulled me with him and I followed him up the back stairs to his room. "What are you going to do with the coin until Monday?" I asked.

"I already did something with it. I shoved it under the floorboard in the barn, right under the arsenic box. That was one place they certainly didn't look."

"Yeah, that's a good place. I feel so bad for your mom."

Andy looked at me for a moment and sighed. "She's upset of course, but now she's saying she wants to have the house ready to sell by the end of the summer and leave. That's only a few weeks away. She says she doesn't feel safe here. I suppose anyone who has their house broken into would feel that way, no matter where it was. Anyway, she feels like we're too isolated out here in the country. She's wondering if we should go get an apartment in Boston right now."

"Oh." I didn't know what else to say. Andy stared out the window. There would be no reason for Andy or his family to be here, once they sold the house. I knew that had always been the plan, but it felt like someone had punched me in the gut when I thought about it being any time soon.

"Don't worry Megs, we'll figure something out."

"Ok." I replied. I felt sick with dread and fear.

He turned to look at me. When he saw the look on my face he came and sat beside me, and pulled me into his arms. "You don't get it do you?"

"What do you mean?" I replied hesitantly.

"I mean about us. We're not going to let this pull us apart. Not this and not anything. We'll find a way to stay together, you can count on that."

I looked into those liquid blue eyes, and I could see that he meant every word of it. He wasn't just trying to cheer me up. I suddenly felt better. Stronger.

"I mean it Meg," he said.

I believed him. Together, we could overcome anything. We sat in silence for a few minutes.

"You know what Megan?" Andy asked. "We should go do something fun tomorrow, to take our minds off all this. You're off tomorrow, right?"

"Yes, tomorrow and Monday."

"Let's go out to the lake. Do you mind if I ask my whole family to go? It would take all our minds off it. We could even take your brothers and make it a real family outing. It's times like this when you realize how important family is."

"Of course I don't mind, I think that's a great idea," I said.

When we asked them, Andy's parents did too. "Yes Meg, ask your little brothers. We'll teach them how to ski."

I smiled. "Ok, but you haven't seen how they idolize Andy. You aren't going to get any time with him, you know that, don't you?"

Mrs. Garrett said, "Well, Andy did say they seemed to like him pretty well."

"I'm afraid that's a bit of an understatement," I said. "But they're good kids. I'll ask them. They'll be thrilled."

"Ok, why don't you bring them over about nine in the morning then," said Mr. Garrett.

"Sounds good, I will," I said.

Andy walked me to the door. I called my mom quick, to tell her I was on my way. "Are you sure you're going to be ok?" I asked Andy. "You could all stay at our house or even in a hotel."

"We'll be fine, with my dad here and all. The police will be checking on us too. I'll see you in the morning."

"Ok. I miss you already," I said.

"I miss you too. I always miss you when you're away from me."

I hugged him tight, and then turned to go.

I drove home, suddenly feeling exhausted. Then I thought about how excited Justin and Nick would be and smiled. They adored Andy. I parked in the driveway and went inside. I could hear the TV blaring in the family room, so I headed that way. I stood in the doorway and watched my two little brothers with their eyes glued to the show. They were pretty cute.

"Guess what guys?" I asked.

Justin turned to look at me. "What?"

"Andy wants you two to go out on the boat with us tomorrow."

"What?" yelled Nick.

"Would you like to go?" I asked. Stupid question.

"Are you kidding?" asked Justin. "He really asked us to go?"

“He really did,” I assured them.

“Woo hoo!” Justin yelled.

I turned to my mom. “Is it ok?”

“Of course it is honey, it’s great.”

“Ok guys,” I said. “We’re leaving at 8:45, so you need to be up and eating breakfast by 8:15, ok?”

They were back to watching their show already. I wandered into the kitchen, and my mom followed.

“I’ll help you get them up Meg,” said my mom. “That’s so nice of the Garrett’s to ask the boys to go.”

“Yeah, it is. It will be good to get everyone’s mind off the break in and all.”

“Well, what happened over there - did the police come and all?” she asked.

“Yeah, and they can’t find that anything was taken – it just seemed like they were looking for something specific. That’s why we think it was the coin.”

“That’s just so scary Megan, I’m so glad nobody was home.”

“I know, the whole thing is just awful.”

Sometimes, no matter how old you are, you just want your mom. I went into her arms, and she held me tight. “I love you Meg,” she said.

“I love you too Mom. I’m going to go to bed, I’m so tired.”

“Ok sweetie, good night.”

It felt good to be safe and secure in my bed.

Saturday morning was sunny and warm. I woke to Nick jumping on my bed. I should have known I wouldn’t have to get them up.

"Come on, come on!" he demanded.

I threw the blankets over him and rolled out of bed. He laughed and kicked out of them, and tore around me. I heard the thunder of his steps pounding down the stairs, and hoped my mom and dad weren't still trying to sleep.

The reality of yesterday rushed back to me. Andy's mom wanted to move. Because somebody had broken into their house. A stab of fear shot through me. How did all this happen? How could it even be possible that Andy might be torn away from me? Would he let that happen? Would we let it happen? I pushed those thoughts out of my head. Today we were not going to think about any of that, we were just going to have fun. Everyone needed a break from all the stressful thoughts.

After our instant oatmeal, I confirmed the boys were ready to go.

"Swim trunks?"

"On," replied Justin.

"Nick?"

"On," he repeated.

"Towels?" I asked.

"Check," replied Justin.

"Sunscreen?"

"Yes," they chorused in unison.

"Anyone need to go to the bathroom before we go?"

"Megan, geez," Justin said. "We're not babies."

"Ok, ok," I said. "You're right, my bad. Let's get going then. Bye Mom!" I yelled toward the kitchen.

"Bye guys, have a great time!" she returned.

"Shotgun!" Nick yelled.

I took a deep breath as they piled into my car. We made it to Andy's house with both boys intact. I introduced them to Andy's parents and sister.

"Are you sure about this?" I asked only half joking, looking at Mr. Garrett.

"Oh yes, it'll be fun," he replied, as he strapped a set of small water skis onto the top of the SUV.

We all crammed inside, with the boys in the back row seat, and me, Andy and Sam in the middle seat. Mr. Garrett drove us to the lake and parked. The boys jumped out of the car and started running toward the dock.

"Hold it!" I yelled.

They stopped and turned around. "Huh?" Justin ventured.

"Come back here. Everyone has to carry something."

"Oh."

Mrs. Garrett laughed, "You guys are just like Andy when he was younger."

I found it hard to believe Andy was ever this annoying. Mrs. Garrett handed Justin a cooler and Nick two life jackets. They turned and started toward the dock again.

"Do you know where you're going?" I asked.

"It's ok Meg," said Andy, as he trotted past me to catch up to them.

"Come on guys," Andy said to them. He would have made a great big brother.

We all piled into the boat, and Andy showed the boys where to sit. As the boat started to move, they couldn't contain their excitement.

Mr. Garrett said to Justin, "You want to see how it's done?"

"Yeah," Justin exclaimed with great enthusiasm.

"Ok Andy, you're up first," said Mr. Garrett.

Andy smiled like a kid himself. He stripped off his shirt, kicked off his flip flops, and buckled into his ski vest. I watched his muscles ripple as he moved like a lanky tiger. Muscular, but entirely graceful. He tossed his ski into the water, where it sliced away across the surface. He slid into the water himself, and paddled after it with powerful strokes. Mr. Garrett tossed out the rope where Andy could reach it, and then Andy got himself into position while Mr. Garrett slowly chugged the boat away, pulling the rope taut.

"Hang on guys, we're going to start fast," I said.

"Ok!" yelled Andy.

Mr. Garrett gunned the boat and Andy sprang out of the water.

"Whoa," said Nick, clearly impressed.

I agreed, 'whoa' was right. But I was probably thinking it for different reasons than Nick. Andy was beautiful to watch, slicing back and forth across the wake and the glassy water. Justin and Nick were entranced. When Andy finally threw the rope into the air and sank gracefully into the water, the boys couldn't contain themselves.

"I want to do that!" said Justin.

"It's not that easy," Nick said to him authoritatively.

"Andy can show me," replied Justin.

"All right guys, who wants to try it first?" asked Mr. Garrett.

"Me!" they shouted in unison.

Mr. Garrett looked at me helplessly.

"Rock, paper, scissors," I said dryly. "Ready guys?" I asked. "One, two, three."

We heard the pounding of two fists in two hands. Thump, thump, thump slap.

Justin got scissors; Nick got paper, making Justin first.

"Woo hoo!" shouted Justin.

Nick, wanting to show he was older and more mature, took it well.

Mrs. Garrett made sure Justin was firmly buckled into his vest, and then she wrestled his feet into the ski's boots. She must have been a good mom for a little boy. Mr. Garrett grabbed him by the shoulders of the vest, and dangled him over the side of the boat.

"Drop him!" shouted Nick.

"Slow or fast?" Mr. Garrett asked Justin.

"Uh…" Justin considered it.

Mr. Garrett opened his hands, and Justin plunged into the water.

Justin shrieked, "I wasn't ready!"

"I know, I'm sorry," said Mr. Garrett. "But it's really easier that way. Now swim out toward Andy."

Justin started struggling through the water, dragging his legs behind him. I looked at Andy, who was patiently sitting in the water waiting. I loved him. The way the sun shone across the water and the air felt just right made it hard to remember anything was wrong. That was exactly what we had hoped for. Andy ended up paddling toward Justin, since Justin was moving so slowly. He got the boy situated in the water, just as he had for me, and I could see him talking into Justin's ear.

"Ready!" shouted Andy.

Mr. Garrett gunned the boat, and Justin flew over the top of his skis into a belly flop and dragged through the water.

"Let go!" we all yelled, as Mr. Garrett cut the throttle.

Justin came up spluttering. After three more tries, he'd had enough. I could see that he was disappointed as he struggled back into the boat.

"Dude, you almost made it on that last try," Nick consoled.

Mrs. Garrett wrapped Justin in a towel and gave him a piece of jerky. He was happy in about ten seconds. Nick was next, and made it up for about twenty feet on his second try. We all cheered madly. His third and fourth tries were not as good, but on the fifth he skied for about a quarter mile. We were all thrilled.

"They sure remind me of how Andy used to be," said Sam in my ear.

"Did you find Andy just as annoying?" I asked.

"Yes, I beat him up all the time," she replied.

"I don't have to do that – they do it to each other just fine," I replied wryly.

"My turn Dad?" Sam asked Mr. Garrett.

"Yes honey," he said.

Sam stripped down to her swimsuit and slid gracefully into the water. As I had guessed, she was a beautiful water skier also. She wasn't as talented as Andy, but everything she did was smooth and graceful, and she obviously knew what she was doing.

The boys were thoroughly exhausted by the time we got to Andy's house, both from the sun and the physical exertion. They sniped at each other all the way home, and I was only too glad to turn them over to my mom. After a late dinner, I called Andy.

"Is everything there ok?" I asked.

"Yeah, we're just going to bed early. Nothing to worry about."

"I know, it's just hard not to worry," I replied.

"It's all going to be ok Megs," he said in his silky voice. That voice could make me believe anything. I smiled with how warm it made me feel.

"Ok, good night," I said sleepily.

"Good night sweetie," he replied.

29 LOST

Sunday, and there I was making sandwiches again. It had been a busy afternoon, and I wasn't getting off until eight o clock. I had just peeled an entire case of potatoes, sliced two days worth of meats and vegetables and cleaned everything too. At least it was mindless. The dinner rush was just starting.

I heard someone approach the counter. I looked up, and Mrs. Garrett stood there with a worried look on her face.

"Hi," I said, smiling but concerned at her expression.

"Have you seen Andy today?" she asked.

"Well no, but I've been here since noon." A flash of fear shot through me. "Can't you find him? Did you call his cell?"

Her look answered the questions. "Yes, I saw him early this morning, but he drove into Ware for some gardening supplies for me hours ago, and I haven't seen him since."

I looked at her, uncomprehending.

"And no, he isn't answering his phone," she said quietly.

Fear gripped me. "That's not like him, to be out of touch," I said.

I grabbed my phone and texted him, "need 2 talk." He had never failed to respond to me.

Panic started to rise through my body as no response came. I didn't want to look at Andy's mom, but I couldn't help it. Her eyes filled with tears as mine did too. There was just too much weird stuff going on all of a sudden, and her reaction really scared me.

"Are we blowing this out of proportion? Andy can take care of himself, right?" I hesitated as she didn't answer or reassure me. "I'm going with you to go look," I said. I certainly couldn't sit around here and do nothing with this panic coursing through me. I turned to Donna, my co-worker, who was trying not to eavesdrop.

"I'm leaving because I have a family emergency."

"Sure, no worries hon," she said with a concerned expression.

I grabbed my stuff and followed Mrs. Garrett to the parking lot. We got in our cars and I followed her back to their house, calling my parents from my car to tell them what was happening. They wanted me to come home immediately, but understood that I wanted to see the Garrett's first. I silently followed Mrs. Garrett into the house, which felt empty and forlorn without Andy there. There was this gnawing feeling in the pit of my stomach that just wouldn't go away. I didn't know what to do with myself. I felt like screaming and crying, but I didn't want to upset Andy's mom any more than she already was. Mr. Garrett came into the kitchen and looked hopefully at his wife.

"Anything?"

She shook her head slightly.

"Did you get a hold of Sam?" she asked. Samantha was staying at a friend's house in New York State for a few days.

"Yes and she hadn't heard from him. She wants us to call as soon as we know anything at all. I told her to just stay put." He turned to me. "You two didn't have a fight or anything right? You don't know of anything he was planning on doing today that he might be doing?"

"No, no." I didn't know what else to say.

The phone rang. Mr. Garrett picked it up immediately.

"Hello?" He listened. "I see." He hung up.

He turned to us. "The police found his car just outside Ware. He's not with it though. I guess the good news is that he didn't crash. They don't know anything else yet."

Mrs. Garrett threw herself into his arms and started sobbing. I wrapped my arms around my middle, trying to squash the pain in my stomach, in utter disbelief.

"Can I go up to his room for a minute?' I asked.

"Yes, of course. Do you know something?" Mr. Garrett asked.

"No nothing. I just want to think for a minute. Touch his things."

"I understand," said Mrs. Garrett. "You just need a moment. Go ahead."

"Yes. Thank you."

I went up the steps to Andy's room and stepped inside. Sunlight was streaming through the window but the room felt empty. Allie's quilt was folded neatly it its box on Andy's desk. I carefully picked it up and sunk onto Andy's bed. I gently stroked the fragile squares, and then hugged it against myself as the tears came. I knew I shouldn't be so rough with it, but I held it against my face and my tears started to make the poor bird square damp. I hadn't really noticed that one before, but it must have been an eagle, since its head was white. Well, now it was kind of yellow, but it was definitely meant to be lighter than the brown body.

"What do I do Allie?" I asked the quilt. I laid the quilt on my lap and dabbed at the wet bird. It looked a little like a turkey. As I pushed it against my leg, I noticed that the bird seemed to have a hard spot in its middle. The quilt was padded with stuffing, but this wasn't just a thick spot, it was a hard spot, like there was a small stone inside or something. I squeezed the bird square in my hand, and felt the outline of the hard spot. It was round. Another coin? "What is it Allie?" I whispered.

I examined the hard spot. The edge of the bird square was frayed, and the stitching holding it to the fourth of July square had started to unravel. "Should I open it?" I asked softly. "Can you hear me? Can you help me find Andy?" Who was I talking to? I thought I should feel silly, but I didn't. She could hear me, I knew it.

I gently tore the bird square away from the fourth of July square until there was a gap about an inch long. I found the hard object and worked it to the edge of the square. I pushed it a little further, and it popped through the gap. A button. Wayne's button. It was tarnished and grey, but I could see it had an eagle on it. The eagle was holding a shield, and there were stars all around the outside. I turned it over and saw that 'Shannon Miller & Crane' was stamped on the back, along with the words 'New York.'

"What are you telling me?" I asked. The button felt warm. Wayne. All that mattered was Wayne. All that mattered was Andy. That was it. I was to do whatever it took to save Andy. All that mattered was Andy. That message was loud and clear. "Thank you Allie," I breathed. "But how? I know he's the only important thing. How do I do it? How do I keep him safe?"

I hugged the quilt to me again, and it almost felt like it was feeding strength into me. My phone chirped with a text message.

It was Andy. I sucked in my breath. Why would he text me instead of calling, when he must know we were all worried sick about him? I looked at the message. "You have something I want I'll trade for what you want, talk?"

Was he flirting with me? Was it a joke? I immediately texted back, "where r u? y haven't u called?"

The reply paralyzed me. "I'm not Andy stupid, only his phone, do you want him?"

I was crying by then. "yes" I texted back.

"are you alone?"

I looked around. I was alone in Andy's room. "Yes" I texted. I didn't know what to do.

My phone rang. The number showed it was Andy's phone.

"Hello?" I said, my voice quavering.

"I'll talk, you listen," said a low male voice. "I know who you are. I've been watching you. Put the coin in a brown grocery store bag and drive to Worcester. Go to the far west side of the parking lot of the VFW hall, and put the bag in the light blue dumpster there. I will expect you within two hours. I don't want to hurt anyone, I just want the coin, but if you tell anyone, or if anyone follows you, someone will get hurt, and I think you know who I mean. Do not take any chances on this."

The phone line went dead. I didn't know what to do. Hadn't my parents told me they would protect me from anything and everything since the day I was born? But this voice had said he'd been watching me. I felt cold.

"What do I do Allie?" I asked the quilt. I knew instantly. "Thank you Allie, you're right of course. I know what you would have done." I shoved the button in my pocket, and then hastily put the quilt on Andy's desk, wiped my eyes and hurried out the door. I forced myself to walk slowly down the steps and into the kitchen. Andy's parents were still there, and they looked at me as I came in the room. I felt terrible seeing the looks on their faces and not telling them what had just happened. I couldn't take the chance though. I willed them not to ask me about the coin. They didn't. Maybe they thought Andy had it with him. Maybe they thought it was unrelated.

"I need to go home and talk to my parents about what's going on," I said. "I'm so sorry." I started to cry again.

"Yes Megan, go ahead. Please call us if you hear anything at all," said Mr. Garrett.

"I will. And you call me too, that is, if you hear anything."

"Of course we will," he replied.

I got out of there as quickly as I could. I hadn't exactly lied. I'd said I'd call if I heard anything, not if I had already heard something. I knew it was stupid not to tell anyone, but I only had two hours. What if I just got the coin and did as I was told? What if I told someone and they scared this guy off, and he hurt Andy? I couldn't take that chance, even though it might mean I would get hurt too. I would not do anything to harm Andy. It was a stupid coin, and they could have it. All that mattered was that Andy be safe. Allie would have done the same for Wayne if she had been given the choice.

They would have no reason to hurt Andy if they got what they wanted, right? This guy couldn't want to make the situation worse any more than I did, right? I had no choice but to believe that I could save Andy by doing what I had been told to do. All that mattered was Andy. Besides, I could call 911 at any time. I just needed to be careful, follow the instructions exactly, and not put myself into any dangerous situations. This stupid coin messed up Allie's life. It wasn't going to mess up mine too.

I turned out of the driveway as if I were headed home. When I reached the dirt road, I turned right instead of left, and drove deeper into the woods behind Andy's house. I knew my parents wouldn't miss me yet. I parked in the woods about a quarter of a mile further down the road from the Garrett's driveway. It was twilight, and the shadows were starting to deepen in the woods. I crept through the woods, avoiding the poison ivy. When I got to the path that led toward Andy's house I took it. As I got closer to the stone wall I peered around it, making sure nobody could see or hear me coming. I felt like *I* was the criminal.

I skirted around the edge of the wall and over to the woodpile. From there, I could see the back of the barn, which was well hidden from the house. I hurried over to the barn and pressed myself against the wall. The back door to the barn was locked. I felt around for they key above the dirty window and found it. I quietly eased it into the lock and then turned the knob.

The door squeaked a little as I started to open it, so I eased it open very slowly, just enough to squeeze in, then gently pushed it closed again. It was very dark inside the barn. It was also dusty and damp and scary, but I knew where I was going. It would have been a very dangerous place if I hadn't. I edged slowly along the side of the barn feeling the familiar objects – the lawn tractor, the barrel, the pile of old sacks, the pile of farm tools. Each step was slow and quiet as I crept along. I came to the wall where the box of arsenic sat, and felt for it gingerly in the dark. I found it, then ran my hand down the side of it to the smooth worn board underneath. I felt the cracks in the board, and the head of a nail sticking up. I ran my finger slowly along the side of the board, being careful not to get a splinter or snag it on something rusty. I could feel that there was a gap under the board, and I pushed my fingers into the gap.

I felt a little piece of fabric and tugged gently. Out came the sock, with the round hard coin obviously inside. I tucked the sock into my pocket and retraced my steps slowly to the back door. I eased out and re-locked the door behind myself. It was darker now, and I felt panic rising. What if I was late? I stumbled quickly back through the woods, scraping my arms and legs as I pushed through the underbrush. A tree branch slapped my face, leaving a thin deep scratch, and a drop of blood trickled down my cheek. I started to cry, feeling almost hysterical. I had to get a grip. Andy was depending on me, whether he knew it or not. I collapsed into my car, fumbled the key into the ignition and started it. I did a U turn and drove slowly back up the road, not wanting anyone to notice me. I gulped some deep breaths, knowing I needed to try to act normal. What if someone grabbed me right here and now? I had what they wanted, didn't I? Terror rushed through me.

I turned onto the pavement, headed toward town. I stopped at the grocery store and bought a six pack of Coke. "Paper or plastic?" the motherly looking clerk asked.

"Pppaper," I replied. I needed that brown bag.

"Are you ok hon?' I could see she was genuinely concerned.

"I'm ok," I replied. "My dog just died." Where did that come from?

"Oh, I'm so sorry. That's never easy," she said.

"Yeah." I just wanted to get out of there.

I got in my car, wondering what kind of trouble I was getting myself into. I told myself I was only doing what I had to do, and everything would be fine as soon as I saved Andy. I eased my car onto the highway, headed for Worcester. My mind raced in every direction on the hour long drive. Should I call my mom? Should I call Andy's mom? Was I being stupid? What was the worst that could happen? What if someone had hurt Andy? Should I have a backup plan? Was there anyone I could tell? What would Andy do? I felt sick and worried and like I was going to throw up. What if I was too late? What if I couldn't find the VFW? What if the coin wasn't even real? All I wanted was to be in Andy's arms and for us both to be safe. How did this all happen?

I had to concentrate to drive the speed limit. Getting stopped was the last thing I needed now. Finally I pulled into Worcester and drove down the main street. When I got to the downtown area, I took a side street toward the VFW hall. I could see why this was the chosen spot. It was deserted and dark and creepy at this time of night. This was not the best part of town. I slowly pulled into the parking lot, wondering if I was being watched. I looked around, trying to plan how I would escape if I had to. I felt completely alone and terrified. What if something went wrong? Who would ever know where I had gone or why? I decided I needed a better back up plan than I had.

I saw the dumpster pushed up against the back of the building. I drove past it and couldn't see anyone on either side of it or anywhere near it. There appeared to be no immediate threat to me if I stopped and got out. I came to a stop on the far side of the lot and turned my car around. Suddenly I had a good idea. I pulled out my cell phone and typed in a text message, "I am at VFW in Worcester, Andy in trouble, if you're getting this, call the police." All I had to do was push the send button if I needed help in a hurry. I drove slowly back toward the dumpster. I put my car in park, but left the motor running. I still didn't see anyone around. I put the sock in the brown paper bag as I had been instructed, folded over the top, and slowly got out of the car. There had to be someone watching me. I was sweating. I tipped open the door of the dumpster, dropped the bag inside, and hurried back into my car. I wasn't sure what would happen next. I drove to the far side of the parking lot, where I could still see the dumpster. I locked the car doors and sat there, terrified. Was I supposed to leave? Though the night was warm, I was now freezing. I didn't have to wait long.

A dark colored four door sedan drove up and stopped by the dumpster. Nothing happened for a moment, and the car's lights remained on. I didn't know what to do, but my mind raced. Call someone? Wait? Get out? Drive away? I was paralyzed with fear, and couldn't take my eyes off the car.

Someone, a man I assumed, in dark clothes and a full face ski mask got out of the car, walked to the dumpster, lifted the lid, and shined a light in it. I sat frozen. There was no indication anyone had any interest in me, but I was still petrified.

The man reached into the garbage and grabbed the sack, opened it, and pulled out the sock. He let the sack flutter to the ground. He held the sock by its toe and shook the coin out into his hand. He shone the light on it, studied it for a moment, closed his hand over it, and put it in his pocket. I felt fear and panic rising in me. Where was Andy? Did I do the wrong thing? Had I just done the stupidest thing in my life?

The man used his remote to pop open the trunk of the sedan. He stood looking in, and then struggled to pull out a huge bundle wrapped in a blanket. He let it drop from his grasp to the ground, then strode quickly to the driver's side of the car, got in, put the car into gear, and drove off. He had done all that without even glancing in my direction. I watched the tail lights leaving, still paralyzed. I realized I had nothing useful I could have told anyone about the car or the man. The car was dark colored, but I didn't know what color. It was a four door sedan of some kind. It didn't have any license plates that I could see. That was it. Was it gone?

The bundle. I focused on its outline in the dark.

30 WORCESTER

Without thinking, I got out of my car and ran to the bundle. I pulled the blanket off. It was a person. There was a full face ski mask over his head, with duct tape around the eyes and mouth. His hands were tied behind him and his ankles were bound together, also with duct tape. Even in the dark, I knew it was Andy. I touched him, and a flood of relief flowed through me as I realized he was alive.

In the movies, the heroine would have pulled out her knife and cut the victim free. Of course I had no knife or any tool of any kind. I pulled at the tape.

"Oh my God, oh my God, oh my God." I realized I was saying it out loud. I grabbed the top of the mask and pulled, and it came off. I looked into the eyes of the person I loved more than anyone in the world. I'd never seen such a look as I saw on his face. It was a mixture of fear, relief, anger and exhaustion. I wasn't sure who was more freaked out, him or me.

"I have to call someone!" I said. "We have to get out of here right now. Are you hurt? Who do I call?" I was babbling and I knew it, nearly hysterical.

"Meg," he croaked.

"I'm here, I'm here. We have to get out of here."

"Get your car," he whispered.

"I can't leave you," I cried.

"Just get the car," he said with effort.

"You're hurt." He looked at me. I turned and ran to my car. I slammed the door shut and rammed the car into gear. I was back in five seconds.

"Help me get in the car," he said.

I pulled him to his feet. He hopped a little and I dragged, and we got him into the passenger seat.

"I have to get you loose," I said, not thinking clearly.

"Drive," he whispered.

It was a relief to have him telling me what to do. I ran around to my side, got in and locked the doors.

"Where?" I asked.

"Anywhere. Find people."

I got it. I drove. I turned into a well-lit grocery store parking lot a few block away and screeched to a stop.

"Call 911."

I did. I gave the police the name of the store, sobbed that I needed help immediately, and then turned to Andy.

"Are you ok?" The quiver in my voice probably scared him worse than he already was.

"Yeah," he croaked.

He didn't look ok. I started pulling at the tape again, and managed to get some of it off his legs. Andy slumped in the seat with his eyes closed, not moving. I was afraid to ask, but had to.

"What did they do to you?"

Andy opened his eyes, and it seemed like he was struggling to focus on me. "I don't know I guess. I feel weird. Dazed." He paused, and the expression on his face turned to puzzlement. "What are you doing here? How did you find me? Why are you all by yourself? They could have grabbed you."

Before I could say anything, I saw flashing lights pulling into the parking lot. I flew out of the car and started jumping up and down and waving my arms. The policemen parked and ran over. I started to sob with relief, and then started babbling like an idiot.

"Andy, he's tied up with duct tape and I can't get it loose, and I don't know if he's ok, and he might need an ambulance. They took him, but I found him. I don't know what to do. Help him, he's hurt."

One of them cut Andy loose, while the other called an ambulance.

"Ok miss, calm down," the friendly looking one said. "Let's start at the beginning. He's going to be ok. I'm Officer Stanton, and that's officer Warzinski," he said, pointing to his partner. "We'll take you to the station and talk about what happened, ok?"

"Ok," I replied meekly.

I clung to Andy, who was sitting sideways in the car with his legs hanging out. He was flexing his feet as the officer helped him sip some water.

"Oh my God, I have to call your mom," I said.

"Yeah, please tell her I'm ok," said Andy.

Mrs. Garrett picked up after one ring. "Megan?"

"Yes, I found him. He's ok."

"Oh thank God," she said. "Where are you?" she asked anxiously.

"We're in Worcester," I said. "It's bad." I heard her suck in her breath, and hurried to say, "I mean, it's not bad now, Andy's ok, but someone did take him."

"What?" Her voice was horrified. "Did you call the police?"

"Yes, they're here now, and an ambulance is coming to check Andy out."

"Should we come there? Oh my God. Jim!" I heard her calling Andy's dad.

I didn't know what to say. I just wanted to be off the phone and making sure Andy was ok. "Let me ask them."

I turned to Officer Stanton and said, "Do you want his parents to come?"

"Yes we do," he replied. "Please have them meet us at the station."

"Ok." I spoke back into the phone. "Yes, they want you to come. They said to meet us at the police station here."

"Ok, we're on our way," she said. "Megan?"

"Yes?"

"He's not hurt?"

"I don't think so," I said.

"Don't leave him, no matter what, and we'll get there as fast as possible."

Andy hadn't moved. I reached out to him, and he took my hand. "They're on their way," I said.

"Good," he said hoarsely.

I called my parents and they were horrified as well. As much by what I had done as by what had happened to Andy. I assured them the Garrett's were on their way and that we were safe with the police, and that I would call them back with an update.

The ambulance arrived and the paramedics rushed over. Officer Warzinski nodded his head toward Andy. The paramedic addressed Andy. "Can you walk to the ambulance with us?"

Andy nodded a slight yes, but didn't say anything. I helped him to his feet, and he seemed wobbly. The paramedic got on his other side, and we walked slowly to the ambulance, where the other paramedic who was waiting helped him step up into the back. I followed. They eased Andy onto the bench. They gave him a bottle of water, and he sipped a little. They took his blood pressure, looked in his eyes with a flashlight, and poked and prodded him.

Andy spoke quietly. "Nobody hurt me. They just tied me up and were rough when they moved me around. My arms and legs only hurt from being in the same position so long. And I haven't had anything to drink or eat since this morning. I also hit my head on the steering wheel when my car went off the road."

"That would explain the cut on your forehead," said the paramedic. "You could have a mild concussion, but it doesn't look like anything too serious." He handed Andy a package of cheese crackers and a sports drink. "These will help you feel better."

"Thanks," said Andy.

I felt useless, yet very important, because Andy didn't want to let go of my hand. I didn't want to let go of his either, but I had to, to open the package of crackers for him. I gave him one, and he started to chew slowly.

Officer Warzinski came over and asked, "Do you feel ready to come with us now?"

I nodded and looked at Andy, who also nodded. We followed him to his police car and Andy seemed a little stronger already. The officer opened the back door of his car for us and we got in. Andy laid his head against the seat and closed his eyes. The drive to the police station was quick. I had never ridden in a police car, and it was interesting to see all their gadgets in the front seat, which was blocked off from the back seat by a metal grate. Not for people like us, I thought. What are we doing here though? This is so unbelievable. The officer parked the car and jumped out to open the door for us. We got out and followed him into the building. He led us to a sofa in a hallway of offices.

"Can you two wait here for a while? I think your parents will be here soon. Would you like something to drink?"

"Yeah, a coke please," said Andy.

"Me too," I said.

Officer Warzinski returned with our drinks, and we sat sipping.

"What happened?" I asked, now that we were finally alone.

Andy looked at me in a mixture of exhaustion and disbelief. "This car drove me off the road, just like in the movies. I thought it was an accident of some sort, even though the other driver seemed in control. I got out of my car to get his insurance information and stuff, and two of them stepped out of their car. One pointed a gun at me. There was nothing I could do. There was nobody around.

They put a hood over my head and tied me up, and the next thing I knew I was in the back of their car, and they were demanding to know about the coin. I guess I should have denied that I knew anything about it, but I was so surprised that they even knew about it. I refused to tell them where it was, because I didn't want them going to my house and finding my mom and hurting her, but they said it didn't matter, and that I didn't need to because they had a better idea. They put tape over my mouth, drove us somewhere, and took me into a room somewhere and shut the door and left me there a really long time, until they dragged me back to the car and threw me in the trunk. I think the rest you pretty much know. What happened to you?"

"Oh Andy, it's so horrible." It just occurred to me that I had given them the coin. "I. I gave it to them."

"You did the right thing, don't even worry about that. But what…"

We heard noise from the end of the corridor, and Andy's parents were running down the hall. Andy smiled. Mrs. Garrett flung herself onto the couch and pulled Andy into her arms. Then she was crying. She grabbed me too, and then we were both crying.

"What happened?" she sobbed.

"It was someone who wanted the coin," I said.

"The coin? This is about the coin?"

Andy nodded. "They didn't want to hurt me, they just wanted the coin."

"I just don't believe this," said Mr. Garrett.

"I gave it to them," I said guiltily.

"How could you not tell us you knew something?" demanded Mr. Garrett angrily.

I felt ashamed, as if I had committed a horrible crime. "I really didn't know at the time you asked me."

"Then when?" he insisted.

"It was all very sudden. Someone called me from Andy's phone, and I was afraid they would hurt him if I didn't act immediately," I said in a small voice.

Andy took my hand protectively.

"You could have been killed for God's sakes!" yelled Mr. Garrett. "What the hell were you thinking?"

Officer Stanton returned and said, "Can you folks come with me?"

We followed him in silence. He led us to a small conference room, where we sat around a table. Another man entered the room. "I'm Detective Wright. Are you able to tell me what happened son?"

"Yeah, I think so," said Andy.

"It's important that we get it all, if you're up to it," the detective added.

"Yeah, ok. Well, I picked up the plants and potting soil my mom wanted at the nursery. Then I was in my car, driving back toward Hardwick. This big black car pulled around me to pass, but then veered sharply in front of me. I had to swerve off the road to avoid hitting it. My car kind of went down into a ditch. The big black car stopped ahead of me. I got out to exchange insurance information, and two men in ski masks got out of the other car. One actually had a gun, and told me to lie down on the ground, face down. I did, and they tied my hands behind my back. I told them they must have the wrong person, but they said no, they were sure they had the right guy."

"Can you describe anything about them?"

"Well like I said, they had ski masks on. And dark colored clothes. They were white guys – I could see their hands. Both about 5' 10", one maybe 180 pounds and the other maybe 220, but with a gut, not in an in shape sort of way. I would guess at least one of them was older, like 40s or something, just from the way he talked."

Andy took a sip of water, and clenched my hand tighter.

"They forced me into their car and put a ski mask on my head, but with duct tape over the eyes so I couldn't see. I asked them what they wanted, and they told me it was the coin, and said that if I told them where it was they wouldn't hurt me."

The detective looked at him quizzically.

"Megan and I found a very old coin at my grandparent's house, and we found out it was probably worth a lot of money. I don't know how they knew we had it, but they did. They had apparently been watching us for a few days too. Anyway, I didn't tell them where it was, because I didn't want them to go hurt my family. They told me they didn't want to hurt anyone either, that they weren't killers or anything - they just wanted the coin. They gave up on me pretty quickly though, because they came up with a plan to get Megan to bring the coin. They had apparently seen us together, and knew she would care. I think they figured that would be the easiest way."

"They were right," I said, and started to cry. Andy squeezed my hand. Mr. and Mrs. Garrett looked at me, looking a little less angry.

"They took my cell phone and it was easy for them to call her," Andy continued.

Detective Wright asked, "Do you know anything about them?"

"Well," Andy paused, "like I said, they had on ski masks, and then they covered my eyes. They didn't seem like they knew what they were doing. They took me to some sort of house, and they left me in one room while they were in another. I'm sure they thought I couldn't hear them, but I did hear some of what they said. I also heard a train go by, quite close, at one point."

"What did you hear them say?"

"Well it was kind of muffled, but I caught bits of their conversation. Like, they were surprised at how easily they were able to get me. Then they were really happy that Megan responded to my phone right away."

Everyone looked at me. I smiled weakly.

Andy continued. "They were congratulating themselves on how the internet is a great thing, and made the whole thing easy. At one point I heard one call the other "Morrie" or something like that."

"Morrie?" asked the detective?

"Yeah. Then they were just talking about the details of what they were going to get Megan to do, and what they would do if that failed. The first plan seemed to be to get me to give them the coin or tell them where it was but they didn't want to do any dirty work like beating me up or anything. They just kept the gag in my mouth and left me there in the room."

The officer turned to the Garrett's. "Do you have any idea who would have known you had this coin?"

Mrs. Garrett responded. "I've only known for a few days. I did some internet research on it."

"I did too, internet research I mean," added Andy.

"But I didn't talk to anyone about it except one person, a Mr. Schneider at the National Numismatic Association. I don't think he even believed we could have this coin, but he agreed to meet with us this coming Monday. So that makes me, Jim, Andy and Megan."

"And I told my mom too," I added.

Detective Wright asked, "So how much are we talking about here, as far as what the coin is worth?"

"Well," said Mrs. Garrett, "if it really is what we think it is, it could be worth several hundred thousand dollars."

Detective Wright sat back in his chair, clearly surprised and skeptical. "I see." He thought for a moment. "You said you found it in your house?"

"Yes, Andy and Megan found it. You see, this house has been in my family since 1776, and it seems nobody threw anything away for the last 200 years or so. It's completely full of antiques, but also a lot of junk. We haven't found anything else nearly so valuable, only a lot of sentimental items."

I was relieved that she didn't go into the whole Allie story. It just sounded too farfetched.

She continued. "As Andy said, when we found it, we did some internet research to try to figure out what it was, and found that the National Numismatic Association actually had one, and knew the history of it. That's why we started with them, as far as looking for help in authenticating it."

The detective turned back to Andy. "Is there anything else you can think of that might help us find these guys son?"

Andy thought for a moment. "I can't think of anything. I didn't even deny I had the coin. I was too surprised by the whole thing. There wasn't much discussion about it. It just sounds like a movie or something – how does this sort of thing happen in Worcester Massachusetts?"

"A very good question," said Detective Wright. "We're certainly not used to seeing kidnappings around here. They seem to have known exactly what they wanted, and pulled off a plan to get it from you." He looked around the table. "Megan, what happened from your perspective, is there anything you can add?"

"No, not really," I said. "It was dark at the VFW. I saw a dark four door car, and not much about the guy – he had on a ski mask when I saw him too."

"What about before that, was there anything distinguishing about the phone call or the instructions?"

I thought. "No, it was just a man's voice, the id said it was Andy but it wasn't, and the instructions were very simple – to bring the coin in a paper bag and put it in the dumpster. That's what I did."

"Ok, well if any of you can think of anything else that might help us here, please call immediately," Detective Wright instructed.

"Do you think we're in danger?" asked Mrs. Garrett.

"You know honestly, from the sound of it, they got what they were looking for and probably have no further need to care about you," said the detective. "Especially since none of you seem able to identify them."

"That does make sense I guess," said Mr. Garrett. "You'll keep us posted on any developments?"

"Oh yes," said Detective Wright. "You are free to go now. Do you feel ok Andy?"

"Yes, much better, thank you," he replied.

"Megan, we'll take you to your car at the grocery store, and then follow you back to Hardwick," said Mr. Garrett.

"Ok," I said.

Andy's mom put her arm around me, and I broke into tears. "It's ok," she said. "It all turned out ok. We know you only did what you felt was best for Andy."

I nodded tearfully.

"I'll ride with her, Dad," said Andy.

"I expected that," he replied. "Megan, I'm sorry for yelling at you. You just can't imagine how terrified we were."

"It's ok," I replied. "But I was pretty terrified myself."

"I know, I know," he said. "Please call your parents and tell them everything is alright."

"Yes, I'll do that right away," I said earnestly.

31 APPOINTMENT

Finally Andy and I were in the car alone, being followed by his parents in their car. I took a deep breath. Andy looked exhausted. I felt exhausted. "I would have died if anything had happened to you," I told him.

"Nothing did. It's all ok." He paused and we drove in silence for a few miles. "Where were you when they called you? How did you keep any of our parents from finding out? How did you get the coin without anyone knowing?"

The chain of events replayed in my head. "I was in your room."

"My room?"

"Yes, I had gone home with your mom when we realized we couldn't get a hold of you. We were all so worried and didn't know what to do. Then I had this really strong urge to go to your room, like I wanted to feel your presence or something, and think about what to do. Only, your room was all empty and lonely without you. I picked up Allie's quilt and sat on your bed."

Suddenly I remembered the button.

"Oh!"

"What?" he asked.

"I completely forgot. I found a button hidden inside the quilt. It was under that bird square."

"A button?"

"Yes, it has to be Wayne's button. The one she mentioned in her diary." I fished in my pocket and pulled it out, and then pushed it into Andy's hand. Andy turned on the dome light of the car so he could see it in the dark. He let out a low whistle.

"I know, right?" I asked.

"Yes, it has to be. Why didn't you tell the detective?"

"Oh my God, I didn't even think of it. I totally forgot about it. Do you think it's important?"

"Well, maybe not really important, but if it's really a civil war button, it would lend some credibility to the whole story. Not that there's any doubt in my mind anyway."

"You're right, it might be important. I'll call Detective Wright in the morning.

"Yeah, it's probably best." He switched off the dome light. "I wonder why we only found it now."

"I think because we were being so careful with the quilt. I wasn't careful with it in your room though, I was squeezing it really hard." I hesitated. "I was asking Allie to help me," I said sheepishly.

"And did she?"

"Yes, I think she did. I knew that no matter what, all that mattered was you, and that I had to do anything possible to save you. I knew for certain that stupid coin didn't matter at all." I was silent for a moment. "And then they called, and I didn't hesitate. It was like I had already planned what I would do. That I would do exactly what I had to, if I had the chance. I know your parents are really mad at me. Mine will be mad too, when they understand the whole story."

"I should be mad too, that you risked yourself like that," Andy said.

"Are you?"

"Well, no. You were really very brave. But I never would have forgiven myself if anything had happened to you."

I laughed grimly. "But don't you know I feel exactly the same way?"

He ran his fingers down my face. I kept my hands on the wheel. "Yes, I guess I do. We're both ok, and everyone will have to get over it. We're a team." He took my right hand from the wheel and brought it to his lips and kissed it.

I was flooded with a sense of relief. Everything was going to be ok. It was a bummer that the coin was gone, but all that mattered was that Andy was safe.

I pulled up to Andy's house, and his parents pulled up beside my car. They stood and waited while Andy kissed me goodbye and got out of my car. They took him into their arms and they all held each other as they walked into the house. I noticed three or four lightning bugs twinkling their little lights in the shrubs by the porch. It was as if they were signaling that life was back on track.

I didn't want to leave Andy, but knew my parents were very anxious for me to get home. As I got to the front door, my mom rushed out and threw her arms around me. "Oh Meg, I'm so glad you're safe." My dad wasn't far behind.

"I am, I'm ok Mom," I replied.

"Stacy Garrett called me from her car," my mom informed me sternly.

"Uh oh."

"Yes, exactly. How could you do such a thing?" She started to cry.

"Yes what were you thinking?" asked my dad.

My mom's crying was what made me feel bad, not the fact that I had acted on my own. I would have done it that way all over again if given the choice. "Mom it's ok. It all worked out ok."

"But what if it hadn't?" my dad asked. "We could not have stood it if something had happened to you. It was sheer hell just knowing Andy was in danger."

"I know, but I knew it would be ok," I replied.

"How? How could you know?" asked my mom.

"Well," I paused. "It was Allie."

"Allie?"

"Yes, I begged her for help. She gave me a sign, I know she did. I knew then that it would be ok. I wasn't worried about myself."

"A sign? Oh Megan."

My dad shook his head.

"Yes, I found the button that was her engagement ring. I knew she felt that nothing mattered except Andy, and I knew I would trade the coin or anything else for him. And that was exactly the opportunity I was given."

"I'm glad it made you feel better, but we would have wanted to help make that decision. We needed to know you were safe. I still can't believe you acted on your own like that," my mom said.

"I know," I said gently, "but I'm not sorry. I did what I had to do. You never would have let me go, and things could have ended very differently."

"Maybe so, but the authorities could have handled it."

My patience was thinning. "Yes, and Andy could have been killed. I wasn't willing to take that chance."

"We'll talk about it in the morning," my dad said. "All that matters now is that you're home and safe. Let's all go to bed."

I nodded in agreement.

In the morning at breakfast, everyone was much calmer. Justin and Nick were highly impressed with the whole cops and robbers nature of the story, but I tried to downplay it so as not to further upset my parents.

"I need to call that detective about the button," I said.

"Yes, you should make sure they know absolutely everything possible, so they have the best chance of catching those guys. It seems unrelated, but who knows?" my mom agreed.

I found Detective Wright's card in my pants pocket from the previous night, and called him. I described the button.

"You're right that it's probably not related, but then again, we should check it out. I'd like to send a police officer to your house to borrow the button for evidence, will that be all right? We have gotten the FBI involved, so we'll send it to their crime lab."

"Yes," I agreed.

We spent the next few days settling back into our normal lives. Samantha was back home, and Monday the three of us went out on the boat. We told her the story in great detail, and for some reason, she didn't think I was an idiot. She found the whole thing fascinating. She threw her arms around me.

"I don't know what I would have done if something had happened to Andy. Or you."

"Nothing did," I assured her, returning the hug.

"So do you think Allie wanted you to find the coin?"

"I guess I feel that way," I said. "But I think she would have wanted it to be a positive force in my life, not cause me or anyone else more trouble. That's what I don't get. How could this whole sequence of events happen, only for us to lose it just like that? What if I shouldn't have given it to those guys? But I had to," I said quickly. "I didn't even try to figure out another way. All I cared about was Andy."

She looked at us holding hands. "You two really love each other, don't you?"

I smiled.

"We do," Andy said gently.

"What are you going to do if Mom wants to move?" asked Sam.

"I don't know. I need to talk to her and see where her head is at. I can't leave Megan. There has to be a way we can figure out how to make this work for just one more year until we graduate."

"It's so romantic," Sam said.

Andy wrapped his arms around me and kissed me.

When we returned to Andy's house, Mrs. Garrett was happy to see us. "I have interesting news," she said.

"What Mom?" asked Sam.

"Detective Wright called, and he said that button Megan gave him was indeed authentic and from the Civil war. That gives a lot of credibility to the rest of our story." She looked at me and saw the slightly insulted look on my face. "Not that we didn't already know that," she added hastily.

I wanted to assure her I hadn't been scowling at her. "I guess I forget that our story does sound pretty farfetched to people who haven't lived it. I'm convinced it's all authentic, but proof would be nice too."

"I am too," added Andy supportively.

"Well we all are," said Mrs. Garrett. "This just helps the detectives get a better feel for the whole situation. Even if Wayne Collins and Allie Bruce had never existed, for whatever reason we seem to have some Civil war artifacts.

"Exactly," added Sam. "I wonder when we'll hear anything."

"It could be hours and it could be months," said Mrs. Garrett. "All we can do now is get on with our lives."

"Let's go get on with our lives," Andy said, winking at me.

Laughing, I followed him out to the car. I helped unload all our day's supplies for the boat, and then we carried the water skis to the barn. We propped them carefully against a wall, and then Andy sat on a small table and pulled me on top of him. I straddled him with my arms around his neck and kissed him. Before long, he pushed my t-shirt up above my swimsuit top, and kissed the exposed part of my breasts. I wrapped my fingers through his hair, enjoying the electricity running through me. His mouth moved to my nipple, through my damp swimsuit, and I pushed my body against his, feeling an aching. I could tell he felt it too, between the thin layers of cloth that separated our bodies. I never wanted these feelings to end, but the dirty barn was not the place for this to go much further. Though we enjoyed a long lingering kiss before I got in my car to go home, it wasn't enough.

Tuesday I was working the day shift making a ham and cheddar on sourdough, when I heard my text message alert from my purse. I wrapped the sandwich and handed it to the customer with a thank you, and then grabbed my phone.

"come ovr aftr wk, news" said the message from Andy.

"k" I replied.

I couldn't wait for my shift to end, wondering what the news could be. Finally work was over for the day, and I drove to Andy's house. He met me at the door with a look of excitement on his face. "The FBI called. The FBI! They think they found our coin, and want us to come to their office to talk to them. We're going on Thursday, can you come? They invited Mr. Schneider too, so he will be able to look at the coin and tell us for sure whether it's real."

"Wow that is exciting! Yes, I'll rearrange my schedule. They'd have to let me go for something important like this. Is your mom going to drive us? Is your dad going?"

"Yes, they're both going. Do you still want to go?"

"Oh of course I do."

We grabbed a bag of chips and some cokes, and took them up to Andy's room. We listened to music for a while, and then Andy said, "Want to go for a walk?"

"Sure, it's really nice outside."

We headed out the back door, and out toward the field. We walked along the stone wall holding hands. Wandering along, we came to the 'swing place' where we had found the coin. For an instant, I saw the big tree with the swing. Only for an instant. We sat on the grass and looked out toward the hills. “She must not be done with us,” I said.

“Who?”

“Allie, because I’m still getting flashes of her memories.”

“Maybe she’s happy this whole thing is going to be resolved.”

“The coin.” I stated.

“And us,” he replied. “Unlike her and Wayne, we will be together.”

We lay down on the grass in a tangled heap as we kissed and touched each other. “We should have brought a blanket to lie on,” Andy said. “But that might have looked strange to my parents.”

“Yeah. This is still nice though,” I said, as I moved my hand under his shirt and stroked his chest and stomach. He moved his hands up my shirt and unhooked my bra. He gently ran his hands over my chest, as I was doing to his. I wanted more. Sometime, we would be in a place where we had time and privacy. This was not it though.

“You are driving me wild,” I said breathlessly.

“Good,” he replied. “Now you know how I always feel.”

32 QUESTIONS

Thursday we arrived at the FBI office in Albany, New York at 12:45 p.m. Fifteen minutes to spare. We entered the lobby and told the receptionist we had an appointment. The lobby had a clean but unimpressive waiting area no different than any medical or insurance office. Andy and I settled into a sofa, while his parents took nearby chairs. At precisely 1:00, the receptionist came to get us and ushered us into the elevator. On the 32nd floor, she led us to the office of the chief of the New York bureau's office.

As we entered, he stood and came out from behind his walnut desk to join us in the sitting area of his office. He held out his hand to Andy's dad. "Hello, you must be the Garrett's. My name is Roger Mitchell. Please have a seat."

As I sat, I noticed the incredible view of the city to the west. The sitting area of the office was like a living room, with chairs arranged around a big coffee table. Andy and I sat on an expensive looking brown leather loveseat and his parents sat in matching brown leather reading chairs.

"Can I get you anything to drink? Coffee? Water? Soda?" Mr. Mitchell asked.

"Water would be great," said Mrs. Garrett. We nodded. Mr. Mitchell left through the door we had entered, and was back in a few moments with bottles of water for each of us. He took one of the remaining open chairs.

Mr. Mitchell spoke to Andy's dad again. "Now then, you are Mr. and Mrs. Garrett, and this is Andy, correct?"

"Yes," replied Mr. Garrett. "And this is Megan, Andy's girlfriend, who is also part of the whole story."

"Good good. I have invited Mr. Schneider from the NNA here as well, as we discussed on the phone. He should be here any moment."

We sat quietly, sipping our water. After a moment, Mr. Schneider was ushered in by the receptionist, and we were all introduced to each other.

"I'm sure you're wondering what we've learned, so let me jump right in," said Agent Mitchell. He put his hand in his jacket pocket and pulled out our coin in a baggie. "Is this the object of so much trouble?"

We all looked at each other. Andy stood and took the coin from Mr. Mitchell. He turned it over in his hand, and then plopped it into mine. "It sure looks like what we found sir," he replied. I nodded in agreement.

"How did you find it?" Mrs. Garrett asked the agent.

"A very good question," replied Mr. Mitchell. "It turns out this wasn't just a random theft. I think you knew that, but I mean it was part of a much bigger operation, though this had to be the best item they had stolen yet."

"I don't understand," said Mrs. Garrett.

"It's an interesting story," said Mr. Mitchell. "Do you want to hear the whole thing, or just your part in it?"

"Oh definitely the whole thing," Andy said enthusiastically. "If you're willing to tell us, that is."

Mr. Mitchell smiled, nodded and began. "We had been watching a series of thefts over the past seven years, of similar objects to your coin – other coins, art, and rare artifacts. There had been a pattern, but we were not sure what to make of it. There was a known link with the National Numismatic Association, but up to now we hadn't been able to figure out exactly what was going on. As a matter of fact, the button you found and turned over to us helped us make the link. As I told you on the phone, it is an authentic Civil War Officer's coat button. That gave credibility to the idea of the coin being from that timeframe and being linked to a case we had been watching. Over the past five years we have been watching a series of crimes related to Civil War artifacts, but have never been able to tie them together until now, with your two items. Let me give you back the button, before I forget." He produced a baggie from his desk drawer, and dropped it into my outstretched hand.

Mrs. Garrett drew in her breath and looked at Mr. Schneider. "You mean Mr. Schneider was involved? He had such good credentials, at least from what I could find."

Mr. Schneider looked sheepish, shook his head no, and then looked at Mr. Mitchell.

"He was involved," said Mr. Mitchell, "but he didn't know he was involved until we told him yesterday. In other words, he wasn't complicit in the crime. We took the name you gave us, "Morrie" and again looked at our data related to the National Numismatic Association. We found a person by the name of Maurice Stephenson, who had left the NNA seven years ago. We decided to look into what he was doing now, and found some interesting activity. He is still involved in arts and antiquities, but mostly working as a broker - buying and selling other people's items, not his own. Still, we put surveillance on him. More than surveillance actually, after the crime that was perpetrated against you. We tapped his phones and computers. After watching him for a few weeks, we discovered that he had put electronic monitors in the offices of some of the key people at the NNA. He was monitoring their communications over a very long period of time, and every now and then, when the right opportunity arose, he moved in and stole something of value.

We've now conclusively linked him to these crimes. There are a few more unsolved ones that will probably end up being tied in as well. This was the first time he ever came close to harming any people though. To be sure, the objects he stole were of value, but up to this point, the thefts had been done in a very impersonal way. In the cases we have solved so far, the method has involved switching a real object for a clever imitation, with nobody catching on immediately. When we interviewed people who had known him, it became apparent that his passion was rare coins. That has to be why he was willing to go to such lengths to steal yours. His setup was quite ingenious actually. He had bugs in Mr. Schneider's office, but also in three other places in the NNA building. In the past three years, he had tapped into their computer systems and was able to intercept their emails as if he were a system administrator. Advancing technology can sure be a two edged sword. He must have been very patient, but I guess given the profits he made on some of the items he stole, he could afford to be. Also, during the whole time the crimes were being committed, he maintained his respectable career as a broker."

"Wow," said Mr. Garrett. "The whole thing is so unbelievable."

Mr. Mitchell laughed. "Yes, sometimes the very people who electronically monitor others are the last ones to suspect the same is happening to them. We were able to intercept the beginnings of very discreet inquiries into a market for your coin. We posed as a potential buyer, and were able to trap him trying to sell it to us. I wish I could say there was more drama to it than that, but there wasn't.

I turned the coin over in my hand. You've been a lot of trouble, I said to it in my mind. Andy's hand covered mine and the coin.

"May I?" asked Mr. Schneider. He had been waiting patiently through the entire story.

"Oh of course," I said, opening the baggie, and plopped the coin in his hand.

He put on some sort of magnifying glasses. "Oh my," he said, as he examined the coin.

We all stared at him expectantly.

"I did some very thorough research on this, in case what you had here was real," he started. He looked up and gazed at each of us in turn. "It certainly appears it is indeed real."

We all grinned at each other.

"With all due respect sir, it had to be real," Andy said. "Because nobody had seen it in a hundred and fifty years."

"Yes, yes, but we get plenty of leads and inquiries that turn out to be only wishful thinking. Do you know the history of this coin?"

"You mean before it was on the Garrett's farm?" I asked.

"Yes, during the Civil War."

"No," said Mrs. Garrett. "I don't think any of us do."

"Well folks, it's quite interesting. Just before the end of the war, the leaders of the confederacy were preparing to become an independent nation, even in the face of what looked like a coming defeat at the hands of the union. In January of 1861, the State of Louisiana seceded from the Union, and the Confederacy took control of the New Orleans mint. The leaders of the confederacy had planned to mint coins bearing confederate designs to legitimize their status as a sovereign nation. At the time the mint was taken over, there was enough supply of bullion to keep it operating. The mint continued to produce Union half dollars while the design for the confederate half dollar was being developed. In April 1861 the design was completed. The front of the coin would be the same as the Union half dollar, but the back would show the confederate coat of arms along with cotton and sugar cane, important crops in the south. Four genuine confederate half dollars were produced; but immediately after their production, operations at the mint were ceased due to lack of bullion and little hope of getting any more."

"There were only four?" Mrs. Garrett asked.

"Yes, only four," replied Mr. Schneider. "That's why it's worth so much. One of the coins was presented to President Jefferson Davis, one was kept by the Chief Coiner, and two were presented to local dignitaries. All that is known then, is that in 1879 Jefferson Davis said his coin had been stolen when he was captured in 1865. What is also interesting, is that in 1879 the original dies for the coins were sold to a New York coin and stamp dealer, and that dealer collected five hundred 1861 half dollars and reprinted the confederate image on the back of them. These are distinguishable from the four originals because of the remnants of the old image. Note that you cannot see any trace of any other image on your coin. Many years later, two of the other three also disappeared, but those are different stories. Even at the time of the end of the Civil War, it would have been recognized that one of those coins would have great value at some point."

"Wow," said Andy.

"Yeah wow," I repeated.

"I have no reason to believe this is anything other than authentic," Mr. Schneider told us.

We all absorbed that information. After a few moments of silence, Mr. Mitchell spoke to Andy again. "If I might ask, how did you come to find the coin?"

"That's an interesting story too," said Andy. "Do you want to hear the whole thing?"

Everyone laughed. Mr. Mitchell responded to the cue, "Oh definitely the whole thing, if you're willing to tell us." He smiled. "To be clear, we're considering everything about your part in the investigation to be settled, so I'm only interested for curiosity's sake."

Andy looked at me. "Where do we begin Meg?"

We told the story together, going into great detail about the diary and the quilt. We left out the part about my visions, because that was just too strange to be believable.

"That is quite a story," said Mr. Mitchell. "What are the odds?"

"That's what we thought too," I said. "But why not us, you know?"

"That's right, why not you?" Mr. Mitchell looked at the Garretts. "As we discussed on the phone, given the great value of this coin, we would be willing to escort you to the Sotheby's office in New York City to leave it with them, if that is where you want it to go.

Andy's parents looked at him. "You're sure of what you want to do with it, right son?" Mr. Garrett asked.

Andy looked at me. I nodded slowly. "Yes," he told his dad.

"Mr. Mitchell, we would appreciate that escort to the Sotheby's office," Mr. Garrett said.

"Certainly," replied Mr. Mitchell. "We had two guys lined up, in case that was still your decision." He walked to his desk and pressed a button, and said into the intercom, "Please send agents Roswell and Ebersol in."

We sat and listened to the adults making small talk for a few moments, and two men walked in. I smiled to myself, and glanced at Andy. He got the joke too. The two men looked just like you would expect FBI men to look, like agents in a movie. I wouldn't have been surprised if they had pulled out dark sun glasses right there. They looked very serious, and certainly capable of protecting us. They had to be wearing guns, though I couldn't see them.

Mr. Mitchell said, "This is agent Roswell and this is agent Ebersol. They will drive you to the Sotheby's office for your appointment there."

We shook hands all the way around.

"Thank you again Mr. Mitchell. You can't imagine what this means to us," said Mrs. Garrett. "We just want this whole story to end. Besides that, this should be exhibited someplace, and hopefully someone will agree and buy it for that purpose."

The Garrett's shook hands with Mr. Mitchell, and we left his office. We rode the elevator down to the parking garage, and the agents ushered us into a big black Lincoln Town Car limousine, with dark tinted windows.

Mrs. Garrett, Andy and I sat and looked at each other quietly, all of us a bit overwhelmed. The handoff to the auction house went smoothly, since they had been expecting us. When we were driven back to our car it was almost dinner time, so we stopped at a steak house to celebrate. On the ride back to Hardwick, Andy and I fell asleep, slumped in each other's arms in the back seat.

It was over. The whole thing was over. It seemed like months had passed since we found the coin, but it had only been a few weeks. The coin had been sold, and the money was in the bank, waiting to fund both mine and Andy's educations. The Garrett's insisted that it be that way. It was almost time to start our senior year of high school. It was clear to me though, that we were not the same people who left there as juniors. Our experiences during the summer had matured us as if we had aged five years or something. I was no longer interested in high school, only with getting on with my life with Andy and our future together. Suddenly the idea of high school seemed trivial. What seemed important was pursuing our dreams and making a difference in the world. Life was too short and too tenuous not to.

I arrived at Andy's house after my shift at 8:00, as twilight was settling. I glanced at the house, and felt a flash of happiness and a feeling of home. I smiled to myself and whispered, 'Thanks Allie, I know. It's over and all is well.' Andy met me at the door, and I smiled at the sight of him.

"Let's go out for an evening boat ride, since there's going to be a full moon tonight," he said.

"I love that idea," I replied.

Andy drove us to the reservoir, and we carried our trusty blanket as we walked out onto the dock and got in the boat. Andy guided the boat to the center of the reservoir, where he cut the motor. We cuddled up on one of the side seats and listened to the bird songs as we watched the sun setting to the west, shining across the water. I was perfectly content, and never wanted to leave this place.

"I love you," I said.

"I love you too. More than anything. Will you marry me?"

I pulled away from him and turned to look at his face. Had I heard him right? "What?"

"I asked you to marry me."

"But we're not even out of high school yet."

"I know, I don't mean right now. But we are more serious than a promise ring, or to just be dating. We're forever. I want the real promise between us. So, will you marry me?"

I didn't hesitate. "Yes. Of course. I want to be with you always."

He pulled a box out of his pocket and opened it, showing me. It was a two carat diamond ring.

"You got me a ring?" I asked, in shock.

"Well, I had a little money, you know."

"Oh my gosh. Wow. It's gorgeous."

"I knew you'd like it. Try it on."

I did. It made me feel like a grown up.

"You don't have to wear it to school or anything, but we are engaged, and after high school I will want you to wear it," he said earnestly.

"Of course I will Andy. I'm never going to lose you again. Do you want to get married after high school?"

"I don't know. We can figure it out later. There's no rush of course, we will be together always. I just wanted us to be formally committed to each other."

I thought about that. "You know it didn't take a ring for that, right?"

"Yeah I know, but the ring is fun, right?"

I laughed. "Oh yes. What are we going to tell our parents?"

"I'd say we tell them, but we also assure them we're not jumping into anything right away. We're going to do this right. We're going to college, we're making plans, and somewhere along the way we're getting married. They'll probably be shocked anyway, but honestly, I don't think they'll be that surprised. We can keep it a secret from our friends and stuff - your friends that is. It's probably a little too weird for high school."

I leaned back into him, admiring how the giant diamond caught the last glints of light from the sun. "I know the answer to Allie's question now."

"What question?"

“She wanted to know what good could come from that coin. Here it is. Us. We will live the dream she and Wayne were not able to. This is the good.”

ABOUT THE AUTHOR

Bonny Gainley lives with her family in Colorado, and enjoys writing as a hobby.

44522527R00231

Made in the USA
Lexington, KY
01 September 2015